COMMON DENOMINATOR

JOHN MARCHANT

ISBN 9781920261610

Printed by arrangement with John Marchant for ValidChoice Publishing

25 Palm Springs Village, Mount Edgecombe 4300
P O Box 2033, Umhlanga Manors, 4021
www.validchoice.com
mail@validchoice.com

Published by Reach Publishers, P.O.Box 1384, Wandsbeck, South Africa,

Website: www.aimtoinspire.com

E-mail: reach@webstorm.co.za

Edited by Gail Kruger for Reach Publishers
Cover designed by Gareth Lagesse for Reach Publishers

CONTENTS

PREFACE

"The selection of the new Führer class is what my struggle for power means. Whoever proclaims his allegiance to me is, by this very proclamation... one of the chosen. This is the great significance of our long, persistent struggle for power, that from it a new master race will be born, chosen to guide the future not only of the German people, but of the world."

Adolf Hitler.

ABOUT THE AUTHOR

John Marchant obtained a Cambridge Matric at King's School, Grantham, England after which he served two years in 7th Royal Tank Regiment in Hong Kong. Thereafter, his banking career, over a period of 9 years in England, also took him to Uganda and Ceylon for a number of years. During the time in Uganda, he married Pat. They have a son and daughter.

John moved to South Africa in 1969 where he continued his involvement in various banking services until his retirement in 1997.

Being interested in travel, John and Pat toured extensively through much of Europe, including Greece, Turkey, Spain, Portugal, Crete, Rhodes and the Greek Islands. Later travels enabled then to enjoy offerings of Florida, USA, Namibia and much of South Africa as well.

John's hobbies include woodworking, bowls and he has for many years been an organist. His passion for history prompted the writing of this novel.

Hermann Schmidt and Ingrid Penz

Hermann Schmidt and Ingrid Penz were both born at Bacharach on the west bank of the Rhine River in Germany. When Adolf Hitler was appointed Reich Chancellor on January 30 1933, they were nine and 12 years old respectively. They were still very young when the Schutzstaffel or S.S. was formed in 1925 as a 'bodyguard' for Adolf Hitler. Four years later, Heinrich Himmler took charge.

On June 30 1934, Ernst Rohm, a sexual pervert and the leader of the S.A., the original Brown Shirts, protectors of the Führer, was shot in his cell and other S.A. leaders cold-bloodedly murdered on the Night of the Long Knives. It was a prelude to the acts of supreme terror that would later be perpetrated by the S.S. Heinrich Himmler, Reichfuhrer S.S., Reinhardt Heydrich. Chief of Security Police and Heinrich Muller, Chief of Gestapo created such a ruthless discipline in the S.S. that it earned a reputation for unsurpassed barbarism in the 20th century. Civilisation was deprived of normal liberty by a system of control based on extreme violence and fear.

Social values changed dramatically; all taboos discarded in favour of raw sexual liberty in a society dominated by male chauvinistic principles. Women had no place except in bed or in the kitchen.

"Women have the task of being beautiful and bringing children into the world," proclaimed Josef Goebbels, Minister of Propaganda.

Excluded from all leading positions in the Party hierarchy, married women doctors and civil servants were dismissed after 1933, and the quota of women high school teachers reduced. After 1936 women could not act as judges, prosecutors or serve on jury duty.

"Children belong to their mothers; at the same time they belong to me," Adolf Hitler announced.

Hermann and Ingrid were brought up to believe that they were part of an elite Master Race, and were compelled to join the Hitler Youth movement under Balder von Schirach. This meant compulsory adulation of Adolf Hitler and all those in the Third Reich, as well as accepting as the norm Nazi doctrine, acts of terror, deportations, abuse of power, sacrificing your property and loss of liberty. Thus conditioned, they knew no other status. Dissenters disappeared inside concentration camps. "Arbeit mach frei": Belsen. "We Germans are a peculiar people; we are so loyal," stated Joachim Von Ribbentrop, Foreign Minister.

Whilst venerating Adolf Hitler, who was never seen in public with a woman, being above such a base human emotional need and dedicated to his people, they were taught to despise Gypsies, Poles, Slavs and particularly Jews; to accept atrocities inflicted on them as protection of the state. Most Germans supported the regime and obeyed orders; only those who were very brave or very dead did not. If Hitler restored vitality to the German nation, giving them a new sense of patriotism, it was at an enormous cost.

Hermann was 15 and Ingrid 18 when war was declared in 1939. In 12 years Hitler created a repressive totalitarian state within Germany, where only males of pure Aryan descent could be first-class citizens.

In 1922, on a wine estate in the province of Champagne in France, Henri Saint-Laurent was born of Germanic heritage. Under occupation by the Third Reich it was important to claim such lineage to remain a member of the aristocracy.

Two years before Henri's arrival, in 1920, Raoul Montpelier's first cries heralded his birth in Paris. Like his father, he would collaborate with the Master Race and become an opportunist par excellence.

To youngsters raised and conditioned in this unique period of history, behaviour patterns and values became radically distorted. They were conditioned into accepting the evil inculcated through acts of barbaric cruelty and terror by the elite perpetrators spawned in the system. Displaying the S.S. lightning insignia and skull motif of the dreaded Death's Head squads, these jackbooted, black uniformed brutal thugs were the most feared men in Europe. Whether German born or persecuted Jewish citizen, none would escape the tyranny of these devoted followers of Adolf Hitler.

SEPTEMBER 1920:

WORMS, NEAR MANNHEIM, GERMANY

The German woman was collected from her home by a wine salesman. "I'm taking you to a hotel in Frankenthal. You will not ask any questions! You understand?" the slightly built man was emphatic. She nodded.

"As long as he can perform, Joachim, what do I care?" the strongly built buxom blonde sneered, tossing her head haughtily.

The little man rubbed his spectacles, wondering what it was like to be married to such a slut, German or not. He felt rather sorry for her husband and his colleague, who was being cuckolded.

A number of travellers took advantage of this woman. She was easy meat, a legend in the firm.

'Did her husband KNOW?' he wondered. On one occasion he had found out for himself just how insatiable her appetite for sex was. He couldn't cope!

The escort introduced his friend as Herr Adler. Her mind raced. Taking in the puffy eyes, weak chin and black hair, with its low right-hand parting and quiff swept to the left, she wondered if he was queer. But although he looked like an overgrown schoolboy, his piercing eyes fascinated her.

They wasted no time in getting down to business, although the 30-year-old man seemed sexually inhibited. The flaxen Amazon couldn't understand why, for he seemed perfectly healthy to her. She wanted a man immediately. Desperately. That was the problem with being a nymphomaniac: with her husband away so often, she couldn't resist a man's offer.

Her present prospect appeared to be a better one than the weedy friend of his who had brought her. The previous week she had exhausted the little runt, who had turned out to be hopeless. He had been tired out before she had even got going.

A little adept coaching from her and he started to relax. Pent up now, desperate, she knelt astride him, accepting him, and started moving rhythmically. Savouring her newly found pleasure she bent forward to kiss him, not prepared for her partner's extreme reaction. Acutely embarrassed, he jerked his head away in his haste to avoid close contact, his stiff moustache scraping her face like sandpaper as he did so. She did not attempt to repeat the affectionate gesture, merely concentrating on the orgasm she craved. Then, as his body jerked with convulsions she peaked simultaneously, exploding with him.

He had been a better performer than his puny friend, she thought. They had scaled the heights together and she felt satisfied when she left him. Little did she know at the time that she had departed with more than she had realised.

Eight months and 27 days later she had a son.

WAR YEARS
*****
SURVIVAL

Chapter I

DECEMBER 2, 1943, 01h23:

OFF VIAREGGIO, ITALY

Moonlit cold black waters: formidable, terrifying. Dive in or die! No time to think. Every second was vital; every second meant the difference between life and death. Let the boat sail away. There was a chance in the water. No time to decide, no time to waste struggling to pull boots off. Just do it! Go!

He dived in, acting on intuition. The German was right; his decision to go over the side vindicated; timing within a hair's breadth. A mere 100 metres away the shockwave from the explosion dumped him like a discarded rag doll, winded but in one piece. Any closer and it would have been his swan-song, the end of his story, he thought, as remnants of the shattered boat fell in the sea around him with heart-stopping closeness.

He had overcome the first challenge and had managed to survive. Now this powerful man had himself to beat, no one else. It was up to him to win or lose; live or die.

Pulling off his calf boots was a battle, but progress would be impossible with them on. He gained buoyancy by taking in gulps of air and clamping his mouth shut while he struggled to release a heel at a time and tug off each boot. After four near drowning attempts he managed at last. He was an atheist but found himself thanking God for enabling him to at least get his impediments off. Treading water, he struggled out of his uniform.

Physical training and endurance tests over the years had taught him one golden rule: never over-exert yourself at the beginning, when one is still fresh. Always keep a reserve of strength; pace yourself slowly and evenly, and finish strongly. The post-autumn Tyrrhenian Sea was not too cold, and he knew that the predominantly off-shore winds made the sea warmer at night. Mercifully the wind was mild although occasional white horses broke around him. Wind brought the chill; darkness stirred fear. Although he was three kilometres out, he could make out pinpoints of lights on shore, which gave him some rudimentary direction. He could not even feel the pull of the tide though, and a gnawing fear convinced him he was making no headway. His stomach knotted as he forced the arrows of terror to subside. It seemed forever. One slow arm flopped over his head followed by the other as they splashed in rhythm, his feet so numb with cold that they no longer even felt a part of him, and he had to force himself to kick, to keep going.

Drifting in thought, he latched onto a picture of his mentor and instructor, Franz Wuttke, whose powerful build resembled that of his Titanic blonde protégé. "Never give up until you collapse and pass out with fatigue," he had drummed into them. Franz had been adamant that the human frame could withstand incredible torments of endurance and stress before defeat, that controlling mental faculties was imperative, as the mind would want to give up before the limbs. This ability to go that extra mile distinguished the Master Race from the rest; never give up, keep going. Gulp air, spit water, one arm and then the other; splash, slosh, plough on; endlessly.

'Rest! Turn on your back for a minute, otherwise you are a goner', he told himself. He lay still for a few moments, floating. Then he heard it. It was there, without any doubt. He forced himself to drag his focus away from the immediate pain in his aching body to listen more closely. This time he was sure: it was surf; breaking on the shore.

Sound travels across water and even further with an off-shore wind. Staring through bloodshot salt-stinging eyes he estimated that it could be within one kilometre of the Italian shore; perhaps only 500 to 800 metres! But his power was fading, strength ebbing. Could he make it? Go on until you get there or collapse. Rather die in a coma of utter exhaustion than be conscious of drowning, he told himself. Never give up. So much depended on the backwash and shore currents as to whether or not he would make it. Semi-conscious effort now: splash, splash, one heavy arm after another, delirious with pain and exhaustion.

Chapter 2

1943:

PARIS

At the pinnacle of Nazi power, terminology was designed to have a pure Teutonic etymology to make words almost instinctively comprehensible; an appeal to guts rather than to intellect. The spontaneous outpouring of popular anger was termed 'Volkszorn'; probably best understood as 'folk wrath'. The orgy of looting and burning of Jewish synagogues and pogroms throughout Germany on November 9 1938, was given the euphemism 'Reichskristallnacht', or 'night of broken glass'. The mild criticism implied by the term in no way reflected the scale of the horrors inflicted, and was thus deemed fit to be taken up by the godless State propaganda machine, imbuing the despicable event with an air of Wagnerian Grandeur and operatic unreality. Small talk for the 108 Jews murdered and 26 000 shipped off to concentration camps, the majority to die there of torture and starvation. In similar vein the crime of sleeping with a Jewess was described as 'Rassenschande' or 'race shame'. Self delusion enabled those in authority to interpret rules as they saw fit. To have sex with a Jewess was verboten, but nevertheless common practice in the exercise of racial humiliation. But it had to be under cover, not blatant, to avoid 'Rassenschande'.

Jealousy of his men and burning curiosity possessed the cruel, perfidious little man, who didn't want anyone beneath his exulted rank to enjoy something he didn't. He was the boss. Their jocular boasts and stories of the staying power of the Jewess had him both envious and horny. He wanted her, and the girl was discreetly spirited to his Paris hotel suite where she was bathed and suitably dressed up in a tight dress and alluring underwear. A liberal application of face powder helped to disguise her recent facial bruises.

For a loser nothing makes up the mind faster than having no option. From there, seek opportunity. Inside the sumptuous suite, feeling clean and smelling like roses for the first time in months, the Jewess made up her mind to live each hour of every day of her incarceration with her mind set on the chance to escape. To do so, she had to keep alert. Survive. The dark-haired girl undressed seductively, all the time aware of the piggy eyes lecherously eyeing her body. Starvation conditions had caused her once-plump frame to shrink, ironically making her more attractive. She had heard that this little man was positively dangerous, information that had made her decide that survival depended on complying with his needs. An initial brutish lunging attempt at rape seemed preposterous. The girl firmly persuaded him that there was a more delicate and pleasurable route to fulfilment and put all her skills to best use, taking control of the situation. She knew first impressions were all important, and that a return visit meant staying alive for another day. The Jewess threw in all her experience and won his confidence by overcoming any apprehension of 'Rassenschande' that the evil little man might have harboured. He was keeping this one until he tired of her.

A second, more relaxed dilatory encounter left the high-ranking officer drowsy and content. "For a Jew you're good," he exclaimed, slapping her backside with his flat hand. His satisfied expression became fixed as he closed his eyes to rest on his back.

The third attempt by the temptress to arouse his enthusiasm was brushed aside with an exhausted gesture. Head on soft pillow, loins and heart taxed and wearied from her pounding, light snoring testified to spent slumber. Slowly, very slowly, the perfumed seductress tested his depth of sleep by touching his face. It was as she thought – he was dead to the world. The newly slim girl slid off the huge bed inch by inch, resisting the urge to try the door. 'I bet the swine has a bodyguard outside', she thought as she tiptoed to the French window, clothes clutched under one arm. 'Dear God, let it be open!' she prayed. Hardly daring to breathe, she tried the catch, gently easing it down. It gave and opened. She took in a strangled breath. 'Freedom!'

Heart pounding, in 35 trembling seconds she was dressed and on a balcony two floors above the Paris night traffic. Glimpsing the fire escape, she was gone.

Chapter 3

SUMMER 1939:

PARIS, RAOUL MONTPELIER

"Jews are leeches - bloodsuckers, all of them!"
Raoul Montpelier had been brought up from childhood with this daily condemnation by his father, Edouard, who had a loathing for the Jewish race to equal any Nazi.

"You have seen them for yourself, Raoul. When the American Jews come here to Montmartre with their stinking wealth to buy works of art, do they come to me? No! They buy their objets d'art from their own bloodsucking stinking breed." He was thinking of Hymie Goldberg in particular.

In 1935, when he had first decided to break away on his own, Edouard Montpelier could not accept that it would take time to establish his own business. He expected instant success to rival that of his employer, Hymie Goldberg, with whom he had served his apprenticeship, progressively working up to senior assessor, salesman and auctioneer. Everything Hymie knew or had learned since starting in business shortly after the First World War he had passed on to Edouard, who had been well rewarded for his labours. He was adequately remunerated, and had enough to bring up his family and educate Raoul well.

Nevertheless Edouard had nursed a burning jealousy of his employer for years, which festered into subversive hatred. Imagining exploitation every day of his life, he had fed this diet of hatred to his only son. Edouard had a driving ambition to one day be bigger than Hymie's business near the Eiffel Tower. Raoul was keenly interested in the business and learned quickly. He could read gold and silver hallmarks, date furniture and recognise Old Masters. When

Edouard had started his business in 1935, he had laid both hands on his son's shoulders. "I'm doing this for you, son. We are starting our family business, which you and your sons will inherit. I am giving you a good education, use it well. We will beat those Jewish swine at their own game. They only succeed because of their connections."

It took longer than expected, and they worked hard to get known.

"Our beloved France is the seat of culture. Our family heritage dates back to the aristocracy. Many of our forefathers paid the ultimate price in the Revolution, but the love of beautiful art is in our blood Raoul! The greedy Jews buy and sell to get rich. We are the custodians of a national heritage that will change hands through our agency, to be loved, preserved and cherished for prosperity." Raoul was impressed by this dogma and became fiercely ambitious to succeed.

Then the Germans came, changing their lives.

The German attacks occurred between May 10 and May 13, 1940. German Panzer Divisions smashed through the Ardennes, around the end of the Maginot Line, breaking through the powerful defence structure that had cost the French nation so much to build, rendering it useless. The Panzer juggernaut swept down and crossed the Seine on June 10, 1940, the same day Mussolini declared war on France. The Axis Pact of Steel between Hitler's Germany and Mussolini's Italy was formed.

On June 12, Raoul, now 18, and his father had their heads bent in concentration and fearful expectation as they heard the radio announcement, "The French Government has declared Paris an open city. This decision has been taken to avoid the destruction of our glorious city. The Government will depart for Tours." Three days later the Government moved to Bordeaux. A further news flash announced, "Marshall Petain has asked for an armistice."

It was granted on German terms that were accepted on June 22 at Rethondes in the forest of Compiegne, in the railway carriage in which Marshall Foch had dictated the Allies' terms in 1918. For the French people it was the ultimate humiliation. French surrender documentation completed, Hitler ordered obliteration of the entire area, effectively wiping out history.

Raoul would never forget the German Victory Parade march through the Arc de Triomphe and past the Etoile at the head of the Champs Elysees as he stood with his father and watched in silence. Wave upon wave of steel-helmeted German troops marched abreast in perfect unison, led by standard bearers of the Third Reich as if from the era of the Roman Legions. The troops were preceded by arrogant mounted officers on snorting tight-reined horses, prancing with impatience.

The jackbooted occupation of Paris had begun.

German occupation of France initially consisted of the land north of a line drawn from Geneva via Bourges in mid France to Bayonne in the Gulf of

Biscay. Southern France was an unoccupied zone under the control of the Vichy Government based at Vichy.

Once over the shock of being occupied by an invading force, the Montpelier family prepared to make the best of it. The invaders' conduct on their entry into Paris had been surprisingly restrained.

At dinner Edouard made a pronouncement. "Hell, I'll say this for Petain. He shows an indifference towards Jews, even tinged with distaste for the bastards. He sees them as I do. And that Foreign Minister Laval is clever. He realises that the Nazi racial dogma has presented him with a bargaining counter, and reckons that if the Germans want the Jews so badly they can have them, but for the price of conceding something he might want. Yes; he's shrewd that one."

In Vichy there was no discussion about the morality of handing people earmarked for persecution over to the Germans. It was a matter of expediency. Vichy took the initiative in currying favour and passed decrees against the Jews before being asked to do so by the Germans. Full cooperation came from the Vichy Government.

"If you can't beat 'em, join them I say," winked Edouard. As an opportunist, he could see light at the end of the tunnel. Some good could come from this after all.

"Raoul," Edouard continued, "you can see what will happen to the Jews. The Krauts will grab everything they have like they did in Germany. So objets d'art will be high on the list. That is where we come in. You know the ropes in Paris. If we help Jerry, they may leave us alone. Some might come our way if we play our cards right. We have nothing to lose by volunteering. What do you say?" Edouard looked enquiringly at his son.

"You could be right… it may work," replied his son. "How do we get in touch with them?"

"Embassy I suppose. We need to make an impression at the top to gain influence."

Edouard and Raoul were turned away from the German Embassy on their first attempt. Persistent, Edouard asked to speak to an under-secretary. "The information I can offer is highly valuable to your state. I must speak to the Ambassador," he explained. Edouard's urgency of purpose persuaded the intermediary.

On June 30 1940, Ambassador Abetz was busy with his new orders from Hitler in Berlin, but gave Edouard five minutes.

"Your Excellency, I am an art dealer. I have been in business for 21 years and know of every art dealer in Paris. I also know who has what. My son Raoul here is in business with me. We believe we can be of service to you."

The German Ambassador eyed the stern-faced intense man before him. The bushy eyebrows, penetrating eyes, flared nostrils and steely flat mouth portrayed a bitterness emphasised by his clipped speech. Maybe this man had something.

"Really? And what qualification does this young man have that might impress us?"

"Like me, he hates fucking Jews!"

The Ambassador smiled slowly, then more broadly until he laughed. "You are direct, I'll say that. What do you have in mind?"

"Your Excellency, we believe that we can render valuable service in directing your attention to those houses where art treasures and masterpieces can be found. My son is very knowledgeable. I have trained him since he was 12. He's good."

"Is that so? Well it seems your timing is perfect. I have just received instructions from the Führer to take into custody all objets d'art, whether state owned or in private Jewish hands." He coughed. "This is not expropriation, but a transfer to our safekeeping as security for eventual peace negotiations." The Ambassador had a wry smile on his lips.

"Your Excellency, my son and I will serve you well. We have only a small shop in Montmartre, but we are exceedingly skilled in the trade."

"If you serve the Third Reich well you will be handsomely rewarded. We will see to it that you have a large shop," he smiled conspiratorially, "when we have dealt with these fucking Jews as you so eloquently refer to them." His smile then vanished as he became serious.

"I am expecting Reichmarschall Goering in Paris any day. He has designated Dr Hermann Bunges, who is an S.S. Obersturmfuhrer, to seek out art treasures throughout France on his behalf. If your son is as good as you say he is, then he can be attached to the team searching the countryside. From what you tell me Monsieur Montpelier, your local knowledge of the Parisian art dealers will be invaluable to us. Yes, you can serve us best here in Paris."

"Your Excellency, we are at your disposal as willing collaborators. We share the common ideal to rid our land of these parasites. With respect, Your Excellency, my card," he said, deferentially leaning forward to place it on his desk.

Edouard and Raoul Montpelier were in the service of the Third Reich.

By the autumn of 1940 a Commission had been appointed to purge from public life anyone who had recently acquired French citizenship, and Jews had been banned from the liberal professions and the Administration.

Fascist youths began to harass Jews in public. Young people blockaded the fronts of Jewish shops to prevent customers entering. This was not the first time Jews had felt the wrath of the French people. In 1348 Jews in France were dragged from their houses and burned, as they blamed the terrible plague on their race. Pogroms occurred throughout Europe, with some 6 000 victims dying in Mainz, Germany, and 3 000 in Erfurt. When the plague subsided, only a few Jews were left in Germany or the Low Countries. History was repeating itself.

A series of articles appeared in Au Pilori. "The Jews must pay for the war or die."

At a meeting between German Ambassador Abetz and Best and members of the Verwaltungsstab on August 17 1940, it was decided to examine ways to limit the residence of Jews in the occupied zone and whether or not their property might be seized. A decree passed in September 1940 forbade Jews in the Vichy zone to return to the occupied zone.

Jews were compelled to carry special identity cards, and shopkeepers had to display rectangular yellow and black posters announcing "Jewish business". Publishing houses purged their lists, and 842 Jewish authors were withdrawn.

Edouard was delighted with developments, and even more so with the arrival in September of 27-year-old S.S. Hauptsturmfuhrer Theo Dannecker. His superior in Berlin was Adolf Eichmann, who reported directly to Heydrich and Himmler.

The French Authorities were required to assist within the Prefecture of Police. In October 1940, all Jews were required to register at police stations. The net was widened to include some recent immigrants from countries under Nazism or first generation French citizens whose nationality was open to question.

Dannecker, the German Embassy staff and the military administration met weekly in committee to coordinate policy. Within the military administration, the economic staff members were headed by Dr Michel who developed a further section, the Commissariat Generale Aux Questions Juives or CGQJ for short, to deal with the Jewish question.

Dr Michel sent out a circular to Feldkommandanteurs. "Two points of view are decisions in the action against Jews in the sphere of the economy. The first is to ensure that the elimination of Jews will also persist after the occupation, and the second is whether an apparatus cannot be constructed on the German side that will measure up to the large number of Jewish enterprises. These two considerations have led us to bring in the French authorities on the elimination of the Jews."

After deliberation, a solution was decided upon: nominate French managers to run the businesses, unless major German interests were at stake, with the object of replacing Jews with Frenchmen. "This way the French population can participate equally with the economic elimination of the Jews, and Germans alone are not seen to be replacing the Jews."

Vichy took advantage of the new racism. In October 1940 the Controle des Administrations Provisoires was created, nominally under the French Ministry of Industrial Production, to liaise with the military administration over the sequestration of Jewish businesses and factories.

Regelsberger, an Alsatian and previously an inspector from the Banque de France, now held the title of Director of Economic Aryanisation. He drew up lists of Jews to be arrested and dispatched to concentration camps so that their property could be made available. In this way 21 000 thousand businesses were transferred to French profiteers, from huge concerns to small workshops, factories and warehouses, freeholds, restaurants, shareholdings in private companies; anything in fact which had previously belonged to a Jew. The only stipulation that mattered was that the former owners should never return to claim what was theirs; this prompted every kind of denunciation and accusation. CGQJ was the instrument par excellence of collaboration, which was run by Xavier Vallat.

Edouard had to produce the goods to get into the Nazi's good books. He and Raoul duly completed a list of leading dealers that included Seligman, Wilderstein, Alphonse Mann, Rosenberg and Bernstein, with the Rothchild collection. This was followed by a list of lesser known art dealers and their business and home addresses.

His initiative made an impression on Dr Bunges, whose team, in which Raoul was now a member, systematically rifled the collections. Stocks of the leading dealers were seized together with sundry museum pieces: hundreds of packing cases were crammed into the Embassy and later removed to the Jeu de Paume.

Edouard lusted for revenge for Hymie Goldberg's persecution, and spent time scheming about an opportunity to get his own back. It would be slow mental torture.

"Herr Doktor. It would be helpful to me to have a search warrant with authority to inspect some of the smaller dealers. I am convinced they have some valuable pictures and artefacts in their collections. The genuine Aryan dealers I will ask to reserve their better pieces for the Reichmarschall to decide on. If I see good pieces in Jewish businesses, the authority will allow me to confiscate them for you before they hide them."

"Montpelier, your performance so far has been impressive, I'll grant you that. Yes, you will have your warrant. Good thinking."

Signed by the S.S. Obersturmfuhrer, Edouard's warrant was a powerful instrument of authority.

Trench coat belted, collar up, hands tucked in his pockets, Edouard sauntered into Goldberg's shop, his trilby hat down at the front. He was the picture of arrogance.

"Good to see you again Edouard. You are keeping well, Ja?" Bald, except for a white fringe, the bespectacled round faced Jew came forward to offer his hand. Edouard's hands stayed in his pockets. The old man hid his rejection. He had a natural pout. "What brings you to my shop? Is there something I can get for you?" he enquired, doe eyes in the wise old countenance remaining polite.

The bitter contempt in Edouard's hostile eyes, and gritted teeth barely visible through set lips, conveyed a message before he spoke. "Yes Goldberg. Those years of exploitation are about to be paid for. You are going to pay through the nose for all the business you stole from me. You and your breed are going to pay through your backside for all the humiliation I and those like me suffered in your stinking enterprises."

Edouard threw down his black leather swastika-emblazoned identity. "This warrant entitles me to search your premises, which is only a pleasure. Close up immediately!"

Hymie closed the door and hung the sign. Knowing his way around, it took Edouard little time to find Goldberg's prize possessions. From his walk-in safe he selected the most valuable works of art: a Renoir, two Degas, a Van Gogh and a Monet.

"I confiscate these in the name of Reichmarschall Goering. They are now the property of the Third Reich. The Van Gogh you will keep. It will remain in your stock safe. If I find it has gone missing, then I will make my recommendation to the CGQJ. Monsieur Xavier Vallat will accommodate my suggestion."

At this veiled threat the Jew drew in his breath. He knew well what it meant.

The next day, Goldberg's four valuable pictures were crated and taken to Dr Bunges, who was doubly impressed with the speed with which Montpelier had unearthed such treasures.

"The Reichmarshall will be very pleased with your contribution, Montpelier. I will introduce you and your son to him. You have both done well!"

"Danke! Danke schon!" Edouard bowed.

Chapter 4

RAOUL MONTPELIER CONTINUED

Goering's presence was overbearing. His sheer size impressed people. Reichmarschall Hermann Goering, Commander of the Luftwaffe, enjoyed impressing people.

He had designed for himself a white Reichmarshall uniform, arrayed with jewels and decorations, complete with the wings of the German Eagle and Iron Cross. He felt the uniform made him some kind of Imperial figurehead. Goering relished the luxuries and cuisine in Paris. When he entered selected restaurants and hotels, he liked to be applauded. Considering the majority of patrons were German officers and their girls and mistresses, this invariably occurred.

"Montpelier. Doctor Bunges speaks highly of you and your son. You are dedicated, I hear," he told them, shaking their hands.

"Thank you Reichmarschall. We consider it our duty in the cause. We are pleased to serve you."

"Excellent," he beamed.

Although Raoul was appropriately deferential, the round face, shallow mouth, bulbous nose and piggy eyes portrayed a weak character, however charming he appeared on the surface. Raoul was not to know at the time that Goering took drugs.

He soon learned. As far as Goering was concerned, he would use his powerful position for self-enrichment without batting an eyelid. Compulsory acquisition of items from French collections was his privilege. Works of art that might be considered 'Germanic' or had originated in Germany, in his view ought to be repatriated without hesitation.

Despite his personal opinion of Goering, Raoul became an important art scout for him, with massive powers. A young man holding such fiendish authority soon becomes morally corrupt, especially when aided and abetted by his father.

Raoul was in a position to take whatever he wanted. If he could steal so easily for his masters, he could also feather his own nest. It was easy to exploit the weak and persecuted. This included young women.

He worked hard, amassing a fortune in pictures from the famous art houses of Paris. These were arranged at the Jeu de Paume where the French curator, Rose Valland, received Goering, accompanied by his art consultant, Walter Andreas Hofer, on November 3, 1940. Goering arrived for his private viewing in civilian clothes, in a long raincoat, with the brim of a trilby hat pulled well down on his face. One day was spent making his selection, and he returned again on November 5. He chose 53 pieces, including one each of Goya, Rembrandt and Teniers from the Rothchild, Seligmann and Wilderstein collections, with works by Rubens, Boucher and Frans Hals.

Raoul learned that Hitler overlooked Goering's plunderings. As a token, 15 cases of objets d'art reserved for Hitler were dispatched straight to Munich; a sweetener to allow continued piracy.

Raoul pulled himself up to his full imposing height, set his square jaw which made him look older than his 19 years, and rang the door bell. A middle-aged Jewish woman answered, looking strangely frightened. It was early afternoon. Raoul flashed his identity card, walked uninvited into the conservatively furnished hallway and stood with his feet apart in an authoritarian stance.

"I am here to inspect your house to see what art works you have hidden."

Rosie Goldberg clasped her hand to her mouth in shock at the outrageous implication. "Vee haf only vat you see on zee valls. Vee hide nothing. Kom, see yourself." She led Raoul into the large reception lounge hung with good works of art, but not in the superior class. Raoul nodded.

"Where is your daughter? Perhaps she will know!"

Rosie was in a panic for her 19-year-old Rachael, their only child. She had been born late when Rosie was 34 and Hymie just established at 35.

"She is not vell. She stay in her room," she lied.

"Really! Then I will go to her. Which room?"

It was hopeless. Rosie led the way, knocked on her daughter's door and went in. Rachael was reading at her desk.

"This young man vants to haf a vord mit you Rachael." Rosie was shaking.

"Leave us." Raoul commanded the distraught mother, who left reluctantly, dabbing her eyes with a silk handkerchief.

These bastards want for nothing, thought Raoul. Well I'll show them who is boss now! Father said I was to humiliate them through their darling daughter.

What a pleasure. He kicked the door closed.

"So you are Rachael Goldberg, eh! You have been living like a princess on the fat of the land whilst our family struggled for a crust. Well dear girl, things have changed. Financial power is being returned to Frenchmen. In the meantime I am requesting your full cooperation to tell me where your father keeps his wealth!"

"My father has his account with the Banque de France. As you have been to his studio I am sure you know that." Her words were factual, but not impertinent.

Raoul laughed. "Oh yes. True. It is not that I am enquiring about. All you damn Jews keep gold, so don't deny that you all hoard gold. Where is your father's gold?" He leaned over threateningly, his face close to hers.

"Please. I am sure he has none. He has never spoken to me about any gold. Not once."

"Is that so? Well now, that is very unfortunate; for you I mean, because I will have to resort to… shall we say persuasion to help you remember." With a twisted smirk on his face, Raoul sat on the vanity stool. "Come here!" he commanded.

Rachael hesitated, not sure how best to respond.

"Come here I said," came the command again. She edged towards him.

"Closer!"

She came within touching distance.

"If you do not cooperate, I should explain that Monsieur Vallat of CGQJ is considered too soft on Jews and a stronger police force is being organised. A few words from me and your mother and father will no longer be sleeping here. Understand? On the other hand, I am not without influence. I can arrange that they are left alone. It is your choice!"

Rachael nodded. "I will do anything to keep my mother and father safe."

"Good. Now we have an understanding." Raoul placed his hand under her calf length dress and slid it up to her knee. She flinched but remained calm. His fingers moved higher up along the inside of her thigh. Halfway up Rachael involuntarily buckled forward in reaction to the intrusion of her privacy. Her sheltered life had not prepared her for an encounter like this, and she felt deeply humiliated.

Raoul withdrew his hand quickly. "So be it. Then I withdraw my support. I feel sorry for them."

Rachael was humbly apologetic. Although scared stiff, she thought, 'What the hell'. She touched herself; what difference did it make if a man touched her there?

"I am sorry. Please. It is alright." She stood stoically by his side, head up, staring into space, her defiance masked as she bit her lip. Raoul was enjoying her humility. He realised how resentful she must be feeling, but that she was helpless in his power. His hand returned and slowly moved up to her pelvic area. He could see her grit her teeth in resentment as his fingers pried into her panties.

"It would be nice to see what we have here," he smiled. "Get undressed."

She shuddered but slowly complied. Rachael was not beautiful by any standards. Her face was rather plain and uninteresting, with plump hips and waist giving her a round dumpy appearance. Even her large breasts and brownish nipples looked clumsy. All the same, she was coy about revealing herself.

"Off – all of them," commanded Raoul.

She struggled out of her foundation garment, releasing her flabby belly which, freed from bondage, flopped forwards.

'Hell, I can't believe this', thought Raoul. Normally a healthy, red-blooded individual, he did not find Rachael in the flesh at all desirable. His ardour for her cooled although he remained determined to impress his power upon her. He had to humiliate her further.

"He asked undiplomatically, "Are you a virgin?"

She nodded.

"I'm not surprised." Raoul decided that to achieve his objective he had to give her something to worry about after his departure. "I'll show you something. Here, look at this." He opened his fly and pulled out his penis, not yet fully aroused.

Rachael caught her breath. This was the first time she had seen a man's male organ.

"Here. Hold it. It won't bite you. You had better get used to the idea!" Nervously, Rachael put her fingers gently around his long, still slack manhood. A little later she had him excited. Raoul lay on the bed, pants half down his legs, and gave Rachael her first basic instruction in manually pleasuring a male.

"Good my child," he said, eyes closed. Satisfied on all scores, he left. Two days later he came back and raped her.

Chapter 5

1941 - 1942:

PARIS

" I only found token junk. There was nothing of value in the temple," Raoul informed his father. "The PQJ have names... I expect the members will be pursued and harassed."

Extortion and blackmail had become second nature to the Police aux Questions Juives, or anti-Jewish Police, whose ranks were permeated by Fascists and anti-Semites. A Masonic lodge in Paris had recently been raided by them, in accordance with the scurrilous reasoning of the Nazi philosopher Alfred Rosenberg's book, The Crime of Freemasonry.

An Exposicion Masonique was held to publicly ridicule the society and strongly condemn the ancient Jewish rites, in compliance with Hitler's orders that Masonic temples were to be desecrated and their contents destroyed.

Being well informed, Raoul was not surprised when Vallat was replaced by the fanatical Darquier Pellepoix. The PQJ were to arrest 35 000 Jews altogether, nearly double the 20 000 arrested by the Prefecture of Police under Commissaire Francois.

Whereas Raoul was considered an authority on art, his two compatriots were thugs. The team travelled to estates, wine farms and houses throughout northern occupied France in search of Jewish property. Valuable works of art were confiscated, and their Jewish owners were also robbed of their businesses, farms, estates and lands in the wake of Raoul's team and others like them. Lorry loads of artefacts, precious paintings and priceless furniture were dispatched to Paris. During one such excursion Raoul arrived at Montmort near Epernay and entered the wine estate of Mannie Gaston. They drove thorough an avenue of neatly trimmed vines up to the house.

Mannie opened the door to Raoul's knock and offered his gnarled hand in greeting. It was ignored.

"PQJ." Raoul flashed his identity card and pushed past Gaston, his manner rude, his speech brusque and arrogant. "You are the owner, Gaston?"

"Yes sir." Mannie clasped his hands tightly together.

"When did you buy the estate?"

"My wife and I inherited it from her father. He died in 1936."

"Is your wife a Jew?"

"Yes sir. She is a French citizen, born in France."

"Enfant. Les enfants?"

"No," lied Mannie. Sophie was on the other side of the river, where she worked as a kitchen maid with the Saint-Laurent family. "Do you have any pictures? You had better cooperate, Jew, or we will smash your place up. Understand! And my friend here loves to rape the ladies."

Mannie complied, pointing out his mediocre hangings in the hall, on the stairs and in the living rooms.

"Those chairs, Louis XIV, and that table. They are not in bad condition." Raoul pointed. "Take them." Burly Paul Matisse elbowed Mannie aside and carried the antiques out to their vehicle.

"Books! Where are your books of account?" Mannie brought his account ledgers and Raoul ran his eyes over the pages, inspecting the receipts for grape sales and payments.

"Where are the land deeds?" Raoul looked through the hastily fetched deeds, then gestured to Andre to bring the receipt book. Raoul scribbled down some words, tore out the leaf of paper, and handed it to Mannie.

"We are taking these to check registration."

The grape producer stood back, helpless. Satisfied, they took their departure and drove on to the next wine estate, passing under an arched cut-out metal gate sign proclaiming La Verite. Napoleonic era cannons in profile bordered the estate name. He was met at the door by Henri Saint-Laurent. "Welcome to La Verite. I'm Henri Saint-Laurent and this is my father, Arnaud," he said cordially, turning to introduce him.

"Guten tag! Kommen sie herein! Sie trinken ein glas champagne?" Arnaud knew many German officers and had Nazi friends whom he treated like royalty. He beamed at his uninvited guests in their Renault, quick to have spotted the official number plate.

"Danke schon," Raoul responded appropriately before switching into French, "but I am French, Monsieur," smiling benignly.

"Mais oui! Naturellement."

Henri had made sure Sophie was hidden at the back. Champagne flowed freely in the huge reception lounge.

"How do you find labour in these difficult times?" enquired Raoul, making polite conversation.

Arnaud answered him. "We have some very accommodating friends in the Party who assist us with a labour allocation for our esteemed industry." He was smiling. This was a euphemism for the forced labour from the Royal-Lieu concentration camp at Compiegne, 48 kilometres north of Paris, who worked at the estate for food and shelter. In return, this 'essential industry' would continue supplying top quality champagne to German dinner tables in Paris and Berlin. Certain categories of 'economically useful' Jews were granted an 'ausweis' to continue trades earmarked with priority status by the Wehrmacht, such as cobblers and furriers making boots and clothing for the Russian winter troops.

Raoul stood up and approached a painting as if to admire it. "Henri, this is a fine painting! See the detail." Henri came over. He could barely hear Raoul's quiet question. "Do you have some distraction for these gorillas of mine?" He inclined his head slightly towards the two surly men. "I want to talk to you alone." Then, more loudly, "This detail is magnificent. Duval; '08. Beautiful."

"Yes, I see what you mean. Indeed," and under his breath, "I'll fix it." Henri walked over to the thugs, filled their glasses. "Drink up! Come. I have something that will interest you." He disappeared to instruct his foreman, who strode over to the women's quarters to summon two.

Henri rejoined his father. "That Jew over there," Raoul gestured across the vineyard to Mannie Gaston's estate, "does he have good land?"

"Excellent soil. Produces a fine grape," replied Henri.

"A wine estate like that should be in the hands of a Frenchman. De Pellenoix wants Jews like him out."

Arnaud sat bolt upright. "Is that so?"

"Do you want the place?"

Arnaud's eyes shone like beacons. "What a question! We need to expand… Henri could work that section," he answered excitedly.

"It can be arranged. I can get rid of him and recommend that his estate be combined with yours." He paused. "For a price!"

Henri visualised the considerable wealth coming his way. "What would that be?"

"You have cellars here?" Raoul touched his nose before divulging his conspiracy.

"Yes. Why?" His voice was anxious now, inquisitive.

"I have some works of art I need to protect for an indefinite period. Should I say it would be awkward if others were to find out what I was doing?" He looked knowingly at the father and son, who both nodded, grinning. "Well?"

"But of course! It would be a pleasure!" Raoul and Henri shook hands warmly. "We'll drink to our bargain." After filling their glasses, he raised his, with a 'salute!' The three men clinked glasses and downed their champagne, broad smiles of satisfaction on their faces.

While most paintings were transported to the Jeu de Parme, 30 canvases remained in the German Embassy on August 11, 1941. They were auctioned whilst a decent price was obtainable and profits were made on the side. The Rosenberg staff members were not averse to selling off various lots of works by artists who were not Jewish, although not considered to be of great merit. These included paintings by Bounard, Vuillard, Matisse, Braque and Dufy. Little by little, Raoul secured a quantity of these for himself which he stored with Henri. After all, if Ribbentrop could steal works of art from the Einsatzstab Rosenberg collection, then so could he.

During 1941, Goering sequestrated 25 pictures from the David-Weil collection and 50 from Jacques Stern, as well as securing 10 canvases by Degas, 10 by Renoir, two Monets, three Sisleys, four Cezannes and five Van Goghs, all for his country house, Karinhall.

Raoul assisted in organising the transfer of the proceeds of two days shopping at the Jeu de Parme and sundry raids. Two gigantic freight cars at the Gare de L'Est were crammed full of booty. Robert Scholtz drew up an inventory of 21 903 works of art looted through the Einsatzstab Rosenberg, which included 10 890 pictures and 5 825 objets d'art, as well as furniture, jewellery, even altar clothes and goblets. The rolling stock moved out to Germany.

Works considered by Nazi doctrine to be unfit for retention were taken by military trucks from the Jeu de Parme and stocked in the Louvre. These included some 500 to 600 canvases by artists such as Masson, Miro, Picabia, Klee, Max Ernst, Picasso, Kisling, Leger and Nane-Katz.

Anticipating the almost predictable destruction of such treasures on doctrinaire grounds and foreseeing the inevitable scarcity value the consequence of such actions would have in the future for any surviving canvases, Raoul came up with a bold scheme to save a selection across the board by pulling off an incredible fraud in his capacity of art selector. He knew discovery would mean death, or even death by torture, but he was prepared to take one gigantic gamble. It was either become a multi-millionaire or die. He had the complicity of Henri Saint-Laurent and the security of his cellars, and he, his strongmen and their Renault van were a familiar sight at the Louvre. Raoul gambled on the fact that the canvases designated undesirable would remain undisturbed in the Louvre, or be destroyed. Why review them again after so much effort?

Having power of access he managed to substitute a considerable number of lesser known painters' canvases, gathered on his sojourns in the country, for the best Miro, Klee, Picasso, Max Ernst and Leger canvases from the undesirable section. His hoard went to Henri's cellar at La Verite.

Fortunately his henchmen knew nothing of value or the significance of his actions. If the pictures had impressive frames, they assumed the works to be valuable. Raoul made periodic trips to the family business in Paris to remove the Van Gogh paintings and other valuable works he had stolen, for storage with Henri.

Chapter 6

1942 - 1943:

PARIS

Martin Bormann, Chief of the Nazi Party Chancellery, was a prime Jew hater and propagator of Jewish extermination policies. As personal secretary to Hitler, he was also very close to his superior.

Possessing an oval face, steely jaw line and receding hair, Bormann projected a bitter countenance, angry with the world and Jews in particular.

The process of Jewish extermination was not proceeding fast enough for him. It was hindered by Hitler's other confidant, his Head of German Police, S.S. Reichfuhrer Hienrich Himmler.

Bormann and Himmler were often at loggerheads over Jewish policy: whether to kill them or use them.

Himmler had visions of Jews working as slaves for the Reich in S.S. controlled factories, and was successful to some extent. Saukel and Speer wanted Jews for their labour supply. At Buchenwald and Neuengamme concentration camps in 1942, 5 000 inmates produced carbines, while 6 000 inmates were ordered to produce 3,7cm anti-aircraft guns at Auschwitz, and 6 000 female inmates spent their days manufacturing communication devices at Ravensbruck.

Bormann nevertheless continued to wield enormous power behind the throne.

In late June 1942, Raoul walked into the large objets d'art shop he and his father owned, which had once belonged to Hymie Goldberg.

"Want to hear the latest?"

"What's that?" asked his father, after first making sure no one else was around to overhear.

"Adolf Eichmann is coming to Paris to discuss with Dannecker the objective of deporting all French Jews to Germany as soon as possible."

"In that case you had better withdraw your support for Goldberg's daughter. You might get sent with them!"

Raoul laughed. "Forget it. I've put so many S.S. officers through that whore they dare not make a move against me. There have been plenty. Remember they don't want a dose and at least the bitch is clean. " Raoul laughed, thinking his boast extremely funny. His father grinned sheepishly.

"Better to finger the Goldbergs now than get seen in the wrong light, my boy!"

"I'm listening," his son nodded.

Raoul reported to the right authorities. He was assured the Goldberg family would be arrested and sent to Drancy camp near the Le Bourget Airport Paris. The first Commandant there was called Laurent. Raoul would bear the name in mind.

Raoul Montpelier led a charmed life. Incredible good fortune in time and circumstance enabled him to capitalise on his expertise and enrich himself very quickly at the expense and misfortune of the less unfortunate and exploited.

His position provided unparalleled opportunity to take advantage of women, and he used guile to achieve his objectives with Nazi authorities through soliciting and the sordid perversions of the women with whom he provided them.

But in the flush of his success lay the seeds of his own future mental torment.

Raoul's scheming involved a French Algerian madame, whose brothel was near Raoul's flat in Montmartre. He had assured this most evil woman, who treated her prostitutes badly, of a steady flow of young Jewish girls through Drancy camp. When their fresh bloom of youth faded, they would join the cattle trucks for Flossenberg or Buchenwald. In turn Madame Courtier provided trained young girls to perform discreet services for high ranking officers in Raoul's flat, one S.S. Colonel in particular.

Madame Courtier brought a 12-year-old girl to his door and pushed her roughly forwards. "She's good now. Tell me if he's not satisfied and I'll thrash her!

Emilie Cohen had learned the hard way. Madame Courtier's speciality was pinching their soft flesh until they squealed in pain. It was her great persuader. Emilie learned fast and applied skills the other girls had explained to her.

Well satisfied, the S.S. Colonel left at midnight.

"Please don't send me back! Let me stay. Please." The waif made a direct play for Raoul's groin; no finesse. "Please let me stay." She held more tightly in desperation. Raoul was aroused. "Tonight then. But tomorrow you go!"

But he became addicted to her sensuous young body. Emilie saw her chance for survival and went out of her way to pleasure him; anything to get out of the brothel and away from Madame Courtier for as long as possible.

She also came regularly to his flat to entertain his S.S. and Nazi acquaintances, which accommodated his blackmail scheming.

She stayed on when they had left and Raoul became more agreeable to her presence. Some nights he called for her. He wanted her, lusted for her youthful frame, and his urge to possess her young body became more demanding. She was a necessary drug.

The brothel witch was quietly amused by his addiction. She'd seen it all before – a chance for a desperate woman to gain a tenuous hold over a man. These men were really stupid pigs

The Goldbergs were swept up on July 16, 1942 in La Grande Rafle, The Great Raid. Children were separated from parents; their bitter crying could be heard in the streets. Most Jews arrested were deported to the Reich and not sent to labour camps or settlements, but to their deaths. It was the Final Solution in the extermination camps.

Rachael Goldberg was pulled apart from the heaving herd of humanity by two SS officers who had frequently been with her.

Well satisfied with her services they wanted to retain their free source of entertainment. Raoul had told her that, although she was no beauty, her sexual skills would probably save her life. Clutching at straws, she had accepted this theory. Unfortunately Raoul had oversold his protégé. He now preferred her dead with no trace to their former connection. As long as she remained alive, be needed to keep track of her and await his opportunity. Rachael was duly held captive in Madame Courtier's brothel for the exclusive use of a number of German officers.

At the end of July 1942, Dannecker was replaced by Heinz Roethke, and the transportation of 1 000 Jews at a time to their deaths began. There were other camps deep in the countryside at Athiviers and Beaune-La-Rolande, from whence Mannie Gaston and his wife were railed out to meet their end by extermination. Raoul had kept his side of the bargain with Henri Saint-Laurent and Arnaud: he had made them wealthy and would use them for his gain.

A conference was called on September 15 1942 to discuss the fate of the 50 000 Jews who were to be occupied in factories. The S.S. was represented by Pohl and Kammler. Representatives of industry were propositioned to transfer entire plants into concentration camp factories. However, the industrialists did not want to see unfair competition working against their own interests and dragged their feet over the issue, so the Jews were sent east to extermination camps. Matter settled.

As Minister of Production, Karl Saukel persuaded Hitler to visit a camp and see that prisoners could be of valuable assistance in factories already established in industrial sectors. Hitler eventually accepted the argument that private business should benefit from this pool of labour, a decision which enabled Saukel to guarantee the supply of all manpower demanded from occupied territories.

The conflict of interests in the supreme Nazi hierarchy undoubtedly saved countless thousands of Jewish lives. Bormann however was impatient, insatiable in his maniacal desire to rid Earth of the entire Jewish race.

In 1943 Hauptsturmfuhrer Alois Brunner came to Paris, fresh from murdering 80 000 Jews from Salonika. Brunner was puny and of poor build, with wicked little eyes. Perfidious, pitiless and a liar who cynically exploited human weaknesses, he had no scruples whatsoever about resorting to the most blatant blackmail to achieve his ends, the threat of deportation. His assistants Bruckler, Weisel and Koepler were sadists who starved and brutalised the inmates of Drancy.

Raoul managed to arrange for the Police to raid the brothel and take Rachael. She was sent to Drancy where she was violated without mercy. The by now half demented woman was then dispatched to her doom. Bruckler told him that his problem was now over, his father avenged.

Raoul had gathered a potential fortune, but still needed to possess it. Invasion by Britain and America was becoming a distinct probability in early 1943, prompting him to approach Henri.

"Henri, you have a lot of canvases for me in your cellars. If France is overrun, they might be discovered by the invading forces. Our province of Champagne has seen an unfair share of war in the past. Do you have any ideas?"

Henri's eyes twitched. "My grandfather has a chateau at Zellenberg. They will be safer there; war usually skirts the Rhine away from the industrial centres."

"I'm not happy with them here, Henri. If you can save them, a quarter will be yours! What do you say?"

"It should be fine with the family, but can you get a movement order to get into Alsace Lorraine?"

"Your hoard can be stored at Zellenberg if you can get it there."

"No problem," Raoul beamed.

He would use his influence on his perverted S.S. Kolonel, who Emilie Cohen entertained in his Montmartre flat by prior arrangement. When it came to the exceptionally discreet gratification of demeaning sexual desires, Raoul had found that the recipients did not ask for too much detail for a favour. He obtained the necessary permit and a requisition for a large van to accommodate his haul, on the pretext of raiding homes and properties north of Metz.

On one occasion, he had asked Emilie what she did for the Kolonel that made him so pliable. When she told him, he couldn't believe it.

"Do that to me and I'd kill you!" he said sternly. Then they both burst into hysterical laughter at the thought of how the Kolonel was being ridiculed. Raoul liked Emilie, but it was dangerous.

By late Spring 1943, Raoul's illicit collection was safely walled up at Zellenberg. As he had promised, a quarter of his hoard was Henri's. They were in this together. On May 27 1943 an immense bonfire flared up in the Louvre courtyard when up to 600 canvases by undesirables were burnt to ashes. Raoul was home and dry, evidence of his fraud destroyed.

Chapter 7

JUNE 1939:

MONTMORT, NEAR EPERNAY - HENRI SAINT-LAURENT

Like Raoul, Henri Saint-Laurent too led a charmed life. Brought up on his father's wine estate, La Verite, at Montmort near Epernay in Champagne Province, he had never needed to put much effort into his life. His hardworking father had built an assured future for him, so why bother? He was preoccupied by self-indulgence, with aspirations of becoming a playboy. Nevertheless, he was a highly intelligent young man.

Not particularly tall, Henri had a splendid physique, with a slender athletic build. His lean tanned face gave him a gypsy-like appearance, further enhanced by a narrow nose, prominent black eyebrows, moustache above firm mouth and pointed chin. Dimples below high cheek bones beguiled the unwary into believing him a self-centred man. But it was his bedroom eyes that riveted attention, at times piercing, at others persuasive, always mysterious, as if guarding an inner secret.

Handsome as a youth, women had admired him throughout his life, magnetised by his dormant sex appeal. He was quite young, just 13, when he had his first encounter in June, 1935. Henri thought back to that memorable day next to the stream that marked the boundary of their and the Gastons' estate.

In the warm sunshine midges buzzed around his head as he strolled towards the awe-inspiring windbreak of poplar trees bordering the stream. The rustling leaves and rippling water coursing between the stepping stones in the shallow stream muffled all other sounds, allowing Henri to reach the water edge undetected by the Jewish girl who lay on the opposite bank. Henri could not believe his eyes. Sophie Gaston was stark naked, her eyes closed and mouth open as she massaged her lower abdomen. As if spellbound, Henri was riveted to the spot, eyes like saucers as he gaped at the long legs, slender hips, neat waist and full breasts. Although not strikingly beautiful, Sophie was attractive, with a pretty face that did not reflect her Jewish heritage, and dark hair that showed off her features to their best advantage. At that moment her glorious body made her seem like the most magnificent being Henri had ever seen.

Sophie groaned, raising her knees as she revelled in her self-induced ecstasy. It was then she opened her eyes.

She jumped up like a shot rabbit when she saw him, grabbing her towel in a reflex action to cover up her naked body. "What are you doing there?" she yelled at him.

"Nothing," answered the 13-year-old stripling. Aroused by her nakedness, he was aware of the uncomfortable bulge in his trousers. The boys often discussed sex at school, but he had never come this close to reality before.

"How dare you stare at me!" she shouted in an attempt to cover her guilty embarrassment. She was terrified he would relate what he had witnessed.

"Don't get angry with me Sophie. I won't tell. Can I come over to your side? I feel stupid standing here while you are shouting."

His words were temporary assurance. She saw no advantage in antagonising him. Rather cement his pledge of silence. Sophie felt better. "Sorry. Yes, come over. You startled me, that's all."

Rolling up his trousers, Henri took off his shoes and stepped across the stream. Looking down in the crystal clear water he saw a flash of silver as a fish darted to swallow what he thought was a minnow. One life for another, he thought. Not concentrating properly, his right foot slipped on a wet stone and down he went, soaking the rolled up trouser leg, but he avoided complete disaster and held onto his shoes. Recovering, he laughed with her which released tension in both of them.

Sophie was the same age as his sister, whom he grudgingly respected when she issued reprimands in their mother's tone. He did not know then that his sister would die in an air raid. To Henri a two-year gap between 13 and 15 was a chasm. Sophie was two grades ahead of him at school, where her father took her every morning in his gig. Sophie was very much his senior and he knew well enough that he did what his seniors told him to do!

"Don't stand there in wet pants," she ordered. "You will get pneumonia. Take them off and hang them on that bush. It's warm; they'll soon dry."

Henri hesitated, then obeyed. But now he had lost the cloak that had concealed his feelings. Sophie's eyes popped as she saw the bulge in his underpants. Breathless she gasped, "I can't believe it Henri, can I see it? I'll let you look at me if I can see yours."

She lay down on her towel, opening slim thighs.

"Come. Have a look. Your first time, eh?"

Henri nodded, enthralled by the sight that he would remember all his days. "Like it?"

"Yes," he croaked.

Still not sure, but obeying authority, he dropped his underpants. Sophie drew in her breath sharply. "It is beautiful. I've only seen one other boy's, but yours is big compared to his!" Henri felt quite bashful.

"Come, sit with me." Sophie tentatively put out her hand to slowly grasp his penis in her slender fingers. Her gentle stroking sensation drove him crazy.

Her brown eyes were shining as she asked him huskily, "Have you come yet?" He thought he knew what she meant but not sure. He looked blank.

"If you play with it, does it spurt out?"

"No. It feels funny though. But it doesn't spurt. No."

"Good! She smiled and kissed him tenderly. "Keep quiet about our meeting and I'll give you your first lesson. I know you'll like it! Lie down on my towel."

Sophie gently guided him into her body, gradually lowering herself on top of him. Henri touched her erect pink nipples and made her shudder. He liked her slim figure. He watched her face contort through ecstasy to agony and back again. Slowly she engulfed his whole length, moaning, "Oh no. No!"

Henri couldn't understand it. "Does it hurt you?"

"No silly boy!" she smiled down at him dreamily. "It's gorgeous. Oh, it's lovely," she sighed, as she began moving up and down rhythmically, until spasms shook her uncontrollably. She threw her head back and then let it fall forward. Henri felt contracting muscles gripping him, but it was a dry experience. He realised something was still missing.

That first encounter with lovemaking would affect him psychologically for the rest of his life. He had lost his respect for women, firmly believing that when a woman said 'No' to sex, she wanted it desperately anyway. Sophie did nothing to dispel his theory. She had taken him and that is what women liked. They wanted to be violated, especially Jewish women.

Henri became Sophie's plaything, in constant demand on the river bank or in any place where they could find solitude.

Knowing that Henri was nearing puberty and fearing pregnancy, Sophie did not allow penetration again. They became constant companions, enjoying their exploits together. In fact, she caused him to become addicted to sex and had a huge influence on Henri and his future attitude to women, much to the detriment of her gender.

Chapter 8

LA VERITE, MONTMORT

Henri learned all about vineyard management while he was growing up, attending courses, seminars and lectures. School holidays were spent at his grandfather's estate at Zellenberg in Alsace, so he was never away from cultivation of the grape.

Henri compared management styles between his father at Montmort and his grandfather at Zellenberg, forming his own opinions. He may have been, or wanted to be a playboy, but he was an expert when it came to the wine and champagne industry. No estate manager could deceive him about quality, yield and production costs. Henri owed a debt of gratitude to his father, who ensured that his son would be equipped to eventually manage the family estates. At his father's insistence, Henri had studied economics at Heidelberg University, reinforcing his Germanic heritage and skill in the language.

Henri sat in a quietly mediative mood next to the stream one day, looking over the rows upon rows of ripening grapes, growing the wealth that would one day all belong to him. He thought of the debt he owed his father, Arnaud Saint-Laurent, who had made it all possible. Half asleep in the balmy air he mused on the history of the estate.

Arnaud Saint-Laurent was a visionary. He had courage too. Ruthless, he used any means to achieve his aim of increasing the family fortunes. Fortunately for him, his father, Baron von Zeichenhausen, had given him financial support.

After the First World War, Alsace reverted to French control and he became Arnaud Saint-Laurent by adopting his mother's family name as a matter of expediency.

Then one day his ship had come in. He had been searching for land to buy and discovered a large estate at Montmort, which had been diabolically stamped by the hell of war. Grapes were the most precious possession in Champagne Province, and Arnaud knew that the best champagne grapes grew on the chalky slopes south of Reims. He found a ruined farmhouse, razed almost to the ground, and noticed that a barn had escaped with only half the roof and walls blown away. He went inside, picking his way through fallen roofing, and recognised an old wine press, equipment, familiar stakes and wire bales. Even the rats had left and only musty decay remained. Troops had plundered the wine cellar. He found a rusty steel helmet that had once belonged to the Wehrmacht and kicked it, the clatter echoing in the desolate space. Although it had been raided, the invaders had not destroyed the rows of about 100 000 empty bottles, ideal for champagne.

Enquiries revealed that the farmer and his wife had been killed, and their shelled farmhouse burnt to ashes. Arnaud tracked down the farmer's sister, who had inherited the property. As she was destitute, without the capital to restore the vineyard, she was only too glad to accept his offer for the deeds, considering herself well rid of a pile of churned up derelict ground, pitted by shell holes and trenches, and strewn with war rubbish and the remains of destroyed buildings.

Arnaud learned from the Reims wine academy that the best chalky soil lay between Troyes and Saint-Dizier. However, he had not been able to find land there for sale, and Montmort as second best was a bargain. Some of the finest farmlands had been destroyed in the war, their buildings shattered and abandoned. Arnaud purchased land in this state, registered the deeds, and formulated a plan of action. His first step was to hire two massive steam tractors that had previously been used to tug heavy field artillery pieces around the battlefields. Engines screamed and tortured metal groaned as cables winched massive six-blade plough shares across the land. Piles of shells, cases, wheels, gun carriages, rifles, machine guns, steel helmets, as well as assorted equipment and machinery, including a Ford-T ambulance, were dragged to the surface. Ever the visionary, Arnaud stored a selection of the better pieces for a War Museum.

Bones of men and horses, accumulated like a knacker's yard, became commonplace in land restoration. He bought an early model Ford tractor, and eventually all the shell holes, craters and trenches were filled, tree stumps uprooted, and rubbish burnt. Then he tilled the gentle slopes until the surface was smooth and the soil evenly textured.

Arnaud drove himself without pausing for rest until, after months of gruelling toil, stakes were finally driven in and wires attached ready for planting.

Thanks to the Baron, his father, who financed the restoration of the barn and cellar, coopers were able to restore casks, pails and tubs in readiness for the first harvest. Arnaud was ready.

He had stayed in rented accommodation until the first phase was complete; the house could wait.

The great day came for him when he bought his first vine stalks in Epernay through negotiants in Reims, a town that is still currently prominent in the production and sale of champagne. It had been so ever since the discovery of champagne by Dom Perignon some 250 years previously. At 21, Arnaud was a grower or vigneron.

He was aware of the vignerons' fight for their rights to prevent the importation of inferior wines from southern vineyards into the province of Champagne, where riots in 1910 and 1911 had resulted in a great loss of life. Several champagne houses owned by the Grande Marques had been burnt to the ground in retribution for their feudal treatment of the vignerons, who owned the vines which yielded 85 percent of the grapes used in the champagne industry.

Following the riots, fair market practices were established in what would normally be a buyer's market, with negotiants buying the grapes and providing the accommodation for producing champagne. The wine industry war over, Arnaud was confident that his investment was safe and 'le champagne' would retain its top market position and exclusive panache.

Where others were slow off the mark, Arnaud was established, planted and waiting the growth of his vines, achieving a head-start on competitors. It was hardly surprising that he turned his estate, La Verite, into a highly successful venture.

At a later stage Arnaud built a farmhouse and returned to Zellenberg to marry his childhood sweetheart, Ursula Broch. Their son, Henri, was born at the estate in 1922.

As the years passed Arnaud was not happy to see his grapes go to negotiants. As far as he was concerned, they seemed to profit the most from the arrangement, making him determined to produce his own champagne. Local craftsmen, desperate for work, took pride in restoring the old wine presses to their pristine glory and in building new ones. Arnaud led the field as an independent, while others followed or joined cooperatives. He fought hard for his market share, and after realising that he needed successful advertising to promote sales, he decided to open his cellars to the public. Let them see the champagne making process and taste the result. The idea was moderately successful, but he knew that he needed an additional attraction to draw the people. Then the answer came to him – a War Museum.

In the off season period he employed work-starved peasants to clean and refurbish his stored war materials. The War Museum proved a success, drawing tourists from Europe, Britain and America, many of whom had lost relatives in the terrible war.

The area was steeped in history, an adjunct to the natural wine route. Montmort was situated 30 kilometres from Chalons Sur Marne to the east, where the Battle of the Marne was fought in August 1914. Chalons fell to German troops and in the north, ancient Reims was also captured. The French lost 200 000 men in April 1917, and when sections of the army mutinied 55 ringleaders were shot and 300 sent to Devil's Island. Marshall Petain valued his soldiers' lives and restored morale in May 1917.

On May 5 1918 the Front Line stretched from Soissons, Reims and Verdun to Nancy. Chalons Sur Marne was in the line of attack in 1918 and Chateau Thierry on the River Marne, west of Montmort, was captured by the Germans. The Battle of Belleau Wood in June 1918, near the village of Bourceches, saw the Americans enter the war. As a visionary Arnaud thought that this wealth of history would be a magnet for tourists one day. He was right.

The label on his bottles, which featured a Napoleonic field cannon, acquired a reputation for distinction amongst champagne connoisseurs, and Arnaud's growing prosperity soon led to a fine mansion and further land acquisition. Arnaud Saint-Laurent was rich. Coming back to reality Henri mused over the thought that his father's riches would all be his one day.

The wine estate on the other side of the stream belonged to Mannie Gaston, a Jew, who had married a French Jewess who had inherited the land from her father. Their daughter Sophie, although 15, was a friend of Henri and they had been to school together in 1937. In the hope that their friendship would eventually lead to marriage, Mannie encouraged their association as much as possible. Arnaud would never allow his son to marry a Jewess, but realised that his son needed a friend. He had no intention off ever condoning a marriage though.

When Hitler moved on the Rhineland in 1936, Mannie Gaston realised where developments were heading for Jews, prompting him to speak to his daughter.

"Sophie, the persecution of our race is intensifying. Businesses and properties are being taken without recourse, and Jews are being herded into concentration camps. I am going to ask Henri's father to take you into their home if the Germans invade France. Do you think he would let you stay there?"

"I don't know, Papa. You had better ask him. Henri would agree."

"Perhaps he can help me retain the estate," he said hopefully. He had a better chance of falling pregnant. If all went according to plan Arnaud had his sights set on his land

It took place in 1940, when German troops invaded the village. In desperation, Mannie begged Arnaud to take Sophie, then 20, as a housemaid and to swear that she was neither Jewish nor connected with the Gaston household.

"She does not look typically Jewish," Mannie wheedled. "She could assume an identity as Adele Mathieu, a peasant girl from the village."

Arnaud drew Henri aside. "You are 18, my son, and a good friend of this girl. What do you say about letting her stay?"

"Dad, I would like that. I'm not stupid, and have no intention of marrying her. But right now she is merely my toy. I'd like to keep her for as long as we can." His forthright admission won his father's admiration. No lies, simply a straight admission. Sophie was his playgirl and he wanted to keep her. Why shouldn't he?

"Alright then," nodded Arnaud. She can stay. But any problems and she must go! When we go to Reims I know where we can buy some condoms. If you will be sleeping with her you'll need some." He smiled.

"Father, you are wonderful." Spoilt as usual, he only had to ask.

Sophie was virtually a prisoner as Arnaud had insisted that she remain on the property. To roam would invite trouble. Back from university (Henri went to Heidelberg University in 1939 and became friendly with Hermann Schmidt, whom he met in 1940) Henri was her only diversion, helping to prevent her from going insane with boredom on the farm. In consequence her sexual exploits with him became ever more bizarre and creative, much to his amusement. There was scarcely a part of her delightful slender body which she had not used to entertain him. In the same way, she took full advantage of his creativity.

When a French investigator of precious pictures called at the estate in 1942 he managed to keep Sophie out of sight. As it happened he need not have bothered, as the man in question, Raoul Montpelier, was destined to become his friend and enter into nefarious deals with him.

Then abruptly in 1943 she told him she was leaving.

"I am going to take my chances outside. Your father has abused me and now, only this past night, decided to rape me! I am not making a fuss. I know what will happen to me if I did. But I'm not staying to be raped. I know his abuse won't stop now. It will happen again if I stay, so don't try to stop me."

She left and that was the last they heard of her. During this time he also learned much about the technicalities of champagne production and distribution within the restrictions of the war environment.

Chapter 9

SOPHIE GASTON

In her own mind, Sophie Gaston was dead. She did not exist. So badly did she want to bury her Jewish identity that she invented a new one by becoming someone else, Adele Mathieu. She believed herself to be Adele Mathieu, a Frenchwoman, and this belief became her life.

In earlier schooldays Sophie had been subjected to crushing taunts of 'stinking Jew'. When eligible to attend high school in Epernay, she could bear no more of their cruel jibes and begged her parents to register her as Adele Mathieu. Resignedly they agreed to the subterfuge, understanding her situation.

So began her new life. Adele was clever, more intelligent than many of her contemporaries at school, although she discovered she possessed a sexual drive that demanded far more satisfaction than was usual.

In the same way that other students occupied themselves in hobbies and sports, Adele was absorbed by sex. Experimenting first with herself at an early age, and then with Henri later on, Sophie had unlocked sexual powers that would keep her in their demanding power all her life. As a beautiful French girl, exuding sexual appeal was acceptable, and she determined to put her habits to good use. Not as a prostitute; that was too basic, but she realised that she could use her wiles to her advantage.

Adele was beautiful. Her figure had ripened and she resembled a Grecian goddess, incredibly lovely in proportion. At the age of 15 she possessed a classic hour-glass figure, with full breasts and a trim waist that swelled into perfectly proportioned hips and legs that swept on forever, from gorgeous thighs down to shapely calves and neat ankles. Her back was all sculpted perfection, from the curve of her buttocks to gracious shoulders and rounded arms.

Her face portrayed no trace of her Jewish heritage. Instead an air of classic mystery or merriment was projected by her mischievous hazel eyes and distinctly shaped eyebrows, while her delicate nose and softly curved lips complemented her oval jaw line. When she laughed or smiled, which was often, she revealed perfect white teeth.

Adele was understandably proud of her figure, never failing to keep in good shape through regular exercise. She developed her body to perfection, especially her breasts, using small weights every day. She changed the style of her tawny hair at whim, depending on the season or fancy, sometimes leaving it in tousled confusion that only served to enhance her delectable youthful beauty. In short, Adele was lovely, a radiant sexy bombshell.

Her enjoyment of gymnastics had aided her pursuit of the perfect body, and she both enjoyed the discipline and excelled at it. It led to her first encounter with a girl when she was 16. Monique had seen Adele rhythmically lifting hand weights.

"Why do you use those, Adele?" she enquired. "Do you want to be a body builder or something?" The attractive dark-haired girl always had something to say.

"Not exactly. But they are good for your chest muscles and tighten your breasts."

The gymnasium was deserted as they stood near the stacked equipment and paraphernalia in the corner.

"Look, I'll show you," offered Adele, slipping off her regulation school tunic. "See these muscles when I lift. Put your fingers there! Higher. Feel the movement." Monique complied; Adele lifted. "Stand behind me and put your hands under my breasts and feel the lift."

Again, Monique did as she was asked. "Let me try," she said, taking off her tunic and exposing neat taut breasts. Adele stood behind her and as Monique lifted one weight at a time, Adele enclosed each breast in her palms.

The indignant reaction she was expecting didn't come, which prompted her to keep them there for a few moments.

"These are heavy! That's enough," exclaimed Monique, who then stood up and cupped Adele's more generous breasts, squeezing them. When she saw her nipples tighten and harden in response, Monique whispered urgently, hungry excitement in her voice, "Let's go into the showers."

They clung to each other like lovers, frantically exploring, arousing and satisfying each other. It was just a beginning: their clandestine meetings continued until Adele left school. She was bisexual.

Adele had placed enormous trust in Henri, regarding him as her best friend and male lover.

It was a deeply disturbing and traumatic experience when his father had violently dragged her up to the barn roof and raped her. He had torn into her like a bull.

Exhausted by his exertions, he rolled off her, leaving Adele scared out of her wits. She knew he could murder her and no questions asked. He had the right connections among his Nazi friends.

"Breathe a word of this to anyone and I'll have you deported! Understand?" leering at her. She was too frightened to speak. She nodded in terror, but knew that he wasn't through with her.

She was only too terrified of her rapist's violent temper. Bruised from the floorboards during the assault, she was determined to run if she survived. She was terrified of a repeat performance. Helpless against his power, she realised he would continue to abuse her. Her only refuge was escape. Irrational or not, the trauma convinced her to flee immediately if she got through this ordeal. Sooner or later he would have her killed to keep her quiet. It was not the kind of sex she wanted.

All she wanted was to survive!

 Even let him think she was worth keeping.

Her only thought was to escape from La Verite.

"Sophie! He knows I'm Sophie, knows I am Jewish. I have to run. I'm Adele," were the thoughts that ran through her mind. She readily agreed never to speak a word of the incident as he wagged an admonishing finger at her.

Adele told Henri, with whom she had shared until then a series of fascinating and love-filled sexual experiences.

"Thanks to your pig of a father, that COCHON!" she spat on the ground to emphasise the bitter insult in the French language. "I'm on the run. He raped me, the BASTARD." No more of this for you, my boy," she said, closing her fingers round his slack member before she set off down the farm track.

"Sophie! Don't go!" Henri pleaded. He could never think of her as Adele; Sophie was his first loving partner.

"And you'll stop your father raping me! Forget it! I'm off!" she replied scornfully. Henri watched her go, helpless to challenge his father. He knew he would lose.

Wasting no time, Adele walked to the Chalons road where, tired out, she thumbed a lift. A truck laden with potatoes slowed down.

"I'm going to Nancy. Is that any good?" offered the young suntanned driver, giving the attractive hitchhiker a friendly grin.

"Merci beaucoup!" Adele grabbed the handle and climbed up the wheel into the cab.

"She's slow, but we'll be in Nancy before dark. I'm Charles. And you?" he greeted her, offering his hand.

"Adele," she smiled her thanks.

"Hello, Adele. Make yourself comfortable – there is still a long way to go. So where are you heading for?"

"It is good of you to give me a lift, but... Charles, I don't know where I'm going." She burst into tears. "I've been raped and I'm running away."

"Good God! That's terrible." He was genuinely concerned. "But you must have some idea of where to go! Haven't you?" She dabbed her eyes. "I just had to get away from that brute... I am on my own. I've lost my parents," she sobbed.

"Do you have any trade? A craft? Any skills at all?" questioned Charles as he plunged through the gears, picking up speed.

"I worked as a housemaid. My mother taught me to sew a little."

"Really! My mother's a dressmaker. She gets by; earns a little. Father's a sign writer, but there is not much work these days. Look. If you have nowhere to go, come back to our place for tonight at least. Let's see how we can help you tomorrow. OK?"

"You are very kind, Charles. I've no money but I'll help your mother in the house. I must earn my keep – I can't accept favours and not do something in return."

Taking his eyes off the road for a second, his big hands in control of the huge steering wheel, Charles turned to look at his passenger, his smile showing perfect teeth. "You know, I'm beginning to like you, Adele. You are made of the right stuff. You'll make out with your attitude, just you see. Dry your eyes, it's a lovely day. There is you, me and big Betsy here," tapping the steering wheel affectionately. "Things could be worse, what do you say?"

"Oh, I'm so glad you picked me up!" She smiled back at him, cheered in spirit.

Charles' mother accepted Adele happily, and willingly aided her dressmaking ability. Quick to learn, Adele soon picked up the threads and became competent enough to contribute towards household expenses. She felt better earning her board and lodging.

One day Charles could see Adele was upset.

"What's the matter? Looks like you've lost your purse."

"I've missed my period! I think I'm pregnant from that bastard. Hell, I'm scared! What shall I do?"

"Don't worry. You're in the right house. Mother can fix it for you. She's done abortions before."

In France, backstreet abortions were all too common, and Madame Rougiere agreed to assist. A painful week later, the bleeding stopped, and Adele returned to a normal life. Except for one detail – she would never bear children.

Adele spent three months with the family. Charles' friend, who drove for a clothing firm, told her of the good money to be made doing piecework in clothing factories in Neustadt, where he had a connection. He could get her a job if she wanted one. He took her there on his travels and introduced her to a factory forewoman, Gerda Blom.

Adele soon learned that women could be just as unscrupulous as men in their manipulations.

"So. You vant a job, ja? Any gut mit button holz?" the older Jewish woman smiled.

"Fair," admitted Adele, vaguely trying to remember if she had ever done one.

"Gut! Vee need expertize. Now let me zee you now. Komm here, girl."

Adele walked towards her and Gerda ran her hands over her body, making it obvious from the initial interview that compliance in a special relationship would receive special consideration and an appointment. Sensing what was needed to secure the job which she so desperately wanted, Adele lifted her blouse from her skirt to roll it high and exhibit her breasts.

"As you see, I am quite healthy," she said, offering herself by moving closer to the woman.

Gerda placed a hand on Adele's left breast and fondled it. "Ja, very firm. You vill do fine!"

The unwritten agreement was concluded. Adele had a patron, albeit unpredictable as to tenure in the circumstances.

In her present hopeless situation, Adele accepted being Gerda Blom's lesbian lover, and soon learned the relative power Gerda held in the factory, even though she was a Jewish citizen. There was no way Adele would ever breathe a word of Yiddish, and she broke out into cold sweat at the thought of it. She worked hard in her job and earned a useful weekly wage.

Adele soon settled into her relationship with Gerda and her gentle ways in bed. There were times when she wanted a man to ravish her, but the only men available were the old cutters upstairs who were unfit for army service, and not her ideal of desirable lovers. However, unable to resist being without some male attention, she cautiously herded one fellow from the flock and had a dalliance with him, but she was terrified that Gerda would find out. Still, it was better than nothing.

Chapter 10

HERMANN SCHMIDT

SCHMIDT'S FACTORY, NEUSTADT

The interior was dark, dank and dismal, with grimy windows shutting out even the most obstinate of the sun's rays. Floors were littered with scraps of cloth, machines festooned in fluffy stalactites. This was the sweatshop where workers cooped in caves produced mediocre quality uniforms. Hermann vividly remembered his first stunned impression at the age of 15. It was awful. He would change the grim conditions, he decided.

Every day after school saw him at the factory. Hermann kept his promise to himself and organised a maintenance crew to clean the place up. His father complained at first, then left him alone. Standards improved: waste was no longer strewn about, the workers became more careful. Hermann introduced minor improvements, taking a keen interest in production methods. It was a second life from school, and he was fired with enthusiasm.

Only four years later, at 19, Hermann became factory manager. His performance at school was brilliant, winning him a place at Heidelberg University, where he met Henri in 1940. After two years of business studies his capabilities were far ahead of the dumb swastika-wearing swaggering cafs in power. Educated in management techniques, his skills were vital to the war effort, and his organisational aptitude in work flow and ergonomics pushed up the factory's output of Luftwaffe, Gestapo and Waffen S.S. uniforms.

Hermann was a star, and as he held a privileged position in vital production he was spared active military service. Success was not without a war of his own, however. Karl Schmidt, his arrogant, uncouth father, became jealous of his son's ability.

"What the hell are you playing at? Breaking down the centre to put in a lift shaft? Have you gone mad?" Red faced, puffing, hands on hips, uttering filthy oaths, Schmidt senior was furious.

"You made me factory manager. Judge me on production volume, quality and cost," retorted Hermann. "If I can't make the changes I consider vital, then you don't need me, Father. I'll go into the damn army. Take it or leave it. It is your decision!"

Schmidt senior, all steamed up, knew he was a loser, and that it was best to lose the argument rather than his brilliant son, who was good for business. He gave in. "Right my boy. I'll give you six months."

Still on the boil, Hermann barked back "If it doesn't work out you can change it back to the pig sty it used to be when I first started. Then I'll take off."

The big German put out his hand. "No, you won't." Hermann shook his father's hand, smiled away his anger and, temper spent, clasped his father in a hug for the first time in years. Hermann now had a free hand.

Hermann's production principles were simple. Gravity feed. Reduce movement costs to a minimum. Equip the four floors of the factory with a main centre lift. The ground floor was for stocks, stores, packing and dispatch, while the basement cellar below was for heating and storage space. Working stock requirements were hauled to the fourth floor cutting rooms. And maximum natural light was ensured.

The cut, make and trim process (CMT) took place as the components of the mass production system cascaded down chutes between floors and rumbled in bins along rollers from machine to machine on each floor. Up to 40 people might be involved in making the various parts of one pair of trousers, but the process was fast. The cycle started at the top and flowed down to the packing section on the ground floor. Hermann's productivity philosophy was based on improved working conditions, with better lighting and clean windows. Comfortable seating cut the fatigue factor and achieved better results, faster. Having material and equipment within close reach, with effort going into production rather than into fruitless exercise, and other simple measures, such as needle threaders on the hundreds of sewing machines, saved hours of unnecessary fumbling.

Hermann had a huge steam press installed. Hand irons swung on arms from a gantry; others were suspended on springs from the ceiling. Take away the strain; work quicker, longer, better. The environment was spotlessly clean and pride in the products was encouraged, resulting in improved quality.

He increased the efficiency of the workforce by 30 percent without incurring any costs. The sweat shop had gone, but Hermann still qualified for forced labour from occupied France, where Saukel produced goods for the German civilian population. Such were the skills of Jewesses in the textile industry generally that Hermann had the pick of the labour force for producing the finest tailored uniforms for the Master Race. Besides the 14 cutters, master tailors and technicians and 300 local women, his workforce was complemented by an additional 600 Jewish seamstresses, who worked diligently. They were spared from the brutal horrors that they would have been exposed to with the cruel criminal elements in the concentration camps. The labour force worked a 55-hour week, as according to Himmler, longer hours and fatigue caused unacceptable reject levels.

Schmidt's factory output in volume and quality was exceptionally high, and soon became known to the Nazi hierarchy.

Hermann had the added good fortune of a 45-year-old Jewish woman with rag trade experience in New York, who had been trapped in Germany when the war broke out. As Hermann's expert, he had made Gerda Blom the forewoman of the Jewish contingency. Hermann respected her.

Gerda felt that she could confide in her boss and opened up to him after one technical meeting.

"Herr Schmidt, it is difficult for me, but I must talk to you. You know about your father and the girls?" Gerda meant the Jewish workers, and looked at him to confirm an open secret. Hermann felt ridiculous; he was embarrassed. On one occasion he had found his father with a girl. It was ugly business and he nodded.

"Yesterday afternoon your father and three of his S.S. friends had one of the girls in the executive suite. She was molested continually for three hours. Raped and abused until she couldn't walk. She's in my quarters. She is bleeding badly, and can't stop crying, so I sent for a doctor. I've no money to pay him. Rachael will be off for days. There are girls out there," she nodded to the factory door, "who will go willingly with your father. He's virtually got a harem that I know of. They don't put up a fight for their dignity when the alternative is inhaling fumes in a gas chamber at Buchenwald or Sachsenhausen. But why her?"

Ashamed, eyes downcast Hermann shook his head. "I don't know. Here's money for the doctor."

The thought that his father was a war criminal and that he was implicated troubled him: he was genuinely scared of the outcome. He had seen his bull of a father hit and mistreat the workers, and any rebuke from him had been met with, "You're too soft. Mind your own damned business."

As far as Hermann was concerned, the only value his father had in the business was an undoubted influence with the Nazi Party. Despite an aristocratic background, Karl Schmidt conducted himself like a pirate. In short he was a pig: he had become a true Nazi.

Hermann tried to maintain propriety, as was befitting a descendant of his titled great grandfather, Baron von Eisenstein, and the inheritor of the family wine estate at Bacharach with the castle 'Berghof'.

Karl Schmidt had acquired the Neustadt factory from Rosenthal, a hapless ageing Jewish clothing manufacturer. Schmidt insisted that his young wife, Rosie, stay at the factory for six months to train the Jewish women. She was abused, humiliated, and finally raped on the day she followed her husband Issy to oblivion at Dachau.

By the time Hermann joined the factory, his father's excesses and perverse conduct had made a complete mess of the business. Fortunately for him, the changes his son made soon brought recognition.

A roaring entourage of motorcycle outriders and staff cars escorted a powerful bullet-proof Mercedes Benz limousine to the factory. There was no mistaking the Reichmarschall, Commander in Chief of the Luftwaffe, Hermann Goering.

Schmidt Senior could not bow low enough before such omnipotence, saliva dribbling from his mouth in veneration, bending in contrite awe before one of the most powerful men in the Third Reich.

The jowl dropped. "Schmidt, I'm pleased with your products. You produce excellent uniforms for my gallant men in the Luftwaffe. Well done. Keep it up!" A smirk on his full face caused his granite-faced courtiers to cautiously nod in agreement. After a blitz inspection of the factory, entourage in tow, the Reichmarschall was clearly impressed.

He turned to Hermann. "I have a sketch here for a uniform for myself. Can you do something?"

The young man knew Goering had a white dress uniform. He remembered newsreels of him in Paris. "Certainly, Reichmarschall. One white dress uniform and another in parade beige. If you approve the design, let us know how many you would like. Our honour, Reichmarschall."

The tall impressive man beside Goering thought Schmidt Senior was an idiot. Aristocratic in appearance, Field Marschall Albrecht von Kesselring was accompanying Goering to his command of the Luftwaffe in North Eastern France.

Goering drew Karl aside, cautious to be out of earshot. "Schmidt. In Paris we retained some valuable objects for the Reich. We sent a rail car loaded for the Führer at Bergtesgarten but storage is a problem. Are there any safe cellars in your building?"

Recognising 'retained' as a euphemism for 'stolen plunder' Schmidt spluttered, over-anxious to please. "Ja, Reichmarschall. Dry and secure! Our honour, Reichmarschall."

"Good! Guard them carefully. It is state property." He did not mention that two baggage cars had started out from Paris. One had 'got lost' on the way.

Later on four Luftwaffe lorries delivered the contents of a huge rail car to Schmidt's factory. Crated works of art, some wrapped, artefacts, objets d'art, statues and two heavy strong boxes were secured in the cellar. A strong steel gate, then a corridor leading to the room was bricked up and painted over to conceal their presence.

Secure. That was late 1942.

Hermann Schmidt was obsessed by the presence of such immense wealth. The magnetism of the treasure haunted him every day.

Chapter 11

MARCH 1943: NEUSTADT, GERMANY

HERMANN SCHMIDT AND INGRID PENZ

Hermann Schmidt was scared, for the collapse of the status quo seemed inevitable. When it came, the Devil would reap his reward.

Although young, his position gave him privileged information into the power structure. Nightmares and days of indeterminate fear tormented him. Hermann Schmidt was in the system, and any detection of wavering enthusiasm would be too ghastly to contemplate. He had to go on. Seated at his desk, Hermann clasped his strong fingers together, forcing himself to appear cheerful. Weary eyes inspected his vivacious secretary, whom he coldly regarded as a voluptuous, curvaceous, over-sexed, steely cruel bitch.

"You hate them, don't you?"

Long blonde locks swished around her chin, bouncing on firm shoulders. Dancing blue eyes fixed on her young boss. A puzzled half smile implied Ingrid Penz was not on his wavelength.

"Jews!"

The smile vanished in disdain, white teeth flashing, breasts heaving "What a question!" in icy venom. "You've known me long enough! They've got what they deserve!"

Hermann leaned back in his leather chair, his smile genuine.

"Hell, you're attractive when you're mad!" he laughed. "In the two years we've been together you have never told me why you hate Jews so much. It's obvious though! What makes you so fed up with the Jews? And I don't mean Hitler Youth propaganda!"

"On one condition!" Dimples reappeared on her face.

"What?"

"You do it to me when I've finished telling you."

Hermann's assenting grin was brief though, and he gave her a warning look, his hand raised for quiet. He cocked an ear in concentration. There it was again, an unmistakable drone. "They're back!" The exclamation was breathless with emotion. Just then, the baleful wail of an air raid siren split the early evening quiet.

"Schnell! Im der unterstand! Luftangriff!" he barked, dousing the light. Ingrid rolled into the low steel air raid shelter, swearing as she barged her knees in panic. Hermann crawled on the mattress beside her. Reaching up he unfastened the drop mesh side of the cage, swinging it down. Their chances of survival were fair: the heavy boardroom table above them would break an initial fall of masonry and he knew that the toughened steel cage roof could withstand enormous weight before buckling.

"Thank God the sides open inwards! It's bare hands through the rubble if we get trapped." She clutched his arm at the thought.

Waiting was terrifying, and the escalating throbbing noise of the approaching raiders turned them into a mass of jangled nerves. Waiting brought fear, which caused terror. Goose pimples broke out on his body; cold sweat on his lip, as the droning intensified. Eyes wide in dread, Ingrid curled her arms round Hermann's left arm, snuggling close to him in mounting fright.

The first stick of high explosives struck a kilometre from the clothing factory. Glass shards rained on the floor and littered polished leather upholstery.

WHUMFF – Kerrack! The sound of exploding bombs echoed again through the factory premises, earthquake-like tremors reverberating through the floor. Fine plaster dust drifted gently down, captured in the brilliance cast by the probing search-lights that stabbed the night, directing streams of anti-aircraft tracer bullets at the raiding RAF bombers. After last night's air raid the cracked ceiling would not take much more, like his nerves.

RAF bombers could hit Metz and Saarbrucken on their 375 mile Thunderbolt range on additional tanks. The previous night and this one were test run extensions to Neustadt. The lightning range would soon extend to their factory as fighter bombers streaked for strategic targets at Karlsruhe and Stuttgart.

The unrelenting Allied bombing from the spring through to the summer of 1943 had temporarily abated, switching from Ruhr targets to ports. Hermann knew the bombers would soon return.

Trapped by the hands of fate, Hermann settled down to look at his secretary, whom he knew came from his birthplace of Bacharach. The thought brought childhood memories to mind of the generations-old castle on the family Rhine wine estate. Ingrid was ravishingly beautiful, but Hermann had detected a hard streak in the 22 year old. This hardness precluded love and tenderness from her make-up, but in no way inhibited her unrivalled appetite for sex. She could equally exploit sex to humiliate others.

Hermann peered through the mesh at his desk where yesterday he had raped a Jewish girl. Ingrid had demanded it.

"This bitch is insolent!" she had screamed. "Defiant and resists authority." She threw the slip of a girl across the room. "Mein Herr, stuff her!"

The terrified girl was 15, just in from Metz concentration camp. Hermann reflected how meekly he had complied with the order. There had been other occasions too. This secretary of his enjoyed humiliating her victims to satisfy her salacious appetite. As part of the system he could not allow his secretary to lose face in front of a worker. Management would lose control of the forced labour, which meant that the terror-based system had to be maintained. It was on Himmler's orders.

Ingrid had screamed, "Strip bitch! Quick, before I slap you again." Hermann saw the red patch on the girl's cheek. The skinny black-haired Jewess timidly unfastened her cheap striped dress and pulled it over her head, then took off her vest, revealing very white skin. She wore no bra.

"Off!" Ingrid screamed, pointing to the girl's knickers. She complied and stood naked and vulnerable, shaking in terror, her small breasts heaving, hands covering her pubic area. Ingrid grabbed the girl's wrists roughly, slipping a cord with a running noose over them and pinning her hands together. She pushed her over to the huge office desk.

"Bend over bitch." She forced the girl's face to the desktop, her pelvis at the edge and tied the cord to a drawer knob. Ingrid came behind and kicked her victim's legs apart.

"Screw her!" Ingrid's smile was evil.

For Hermann rape was becoming a habit and after the girl left he vowed that this time would be the last. The day of reckoning was perhaps not too far off.

What had made Ingrid so callous? Hermann was cautious about how best to ask her.

The bombers had gone, leaving an eerie stillness. Would there be a second phase? The all clear seemed a tediously long wait.

"You were going to tell me before this started," he said, nodding at the chaos outside. Hermann listened as attentively as if he had been attending a tutorial at Heidelberg University, where he had been studying economics until two years ago.

"You know our family delicatessen in Bacharach." It was a statement; Bacharach was a small wine town. Ingrid continued. "Papa built up a good trade and we lived well from it. Then some fucking Jew set up in opposition, taking advantage of the French occupation of the Rhineland. That was in '29. The French left, remember, in June '30, after 15 years. In the depression we had a hard time surviving. Hate boiled in our house for that Jew. But they're all the same; steal the living from decent people.

"The Nazis had tremendous appeal for father and other discontented people like him, and they attended meetings where Hitler and Goebbels whipped up wild frenzied mob hatred. These powerful men played on mass instincts and passions, enforcing order and discipline with their S.A. storm troopers, making promises of economic rejuvenation. Particularly promises of the revision of the Treaty of Versaille. The frenzy demanded victims and Hitler and Goebbels lashed out at the Jews. Father got quite carried away by his passionate need to bring about their destruction. When Hitler held the 1934 plebiscite, father backed him, but he had to keep it quiet. National Socialism was not too popular in the area then and Papa could not afford to upset customers and go out of business.

"Father saw Hitler's rise to power as a way to rid himself of the Jewish bastard who threatened his business survival. Some of Hitler's closest associates, like Goebbels, Ribbentrop, Frick and Ley, came from the Rhineland, and Father felt in good company. Instinct told him that Hitler would succeed – it was just a matter of time. So he joined the Nazi Party. He wasn't well off, but made a contribution. He knew Rhineland industrialists made financial contributions to finance the National Socialist movement whilst Hitler was still in opposition. When Hitler occupied the demilitarised zone in 1936 without effective opposition from the Western powers, father knew his winner instinct had paid off. The left bank was German again.

"That's the background I grew up in; I was only a kid at school. Like you, I helped on those steep slopes with the wine harvests. Father got me into Hitler Youth early. Later it was compulsory.

"I was always very fit and enjoyed the physical training. The instructors soon found that I was compliant and I built up strong forearm muscles and wrists to meet their kind of physical training needs." Ingrid laughed. "It was wonderful not having to attend mass. When the Roman Catholic Church signed their concordat and priests offered prayers for the Third Reich, it proved the Church losers to the Nazi regime. I didn't have to confess to some stupid priest when I masturbated."

Hermann smiled at her utter frankness, which was quite in keeping with her brazen character.

"Getting rid of the Jew meant we had enough to send me to Wiesbaden secretarial college. That's why I'm such an excellent secretary!" Ingrid turned on her side to look at him, pulling a face and sticking her tongue out. "You see our Jewish intruder received special treatment from Papa's Nazi friends. Your father and mine became friends at the time. Some said that Jews had been part of the life and culture of our river for 2 000 years. Well we wanted them somewhere else! Father took over the Jewish bastard's business, which is when we started making decent money. The shit ended up in Dachau!"

Even hardened as he was from years of Hitler Youth propaganda, reinforced by Nazi dogma at Heidelberg University, Hermann could see how cold and heartless this attractive German girl at his side was. She had been brainwashed.

Hermann, highly intelligent, kept a balanced vision. The factory he managed for his father had been stolen from the Jewish proprietor for a pittance. Any comeback had been insured against by a one-way trip to Dachau. True at least to himself, Hermann thought that they would one day pay dearly for their outrageous behaviour. 'That may not be that far away', he thought, as he surveyed broken windows and plaster dust, a prelude to future devastating bombing sorties in a mindless war of attrition. 'In the meantime, plan to stay alive', was his secret motivation. 'Be a survivor'.

Being both friends and Party members, Karl Schmidt had invited Heinz Penz to allow his daughter, Ingrid, to begin working at his clothing factory. She was 21 when she joined. Hermann had to admit that she gave him competent secretarial support. They had made love in the first month and ever since then. An immediate concern for Hermann was whether he could trust her.

Chapter 12

JUNE 2 1943, 12h00:

HAMBURG

'Hell! What do they want me for?' Nervously the brilliant naval engineer glanced at his immaculate finger nails and rose from the waiting room chair, looking in the mirror to see if every hair was in place, his tie straight. Klaus Fischer was a perfectionist, and had enjoyed a meteoric rise. At 33, he was a specialist designer of Walter turbine submarine development, and assistant to Professor Helmuth Walter. No matter how brilliant though, he did not delay in obeying a Gestapo summons.

A door opened, and he was beckoned peremptorily by a secretary, flaxen hair in a bun, who pointed to an inner office. An S.S. Obersturmfuhrer pompously saluted. "Heil Hitler!"

Klaus shot out his right arm stiffly. "Heil Hitler!"

"Sit!" The black snake indicated a high chair opposite his desk and slumped down in his executive seat. He sneered indulgently at the engineer, revealing yellow nicotine-stained teeth. Slouched, fingers steepled, his tone was taunting, his attitude disparaging. "Smart boy, hmmm?" He enjoyed mocking intellectuals. Pricks!

"Reichführer Himmler says Speer speaks highly of you." His attitude was as sour as a lemon. "But what else could the Armament Minister say of his cosseted engineers?" he added, sneering. He picked up a report. "Diligent, dedicated hard worker," exaggerating surprise and pulling a face, "meticulous in detail, does not give up easily. Whatever he is entrusted with, he does it well!" He looked up. "Bloody hero! A fine product of the Fatherland, Ja?"

Klaus moved uncomfortably on his chair, feeling tense. 'What next?' he wondered. "I've always done my best," he replied politely. "Indeed!" came the mocking reply. "That's why I'M an intermediary for THE most elevated in the Reich. They want to make a proposition." Black snake believed himself privy to top secrets, unaware that he was being deceived by his superiors. "The elite want a presentation explaining the advantages of Walter turbine U-boat development compared to conventional types. A strategic planning meeting is being held to which you are highly privileged to attend. It is to remain confidential – absolutely! Any leak is treasonable. That would mean number eight Prinz Albrecht Strasse for you! Do I make myself absolutely clear?" The Gestapo Headquarters was the most sinister address in Berlin.

Full of self importance, the black-clad S.S. Officer smacked his desk with a black leather riding crop, making Klaus jump. The Gestapo man enjoyed the reaction. The Geheime Staatspolizei or State Secret Police roused feelings of dread in the German population at large.

Klaus assessed the black uniform, riding breeches, black jackboots, swastika arm band and cap decorated with the skull 'Death's Head' symbol with utter contempt. Their fear-provoking presence had certainly worked on him. The S.S. from Schutzstaffel or bodyguard squad was formed in 1925 to protect Adolf Hitler. Klaus compared these despicable thugs with the indomitable courage and spirit of the brave submariners who were, he thought, real men.

Klaus accepted the commitment, saluted and left. Outside he spat on the ground. "Shit! Pigs!" He felt better.

09h00, June 9 1943.

Survival is all powerful in the human spirit. Especially in bullies.

A group of ruling Nazis had a common theme: survival. Wielding unchallenged power in the Third Reich, they knew its collapse would mean their extinction. The situation looked bad in June 1943. Animosities set aside in common conspiracy, the clique had enough authority to plan a store of wealth outside Germany. To the Führer or Goebbels it would be treason. Betrayal.

Goering founded the master plan supported by Himmler, Heinrich Muller, Chief of Gestapo, Ernst Kaltenbrunner, who had succeeded Heydrich, Himmler's Deputy assassinated in 1942 and Von Ribbentrop, Foreign Minister. As Goering needed the services of Speer as Armament Minister for logistical purposes, he included him too.

Bespectacled, flabby cheeked and mean in expression, Himmler spoke. "It can never be admitted that a fall of the Third Reich is possible. But the reality of the situation cannot be ignored." The 43-year-old Reichführer S.S. Chief of German Police was not particularly clever, but he could see that his original plan to create a Slave State would no longer be a reality. He had planned to enslave four million permanent captives from eastern European Slavonic countries to provide German factories with human resources in a peacetime Thousand Year

Reich. His vision of having thousands of women from those countries sent to brothels would also remain a pipe dream.

He continued, "Consider. The enemy established the previous year that unconditional surrender was a precondition for peace. There have been conspiracies to assassinate the Führer. The loyalty of our generals has been questioned! The Sixth Army surrendered in Stalingrad on February 2; recent Russian counter offensives have been strong, while on May 11 The Afrika Corp surrendered in North Africa. It follows the enemy will attack Italy. Will the Italians stand and fight in our Pact of Steel? We must prepare for the future. We must secure some of our wealth beyond the grasp of invaders."

Himmler was referring to gold bullion, a hoarded product of extermination camps, extracted from teeth in shattered skulls and fingers crushed for the wedding rings they had once worn. This accumulated gold, together with golden artefacts from Jewish homes, was smelted into ingots and stamped with the S.S. insignia. But Goering, accustomed to luxury, wanted to take out insurance against the likelihood of losing the ingots and priceless works of art pillaged throughout Europe in a burning Fatherland. He stated their cause.

"It is agreed Gentlemen that sufficient treasures must be exported to South America; to Uruguay, Paraguay and Argentina to secure resettlement befitting our style should all be lost in our beloved Reich. Gold and works of art are always negotiable." He smiled like a benefactor. A man with an openly masculine nature, their informal leader possessed a great personal charm. "Deceit will be essential in deploying resources under a valid guise," he informed him. In this skill they needed no guidance.

By now Goering believed Hitler was insane but could do nothing about it. A secret transcript was produced by the Reichmarschall.

"Here's Doenitz's report to the Führer at Rastenburg HQ on May 14. Just three weeks ago they discussed the need for keeping Italy in the war. If the British and Americans can free the Mediterranean of our Navy, the enemy stands to gain two million tons of shipping space. The Grand Admiral told Hitler, 'We are facing a U-boat crisis. The enemy has new systems for locating U-boats, inflicting heavy losses on us; 15 to 17 U-boats a month. Biscay is the only attack route for the U-boat war. The narrow lane is so full of obstacles that it takes our U-boats 10 days to overcome them'."

Goering looked up, "Doenitz is not frightened of Hitler! He took over as Commander in Chief of the Navy from Raeder on the losing end of the U-boat war. He is like a headmaster! Hitler respects him. Doenitz can tell the truth whereas we get tirades of abuse!" He smiled; the others had experienced it too. He continued.

"Doenitz told the Führer on May 31, and I quote, 'Losses risen to 30 percent of U-boats at sea. I have withdrawn from the North Atlantic to the area west of the Azores'. Unquote. He speculates on an enemy detection device that we cannot counter. Hitler agreed to increase production of U-boats from 30 to 40 a month. In 'Black May' we lost 41 U-boats from five a month."

Speer nodded at the statistical accuracy.

"We have no time to waste," announced Goering. Summarising, he counted on his fingers, "One. Surface shipping will most probably be sunk.

"Two. The North Atlantic is too dangerous for U-boats; they are easily detected.

"Three. Our U-boats are trapped in pens at La Rochelle and La Pallice. Ten days gauntlet to run Doenitz reports to clear the Bay of Biscay.

"Four. Only the Azores area is still relatively open.

"Five. The Mediterranean is still marginally under our control, but slipping away fast. The enemy's supremacy at sea and in the air is increasing. North Africa is lost to the enemy.

"Six. The Italians are wavering in our Pact of Steel. Can they be relied upon?" nodding at Himmler.

"What are our options?"

Despondent faces waited expectantly for salvation. 'Radar' was yet unknown to the Germans. They knew only the devastating effect it was having on their U-boat fleet.

"Options are becoming fewer by the day," Goering went on. We still have Italy and the French seaboard. I am in favour of loading a large submarine in our Mediterranean submarine base at Toulon. We still have Italy, so that is our safest route. The west Italian coast is now vulnerable. We can send a small fast submarine from Toulon. We dare not at this stage raid the Vatican, but there is unbelievable wealth in gold in the goldsmiths' shops along the Ponte Vecchio. We raid Florence and meet the submarine off shore at Viareggio. Again liaise with Monte Cassino HQ and meet off shore, say at Ischia, Naples. The subs meet in mid-Tyrrhenian Sea, transfer goods to the big one and sail to South America."

He noted nods of excitement for his plan. "However we have a. serious problem. Submarines are slow, seven knots under water. Water in the Mediterranean is clear and they can be spotted more easily than in the Atlantic." More nods. Speer was agitated, but dare not interrupt.

"Professor Walter has advanced his turbine and carried out successful tests. Albert can perhaps enlighten us."

Speer straightened up and coughed. "To put you in the picture I have Professor Walter's assistant, Herr Klaus Fischer, Engineer. He is a brilliant nautical architect and engineer. He knows nothing of our plan of course. We'll say we want to blockade Malta again." More nodding as Speer went to the door.

Slightly balding, with a receding hair line, the good natured Klaus did his best to appear enthusiastic and confident. He looked highly intelligent. Introductions made, he commenced his presentation, smiling away nervous apprehension.

"Your Excellencies. To appreciate advances in submarine developments, a basic knowledge of construction is necessary." He pointed to his flipchart pictures. "A submarine is a metal tube containing engines and equipment. At the sides a second skin forms water tanks, which are open at the bottom, and have valves or flaps on top. When these are open, air escapes, water rushes in at the bottom, so the submarine sinks or dives rapidly. To surface we close the valves, pump in air and water is forced down and out the bottom. The submarine becomes lighter, rising on two pockets of air." He looked around at his audience, then went on. "Horizontal hydroplanes fore and aft steer the U-boat up or down. Rudders steer port or starboard; left or right. Trimming tanks maintain neutral buoyancy to keep balanced. It is easier for the operator to keep balanced when moving. Control is lost when the submarine stops, as the submarine slowly sinks to the seabed. As diesel fuel is consumed, weight loss must be compensated for by trimming. When torpedoes are fired, the U-boat becomes lighter by a matter of tons in seconds and must be quickly stabilised so as not to rise upwards too rapidly and betray itself, particularly at periscope depth.

"Propulsion is by two methods, above water, by diesel engines and below water by electric motors. When submerged, diesels cannot be used as they need to consume fresh air. Electric motors derive energy from batteries that are heavy and bulky, their size limited by the U-boat width. Energy is soon exhausted under heavy loads and the submarine has to resurface to recharge batteries with its diesel engines. It must surface to replenish fresh air, which diminishes under water.

"To cover long distances a conventional V11C series U-boat of 760 tons must travel mainly on the surface; top speed 19 knots, range 24 000 nautical miles at 12 knots. Its underwater capabilities are reserved for shipping attacks and to evade attack, speed limited to seven knots. It has limitations."

Klaus turned away from his flip chart, resting his pointer, eyes bright with enthusiasm.

"To find the perfect submarine we had to overcome these major limitations. We needed propulsion without having to surface and charge batteries. To stay submerged for indefinite periods meant increasing speeds. Professor Walter invented a power unit driven by hydrogen peroxide and developed a turbine. We incorporated this into a U-boat where steam is generated by 'perhydrol'. The submarine does not depend on fresh air and can stay under water indefinitely, evading the British invention, which can detect our subs on the surface even at night. Expelled residual CO_2 gases combine with sea water and leave no bubble track, while the sound neutralises the engine noises and cannot be picked up on Asdic, the undersea sonar detection system."

Klaus added that they had produced four experimental boats; Type XVII, 34 metres long, weighing 236 tons, with a cross section profile oval like a fish for high underwater speeds. The boats had achieved 28 knots, but 26 knots was standard, whether submerged or surface.

There were gasps from his audience, before he went on.

"Fuel consumption is very high, which means a short range. It has four torpedoes in two tubes. Until we can improve on fuel consumption we have developed an intermediary step using the Schnorkel. We draw air in through a tube. So we have built what we call the 'Electro-boat', which has the same shape as the oval fish profile. It is powered by two double motors, two further double motors for slow speed, one double for high and a single motor for very slow speed; very versatile.

"The boat can dive to 250 metres in 28 seconds. We had one submerged for three days on trials, without any problems," Klaus told them, aware of the expressions of amazement on their faces.

"At a cruising speed of 10 knots the boat has an action radius of 16 000 sea miles – the distance from La Pallice to Cape Horn and back or a round trip to Cape Town, underwater or surface."

Glee was now evident on some faces, which puzzled Klaus. "The speed is not as high as the Walter U-boat but experimentally we have achieved 17 knots under water for six hours. It is certainly fast enough to evade pursuers." Looking at Speer he commented, "We hope to go into production by August, prefabricating eight sections in different factories for final construction in Hamburg."

Goering spoke. "Is there an Electro-boat serviceable?"

"Yes Reichmarschall. One is seaworthy. Others are partially stripped or are being modified."

"We want it! And the small ones, are any of these seaworthy?"

"Yes, the U793 is undergoing trials."

"The range is limited you say. Can it get to Italy?"

"No. It would need a support U-boat tanker in constant supply. It would be easily detected and sunk in the Bay of Biscay."

"Ah! Can you get it to the Mediterranean by river and rail?" Klaus recalled that submarines had been transported and assembled in the Mediterranean in the First World War. "We could send it down the Rhine to Strasbourg then on flat beds by rail to Marseille."

"Good! We must upset the British at Malta! We want the XXI Electro-boat at Toulon by December 2. Get U793 to Marseille by November 15 and reconstruct it – Minister Speer will give you all the resources you may need."

It would be a tall order to load 236 tons of submarine on tank transporter beds but Klaus accepted the challenge. 'They're the bosses and I know the consequence of failure. Maybe they're repeating the 1942 siege of Malta', he thought.

The trials had been successful; the U-boat was ready. At the dockyard, looks of astonishment greeted the huge XXI Electro-boat, with its revolutionary new design prototype, as it emerged at Toulon on November 30 to refuel. Hoards gathered to ogle the symmetry of 'La Belle Fille' in the submarine pens.

Commander Mueller had orders to proceed to Toulon without surfacing, as the enemy's capture and occupation on September 9 of Taranto, the second most important Italian naval base, had made a direct underwater voyage to Toulon a necessity. The enemy's air supremacy in the Mediterranean called for the talents of the Electro-boat. Moving quickly, the big fish was in Toulon in good time. Topped up and provisioned, 10 of the 24 torpedoes were removed to provide storage space for the cargo of art treasures, and for weight compensation of gold bullion.

Commander Mueller's orders had been to rendezvous with U793 on December 6 at 00h01 off Ischia, longitude 13,2 degrees east and latitude 40,7 degrees, to take on further cargo at sea. If necessary, four more torpedoes were to be jettisoned. Instructions were to break open the sealed orders in his possession and proceed accordingly after securing the additional cargo from U793.

He wondered where they were sending him and what the instructions contained.

Being a true Nazi, he had a good idea.

Chapter 13

DECEMBER 1, 1943, 00h01:

FLORENCE

S.S. Lieutenant Erwin Ehrhardt enjoyed a challenge, which made the Ponte Vecchio robberies appealing to him. He detailed two good men in his blitz group to work on the famous bridge.

Blackened faces matched their uniforms. Trained killers, their skull Death's Head badges epitomised the ruthless nature of the contingent.

Curfew silenced a sleeping Florence, moonlight casting a clear reflection on the River Arno's lazy waters as they slid under three arches of Florence's oldest bridge. It was midnight and balmy.

Silent in their precision, Corporal Martin Esslinger signalled Stormtrooper Adolf Pleister to close up. They crept along Vacari's famous corridor high up on the left side of the Ponte Vecchio, which connected the Uffizi Gallery to the Pitti Palace. At the central point, Esslinger's rubber-soled progress stopped. Strong fingers unfastened a black Alpine climbing rope from his waist belt, and tied it around a stone pillar. Pleister, the more experienced climber, tested the knot with a violent jerk, then forced a window and looked down, checking that they were directly above the open middle section. Satisfied, he uncoiled rope over the side.

Nimble as a rat on a ship's hauser, Pleister slid down hand over hand, legs in a scissor grip, to the thoroughfare below. A shake signalled his safe landing and he was joined in moments by his corporal.

Then they froze, melting into stonework shadows. Old Luigi Continelli shuffled from shop to shop on his nightly vigil, rattling each door. The routine kept him awake, otherwise the warm stillness would tempt him to sit and doze off. Half asleep from boredom, he had little comprehension as a black gloved hand closed on his mouth. Esslinger's steel blade claimed Luigi's last breath of life as it pierced his rib cage. A mere 30 seconds later the lifeless body slid over the parapet into the dark waters with barely a ripple. Corporal Esslinger flashed his shrouded torch, signalling his comrades to join him as he unlocked the bridge gates. In minutes systematic burglary of the jewellers' shops began. The team moved with regimental precision, their S.S. lightning bolt insignia appropriate as the acetylene cutting torches melted protective metal and safes.

Rebuilt in 1345, Medici rulers had decreed the Ponte Vecchio's shops be given to goldsmiths. The convenient access to the clustered jewellery shops made the plunderers' task so much easier.

"Schnell! Into the lorries!" directed Lieutenant Ehrhardt.

Two hours after their start the gold was in a waiting lorry in the nearby Borgo San Iacopo at the junction of Via Guicciardini. Colleagues had laid mines in the Borgo San Iacopo to hinder pursuit.

Meanwhile, Florence slept on, with only the occasional bark from a watchful dog disturbing the peace.

"Climb on, schnell! Let's go. GO!" Ehrhardt's commands were muffled but audible to his crack team, who scrambled into one lorry to return to barracks. At 02h00 the second lorry with the gold on board sped down Via Pisana towards Pisa.

A few hours later, Florence awoke at daybreak to horrendous explosions in the Borgo San Iacopo. Detonated mines, heralding the violation of the famous bridge, ripped apart the early morning quiet. The message was clear: the stamp of force, disgusted with the wavering change of heart in its former Pact of Steel ally. The weak go under the jackboot and will not inherit the Earth!

In the dark cab, Ehrhardt smiled as he fingered an exquisite gold bracelet. What a trade in sexual favours he would extort from his Italian girlfriend!

"Press on north to Viareggio," he instructed Adolf Pleister at Pisa. "There's the turning. Near the docks we pull into a double garage Left here, now straight on. There – on the right. Slow down. Corporal! Open the door. Guide him in." Nimble as a mountain goat, Esslinger jumped down and swung open the garage doors, closing them after the small lorry had entered. Their precious cargo would be concealed when they packed the gold.

"We can't have lights on… they will be seen outside. Get some sleep. Corporal, you are on guard for two hours. Then you, Pleister. Wake me after three hours. I'll get us some food. I speak passable Italian."

Ehrhardt was soon asleep, stretched across the seats of the cab.

Adolf Pleister felt a playful kick as he became conscious.

"Hey. Shithead. Time to get up! Move it! My turn to sleep."

Strict training had taught Adolf to be awake and rested in moments, despite the hard lorry floor. An hour later he woke his officer. Corporal Esslinger slept on.

"Pleister, stay on guard. I will be back soon."

The trooper watched his officer go to a small car parked in the garage, open the boot and change into civilian clothes. Ehrhardt disappeared and returned half an hour later with bread, cheese, hardboiled eggs, pizza, milk and some Chianti. The food tasted wonderful.

Rested and fed, Ehrhardt showed his men how to pack the gold pieces into tube shaped containers which had been hidden under sacking. Satisfied they had got it right and the sealing process perfected, he left them again. "Have a leak now! I'm locking you two in from the outside. No smoking! I'll be gone for about three or four hours. Corporal!"

"Sir!" He was ramrod straight.

"You are in charge."

"Jawohl, Lieutnant!" Click went his heels.

Ehrhardt drove off in the Fiat towards Pisa for his rendezvous at a safe house on the outskirts of Viareggio. He would pick up two canisters from a courier drop. In the right hands the value of the contents was beyond estimation. When Goering devised his Master Plan, the emphasis had been on rehabilitating the Nazi hierarchy at a later stage. For this, several pieces had to be in place on the chessboard. In the two canisters were lists of top Nazi conspirators, together with the names they would adopt in South American states. The second canister held the names of Gestapo and Nazi collaborators, with details of the war crimes committed to solve the Jewish problem. Included was documentary proof of property to which the present owners were not entitled; this had in fact had been stolen from Jewish families. There were many, including a factory at Neustadt and a large vineyard in Montmort, Champagne Province, France. Users of slave labour had been tabulated. The objective of Goering's cunning plan was to provide material for the extortion, manipulation, coercion and threats of exposure of prominent people who had benefitted from the Nazi regime, and the assurance that 'safe houses' would offer accommodation in the process of rehabilitation when the wrath of war had subsided; retribution stilled. Ex-Nazis would be able to lead comfortable lifestyles.

S.S. Lieutenant Erwin Ehrhardt was the product of Himmler's evil, and a model of the 'blonde God', Reinhardt Heydrich, Himmler's deputy.

Schooled in Nazi indoctrination, adulation of Hitler was unquestionable to him. He had proved his fanatical loyalty and obedience to the Führer by killing his pet dog with bare hands during S.S. training. With other brutish louts he practised killing as an art on Jewish inmates and political prisoners in Dachau concentration camp. They beat up sick women and hit pregnant women with clubs, especially Jews. Rape was a matter of course to this despicable gang. In recognition of his enthusiasm, Ehrhardt was chosen to carry out daring raids. He showed leadership qualities, was commissioned and allowed to select a ruthless gang of killers, who made up his blitz or hit squad. Erwin was extremely ambitious and knew that a successful operation would enhance his prospects of promotion to Kapitan. His superiors were confident that he would not open the canisters, and that their secrets would stay intact. They were equally confident that he would obey his orders. He felt nothing when told to break the chain which could lead back to his superiors. The intermediary at the courier drop was not to remain alive. He enjoyed killing people.

Ehrhardt drove past the house, parked up the road and waited for the exact meeting time. He walked back, opened the garden gate, strode down the short path and rapped on the front door, flesh tingling as adrenalin built up. He had an erection from excitement, which always happened when he was about to kill. His right fingers felt the stiletto in his trouser pocket for assurance.

The door opened quickly. Erwin was momentarily thrown off balance – he had not expected a woman.

Identification proceeded. "Buon giorno, Signora."

"Giorno! Lei ha una macchina?" She appeared to look for his car.

"Si, Signora. La." Erwin pointed down the road, then stood back to admire the house.

"Quando saro ricco, comprero una bella casa." (When I am rich I shall buy a beautiful house.)

"L'abbiamo comprata." (We have bought it.)

She invited him inside and closed the door. Erwin guessed she was about 40. Attractive; not bad at all, with long legs. Her movements were smooth, her breasts nice too.

"What's your name?"

The Italian beauty looked him straight in his blue Aryan eyes and slowly breathed, "Caterina. And you?" She thought him handsome. Not like the ugly pig who had called before with the grip bag. If only she had known.

"Erwin." She was going to die, so why pretend?

"Would you like something to drink?" Her eyes carried a message.

"Thank you, that would be nice." She was leading him on. 'She wants it', he thought, just like that.

Caterina brought two glasses and poured the wine.

"You will be wanting this!" she said, pointing to a grip bag on the floor. "A really ugly bastard brought it an hour ago, right on time. He didn't say a word after telling me the code. He gave me the shivers. The bag is heavy, whatever's in it."

Erwin went to the grip, unzipped it and saw two large canisters. He picked one up; it was securely sealed; so was the second. There had been no time anyway – that was the schedule. Satisfied, he zipped it up again.

Caterina peered at him over her glass, eyes sparkling. "Salute!"

"Salute," he smiled in return.

"Do you like Italy?"

"Sure."

"Italian women?" she teased provocatively.

"Definitely."

"Would you like to have me?" she murmured, opening her blouse.

"You don't waste much time, do you?"

"It is not every day I get a gorgeous man in my house," she replied. "My man has been away in the army for five months, and a woman gets lonely."

It was a pity he had to murder her.

Can we have a shower first?" Caterina agreed.

"Turn on the water, I'll join you," he called after her.

She adjusted the shower, then called to him from the cubicle.

"It's fine now." The glass screen was already steaming up. Erwin clutched his stiletto, a towel draped over his right hand, and wandered into the shower.

"Goodbye, Caterina."

Her eyes bulged as the blade ripped into her rib cage and tore into her lung. Mouth open, one word gurgled from her throat, "Why?"

"Orders! Pity, but there it is." His voice was smug, resigned. A second thrust to the heart and she was dead.

He showered off the blood, dried, dressed unhurriedly and picked up the grip. Ensuring the front door locked behind him, he strolled to the car and drove back to his men.

At the quayside they smuggled the containers onto a fishing boat in the early evening.

An hour after midnight, three kilometres off-shore, they waited at the arranged grid bearing until a grey mass emerged from the depths and broke the surface of the sea.

Approaching stealthily, the small German submarine looked eerie in the moonlit sea.

Chapter 14

DECEMBER 3, 1943, 00h00:

OFF VIAREGGIO

Tension spread through the U793 crew. The Walter turbine driven, hydrogen peroxide powered submarine prepared to surface. First close shore. Crew knew by instinct. The only sound in the control room was from Captain Gerber's shoe scraping on steel decking as he moved to position himself at the periscope. In command position, it meant one thing – they were going up.

The order came. Their position was three kilometres off-shore of Viareggio.

"Zwanzig metres." The Captain's command broke the silence.

"Jawohl, Kapitan," acknowledged the First Officer quietly, relaying the command.

Klaus Fischer picked up the tension like a magnet attracts iron filings. A hidden force. As a marine propulsion designer, there had been many dives on experimental U-boats commissioning revolutionary craft. Active service was very different. The apprehension among the 17-man crew of the small 34 metres by 3,5 metres submarine was endemic. In this game of cat and mouse a U-boat killer could be up there. The Mediterranean was densely populated by enemy shipping, and the clear waters offered very little protection near the surface.

The 234 ton experimental prototype XV11A U-boat was intended for short range, which made it ideal for operations close to the coast. It was easy to manoeuvre, fast, and offered simple depth keeping and a small surface for location or attack. Its propulsion system allowed it to remain submerged as it was not dependent on fresh air to run the motors. As it was completely silent, the enemy had to sense the presence of a U-boat, rather than obtain clear proof of its position. Heavy fuel consumption, even at short range, was the U793's main drawback. Consequently, it had to refuel from a Type X1V U-boat tanker, which carried 203 tons of fuel.

Sweating in sympathy, Klaus Fischer watched two planesmen carefully turn steering wheel hydroplane controls to alter the pitch of fins fore and aft, skilled eyes focused on depth gauge needles on large dials. Under each one was a long curved glass tube of green liquid, each containing a suspended bubble. The position of the bubble indicated the angle or slope of the submarine to the planesmen. By watching depth needle and bubble level, they were able to move the hydroplanes and steer to the desired depth, as well as keep level when blowing ballast to avoid discovery by emerging too soon. They were calm but tense with concentration. Forward of the control room a helmsman steered the course. Vital controls were in the hands of three men.

A sailor slammed several levers then reported, "All vents shut, Sir." The First Officer bellowed, "Blow ballast!" The immediate roar of compressed air forcing its way into ballast tanks outside the pressure hull broke their silence. As the sailors turned control valves, the First Officer watched the depth gauge needles creeping round the dials. "Zwanzig metres, Kapitan," he sang out. Klaus knew it was easier to control a U-boat in motion. Motionless, it was uncontrollable, its rudder and hydro-planes unresponsive.

"Funf knots, zehn metres," ordered Captain Gerber, ready to take the periscope at 10 metres.

"Zehn metres," called First Officer.

"Up periscopes," commanded the captain. A rating pulled a lever and the bronze periscope column started gliding up from its well. Bending down, Captain Gerber jerked long handles out from their folded position, eyes glued to the eyepieces whilst the periscope continued moving smoothly upwards. When fully extended, Gerber stood up, eyes searching the sea. Using the handles, he gradually turned full circle, walking slowly round the well. By the time he had ensured no enemy destroyers were waiting, a minute had passed. His crew waited on tenterhooks for orders to dive instantly in the presence of danger.

"All clear!" Sighs of relief came from the crew.

Satisfied, he reversed a quarter towards shore and twisted the right handle to 'high power' magnification, altering pitch with the left hand. The fishing boat he was expecting eventually appeared in the crosswires, clearly visible under the almost full moon. He glanced at his watch; one hour after midnight. "Es ist ein Uhr! Das fischerboot kommt jetzt!" he told his First Officer. "Surface!"

He climbed up through the lower hatch into the conning tower.

"Blow main ballast!" bellowed the First Officer, calling out the depth above the roar of compressed air so that Captain Gerber could hear inside the conning tower. "Neun metres, acht metres, sieben, sechs, funf metres…"

As they neared the surface they could feel the motion of the waves. A moment later the captain opened the top hatch and climbed out on the bridge. Klaus followed, filling his lungs with deliciously fresh sea air.

The fishing boat with sailors fore and aft moved cautiously alongside, bumping gently in the swell.

"Heil Hitler!" The captain greeted them. "I'm Captain Gerber. Our Engineer, Herr Fischer. Welcome on board," extending his hand. Lieutnant Ehrhardt returned the salute stiffly in true S.S. fashion, then shook hands with both men. "Thank you Captain. I will be glad to see my consignment safe inside your tin fish! Corporal, pass those tubes. Careful. Watch the swell."

Following strict orders, the cargo of loot was secured below. Lieutnant Ehrhardt was pleased with his successful mission. Nevertheless, skilled in Nazi operations, he remained alert as a cheetah. Something in the captain's manner perturbed him.

"All stowed. Come below, have a Schnapps to keep out the cold," Captain Gerber invited.

"My first time in a sardine tin! It is a new experience for me. But I will try anything once! " Ehrhardt climbed down the vertical conning tower ladder. They sat in the tiny wardroom, chasing beer with Schnapps, smiling artificially at each other while they shared the latest war news.

Captain Gerber hated Nazis, but carried out naval orders. From their brief conversation he judged Ehrhardt a real Nazi. The man was arrogant; he didn't like him. Going over the sealed orders in his mind allowed him to salve his conscience. 'Imperative annihilate fishing boat and crew. No survivors. No trace. Heil Hitler.' Captain Gerber, loyal to the German Navy, had no intention of becoming a war criminal. Refusal to obey orders meant a court martial and death. He would not, however, commit cold-blooded murder. Had the tables been reversed, the Nazi would not have hesitated. Gerber thought through his alternatives. U793 had no external armaments. Good. To mow down the crew would sicken him. Murdering defenceless men and scuttling their boat was equally repulsive, an act he would not commit. The third disgusting alternative was to torpedo the boat. At least it could be construed as an act of war; firing on suspected enemy shipping. To rid the world of a Nazi like Ehrhardt would be a service to the German people and the human race.

Ehrhardt was a survivor, and his intuition detected unease in the captain's manner. He put it together. If he had to kill his own contact in Viareggio, then they in turn would have to take him out to break the chain. When though? It had to be now! He would watch their every move like a cat. Take some with him!

"It is dangerous on the surface, Lieutenant. We must go. Your receipt," said the Captain, handing a paper to him.

The captain was anxious to sail. Would he torpedo them? Ehrhardt thought then that they might shoot him as he climbed the ladder.

It didn't happen, and he saluted as the fishing boat cast off, slipping across the silver moonlit sea towards Viareggio.

"Dive, dive, dive!" the order rang out.

Captain Gerber closed the hatch and gave rapid orders. "Full ahead." A speed of 25 knots soon put U793 well ahead of the fishing boat. The next command had the U-boat executing a rapid circle to head off their target. Peering through his periscope, Gerber aimed a bow cum broadside shot. The fishing boat would sail into their torpedo track. "Feuer Eins!" he bellowed.

There was a hiss as a sailor punched a red firing button and a silver fish streaked to its target. Scoring a direct hit, it blew the boat to smithereens. Observing the destructive result Gerber commented flatly, 'Was fischerboot wird versenkt," for the ship's log, closing periscope handles as it descended. He was disgusted by the heartless act of elimination.

Chapter 15

DECEMBER 5, 1943, 23h00:

OFF ISCHIA, TYRRHENIAN SEA

The U-boat crew was tense, sweating in the narrow space, nerves jangling in anticipation. It happened every time: adrenalin coursing through veins and imagination playing havoc with minds and brains. Prepare to surface. They would soon lose comparative security at 40 metres, well aware that submarines were easily detectable in the clear seas of the Mediterranean unless below 15 metres. Oh for the North Sea where even at periscope depth they were unseen. They would soon shed their swift 25 knot speed, another safety factor, and they were all scared.

To occupy his mind Klaus Fischer thought about the sister U-boat U792, commissioned on November 16 at Keil. The first 'true submarine' had entered the service. U794 had been launched on Sunday November 14, but had not yet been commissioned.

Rome had been occupied on September 10 by the German Army and Naples had followed suit on October 1. Land battles raged. Allied landings would soon be attempted on the Italian west coast. They heard the latest news from their 'milch cow' whilst refuelling 40 tons of perhydrol at sea off Anzio. The Tyrrhenian Sea bristled with a huge concentration of hostile warships in the waters above them, some already sighted. The latest news was that the Americans were coming in force.

Both planesmen gripped their wheels, eyes glued to bubbles and depth gauge needles as they maintained trim. The captain had to maintain at least five knots of speed or they could lose it. If they came up too fast the bow would break surface out of control, leading to discovery. Concentrate.

"I wonder what's waiting for U3 up there?" whispered one crew member. A bloody destroyer?"

"I'll give you some clean underpants if there is!" his mate answered. "The bastards can see us damn easily in these waters. It's night up on top, but they can still spot us in the moonlight. Shit!" He concentrated even harder to still his fear.

Their position was off the island of Ischia, passing by the Gulf of Gaeta to the Gulf of Naples; their mission to meet another clandestine boat and take on more spoils, this time from the Nazi HQ at Monte Cassino which was practically under siege.

It was a repeat of the cargo transfer off Viareggio three nights before. The small 234 ton U793 rose slowly from 40 metres, compressed air blasting water from the open bottom of both side ballast tanks.

"Funfunddreissig, vierunddreissig," said the First Officer, who was busy monitoring the depth gauge needle. The crew members were usually tense when surfacing, and would have been more so if they had known what lurked in wait above and 80 metres forwards of them.

Allied landings at Anzio had been planned. To contain Axis shipping movements a British submarine had laid a cordon pattern of mines from her torpedo tubes. One mine floated 10 metres below sea level, an inert force of destruction until a horn was struck. Waiting.

"Sechsundzwanzig, funfundzwanzig." Leaning into his spoked wheel the helmsman at the forward end of the control room kept his steady course. The First Officer checked compressed air pressure dials in a flash, then turned his eyes back to the depth gauge, "Zwanzig," he called.

Periscope depth would be reached at 10 metres; 10 more to go. Outside, the mine hawser wire touched the bow of U793 and as the U-boat rose, the mine positioned to strike high on the hull, astern of the conning tower. The noise of forced compressed air drowned any extraneous sounds as the cable gently scraped by the hull. The mine came slowly nearer.

"Funfzehn… vierzehn."

Palms were sweaty. They would soon be visible up there. The Captain stood poised to accept the periscope from the well.

"Dreizehn - zwolf - elf – zehn-"

B - A -N-GGG!!!

The submarine shook from bow to stern, reverberating like a giant bell struck by a sledgehammer, the sensation that of a locomotive smashing into buffers. Unable to release his grip quickly enough at the split second of impact, the helmsman was flung down bodily by the spinning wheel reacting to the rudder, which had been smashed by explosive side forces searching for peripheral equipment on the hull to rip and destroy. The port hydrofoil spun off into the depths. The port decking had received the main force of the impact, which had torn a gaping hole through vents, and ripped jagged strips from the port ballast tank. Incredibly the explosion was partially cushioned by air trapped in the ballast tank top. The blast spent its fury on the port outer shell, which acted like a trilby hat, cushioning skull damage against a windscreen. The pressure hull held intact with minor stress leaks.

Utter chaos reigned inside the U793, with not one man left standing or sitting in place. Pressure valves had burst, spraying a mist of water, while a depth gauge had cracked, hit by a valve control flying across from the side of the explosion. A port list had developed immediately, the submarine hanging, suspended by air in the starboard ballast tank. What remained of the port tank filled up fast. Crew crawled and stumbled over equipment attached to the port side, which was underneath them as the U793 slowly rolled, then descended in a side-slip. The serviceable depth gauge, now over their heads, registered their continuing descent. Forcing air into starboard ballast had no effect, and it continued escaping from the open bottom of the tank, now horizontal above them. The U793 went down slowly, with motors still running and lights on. Crew members were hysterical with fear; helpless, terrifying of dying in a tomb, buried along with a wealth of secrets and gold to rival that of the Pharoahs.

The aft planesman fell backwards off his seat, shrieking as his head struck the periscope, which hung horizontally. Blood poured from his gashed ear and torn face. A sailor screamed out as his leg snapped, his foot twisted between the valve pipes beneath him; unable to correct his fall in time. Captain Gerber clung to the periscope like a drowning man to driftwood.

Klaus Fischer was fortunate. On the port side as it rolled off balance, he was compelled to sit down ungraciously on the uncomfortable dials of the port instrument panel. The First Officer next to him helped him to sit up. Rigid naval discipline gave way to panic among the crew. Screams forward pierced the confined space as a torpedo broke loose, crushing the life from a loader, leaving him mangled against the hull. He took six squealing minutes to die, his screaming crescendo ending as he coughed blood, choking to death. The second planesman and helmsman, both unhurt, were dumped on the port side, the depth gauge above them reading 110 metres, and still dropping.

A grinding bump stopped U793 as she struck a rock pinnacle at 200 metres, bringing a shout from the crew. "Halt!" shouted Captain Gerber, to stop all movement. Most of the men were on the temporary port floor anyway, and had no option. A grinding wrenching noise echoed as U793 jolted to a stop, then quickly corrected to normal balance level. Utter confusion reigned as reclining bodies pitched to the steel flooring. Lights flickered, went out momentarily and came back on again.

Klaus, the marine designer, had been anticipating an explosion. It was a miracle the turbines had not faltered and blown up under the intense pressure. They continued to perform, a tribute to their engineering. The engines would continue to run until the fuel ran out. At least they would have lights for as long as the generators turned. Air would circulate and be scrubbed for a time.

"Close bulkheads! First Officer. Assess damage. Report injuries."

"Jawohl Kapitan!"

Settling himself, the captain meticulously wrote up his log, recording every incident; strict naval background sustaining him to the end. Gerber, Klaus and First huddled in his tiny wardroom.

"We all know it's hopeless. Be realistic. Three dead, four injured, one badly and bleeding. Fuel is low. Give us 12 hours and that's it." The two men felt pity for the first class seafarer who they knew had to make a dreadful decision. Hang on or hand out pills for a final sleep. Wait too long, and have an uncontrolled mutiny of madmen. Only seven crew members remained. Captain Gerber took his keys and opened a steel cupboard and brought out a Mauser pistol, checking to see whether it was still loaded. "Just in case." A wry smile flitted across his weather-beaten face.

"May I suggest you offer relief to the injured now, Kapitan," ventured Klaus, his heart torn by the agony of the battered few. First Officer nodded his agreement.

"The men have a right to do whatever they wish before taking their lives. Some may wish to meet their Maker and some may go to the 'other' place, if we have not already arrived." They admired this wonderful man. "I retain the right to go last as any captain and write the last words in the U793 log. You never know, it may be found one day!"

It was a terrible end, all the details recorded in the log in neat Gothic script.

He hated the Nazis and Gestapo and what they had done to terrorise Germany and Europe. He had let out exactly how he felt.

Some elected to get blind drunk and then took their pill. Two prayed together as they placed the fatal cyanide pill on their tongues, crushing them between their teeth. Klaus thought of his mother as he died. Others sought past childhood memories as they administered the fatal swallow. Captain Gerber sat bolt upright in his ward room, surrounded by his dead crew members.

As the light spluttered over his last words in the log, he placed the Mauser to his grey temple and squeezed the trigger.

Chapter 16

NEUSTADT

Hermann's fateful prediction crept closer by the day. Ruhr industries continued to be annihilated by waves of Flying Fortress bombing raids. These had peaked in the momentous impact of the Dam Busters on the evening of May 16 1943, which breached a ragged 100-metre diameter hole, causing 134 million tons of water to crash into the valley below in a 65-metre torpedo. Three kilometres away, the sleeping villagers of Himmelpforten would never see another day. The 'Gates of Heaven' were removed.

That same night the Eder dam was breached, spilling 200 million tons of water into the sheer-sided valley. Foaming floodwaters hurtled down the valley at a speed of 10 metres per second. A car raced in front in a desperate attempt to outrun the rushing monster, headlights shining like two eyes in the dark. It was not fast enough though, and the raging water serpent swallowed it whole. Wuppertal was devastated, without food or fresh water. Factories, if not destroyed in the flood, were unable to function without water, and came to a dead stop. The single, most stupendous blow to German morale had been dealt that night.

On July 9 1943, Allied armies invaded Sicily. Mussolini was driven from power and imprisoned. By September 3 the Allies had taken Reggio di Calabria on the toe of Italy. The Italian Government surrendered on September 8 and the main element of the Italian fleet sailed for Malta. Taranto Naval base was occupied on September 9th and on the same day the Fifth Army under Field Marshall Montgomery landed on the beaches of Salerno. Foggia was captured on September 27 and Naples occupied on October 1, 1943. Was it a salute of nature that Vesuvius erupted in March 1944?

Field Marshall Kesselring was sent to hold the German Army together and the final bastion of Monte Cassino fell in May 1944. The German armies on the Russian front were driven back and destroyed under the maniacal orders of Hitler to stand fast to the last man. Russian barbarism matched the hideous brutality of their invaders: an eye for an eye for the vile atrocities committed against the Slavonic peoples.

The vice was being screwed tighter. "Enemy forces are being repulsed on Normandy beaches."

Hermann had heard propaganda lies like these before, from Goebbel's newsreaders, so his imagination adjusted the distorted newscast on the morning of June 6 1944 to read, 'Allied Invasion'.

That was enough for him.

At that moment Ingrid entered his office.

"Hell, you look tired!" he commiserated.

"Not too tired to look after you though!" smiled Ingrid, pursing her lips for a kiss.

"Not a chance! I'm finished – I have been awake most of the night."

Hermann's bloodshot eyes and shaking hands told a tale of utter exhaustion and blinding fatigue. Night bombers had streaked over Neustadt to Stuttgart, chased by anti-aircraft tracer bullets. Incessant bombing and noise was stretching his nerves to breaking point: he was on the edge. Hermann gazed at Ingrid, still provocatively beautiful through her veil of tiredness. She was no quitter, he had to admit, despite the fact that she was trying to cope with tiresome problems, and was struggling to maintain productivity schedules and deadlines.

"Has that serge arrived yet?" he enquired tiredly.

"No, not yet. The phones are still out, so we cannot get through."

Hermann swore loudly. "They're screaming at me for S.S. uniforms, the usual threats. Put another run of Luftwaffe through in the meantime then."

Ingrid waved her hand down in a gesture of, 'you haven't heard anything yet'. "I have just been upstairs! The top floor windows on the south wall have gone; the east wall has a gaping hole, a metre or two across. The roof leaks a bit on the south end but we'll manage!" She was still smiling through it all.

He looked at her lovely blonde hair. She still looked gorgeous.

"The extra hour a day. Has it caused any problems?"

"Bugger them! They can work it or go to Auschwitz! It's not a health resort we're running." Ingrid's nostrils flared.

"Come here!" He put out his hand and led her to the settee. "Listen to me." He turned to look directly into her crystal blue eyes. Her loyalty now would make or break him.

"You realise it is only a matter of time before we are defeated?" Ingrid shook her head in righteous indignation; Nazi indoctrination was deeply ingrained. 'Deutschland uber alles!' After a pause her shoulders dropped. Resignedly she nodded.

Hermann took her hands in his. "One night this factory will probably be destroyed. We have had some close escapes already. I don't want to die suffocating under a pile of rubble. Also if we sit here and wait it out, we'll certainly be arrested for using forced labour. They'd call it slave labour! Either way, if we stay we lose out in the end. If we survive and are taken by the British or Yanks, perhaps it won't be so bad. But can you imagine the Russians! You've heard the stories!" Hermann watched her eyes. However reluctant, he could sense she was in agreement and scared as well.

He continued. "You've been good to me and I want you to get out with me. I have a plan. Will you join me?" Ingrid Penz looked at him, placed long fingers on his right cheek, moved forward and kissed him tenderly on the lips.

"I'll even go to Hell with you! You're good for me too, you brute!"

Hermann sighed, wondering just how to tell her about the store of treasure below. "For some reason they never came back for them. Circumstances have changed so much, they could possibly have been forgotten. It's my plan to get the goods to the Berghof castle cellars in Bacharach. If I leave them here they will most probably be destroyed. Ingrid, you realise the risk involved! This is stolen Nazi booty and I'm stealing it from them! I could always fall back on the story that I'm safeguarding the pictures for them. If the factory goes up in smoke, the treasures perish with it. When the war is over, we would have assets to sell. Our money will have no value after the war. It is always so after wars. With the factory gone I would have nothing. At least we can go to the castle and farm the vineyard, sit out the invasion and watch the outcome of hostilities from a quieter spot. The Yanks and British will come in and give the Rhineland back to France! Just you see if I'm wrong! What do you say?"

"Yes Darling! As long as I can stay with you!"

"Good. I've been planning for months. Come and see my collection." Hermann led the way to the cellars, entered a small room and locked the door behind them. Opening a cupboard he pulled out a tailor's dummy dressed as an S.S.Untersturmfuhrer, high peak cap with the Death Head's badge perched on the centre knoll. Jackboots followed. A drawer contained a black belt, shoulder strap and holster, complete with Mauser P42 and lanyard.

"Christ. Where did you get those?"

"Off a man who was killed in an air raid three months ago. His head was crushed when a building fell on him. I found him bleeding to death. He was a terrible mess; a hopeless case. I put him out of his misery."

"How? Did you shoot him?" Ingrid was open-mouthed.

"No, with a piece of iron railing. Bullets tell tales and I didn't need problems.

It was night, so no one saw me. His uniform was ruined; covered in blood. So I stripped it of all badges of rank and insignia, and took everything from his pockets. We produce uniforms, but I needed his cap which had miraculously survived; must have blown off; his boots, belt, side arm and holster and most important, his identity card. I've fixed that too!"

Ingrid looked at Hermann's face in the identity of S.S. Untersturmführer Kurt Neethling.

"I need your help and two of the Ukrainian girls for my plan to work."

"You are crazy! Why bring them into it? Can't we do it alone?"

Hermann pulled a sardonic smile. "You forget dear girl, they have no origin or status. They won't live to tell the tale. I need a second driver and their strength to carry the stuff."

Ingrid smiled. "I see!"

"You will be dressed in Luftwaffe auxiliary: you as a corporal, and Olga and Nashka with no rank. I have forage caps, badges, belts, boots and false papers too. Make sure your uniforms fit well and look smart. Fix the stripes and check the insignia is correct. This is very important. Here; look through this manual. I believe audacity has the best chance of success. We drive straight past them in broad daylight! I am relying on the arrogance of the S.S. Lieutnant to be sufficient to intimidate the simple 'Michaels' on duty at the checkpoints. Remember, the German private soldier expects to be pushed around and shouted at by his superiors. He gets just that rough treatment! He obeys without questioning authority or his superiors. It is a distinct weakness in the whole military system. It is their Prussian heritage. No one thinks for themselves, they just take orders. We will exploit that weakness if we can. Use two Luftwaffe trucks to carry a genuine consignment of uniforms with our booty underneath. I want you to make up invoices, delivery notes, certificate of origin and manufacture; the usual rubbish. Consign to Koblenz. I taught Olga how to drive our truck. She will drive me; you drive Nashka. That way we will handle any conversation at the checkpoints.

"Like you, Olga learnt to drive on tractors, so I need to be with her. We set up to go on Thursday 14th. We break open the wall on the Tuesday; stencil the boxes to coincide with your invoices. The girls will load on Wednesday. Take care! No stupid slip-ups!"

"There won't be. You know me."

The light summer rain had stopped and the tarred streets of Neustadt glistened in the early sunshine. At 06h00 the town was not fully awake as the two trucks slowed at the exit checkpoint.

Tired and wet, waiting for his change of guard and looking forward to a hot breakfast, Hans Blucher stepped out to meet the vehicles. He soon recognised the S.S. officer, saluted, noting the disdain for lower ranks apparent on the officer's face. A clipboard holding the movement sheet was pushed arrogantly under his nose. The private glanced briefly at the document and handed it back promptly in deference. He hurriedly saluted which was casually acknowledged. Leaning his weight on the road barrier; the pole lifted against the counterweight. A roar emitted from the diesel engine and the heavy lorry passed through, followed by Corporal Ingrid. It went without a hitch.

They headed west to Frankenstein, turning off north before Kaiserslautern, and heading for Winnweilen, Rockenhausen and Bad Kreuznach. The town's entrance barrier was down as Olga shifted gears, slowing the big Luftwaffe truck down well before the barrier, following the discipline Hermann had instilled into her. The last thing he needed was a gate crash. Olga inched the lorry up to the checkpoint in first and braked, engine ticking over. A corporal approached the driver, signalling for her to cut the engine.

At first Olga did not comply, not sure of his instruction. Hermann whispered to her to switch off. The corporal saluted, accepted the clipboard, not intimidated by the S.S. regalia. He had his duty to perform. He examined the sheets.

"Sir, I must see inside the canopy."

Hermann waved nonchalantly to Olga to follow orders and open up for inspection. The efficient corporal raised the flap and looked at the neat boxes, checking to see that their markings corresponded to the entries in the documents.

"How many in each box?" he asked Olga. Before she could speak Hermann shot out, "Ten uniforms in each box. What is the problem Corporal?"

"Nothing. Sir! Just checking. All correct sir." Hermann snatched the clipboard from his hand, signalled authoritatively to Olga to get back in the driving seat. He climbed in; composed himself. Olga switched on, pressed the glow-worm and pushed the ignition.

It did not catch. She tried again, still nothing.

Sweat trickled down Hermann's armpits.

"Out!" he commanded. Olga jumped down and Hermann moved across into the driving seat. He tried again. Nothing.

"Hell! We should never have switched off," he fumed angrily. He shouted back to Ingrid. "Corporal! We need a push start. Come up behind." Trying hard to disguise his panic he switched on again and felt the truck slowly roll as Ingrid's truck nudged, pushed and gathered speed. Letting out the clutch in third, the truck coughed, fired and came to life with a roar. Hermann signalled success and Olga scrambled back in to the driving seat once more. Phew!

They were on their way again, north to Stromberg and Rheinbollen, then east down the winding road to Bacharach. The twinkling Rhine welcomed their arrival. Never before had they been so pleased to see the steep sloping vineyards and the 13th Century church of St. Peter in the village.

Home again. They had made it. But tired as they were, they did not dare rest until the boxes were safely locked away in the castle cellar. Finally all the uniforms were stacked into Ingrid's lorry for the final phase of securing their alibi.

The next morning Hermann and Ingrid set off together and arrived in Koblenz, delivering the consignment against receipt. This time Hermann was in his civilian clothes, with Ingrid still dressed as his Luftwaffe corporal driver. That evening at the castle they dined well and drank to their success. They toasted the next load. "Cheers, my darling!"

Later, in his bedroom, Hermann looked into the mischievous eyes of this determined woman who had become such an integral part of his life, thinking that she was his right arm, confidante, sexual companion and friend. She had never been possessive, or tried to own him. She valued her freedom and respected his. It was a good arrangement. Hermann playfully held her chin between his finger and thumb before he asked, "Would you really like to live here? With me I mean?"

Even though she was snuggled up against him, Ingrid managed to blow him a kiss. The clean sheets of his massive bed felt delicious. She slid her leg over his thigh and massaged her mound against his muscled leg. "Need you ask?" she whispered.

The second trip was easy. Hermann had insisted that the authorities institute checks on his previous journey that the delivery had been executed at Koblenz. His second movement order came through without a hitch. But this time two full truck-loads of treasures would be going to the castle, disguised with only a few boxes of uniforms. Hermann decided to go precisely a week after this, and counted on the same men being on duty at the same times, with precise Germanic repetitiveness. His hunch was right and they sailed through. The transfer to the castle was accomplished.

Hermann thought that bricking up the wall would provide the best security, and bought bricks, cement and sand. They completed the job with the Ukrainian girls' help, making sure that the evidence was neatly plastered over.

His next problem was secrecy.

"I am so delighted with our transfer I think we should celebrate," announced Hermann. He opened some bottles of wine and the girls were soon tipsy. He pressed more and more on to them, which they eagerly consumed.

"I want these two almost drunk," he whispered to Ingrid, who giggled to give them the impression that over-indulging was acceptable conduct. They were soon quite drunk.

"I will take you to see the most beautiful part of Bacharach, at the mouth of the valley of the Steeg. The only way to appreciate it is from the Rhine! We will hire a boat and go in the early evening," Hermann told the giggling girls.

Such were the delights of the breathtaking scenery that they even managed to penetrate the Ukrainians' alcoholic haze, but their enjoyment came to an abrupt end in the middle of the Rhine. There were two muffled reports as Hermann shot them in the head at close range, and dumped them overboard. Ingrid smiled as their bodies slipped silently to the bottom of the world-famous river, completely unmoved by the cold-blooded murders. In fact she was so turned on she made passionate love to Hermann when they returned to the castle. It had been necessary. They now had a bond more binding than just sex.

"Ingrid, no matter what happens to us, this event must never be spoken about! When we are back at the factory say that the girls are employed on the estate. No one will ever be the wiser. Agree?"

"Yes," pledged Ingrid.

They were well aware that the penalty for the peacetime discovery of their two secrets would be death.

Gerda Blom was waiting for Hermann in his office when he returned.

"Herr Schmidt, we have had a revolt on the third floor."

"WHAT? Why? What happened? Tell me!"

"Your father. He is dead."

"WHAT? Dead! How?"

"He went too far. I did warn you, Sir. He was beating a young Jewish girl who was standing near the windows, and some of the girls rushed over and tried to push him away. He fell through the window and broke his neck. I dragged his body into the loading dock."

Hermann was stunned. Anger rose in him, then subsided. He knew all about his father's excesses.

"Yes Gerda, you did warn me, and there is a limit. He's dead. If the Nazi friends find out what happened, every one of the Jewesses will be transported or shot."

Hermann looked at Gerda and then said, "And you included! If that happens, I too would be judged a war criminal after the war as no one will believe that I didn't order it to be done! I don't want that! I don't want 600 murders on my conscience either. Gerda, we will say he was killed in an air raid. There's one practically every night. Help me clear up this mess."

"Thank you Herr Schmidt. You are a good man. We all respect you as a decent German."

Karl Schmidt was entered in statistics as yet another air raid victim, the secret buried with him.

Chapter 17

MARCH 1944

Time dulled expectation, leading Hermann to become complacent about his double-cross. Then one evening when the factory had closed down for the night, Ingrid announced the arrival of S.S. Hauptfuhrer Bockler. Hermann took an instant dislike to his visitor, whose arrogance made Hermann want to strike him.

"So you're Schmidt," he smirked, placed his black gloves and swagger cane on the desk with a disturbing deliberate gesture. "I have privileged information that you have in your keeping treasures of the State. I take it they are secure?" Hermann nearly had a stroke. His eyelids twitched. The visitor's manicured fingers opened a gold cigar case and withdrew a square Villager. He did not offer one to Hermann. From one pocket of his black uniform he withdrew a gold lighter, lit the cigar and puffed smoke in Hermann's direction.

'Pig', thought Hermann. "Why of course," assured Hermann, mustering false bravado. "1 can see you are a man of good taste. Can I offer you a glass of Rheinbleicherte? We can see the things later." He hoped his rigid smile would not betray his panic. An agreeable nod maintained the arrogance.

"Schmidt, I have removed a copy of a detailed catalogue from Central Archives. I do not know where the original is, but it is enough to know what you are storing. I want half of these treasures. Understand?" No negotiation; just a straight demand.

"A moment bitte! I'll get the wine organised. For such a distinguished visitor, perhaps I can offer schinkenbrot, wurst und kase, Ja?" with a servile bow. "Then we discuss, Ja?" Acceptance of his servility gave Hermann the chance to speak to Ingrid outside.

"Listen! I want you to screw this sod. Get him in the cellar room and kill the bastard! I'll put a gun halfway down the right side between the mattress and base set. Be too obvious under the pillow. Cocked, catch off. Bring ham sandwiches, sausage, cheese. I'll talk a bit, then leave for wine. You do your thing. Get him down there. Right! We are in big trouble if this character leaves this place alive. I'm not going to Dachau; I don't know about you." Ingrid was green with fear – he knew she would do it.

Hermann returned with two glasses and his estate wine, pulled the cork and poured. "Hope you like it. Good health!" he toasted, raising his glass. The S.S. man relaxed, dropping his guard.

"You must be very busy with your duties, Sir. It must be taxing, with little time for leisure." The blatant flattery was soaked up, self importance glowing on the pinched face.

"We are kept constantly on our toes in the affairs of State. The Jewish problem is a constant reminder of the undermining of the State. We have the final solution of course!" He smiled, "unless they are useful to us, like your workers."

"The nation needs you to protect us from these evil forces. You do a fine job for our glorious Reich." Hermann then appeared to be hesitant. "Sir, without being too forward, do you get much opportunity for," he paused for effect, "light relief shall we say?" He winked knowingly.

"It is not easy. I miss Hamburg," came the reply.

"If I might suggest, without offence Sir, my secretary is, how shall we say, 'accommodating' to our distinguished visitors. Such as you, Mein Herr." He smiled conspiratorially.

"Is she indeed? I'll bear that in mind."

Ingrid came in at that moment having listened outside, wearing a sexy black dress with a revealing lace-up bodice and ruffled sleeves, which exposed her shoulders and breasts to their best advantage. Her blonde hair was tied back with a black chiffon scarf, which trailed down to her bosom. Hermann tried not to notice the Gestapo's sharp intake of breath. He was hooked.

Ingrid's look was one of sheer seduction. She put the ham sandwiches on the table, arranged neatly on a plate with sliced sausage and cheese. Moving to their guest, she picked up a morsel of sausage and placed it on her tongue, caressing it as she slowly drew it into her mouth.

"Gorgeous," she murmured, closing her eyes for a second. "Would you like some?" she asked, fluttering her eyelashes. Deliberately and slowly, her fingers carried a piece of wurst to their guest's lips. He took it like a fish takes bait. The loose lacing of Ingrid's dress gaped with her movements, the top gradually dropping lower until her pink nipples were exposed. The S.S. man was clearly disturbed, moving awkwardly on his chair. Hermann's offer to refill his glass a fourth time received a nod.

When Hermann excused himself to replenish the wine, Ingrid wasted no time with her advances to the Gestapo pig. She placed her long fingers on his thigh. "We could go downstairs," she whispered seductively. "There is a bed there." She led him down cellar steps to the bedroom they used when they slept over. Once inside, the suspense was too much for him. He roughly grabbed at Ingrid's dress, ripping the front, then snatched at her underwear, cutting her thighs in the process. In a flash his pants were down and she realised that he intended to rape her. He lunged at her, dragging her down onto the bed. She knew better than to put up any resistance. She didn't want her hands pinned down.

Her rapist achieved a clumsy penetration, and Ingrid realised her chance. She threw her left arm around his neck as if in mock ecstasy, distracting his attention as she pulled his face down to hers for a passionate kiss. The fingers of her right hand searched desperately under the mattress. Encountering cold steel, she withdrew the gun and applied pressure to the trigger. The next events happened in seconds. Pressing the gun to his temple with practised skill, Ingrid fired. She was deafened. He was dead, his blood splattering her arms, face and body. She swore, moaning and shuddering in disgust as Hermann rushed in and pulled the corpse off her.

For once Hermann was glad to hear the air raid siren wailing. Cleaning liquid, a match and a bombed out building nearby would provide a means of disposal for the corpse. It was not necessary. Ingrid grabbed her things and rushed upstairs to the executive washroom. The bombers were arriving.

"Quick. The shelter!" Hermann screamed. They ran through the building to the office and scrambled into their shelter.

In the clear night a British bombardier detonated a stick of 10 tons of high explosives from the bomb bay of the aircraft. The cluster fell in tight formation, the leading bomb landing 10 metres from the Schmidt factory corner. The rear gunner saw the complete north-east wing of the factory collapse amongst a ripping blinding fury of explosion, burying the unwelcome visitor under 50 tons of rubble.

Hermann and Ingrid escaped alive. With the factory ruined it was time to go to Bacharach. "I'm taking Gerda Blom with us."

"You are WHAT – are you mad? Harbouring a Jew?" Their Jewish workers would be employed as slave labour in similar conditions in factories, or returned to concentration camps and probably herded with bureaucratic efficiency to their extermination in the 'Final Solution', which was now operating at fever pitch.

"If I ever get started up again, I want Blom as my shop floor manager. It would be a waste to see her expertise go up in smoke, literally…" Sick humour had become commonplace. "I'll report her dead in the air raid, and hand over the others. War will soon be over. Germany has had it."

"Hell, you like taking risks, don't you? But you are right – after the war there will be few experts left if all the men are killed at the front. At least the cow can help us get going again. I see your point," admitted Ingrid.

Gerda was speechless. "Herr Schmidt you are a gut man! Vat a risk you are for me taking. I appreciate. If you get into business again I vill verk for you." She looked a bit sheepish then asked outright. "If you take me vif you, can I ask an enormous favour off you. Vould you plees take also another girl. She is French; she has been here six months. Very gut girl. Lost her people. Plees. Ve vill verk hart for you on your estate, Herr Schmidt. You vill not regret. She vould be gut company for me." Gerda smiled apologetically.

"Lesbians aren't you?" Hermann went straight to the point; he had spotted her concern. "Lovers?

"Ja, Mein Herr."

Thinking quickly, Hermann decided it could work for him.

The arrangement would keep Gerda from straying and could also be good insurance. "If she comes, you two do not move off the estate until the war is over. Agreed?"

"Ja, Mein Herr. Danke schon."

"Officially you two died in the air raid. What's the French girl's name?"

"Adele Mathieu, Mein Herr."

POST WAR YEARS
*****
REVIVAL

Chapter 18

1949:

ZELLENBERG

Henri was 27 when the moment of truth hit him. His father had died suddenly in 1949 and he owned two large vineyards and estates with a champagne distribution network. The awesome responsibility gave him a jolt, and the nervous twitch in his left eye became more frequent.

Highly intelligent, Henri realised that he had to protect his business empire. He had no intention of losing the golden goose that had afforded him so much pleasure, but he had no desire to work too hard in the process. Estate managers could do that for him.

The body of the murdered Arnaud Saint-Laurent was buried in the winelands of his birth. Henri knew his father would have wanted it so. The funeral over, Henri had to think seriously of his future.

He gazed down on the charm of Riquewihr, snuggled in a blanket of vines; a working village dedicated to the Riesling grape. Cobbled streets lined by ancient half-timbered, gabled buildings were dominated by a towered church bearing aloft a gigantic four-faced clock, whose weathercock reigned supreme over the huddled, steep-tiled roofs beneath.

Henri thought about his father's murder; the senseless revenge of the French Resistance partisans; retribution for Nazi collaboration.

Looking over Riquewihr, Henri's eye traced the wine route leading to Ribeauville as it wound through the cleft of the gently swelling hills skirting the family chateau at Zellenberg, over the first rise. A patchwork of vineyards spread all round this important wine producing region, a legendary relic of the Romans, who had brought their vine clippings from Italy some 2 000 years before.

The wine producing area of medieval Colmar, between Mulhouse and Strasbourg, was largely a German speaking area, with the Route des Vins passes through picturesque villages such as Mittelbergheim and Kaysersberg. Henri's inheritance had made him a prominent vineyard owner in the district, with power and influence to rival the weathercock. He was the master of the family wine estate, its chateau and cellars bequeathed through his grandfather's aristocratic heritage as Baron von Zeichenhausen. He had also inherited the large wine estate at Montmort and the distribution company. The family had maintained their Germanic background but adopted the French family name of Saint-Laurent from the Baron's wife's side, after the First World War.

Alsace-Lorraine had changed hands between German and French rulers four times in 75 years since Napoleon's gain reverted to Prussian control in 1870. In the German Empire it was a Reichland. Although the population stubbornly refused to accept their new status as Germans, political developments in France moderated their enthusiasm for the Third Republic. In 1918 the area once again came under French control. The majority of Alsatians have both a French conception of state and German conception of nation, never wholly at ease with either. They learned to adapt. Alsace fell under German domination again in 1940, when Henri was an impressionable age, especially under Nazi indoctrination at Heidelberg University.

In spite of his fortune, Henri was disturbed. There was a skeleton in the cupboard. A threat hung over him like the Sword of Damocles. His father had been murdered. Would this satisfy their lust for revenge? His left eye twitched at the thought.

Henri had a friend he could trust; Hermann Schmidt. He set off in his car for Bacharach, looking forward to their reunion.

As the car crunched to a stop on the gravel, Hermann opened the door, arms spread wide to welcome his old friend.

"Good to see you Henri," he said after their warm embrace. "We should get together more often. Sorry about your father; his death was really tragic. Come inside."

Henri entered the baronial hall, draped with tapestries, swords, shields and suits of armour, unchanged from their graduate days when they had vacationed together here and at Zellenberg.

Hermann led the way into a magnificent drawing room hung with breathtaking works of art. A huge leather armchair looked inviting, and Henri slumped down to relax after his journey.

"Well my good friend, what's new?" After chatting about wine, market prices and economic prospects, Hermann looked at Henri.

"You didn't come to see me to talk shop, Henri. What's on your mind?"

"It's La Verite. I don't really own half of it." Twitch went his left eye.

"What! How can that be?" Hermann appeared shocked. "You never told me that before. What happened?"

"To make sense I had better tell you how father got started at Montmort, then you will understand what that land meant to him." Henri related the history of La Verite.

"Sophie stayed with us until 1943, when she was 23, and then she went her own way." His left eye fluttered again. Hermann put up his hand. "Wait my good friend. Let us enjoy a glass of Rheinbleicherte with your story..."

Leaving the room he returned with glasses and wine tasters and proceeded to pour a little in the tasters. Holding the stem, Henri lifted the slender necked glass up to the light and observed the pale red wine. A twist of his wrist rolled the wine around the sides, then he placed his critic's nose to the edge and sniffed carefully. "Excellent aroma. Year?"

"Forty-five. A good year."

Henri sipped, holding the liquid in his mouth, moving it slowly around his tongue. "Congratulations! You must have done well with this."

"We have indeed." Hermann filled regular wine glasses. "So tell me more," he prompted.

"Father's Germanic heritage saved us and stood us in good stead. He welcomed the Nazi occupiers. Welcomed them to his mansion and gave them cases of champagne. They ensured that we had no shortages to hinder production." Henri looked knowingly at Hermann. "Yes, we used forced labour from concentration camps to cultivate, harvest and prune. Life for Mannie Gaston was made intolerable. One evening a high ranking S.S. Colonel came to the Gastons' home, and Mannie was coerced into signing over the deeds to his estate. He didn't put up a fight in order to save Sophie. Within the week Mannie and his wife Rosie were interned. We never heard of them again. Gas chambers I imagine. We ran their estate as ours.

"But here is the problem. To keep a hold over Father, the Nazis kept the temporary title deeds. They have never been registered of course. We have cultivated the vineyard to this day, absorbed it into La Verite. If Sophie got hold of the deeds she could lay claim to the land; insist that her father had signed under duress. I think that she would be believed too. Although we sheltered her, she hated my father. I think she had him murdered." His eye jumped three times.

"Why would she want to murder him?" cut in Hermann.

Henri smiled wryly. "Father was no gentleman. He humiliated and struck her a few times. Raped her once; she told me. That's why she left."

Hermann looked at Henri. "Did you?"

"No. We had a thing going. Her eyes held deep burning resentment at being so badly treated; hurt in her eyes for the broken pledge to her father. I was shocked, but did nothing. She may have hated father enough to want him dead, I don't know. She ran away in the end. Whether or not she hates me enough to set the old Resistance on me I don't know. Perhaps I've got it all wrong, but it's the uncertainty that gets me."

The tick again. There was a pause before Hermann spoke again. He was pensive.

"Those ex-Resistance fanatics can be real bastards, and a woman scorned is unpredictable. Take precautions is all I can suggest. What about a bodyguard? Why didn't you help her if you had something between you? Some bad character you are." Hermann was smiling. He could talk this way to his old friend.

Henri replied, eye twitching again, "One, I was scared of my father. Two, I didn't want to compromise my position with the Gestapo by seeming to help a Jew. Three, we were keeping her alive and safe at considerable risk to ourselves. She used ME as a youngster! I figured I owed her nothing. She liked getting banged. Loved sex. Women make a lot of fuss, but like it all the same. What's a screw anyway? Better than being in a labour camp."

'He is just making excuses for doing nothing. But he is still my friend for all that', thought Hermann.

"Henri, as for the deeds, who knows, they are probably destroyed. Most officials were Nazis, and they vanished in the last hours before surrender. One minute they were driving sleek black cars; the next, they disappeared. They either slipped into men's lavatories, changed into civilian clothes or stopped and changed behind a tree beside the road then melted in with refugees. Who would want to get caught with incriminating documentation like that? Forget it. If something crops up, deal with it then. Don't sell the land and stir up an enquiry." He was smiling. "Besides, you should have seen the bonfires when the Nazis destroyed their files. Christ, it was like enemy bombing."

"Hermann, I have this concern, but I don't know for sure if she is alive. The sins of our fathers, not so?"

Chapter 19

1949:

BERGHOF CASTLE, BACHARACH

"Relax. We can't throw stones!" Hermann looked like a model of the Nazi Aryan concept; blonde and square-jawed, with a sparkle in his blue eyes. "You told me your story. We had 600 Jewesses on forced labour in our factory making uniforms! That alone qualifies one for a jail sentence!" The serious tone changed to a grin. "Let me tell you about the 10 Ukrainian girls though, who were sent to us in April '42."

On the Fuhrer's orders, Sauckel had brought half-a-million healthy strong girls into the Reich from the Eastern Territories to be employed as household help. Then another half-a-million Ukrainian girls were brought in to solve the servant problem for Party functionaries. This had caused a lot of talk amongst the people.

"Our 10 had been accustomed to sparse living conditions. They were mostly peasant stock, used to hard work, long hours. Surprisingly they settled in quickly. They were willing workers, of limited intelligence, but good for pressing, packing, moving stock. Communication was a problem, but we managed. After only a couple of days they were into the men. They were sex mad! We put it to good use though – promised the cutters a night with one for achieving short-term targets. Otherwise they were off limits. It worked a charm!

"But my father," he went on, shaking his head and looking up at Henri, "was a bull! But he soon took advantage. He sent three of them here to the castle to help at harvest time and more. He would invite his Nazi pals here for wild drinking sessions and orgies. The girls spent most of the weekends on their backs! They may not have been particularly attractive, but they knew how to screw. They seemed happy enough to be here, and they were better off than they would have been in Russia. So we certainly exploited our opportunities. Henri, you told me your secret, I'll tell you mine.

"Two of the brighter Ukrainians helped me bring some canvases from the factory to the castle during the bombing. They were physically strong but more important, virtually untraceable, expendable. Do you follow me?" Henri picked up the inference. Hermann refilled their glasses.

"One day in November '42, Goering came to the factory with his entourage to check on our output. Brought Kesselring, Commander of Luftwaffe II stationed in north-eastern France. We produced good Luftwaffe uniforms and got the choice of the best Jewesses for the war effort; top priority. Goering asked father to store objets d'art from Paris. We hid the goods in our cellars behind iron grilles, then bricked them up. When I decided it was time to go I faked a delivery to travel to Bacharach in Luftwaffe trucks with canvases stolen from the Nazis. The collection is still here in the cellars, bricked up." Hermann watched the look on Henri's face.

"What? Fantastic!" gasped his visitor.

"We kept our heads down when the Yanks arrived. Hell, there was retribution when they first arrived! They dished it out for the Jews alright. At the internment camp near Nattenberg, north of Munich, the American Military Police in the American Sector lined men and women up against the wire, systematically beat up the men one by one and raped the women. But we can thank God we were on this side of the river. The slaughter in the Russian Zone! Some say six million Germans died in the last six months of the war. Cattle trucks repatriating Germans to Berlin were broken into through the roof by Poles, who took every stitch of clothing. Many died of cold. We laid low here until the venom had subsided.

"We had to report of course. Then a Yankee Colonel came here, asking some difficult questions. How had I avoided military service? I told him I had T.B. and produced false hospital records I had ready, just in case. I also passed off Ingrid as my private nurse, explaining that she had stayed on with me as her parents were dead and there was no work elsewhere. He asked questions about father. I told him that he had once owned a bombed-out clothing factory in Neustadt, and had been killed in an air raid. I knew he was suspicious about my story, but it was the last I saw of him."

"So what has happened since?"

"Let's fill up and I'll tell you." Hermann poured more wine and settled himself.

"Recovery after the war has been called a miracle. My friend, on the Rhine the only miracle was survival! At one time people survived for a day on one potato and two slices of bread. Some people lived on less food than concentration camp victims on deliberate starvation diets! So when folks here built houses, fixed roofs, windows, painted their neighbours' houses and so on, they did it for a plate of food. A bicycle then was worth more than a car. There was no petrol!" Hermann shrugged his shoulders.

"American Marshall Aid was introduced to try and restore the economy. It was time to tell them I owned the bombed factory, which meant further questions to answer about the business. I could never admit to having been involved with forced labour! I told them that I felt capable of carrying on the business if the factory was restored, as I had studied economics at Heidelberg and so on. Another difficult question came. What did I know of the skeleton of an S.S. Hauptsturmfuhrer that had been found in basement rubble, with his head half blown away? Did I know anything? I looked blank… how was I to know! I suggested suicide, like many S.S. officers when they knew it was all over. I told them father's factory had been commandeered to make uniforms, and that senior men in the services often visited him. It seemed a reasonable story, but I couldn't totally convince him. Anyway I was acknowledged rightful owner of the factory. They told me that clothing was desperately needed for the population. Could I get the factory going, making coats, suits and so forth, to start as soon as possible? I told them I could, if I were given a grant to restore the property. I needed working capital too.

"As you can imagine this opened up enormous opportunities for me, but I should first outline the situation for you so you understand the background. In the Western Zone, well over one million Nazi Party members and hangers on had lost their jobs, their property or both, while tens of thousands still languished in internment camps. In Heidelberg 122 out of 469 bank employees were sacked in 1945. Americans dismissed 141 000 people, including 80 percent of schoolteachers, half the doctors and in some towns, the entire staff of health departments.

"Henri, I had to ensure that they had no idea of my contact with the Nazis. Father was dead and our connection died with him, I hoped!

"In the Western Zone there were one and a half million surplus women pre-war; there was now a surplus of over seven million, so I had plenty of potential female labour. The general poverty and misery was greater than at anytime since the Thirty Years War! Women opened their legs to the Yanks for a packet of cigarettes or a tin of coffee.

"The Allied Authorities decided to cancel the old Reichmark at an exchange value of 6,5 Deutschmark to a 100 Reichmark. We Germans considered the old RN worthless anyway; we had mentally written off any savings. The Western Allies made a brilliant psychological judgement as the German people believed in the new money. The reduction in marks was so drastic that people assumed that the new notes must be worth what was printed on them! It was a giant conjuring trick, but it worked!

"Goods appeared in the remains of blown-up shops like magic; clothes, shoes, kitchen utensils. The black market shrank. At first the population enjoyed a buying spree of food, followed by household goods, blankets, tablecloths, radios and then clothes. They spent whatever savings they once had in the new currency. The first priority was to buy shoes, then a coat. This is where our factory became so important to the authorities. People then wanted some colour in their lives: suits and so on. Women took an interest in their appearance again. There was an enormous market potential for women's clothes and we wanted to get in there. Quickly.

"We had the factory rebuilt and started production in April '48 on Marshall Aid. Folks were desperate for work, even for really low wages; so by paying over the going rate and adding goods in kind and some food to supplement the wages, we attracted good staff. We picked the best. I even employed some Jewesses who had escaped the ovens!" Hermann laughed. "I took a chance. I reappointed Gerda Blom who had once been my forewoman. She answered the call, believe it. Today she is Production Manager. In fact what I'm doing is buying her silence. She has an excellent position, profit incentive and a lot at stake. She needs me and I need her. She really knows her stuff. She is very good.

"Now let's look at the financial side. Dr. Erhard believes in private enterprise and forces of competition. Instead of rationing he believes that if individuals are given a chance they will provide for society's needs more quickly than State controlled apparatus; that competition from abroad will keep down prices and avoid exploitation. Erhard has abolished import duties on many consumer goods, so that if German producers try to take advantage of the general shortage, we would be undercut by competition from foreign countries. It has worked like a charm!

"From the sale of illegally hoarded stocks, high profits have been made – these are tax free when ploughed back into the business. Industry grows. This is why I need an influx of capital into the business now. I need capital to grow. Now is the time to expand. In five years time it may be too late or too expensive to get big enough.

"Taxes are minimal. Overtime is virtually tax free so there is no difficulty in getting the workers to work longer hours. Our income tax allowances as employers are so generous we can live well off the business. We were allowed to revalue our assets arbitrarily at the time of currency reform, which meant I could write up our assets and then write off large amounts against tax over the next five years, thereby generating extra cash. There are special depreciation allowances for capital expenditure on repairing war damaged property, and we have claimed against the cost of restoring the factory. The same applies for machinery and equipment, even in the office. We're making money.

"We have a good banker, Heinz Bloch. He has helped me considerably. Whilst we only had a half destroyed factory building, it was collateral enough for him. The family heritage and estate is important too. German bankers sometimes claim they lend more adventurously than others; get closer to the economy. But they were forced to lend on the flimsiest collateral to get this country moving again. There have been comparatively few failures though, Heinz tells me!

"By keeping money tight, the banks not only force business to plough back profits, but set a limit to the amount Germans themselves can buy. Bankers are encouraging exports as much as possible. We cannot manufacture arms, so we concentrate on everything else; the capital goods that industrial countries are crying out for. Look at Grundig for example. He is doing extremely well. The Federal Republic of West Germany is going places, just you see.

There are already some fantastic success stories; Wilhelm Becker with Auto Becker and Willie Schlicker, steel magnate and shipbuilder. I want to be one of them!

"So I need capital! I want a second factory for women's fashions. Ingrid is a great designer. She has good sexy ideas that I'm confident will sell. Women want to be women again!

"I need the capital NOW. Can I risk selling off some canvases? THAT is my dilemma. Is it too soon? Where do I sell? To whom? How much? So many questions I don't know the answers to."

"The thing is, do you know what you've got? Their value?" asked Henri, eye twitching.

"No. I don't know their value to be honest."

"Then you risk being robbed! Look. I've got just the man for you. Raoul Montpelier. Young guy, our age. Expert on art, with an objets d'art business in Paris. His father taught him the game. Both collaborators with the Nazis! They stored stolen loot at La Verite and later transported it to Zellenberg for safe keeping; I got a quarter.

"I met Raoul at La Verite in '41. He was raiding Jewish estates for canvases at the time. Through him we got Mannie Gaston's place! We did a deal. He's bloody good I tell you. Can authenticate and value your lot for you. What do you say?"

"Excellent! But can you trust him to keep his mouth shut? I'd be in big trouble if he blew the whistle on me."

"Hermann, Raoul is as bent as a corkscrew, but he's not going to split on me or you, my friend, he has too much to lose! If one goes down, we all go down! No. He won't stir up trouble. He can only come unstuck himself. He doesn't want to be known as a collaborator. Some get eliminated!

"I'll introduce you. You'll be all right with Raoul, I promise you. Take a chance?"

"Fine. Yes, please arrange it then. Thanks Henri," nodding.

Chapter 20

BACHARACH CONTINUED

Worries shared, able to help his friend, Henri relaxed. Talk of Heidelberg days brought fond memories and amused laughter, then Ingrid burst in.

"I'm back! Oh! Sorry. I didn't know we had a visitor," she exclaimed, flashing a smile, revealing white teeth. Ice-blue eyes fixed on Henri, her face shining.

"Ingrid, meet Henri, my university friend remember? He is here for a couple of days. Henri, Ingrid."

Inquisitive eyes did not leave Henri as she offered a manicured hand. "It is nice to meet you. Hermann often spoke about your days together at Heidelberg. Welcome to Bacharach. I hope you enjoy your stay."

"Thank you, I'm sure I will," replied Henri, reluctantly releasing her fingers. Those eyes tingled with a message. Ingrid flung herself down in a leather armchair, crossing her shapely suntanned legs seductively. "I'm exhausted. Shopping gets more tiring. So what have you two been discussing? Don't tell me!" she put up her hand, "all those girls you had at university!" They all laughed together.

"No Ingrid. Unfortunately Henri came here to bury his father at Riquewihr," said Hermann quietly. Ingrid felt stupid; became serious. "Oh I'm so sorry! I shouldn't have."

"No. Please, how could you know," Henri cut in quickly, dispelling embarrassment. "Just one of those unhappy duties," he reassured her, looking deep into crystal eyes for as long as he dared. She darted a look of gratitude at him and looked quickly away. She knew Hermann would quickly pick up the vibes.

"So you see Ingrid, Henri is a wealthy man. He has inherited all the problems that land and business bring."

Ingrid became interested in their visitor, fascinated by his eyes, neat moustache and hairstyle. What a gorgeous man. They all walked around the grounds, chatting. Henri was tall and he walked with a rolling cowboy gait. He was supremely fit with powerful shoulders, and Ingrid was excited by the muscled thighs and buttocks moulded by his closely-fitting trousers. "Do you do much walking?" she probed.

"Sure. Walking through the fields at harvest time; supervising pruning, cleaning the ground. La Verite covers a lot of land. I enjoy walking though. Do you?"

"Well, I try to keep fit." At 30, Ingrid had reached maturity of beauty. There had been no children to 'spoil her figure', which she had been careful to keep in good shape.

"Well you have a splendid figure, I'll say that." Ingrid preened at his compliment. What a lovely man.

Hermann cut in. "Henri is going to help us turn some pictures into cash." He explained their arrangement.

"That's fantastic. But enough of business. If you like walking I'll show you Bacharach. There are wonderful walks to the Rhine, and I will show you my family delicatessen where I was born. What do you say?"

"It sounds marvellous – it would suit me fine."

Early on Sunday the three strolled through Bacharach, Ingrid pointing out places of interest, touching Henri's arm or hand on the slightest pretext. She bumped him behind Hermann's back, drawing Henri's attention. Gazing over a parapet at the Rhine, she felt Henri's palm on her bottom. She pressed back to signal approval. It was like a neon sign between them. She felt behind her and touched his hand for a second. They moved away, contract made. The game was on.

On their return they called at the delicatessen and Ingrid introduced him to her family. "So this is where I was born and brought up," she said, looking innocently at Henri. "Come. Let me show my old room and the view. It is beautiful from there!"

They climbed the stairs to a small bedroom, where she kissed him urgently. He cuddled her. "You poor darling, you must be desperate. God, I want you!" she confessed. "Stay tomorrow morning darling. Hermann leaves early for a meeting at Neustadt. Say you are leaving early too, for Zellenburg. Yes?"

Henri nodded, love pact formed. Ingrid kissed him and they went down. He was a wealthy man and she was hedging her bets. Over Sunday dinner Henri thanked his hosts. "It has been a splendid weekend after the funeral, and has cheered me no end. Thank you for showing me around Bacharach. It has been delightful. Tomorrow I will go to Zellenberg to sort out my affairs. I'm sure I can get Raoul to help you Hermann. Leave it to me."

"Thanks Henri. It has been a pleasure to have you," assured Hermann. "I have to be in Neustadt tomorrow for an early appointment, so I'll say my goodbyes now. Once again Henri, thanks for your help."

"Only a pleasure, my friend. I'll be off myself after breakfast. Have a good trip." They retired after a nightcap.

Within minutes of Hermann's early departure Ingrid appeared in Henri's room, fully dressed. "Hello," she pouted, bending to kiss him. "Like a little treat?" she whispered mischievously.

"Why not?" he smiled.

Ingrid performed a strip routine until she stood in a black lace-trimmed slip, black suspenders and stockings. Placing her palms on her hips, elbows out, she pushed her full breasts forward, until they fought to escape the lace trimming that barely contained her nipples. Ingrid's almost white-blonde pageboy hairstyle contrasted strikingly with her black costume, and she was aware that her almond-shaped eyes, pert nose and seductively parted blood-red lips stirred up the lust she wanted. Her panties were miniscule.

"You like my outfit?" she purred.

"Gorgeous!" replied Henri, mouth dry.

"I designed it myself. It will be going into production soon," she teased, wrinkling her nose.

"Come to bed," Henri pleaded.

"Oh no! You're not ready yet. We have the run of the castle; the staff members are all banished to the kitchens. But first, breakfast. Come, get up you lazy thing. Here's your dressing gown." She threw it to him.

A delightful breakfast awaited them on the terrace. "Enjoy it, love." Ingrid blew a kiss.

Henri could not take his eyes off her. The scantily dressed beauty fanned a lust in him he had never quite experienced before, and her hard swollen nipples relayed her answering excitement. It was unbearable. Somehow they ate breakfast, tension building.

"I'll show you our castle. My way!"

Once in the enormous baronial entrance hall, Ingrid climbed on a huge oak table and proceeded to pose provocatively, one leg seductively in the air, rolling and squirming like a cat. In these circumstances, it was the most erotic encounter Henri had ever experienced. Ingrid posed on the massive stairs, gliding, sliding, crawling on the steps, leaning over the banister and finally writhing before a huge shield and crossed swords on the landing of the stairs.

"Open your dressing gown," she commanded. "How are you feeling?"

"Randy. Why?"

"Let me see. Ah. Good," she murmured, admiring him. "You have been a good boy. Sit on that step and watch." Ingrid pulled down her shoulder straps, freeing her breasts from the restraining fabric. She touched a nipple with her finger tips. "Like them?"

"Lovely." He was breathless.

"Do you want to make mad passionate love to me? Let it all out?"

"Oh yes, YES!" Henri was pleading.

"Watch," she pouted, pulled down her panties, dropping to her knees and with legs apart, buttocks in the air like a bitch on heat, turned a full circle until he could see her treasure house.

"Want me?" she asked cheekily.

"Wow! Yes," he spluttered, beside himself. "Come here and I'll show you how much."

"Yes I think you are ready. To bed!" she waved dramatically. They cuddled and stroked and kissed, both wet with passion, his fingers inside her. "Take me now! Let it all out first time! Bang me! Please NOW Henri." Ingrid had lost control. "Oh. OH!!" They rode in a storm of passion, exploding in blissful unison. Exhausted, they lay curled together to recuperate.

"That was the most incredible experience of my life," Henri admitted, kissing her. Ingrid nibbled his ear. "Don't think you are finished yet, good sir! But next time I'll be in the saddle. Oh you are lovely Henri, lovely, lovely," as she stroked his chest, stomach and manhood. "Doesn't it ever go down?" she teased.

"After that, how can it!" he laughed, licking one of her nipples. She threw her head back in ecstasy as his finger penetrated her, shamelessly revelling in her magnificent body.

"Lie back, big boy," Ingrid commanded, sliding her thighs across him, lowering herself on top of him. "This we won't rush," she promised, smiling down at him, her generous breasts swaying gently in a slow rhythm.

Half demented, Henri breathed, "You are FANTASTIC, Darling."

"I know!" she whispered smiling. "Shush now." Ingrid built slowly up to a crescendo. When Henri exploded, he felt as though he had been blown out of one world into another. Ingrid screamed as she hit the pinnacle of release, lost in a wild sea of sensual bliss and passion. Her violent gyrations ceased as she slumped forward, groaning, gulping air; every atom of energy expended in a galaxy of pleasure. They lay gazing at each other for a long time, kissing, resting.

"I want to see you again, darling," Ingrid implored him. "And this," she touched him playfully.

"Agreed. I'll telephone when I'm coming this way again – perhaps on the way back. But what about Hermann?" Guilt gnawed at him – he was betraying his friend.

"He must never know, that's all. We aren't married, you know.

"Hermann and I just happen to like each other. But I like a change now and then, like anyone else!" She was practical as ever. "I'll always be here for you, Henri, anytime you want me, oh great lover!"

Ingrid dressed him, not allowing him to do a thing. Still naked she brought him a glass of wine then raised her own glass. "To our great day of sex," she toasted. "To my gallant knight!"

With that, she slipped into her black creation and threw on a negligee before leaving the room, returning later with a trolley.

"Lunch."

They ate like lovers, feeding each other like honeymooners.

Henri left for Zellenberg, waving. He was satisfied, content. Ingrid had established her first foothold of control over him. He would come back for more; she was sure of that. She wanted some of his good fortune.

Chapter 21

BERGHOF CASTLE, BACHARACH

The telephone call a week later came as no surprise to Ingrid. "No. Back Friday. What? Of course, darling. You know that you are welcome. Oh! Suggest that you bring three canvases you want to sell… it will be a good alibi. Can you do that? Good. See you Wednesday afternoon. 'Bye!"

Outside, Ingrid welcomed Henri to Berghof formally, until they were alone in the drawing room.

Henri twitched nervously. "I feel guilty being here. I almost phoned back to say I wouldn't come. But I wanted to see you!"

"Silly boy! You're welcome anytime." Ingrid's fingers slid down to the bulge in his trousers and squeezed. "But it's tricky you know: you are his friend. Although we have an arrangement, I wouldn't want him to know about us."

"He doesn't mind you having a fling then?"

"No. Not normally. But as I said, your being his friend is a bit different. He would be hurt if he knew."

"Yes. I feel bad, as I already said. Ingrid, let's go to a hotel in St. Goar. It isn't far. What do you say? Please!" Henri's eye twitched again.

"He is certainly going for the bait," thought Ingrid.

"Well if you feel that way, perhaps we'd better. Get me back early though as he may 'phone. We'll say we went for dinner. I will be ready in 10 minutes."

They drove the 13 kilometres to St. Goar. Ingrid sat scheming, until her thoughts were broken by Henri.

"This is a crazy thing to ask, but will you marry him?"

Ingrid put her long fingers on his leg, sliding them along his inner thigh.

"He hasn't asked me yet. If he asks I suppose I'll accept. I will not push him or trap him though. He's only 25; I'm 30. He'll settle down when he's ready. A young man needs some freedom and variety," she added, looking at Henri as she stroked his erection. Henri smiled back.

"I still fix him up with an occasional factory girl. He's still a young buck really, and needs to get his urges out of his system. I'm genuinely fond of him and we've been good for each other, but we don't own each other, you understand! I'm me and he's Hermann. I have my freedom and he has his. We have been together eight years, and have had some good times, some hard times. I guess we are stuck with each other. If he screws around he always comes back to me! Turns me on, be does," she added, grinning.

"Go on! How's that?" asked Henri, smiling at her frankness.

"He touches my tits. He knows I can never say 'no' after that. Circles his palm on my nipples. I go mad. Nearly die!"

Henri laughed out loud. "You are certainly direct, I'll say that, Ingrid."

"Oh, Poor Henri. You've been neglected! I tell you what I'll do – I'll give you my special room service, but for God's sake never EVER mention it, even in fun! He'd know!"

"I can't wait," announced Henri, as he pulled to a stop at the hotel. Once they had checked in and were in their room Ingrid touched his forearm.

"I also feel bad, but not about Hermann. Pour me some wine and I'll tell you."

"So what's the big secret?" he asked, handing over a wine glass, fingers trembling with impending excitement. He was always like this before sex.

"One of our girls, Natashya, came from the Ukraine in June in 1942, when she was 17. She's 24 now, not bad looking. She'd seen enough poverty, starvation and misery to last a lifetime. The first real civilisation she had experienced was with us. She knew there was no future for herself in Russia after the war and begged us to let her stay on at Berghof. We were happy to keep her. During the war we entertained Nazis and army officers. Natashya enjoyed it – she would rather have sex than scrub floors or wash dishes, and made sure the men wanted her. So now when we have male house guests she still expects to get in on the action. I never told you about her and Hermann leaves that side of things to me. He naturally assumed she would be invited to be with you. I left you alone all night because I wanted you to be starving for me! Desperate! I hope I made up for her!"

"Need I say! I'll forgive you; thousands wouldn't." Henri laughed as Ingrid put down her empty glass and began to undress him. Then she did a seductive strip for him.

The servant had watched her mistress leave. Natashya saw her role somewhat differently. She was loyal to Hermann, who she thought a reasonable employer.

He had been fair to the girls by German standards and let her stay on. But she despised Ingrid. As far as Natashya was concerned, she was a typical racist Nazi who looked upon Ukranians as 'objects'; rubbish, lesser beings to be used, worked, exploited and humiliated. Etched in her brain were those experiences when Ingrid had triumphantly lorded over them as 'Madame', ordering them to sleep with Nazi officials. The girls had been simply slaves to her.

"If the men want to touch you, you let them, understand!" They knew better than to disobey her. She believed Ingrid had derived sadistic pleasure from their humiliation, for to her the defenceless girls were mere playthings, not people.

When Hermann telephoned; Natashya answered. "Madame has gone off with a gentleman in a motor car." She spoke good German. "She said that she would be back in the early evening, Mein Herr." There was a pause. "At about 16h00, Mein Herr." Pause. "Ja, Mein Herr. He stayed the previous weekend." Pause. "Nein Mein Herr, Madame didn't tell me to." Pause. "I don't know Master. Madame gave us the day off." Pause. "Gut, Mein Herr. I will tell Madame my Master is coming on Thursday evening. Ja, Mein Herr. Danke."

'Let her talk her way out of that', she thought, smiling. 'I only told the truth'.

Natashya had ambition, even if her chances were slim. It was difficult with Ingrid. She had managed to get hold of Hermann on a couple of occasions, but it wasn't easy. But there were many days in a year, her Russian patience told her.

Ingrid bent down and kissed Henri tenderly on the lips. Very gently she asked, "Was that nice, darling?" smiling sweetly as if she needed an answer. His fluttering eyes told the story. They curled up in each other's arms for a few moments, enjoying the delicious sensation, then disengaged.

Ingrid curled next to him, gazing at him. "Henri," she broke the reverie.

"Yes darling."

"You won't get too fond of me, will you? You can have me if you can arrange it, darling, but don't let's get carried away. Understand?"

"Yes. I think I do," he said looking straight into her blue eyes. "You're beautiful, Ingrid, and what a lover!" he murmured, stroking her golden hair. 'Independent, this one', he thought – 'but what a woman'.

Ingrid hoped her ploy with Henri would keep him wanting her. If she made it difficult for him to meet her, and confused him, she would increase the need for him to come back to her even more.

If Hermann was not a success, then Henri was already wealthy. The next two years with Hermann would decide her ambition. She was going to be rich, and Hermann and women's fashions could be it. She wanted half. If she didn't get it, then Henri was a splendid second choice.

"Come on lover boy! Better take me back."

Later on, when Natashya told her mistress about the conversation with Hermann, carefully suppressing her glee while she did so, Ingrid put her alibi into effect. Poker-faced, she addressed the servant girl. "Our guest has a long way to travel tomorrow after his stopover, so I think he should go to bed early. Monsieur kindly took me to dinner, so I think you had better show our guest the special Berghof hospitality!" she announced, with haughty levity.

Natashya nodded, confused. This was not the behaviour of a woman in love! Perhaps she had got it all wrong after all.

"Natashya, see Monsieur is up for an early start. Knock on my door when you go down to make breakfast as I will have breakfast with Monsieur to see him on his way."

"Yes, madam.

"A nightcap, Monsieur Saint-Laurent?" she enquired, stiffly polite.

"Thank you Mademoiselle," as the girl left.

Ingrid whispered. "See you tomorrow," kissed him, squeezing him one last time.

Ingrid's plan worked like a charm and she waved goodbye with a straight face and a cautious wink as he drove off smiling next day.

"So where were you when I phoned?" Ingrid didn't bat an eyelid.

"Henri dropped off three pictures to sell when we sell some of ours. I'll show you. He insisted on taking me to dinner. Left early this morning a bit the worse for wear," laughing. "I put Natashya in with him!"

"Really! And last time?" He was still stern, mocking.

"No. Well, being your friend I felt a bit stupid. Last night I thought, 'what the hell'! Anyway he was alright last night. Shy this morning."

"When he left the previous Monday you let the staff off. Why?"

"They were on duty all weekend without a break, as Henri was staying with us. You'd gone away, he was leaving, so I thought they deserved SOME time off. Why?" with such innocence.

"Oh, never mind." The story seemed feasible, and Hermann decided to accept it. Especially after a few words with Natashya which helped to dispel his suspicions. 'These servants sometimes see and imagine things that don't exist', he told himself.

"Lovely to have you home early," she cooed, cuddling up to him. "Is everything in order at the factory? I must say I'm enjoying my break. I needed to get away a bit."

Hermann was smiling once more. "Excellent. Heinz has agreed the loan advance against a new mortgage on the factory, with amortisation over 10 years. With the present soft tax rebate we will eat it. And with a new influx of capital, I've got just the factory to buy – with luck we could be in production in November! Get cracking with your designs. I need you there. We're going into ladies' underwear. This will be your thing. Do you see yourself as managing director of a new company?"

"Oh Darling, DARLING! I'll show you just how much!" she responded, pulling his hand. "Come with me."

Three weeks later Raoul Montpelier came to Berghof at Henri's request and assessed the haul. Impressed, he arranged to sell sufficient canvases to meet Hermann's immediate capital needs.

Hermann took to him; Ingrid did not.

"Frankly I don't trust that man," she blurted out once he had left. "He is opinionated, arrogant and full of himself! He thinks he's God's gift to women," Ingrid scoffed. "He nearly raped me with his eyes – he stripped me off I don't know how many times in his mind." Normally she enjoyed men admiring her, but this one's lecherous glances did nothing for her. Henri was different.

"Well he's a clever guy. He saw his chances in the Occupation and took them, made a fortune, and now he is helping me out. He did alright by Henri too. Raoul is a sharp operator, and I'm grateful to him."

"Fine. Just be careful that's all." Ingrid was still unconvinced of his credentials.

Hermann went to Paris on a number of occasions and found Raoul very accommodating. They got on together very well and enjoyed the same pursuits. When Hermann went away, Ingrid managed the businesses. With advance notice, she would contact Henri, and arrange for him to meet her in a hotel in Neustadt.

When Ingrid visited Paris to catch up with the latest fashions, Henri would entertain her lavishly in superior hotels. Ingrid enjoyed the best of two worlds for a time while she had fun with her lover. Like all good parties though, it eventually had to come to an end.

Chapter 22

SUMMER 1951:

HEIDELBERG, GERMANY

The inebriated ex-submariner was amusing the jovial gathering in the Heidelberg inn with harmless boasts of U-boat exploits in the Atlantic. Jolly buxom wenches in pinafores replenished flagons of beer as the men slammed fists on scrubbed tables and slouched forward on their benches.

"If we had more time to develop the Electro boats we could have won the war! And those top Nazis in South America live well today; thanks to us!" He rambled on, speech slurred, while he stuffed a chunk of wurst in his mouth. "We were the stupid bastards who risked our lives for them to live like kings." Nibbling a piece of pumpernickel bread, crumbs in his beard, he burped and muttered again. Seated at the next table, Erwin Ehrhardt listened carefully,

The ex-sailor droned on, his audience now half attentive. "We took plenty. Loaded that Electro boat, bloody fast she was – pictures and stuff; all bloody expensive, worth a fortune!" Beer dribbled in his beard from another long swig of beer. "At the end of the war another E-boat went to Mont... Montevideo," he laughed, drunkenly reminiscent. "The Brits found it; captured it. Tried to get it going and the fucking thing exploded." He laughed heartily at his own story. By now the others were ignoring him... all except Ehrhardt. As a trained killer he had infinite patience. He waited for the party to break up, when the 37-year-old ex-submariner decided he should go home too and rose, swaying a little on his way to the door.

Erwin followed him home and stopped him before he got through his gate. "I've been listening to you in the pub. I was also in the Subs," he lied, "at La Pallice. I'd like to meet you... talk about the old days. Buy you lunch and beers tomorrow. Meet you at the Corn Market at 12 noon. Agree?"

The man nodded, "Jawohl," beaming drunkenly, "Gut Mein Herr, zwolf uhr..."

At noon the next day, when Ehrhardt saw him approaching, he was surprised that the arrangement had penetrated his drunken haze; but he had known where to find him anyway. This man could be a mine of information.

"Guten tag! Come. Let's go in the pub for a flagon and a meal." Erwin wanted to control his drinking acquaintance this time.

"Went to Trieste and loaded that Electro boat to the gunwales in a manner of speaking. Even took out torpedoes. Mind you, we had to leave space for a pick-up at sea off Ischia..." Erwin pricked up his ears. "...from another U-boat. Never happened. Never saw it!"

"When was that?" Erwin probed.

"Italian invasion time, during December 1943. Reckon that other U-boat was sunk. Enemy everywhere. Shit, we were scared; even with our speed."

"What was the other U-boat's number. Can you remember?"

The prematurely old ex-seaman screwed up his eyes, thinking hard. "7-93. That's it, U793. I remember because Captain Mueller told me it was a small experimental Electro boat. I was on watch. They never found her."

Ehrhardt was now convinced that U793 went down between Pisa and Ischia with secret canisters and gold, but where? There was a fortune in that U-boat.

"Do you know the meeting point? Ischia you said."

"Yes, but out at sea off the point. Not close to shore. Too dangerous."

Ehrhardt persuaded his companion that a trip to Heidelberg Schloss would be pleasant and they went up on the bergbahn, or railway tram. At the castle they sampled wine from the gigantic wine vat and strolled around the grounds.

"Did you meet any of the top Nazis in Montevideo?" asked Erwin casually.

"No!" His answer was too quick to carry the ring of truth or any conviction, his panicky reaction showing that he was all too well aware of the death threat should he ever mention the meeting. They would get him.

Ehrhardt had seen the fear in his eyes. "Pity." They were moving towards a deserted part of the castle near the old blown-up tower, overgrown with vegetation. It looked like a giant had rammed a sword through the building, splitting it like an apple, its core exposed.

In a flash Ehrhardt had his right arm looped around the man's neck, left grabbing the man's left arm and yanking it behind the man's shoulder blades. An ankle tap had the man helpless and prostrate on the ground. Ehrhart knelt in the small of his back, intensifying pressure on the bent arm, right hand free to chop the neck if need be. He applied a stiff finger to the man's throat.

"You've got 10 seconds to give me a name or your arm is broken." He cried out. Ehrhardt struck him. "Quiet." Bang again.

"Mendoza!" he coughed. "Man called himself Mendoza… loaded lorries… went to a ranch."

"Where?" He wrenched the twisted arm.

"Fifty kilometres north-east," his prisoner gasped. "Left the stuff; back in one lorry. That's all I know."

Ehrhardt believed him. The edge of his right hand came down on the man's neck with the speed of light with a sickening thud. He was dead.

Still supremely fit, Ehrhardt picked up the body and threw it into the ruins of the tower, where it would be hidden by foliage. It was discovered a few days later. There was no clue and the Police were baffled about what appeared to be an assassination without motive. The case was filed and soon forgotten.

Chapter 23

OCTOBER 1951:

URUGUAY

Ping! A rifle bullet ricocheted off a stone in the road. Ping! A second one made for better understanding. His presence was not wanted. It had not been easy to get this far and he could not give up now. Brave or foolish, he slowly opened the car door 200 metres from the wired perimeter. The guard was pointing his rifle at his head. Raising his hands in the air he gestured he wanted to get out and talk. The rifle moved up in a signal of acceptance before sights levelled on him again. He slowly got out, hands in air, and moved closer, step by step.

Erwin had Austrian travel documents in the name of Dr. Kurt Bachinger, optician, and had spent three weeks asking questions. After getting nowhere, in desperation he left Montevideo and flew to Buenos Aires. He had robbed a jeweller in Hamburg and his expenses were cutting into his dwindling capital.

At last he had made contact with an ex-Nazi in Buenos Aires. After several days of proving himself, the man agreed to help him make further contact. A telephone call assured him he would be allowed to visit the hacienda in Uruguay.

Erwin felt stupid asking, "Sprechen Zie Deutsche?" as he called to the guard.

"Ja! Wat wunschen Zie?" Once within talking distance the guard relaxed and allowed him to approach and be identified. "One can't be too careful."

"Quite right," agreed Erwin, as the guard fleeced him for weapons, missing the knife strapped to the inside of his thigh. Imposing, magnificent, the hacienda reception room was equally spectacular. Standing in front of the decorative fireplace was a figure familiar from newsreels. By all accounts believed killed in Berlin 1945, a man who had once held enormous power in the Third Reich; 55-year-old Heinrich Muller, Chief of Gestapo.

"We have carved ourselves a little piece of paradise here in South America, and you have found us Untersturmfuhrer! What can we do for you?"

"Allow me to serve the Reich in any way I can." Ehrhardt clicked his heels and saluted, arm held stiffly in front of his body.

"Gut. Here we ranch; beef, hides and skins we export. Can you ride a horse?" he laughed. "We have other places in case this one gets too familiar, but quite secluded as you found out." He continued to smile, then became serious. "The Jews want Eichmann badly. He could just lead them to us. A problem actually. Mengele is in Brazil the last I heard. Martin Bormann stays at Caacupe, East of Asuncion in Paraguay. We set up a tobacco drying plant there, with another in Ecuador. We move around sometimes, but it costs a lot of money to keep a low profile! A lot of us are here in South America," he nodded slightly.

"Are there other senior Party members here Sir?"

"Most senior men ended up at Nuremberg. Ernst Kaltenbrunner and Von Ribbentrop were executed on October 16, 1946, while Heinrich Himmler and Hermann Goering commited suicide; Hermann in his cell. Those four planned with me to set up here. Then, on October 16, '46, Frank, Frick, Alfred Rosenberg, Julius Streicher, Seyss-Inquart, Sauckel and Jodl were all executed at Nuremberg. Albert Speer helped us, got 20 years with Shirach; Doenitz 10. Hess, Raeder and Funk got life sentences and the Führer, as you well know, committed suicide in his bunker. As representative of Reich Kommissar for the Solution of the Jewish Problem, Adolf Eichmann is our biggest headache! It is generally believed that both Bormann, Hitler's secretary and Chief of the Nazi Party Chancellery and I were killed in Berlin. We must never be seen of course. So there you have it Lieutenant."

"A submariner told me an Electro boat loaded with objets d'art came here in '43, supposedly to rendezvous with U793, an experimental U-boat. I led a raiding party on the Ponte Vecchio and loaded gold and diamonds in canisters onto that U-boat with two other sealed canisters. As ordered, I killed the pick-up. Must have been important! I know from the ex-submariner that the boats never met. The U-boat is presumed sunk somewhere between Viareggio and Ischia in the Tyrrhenian Sea."

"Now that's interesting! Perfectly correct, we have the main load here; the canisters, no. I filled them. They contained a list of high ranking Nazi officers, Party functionaries and names they would assume here in South America. As Chief of Gestapo I knew the names of collaborators in France. Between Kaltenbrunner, who succeeded Heydrich in the S.S. and me, we knew everybody who made hay whilst the sun shone from our Nazi system. They owed us if things went wrong. This list and documents would enable us to make life very difficult for some of the suspects. Few want to go to jail, so this has good potential for blackmail. Unfortunately only one list was made; on purpose. It was dynamite. Now it's lost. There is another route we can take however. Do you really want to help us?"

"Jawohl, Mein Herr! Anything at all," replied Erwin smartly.

"Good. Now listen to this and don't be frightened to express an opinion. If it works you will be a wealthy man one day. Between 1933 and 1945 there were 10 700 million Germans registered as Nazi Party members. We have found out their files are kept in the Berlin Document Centre, which is located in a cluster of white painted cottage buildings in the outlying Zehlendorf District. It was our Gestapo wire-tapping centre. Bormann substantiates it from another source.

"These files contain the names of prominent Nazi members during World War Two. The information is top secret; worth a fortune in our hands. We could make an excellent living Lieutenant, blackmailing ex-Nazi officials for our silence if you can steal a few hundred files. You raided the Ponte Vecchio; do you think you could pull this one off?"

"It is certainly worth a try. But it's a pity about those canisters in the submarine: they must be worth a fortune."

"Quite so! Big fish are listed in there. But they are at the bottom of the sea and remember, if they get into wrong hands we would be in jeopardy here. We've built up elaborate false backgrounds and identities that have taken time to cement as authentic. That discovery would blow our cover throughout the whole network. Better they stay down there unless we find them first!" Heinrich Muller was deadly serious.

Chapter 24

ERWIN EHRHARDT

Erwin Ehrhardt felt more relaxed in front of Muller.

"A country becomes famous for its drink, Lieutenant," Heinrich informed Erwin. "With Germany it's beer and schnapps; Scotland, Scotch whiskey and France, Cognac brandy and champagne. Ribbentrop told me about Napoleon. He ruled most of Europe, but imported red wine from Groote Constantia estate in Cape Town. He drank nothing else for three years. Ribbentrop was a connoisseur. Did you know he had once been a champagne salesman?"

Erwin shook his head. "No. Father was in wine at Worms, but I didn't know about the Reich Foreign Minister."

"We Germans love French champagne," continued Muller. "During the Occupation we drank hundreds of litres of it," he reminisced, throwing his arms wide. "Ribbentrop made sure of our supply. I particularly remember those cases. Bottles with a Napoleonic cannon on the label." The mention exploded in Erwin's memory. Quickly he composed himself and remained attentive. Think about Adele Mathieu later he told himself. "We supplied forced labour and they maintained the flow, which of course was vital to the war effort you understand," with a knowing wink for bureaucratic priorities. "Ribbentrop was into the Paris art scene too. Goering of course had the lion's share, but large crumbs fell from the table as you can imagine. Some Frog collaborator dredged Paris for priceless pieces. Very effective he was."

He paused, thinking hard, then said, "Montpelier! Yes, that was his name – he unearthed a fortune in canvases. If he hadn't, the Jews would have kept the lot. We could use that fellow today to sell off canvases in the States, as these big league art dealers are a closed shop. If you don't have experts on your side, you get 'ripped off!' as the Yanks say." He looked at Erwin. "Could you find him?"

"I will try. Montpelier you said. Paris."

"Our contacts will manufacture a completely new identity for you with impeccable background, documentation and records. They will be good enough to fool your Mother!"

Erwin duly changed his alias from Doctor Bachinger, assuming the identity of Hans Beckenbauer, who allegedly narrowly avoided concentration camp internment by his reluctance to enthuse over Hitler Youth doctrinaire training. In later years he had voiced timorous religious grounds in an attempt to avoid military service. His attitude was ridiculed in a newspaper cutting from the Frankische Tageszeitung, the Nazi mouthpiece. He carried this with him. It was completely fabricated, but the cover would allow him to sail close to the wind with Semite groups which the ex-Nazis might one day wish to infiltrate. 'One of the good guys in difficult times,' syndrome.

Tracing Raoul Montpelier was easy. After initial fencing and bargaining, Raoul agreed to accept a consignment of objets d'art for sale in Boston and New York. These would be concealed in huge cases of Uruguayan pressed beef, and landed through packed meats importers. From theft to sale, Raoul completed the cycle. Erwin's next objective was to find Adele Mathieu. A few things had fallen into place, making him decide that he had to find her. He needed her – but would she help him?

La Verite champagne continued to enjoy prominence in the market, displaying its distinctive, cannon label, each bottle certified with Estate of Origin and Cultivar; Montmort, Champagne. He had been there once before; two years previously. It all came back to him.

Surviving the swim from the sunken fishing boat to Viareggio beach had provided Erwin with an opportunity to start a new life. Officially Erwin Ehrhardt no longer existed: he had been drowned at sea. Everything had gone according to plan. His superior strength and fitness had enabled his powerful body and muscled limbs to persevere with the long and exhausting swim to shore, an ordeal that not many strong swimmers would have survived, even in the relatively warmer summer seas.

Erwin, above all else, was not stupid. There was enough evidence to show that the cause was lost for Germany and the Third Reich. He headed for Florence and moved in with his Italian girlfriend until hostilities ceased. It had been a clever and provident move to secure a cache of stolen jewellery in the Fiat car boot at Viareggio, which he thought should see him through.

When Erwin was a young boy he had been fortunate enough to live at Colmar, the centre of the wine industry, after his father had been transferred from Worms.

Their Italian neighbour, Mario Cellini, had been in the wine trade. His daughter Rosa was barely seven when she inadvertently began teaching Erwin to speak Italian. They became inseparable, and by the time he was 10 he could converse fluently. In turn, Rosa learned German and French from Erwin.

As special friends in those formative years they had studied their respective anatomies as children will. Finding the human body a source of mystery and wonder, they had inspected every inch with fascination.

Then Erwin's father's transfer came through and their relationship ended when he was 12. The Italian language had become so deeply ingrained that Rosa often joked that he spoke like one from Napoli. It would prove to be a great gift, and had been the motivating factor that had made his army posting to Italy a natural occurrence.

For 18 months Erwin moved in the twilight world of the Mafia as a hit man, plying his trade as a killer. That and burglary kept him in funds as Guiseppe Monteregge from Napoli.

War came to a close and Erwin made his way to Marseilles, where he made contact with Corsican Mafia in sleazy bars. His only trade was killing and for a year he became a contract killer, often acting on penultimate orders from the Maquis to settle scores and take out collaborators for the Resistance Movement. These had been mostly revenge killings. Kill and go! He felt nothing – a dead body was a dead body. Ideology had little place and fanaticism didn't pay the bills. Survival and money counted.

Erwin lived on his wits until he realised that the authorities were finally getting hot on the drug trafficking with the French Connection. It had been time to move out and in 1947 he broke away completely from Mafia links; vanished. He had then made for Kaiserslautern to begin a new life as Andre Cartier, wine salesman, living on a pittance. The hand to mouth existence led him to seek additional financial support. He had established contacts with French Resistance fanatics and offered his services in need. Routinely checking La Monde adverts in the local library newspaper racks, he spotted an advertisement in the Lost and Found column of June 1949. 'Found. Cockatoo. Three tail feathers missing. R.S.V.P: Newspaper Box 1474, Neustadt Office.' His job summons.

They met on neutral ground about equidistant from Kaiserslautern, at Frankenstein, in a cosy inn, 20 kilometres north of Neustadt.

"Adele Mathieu," the dark-haired beauty Sophie Gaston had introduced herself, squeezing into the corner seating in the pub. Her hair was piled high and she wore enormous round dangly earrings. Nail varnish matched her red lips. She looked neat.

"Call me André," he responded, offering a shovel-sized hand. His nose was broad, the flesh around his eyebrows flattened.

Was he perhaps a boxer, she wondered. "I have made contact with people who say you can carry out a job for me." Sophie looked knowingly into his huge face, as inscrutable as the Sphinx. "A debt I need settled," she almost apologised.

Mouth clamped shut, his chin moved up and down in acknowledgement. "When? Where?" He was distant, aloof.

"Champagne Province. Any time, but soon. How much do you want?" Sophie asked through clenched white teeth, brown eyes wide open, eyebrows raised, apprehensive about his response.

Erwin studied her pretty face, so full of concern. She was pretty, he thought, taking in her finely chiselled nose and lovely complexion. Her full breasts and slim, petite frame showed that she was from good French stock. Nice legs too.

"Normally I don't get involved, but can I ask why a pretty girl like you wants a contract?" he whispered. Her mouth set in aggressive contemptuous anger. "Because Arnaud Saint-Laurent killed my father, that's why, and the bastard was never convicted!" Part truth was sufficient. "Will you help me or not?" she asked, leaning closer towards the giant, so near he could pick up her delicious perfume.

Surprised, Erwin withdrew slightly. "Blood feud, eh?" speaking more to himself. "Right. Have you got 10 000 US dollars?" he enquired smugly.

"WHAT?" She recoiled. "You must be crazy! NO one has that kind of money!" Her cheeks were flushed. She looked beautiful to him. "But I have a painting; a canvas by Matisse which is worth a lot. Would you take that? Please." She was pleading now.

His mind flashed to the concentration camps, the women pleading. Not to be raped any more; on their knees. The thought stirred his loins. He hadn't had a woman for a month. Couldn't afford one. 'But this one looks nice', he thought.

"You must want this job done pretty badly!" For the first time the vestige of a smile creased his lips. "Oh yes. I do!" She was pathetically earnest in her desire for revenge.

Erwin had nothing to lose; looked her straight in the eyes. "For the painting and a day in bed with you, I'll do it."

Sophie didn't hesitate. "REALLY!" she beamed. "Oh thank you! Er... today?" noting his grin.

"Why not? I'll book a room." The place did not look too expensive. "Oh. One thing. There will be a small advance for expenses of 100 francs. Can you manage that?" He needed the money; he was almost broke.

"Yes, here." Sophie eagerly scratched in her purse and handed some notes over. Then, carried away in her enthusiasm, she rushed on, "I'll make a repeat offer on successful conclusion!" She saw him soften into a different person. Transformation of the cold and rigidly determined face to a warmth of expression she would not have believed possible. A complete metamorphosis.

Erwin returned in 10 minutes.

"Fixed up. I also have some wine in the room from my car. All set for a good time." She grabbed his huge hand and followed him upstairs.

It was an amazing experience for them both. Totally unexpected, totally spontaneous. Sophie had been tied to Gerda Blom as her lesbian partner for too long but she did not really have any other choice at the time – it was through economic reasons and necessity. She had found few chances to even meet a man. Bisexual, she welcomed a chance to indulge her considerable talents and surrender to a real man. Erwin had precious little chance to take a woman and here was a stunning beauty who responded to his every whim. She could even teach him a thing or two. Fantastic! They created a sexual firestorm. As Erwin slept for a while after Sophie's expert coaxing to perform for a third time in succession, she lay contemplating. If this was what it was like to have a real man, she would break away from petty titillations with her lesbian companion. Agree to hitch up with him, on any terms; she would not even mind if it was only on a casual basis.

They went to La Verite the following day, approaching from the stream, stealing into the yard. There had been some additions but the basic layout remained the same. Sophie knew every nook and cranny of the old buildings.

Habit dies hard and she had counted on the racing pigeons. As they crept into the first floor barn loft, a few pigeons stirred in their coops, an intermittent coo coming from the cages. It had been his nightly vigil to see his pigeons before retiring for the night; Arnaud's only hobby, his racing pigeons. It was in this barn that he had raped her.

It was all worked out. She watched through the grubby loft window then whispered, "There's the bastard; he's coming now." She hid behind a wooden section, very still. The barn latch sounded like thunder in the quietness. A flash of light beamed as he turned his torch on the stairs and started to climb.

Piano wire stretched taut between his black gloved hands, Erwin drew in a deep breath which he would hold until his quarry was within striking distance. Arnaud's tired day's end steps laboured up the stairs, four more, three, two, one, NOW. Erwin pounced. The wire tore into the captive's throat, which emitted a strangled gasp as the monstrous hands tightened their crosswise pull with incredible force. The torch clattered to the ground, beam spinning as it rolled around on the floor. The last thing Arnaud Saint-Laurent saw in the dim torch glow was the servant girl he had raped in the straw of this barn floor. As prearranged, from a metre in front of him, Sophie Gaston scored a running goalkeeper's kick into his testicles as Erwin continued to strangle the life from his body. Before Arnaud expired, the excruciating pain and agony was reflected in his bulging eyes, helping to avenge Sophie's bitterness for the raped daughter whose parents this man had betrayed. They had been exterminated so he could steal their land. Eyes now closed, the body was lifeless. The pigeons settled once again. Erwin allowed the corpse to slump down to the floor and without a sound, signalled to Sophie. With his forefinger raised for 'silence', and hand flat to indicate, 'slow, stealth', they made their way on tip toe down to the yard and then back through the fields to the stream, crossing over by the poplars.

She so wanted to tell him, 'This was my father's land', but then he would know she was a Jew. She had told him that she was a servant girl, intent on revenge. If he knew the truth he might leave her, or worse. He was a killer and there was still hatred for Jews in this land. She knew nothing about this man and had to be careful. Confused, she held his arm to stop his progress.

He turned to her, "Feel better Adele?" the giant asked.

"Marvellous. Elated! I feel wonderful, André!" It was exciting in the weak moonlight. This was her secret revenge on Henri. It was the principle that mattered, full circle.

Staying in a farmhouse for 20 francs on the pretext of a breakdown, Erwin and Sophie, known to each other as André and Adele, made their pact. "Yes, I'll stay with you as long as you'll have me," she promised.

"We can do well Adele! I have contacts and I know how we can make money. It will be tough at first. But I need you!" He looked at her for confirmation. She nodded. "You're on then!" he said excitedly. "This is what we do!" Sophie listened patiently to his daring plan. Audacious, but it could work. She lay by his side in the crook of his big arm. "What's that scar under your armpit?" she enquired nonchalantly, momentarily distracted; almost out of idle curiosity.

"Oh that! Nearly cost me my life that did!"

"Really!" she blurted, keen to hear what he had to say. "Whatever happened?" She was full of curiosity but vulnerable to deceit.

"I told you Dad was in wines, right! Playing ball as a kid in the stacking yards, my friend kicked the ball too hard and it bounced amongst some brandy barrels. Empty, finished they were. Our ball dropped inside one. I got up and reached for it, but in reaching down, the barrel I was standing on moved! I slipped and scored my inside armpit on the rusty band."

For dramatic emphasis he raised his eyes to heaven in a gesture of 'you know what happened next!' then went on. "I got septicaemia and was rushed into hospital. At one stage I was scared I'd lose my arm – or worse!" He stopped to let it sink in. "Fortunately it cleared up or I wouldn't be here today," he grinned, as if it had been absolutely nothing. André was smiling.

Adele thought he was smiling because he was so brave. She never asked about it again.

Chapter 25

1952:

SPRING, BERLIN

Bent, hindered by a limp, scarf muffled, the middle-aged man in the greatcoat leaned into his handcart. The buckets hanging on the extension ladders balanced on the spider-wheeled pushcart were still swinging when he came to rest at the sentry box. His large frame shuffled up to the white helmeted and gloved American on duty. In deference a mittened hand touched his grimy torn cloth cap, "Bitte. Ich komme clean windows." His breath was visible in the crisp Berlin spring air, which still bore the nip of the past severe winter.

"Move on old guy," motioned the guard, night-stick swinging in an unmistakable gesture of riddance.

The man's fingers stroked his stubbled chin, eye sockets grey from hunger and fatigue, leaning in a disconsolate posture of dejection on his ladders. It was an impressive portrayal. Six months in an Italian circus had been well spent, driven there by desperation in the closing years of hostilities. His physique had given him an entrée as a strongman, bending iron bars and lifting midgets on his arms. He doubled as a huge clown, allowing midgets to jump on him and bounce off in hilarious scenes to the peals of children's laughter. Introduction to the art and skills of make-up, wigs and disguise would serve him well, and he was now capable of transforming himself from a fit and athletic young man into a grey-haired, middle-aged individual with a careworn expression and stooping posture. They had taught him well.

Uncharacteristically, a wave of compassion overcame the sentry. "Okay! I will see if I can get you a job!" The toy soldier rang a field telephone, spoke, then opened the gate. Gratitude spread across the bent figure's face as the handcart trundled into the yard. He would become a familiar figure during the summer and autumn months as he scaled ladders with two buckets and leathers, returning every two weeks with clockwork reliability. When collecting the meagre pittance he asked, his cap was clutched in his hands in humble stance. They increased his contract price. Good souls these Americans. The beauty was, the scam continued to work. He smiled in recollection.

Sophie, or Adele to him, had jumped at his proposal. Revenge was sweet, so sweet! What nectar. She wanted more to avenge her father, mother and all her race. Nevertheless, freed of social stigma she decided she would never again admit to being of Jewish line. The entire world hated Jews; this had been her experience all her life. Some chosen race! Strange man this André she thought, with such a driving force of vengeance for the Jews. She knew his body, but nothing of his mind, for he would not talk about his opinions to her. He was simply a man of action.

"Convince them!" André had told her. "How you get the job is your affair, but you must get into that archive!"

Sophie planned meticulously in Berlin, discovering the name of the US Colonel in Intelligence responsible for hiring people as they called it. "Lie if necessary, do anything, promise anything, but get the job," André had insisted. He really meant it. Sophie, applying as Adele Mathieu, looked her prettiest as Tom Malony invited her to sit. As a full colonel he had his wife with him on the station, but it hadn't been much fun lately. He flicked the ash from his cigar. Now she looked something! French and classy too, that was for sure.

"My native tongue is French," murmured Sophie, fluttering her eyelashes. "I write and speak German and English fluently. My father taught me basic Russian. Although limited in vocabulary I can understand and make myself understood."

"Really!" The colonel was impressed. "Is that so?" leaning closer. He liked the way her bosom heaved when she spoke. Sophie continued demurely. "My wartime colleague and friend taught me Yiddish. We have since gone our separate ways." The colonel was relieved to hear that.

"Why do you want to go into the Document Centre?"

"Because there I can be an interpreter and use my talents to best advantage." Sophie gazed at him, moistening her lips ever so slightly, allowing her tongue tip to protrude. The gesture had the intended effect: signal received.

"What do you say we continue this interview in more convivial surroundings?" suggested the medalled soldier of Uncle Sam. Sophie smiled so sweetly. "What a lovely idea," she murmured slowly, leaving no doubt in his mind of her confirmation. Cheekily she touched his hand.

"Do I get the job?" she asked, pouting red lips provocatively.

"Sure do, my little darlin'. Let's go!"

She had been so excited when she got back to their tiny apartment, rushing into his arms.

"André I've got it, I've got it."

"Good girl! Good girl! Now we can plan our robbery. This is what I want you to do. You start in March. Concentrate on your job first and do it well. Get acceptance. Gradually build up a detailed sketch plan of the centre building, piece by piece. It may take a month. Detail routine security procedures, guard system, who is left behind at night, any windows not burglar-guarded. Check carefully how you can steal files and not get caught.

"We can create false ones if there is the need to replace any. Find a temporary hiding place for stolen files. Detail deliveries, routines, rubbish disposal, tradesmen's calls, cleaners, window cleaners and so on.

"After three months start selecting about 50 files, but let it be a haphazard selection to defy detection. Perhaps swap them with new ones coming in. In the spring we will be ready. I know I can rely on you, Adele." He kissed her.

The window cleaner ruse was considered the most ideal.

For Sophie it was the excitement that made her steal. She knew the risk but André was so good to her when she succeeded. Her toes curled up in her shoes as she thought about the way he showed his appreciation! Devastating, unreal, that man. She had a double reward; both vengeance and satisfaction that was out of this world.

Timing was everything. At a precise moment, her man would be at a specifically designated window, one bucket filled with water and another with leather cloths. The files went through the window covered by the cloths. Not a word was exchanged in their procedure, which had been carefully orchestrated the previous evening to provide various pick up points around the building. Descending the ladder, the files disappeared into the trapdoor at the bottom of the handcart.

In the evenings Erwin frequented bars and clubs in Berlin under his alias of Hans Beckenbauer. At last he became integrated into a Zionist society, hell bent on rooting out Nazi war criminals. Their major prize was Adolf Eichmann, who had eluded them for years.

"I feel I should help you in some way in atonement for what my nation did to the Jews," had been his reason for wanting to join them. Suspicious at first, they invited him to be with them.

Hans led them to two nondescript Class Three minor offenders convicted as Nazi war criminals, having first extorted bribes from them for non disclosure. The Zionists made sure they lost their jobs, one being in the employ of the British Military Government. Jobs were hard to find, and some of their victims died.

As he drew closer to the heart of the society, Erwin found the Zionists were getting nearer to the realisation of a Nazi conclave in South America and sent secret messages in code warning of their intended actions. He then dished up plausible disinformation to throw the Zionists off track. One Mannie Mankovitch was a bright leader. He was their best tracker. What a paralysing effect it would have if he should disappear, thought Erwin. Jew pig! The group was mortified when Mannie did not return to them. Hans registered equal concern; his main unspoken concern that the Jew's battered body would not be found for a few weeks in the bomb rubble where he had buried him.

One evening Erwin slipped up. Showering after an energetic game of squash at the club he forgot an important safeguard. When naked, he always had to turn away from people if he raised his right arm. The skin graft was still evident where the S.S. lightning insignia had once been tattooed. To those in the know, it was a dead giveaway.

It all happened so suddenly.

"A game tomorrow?" called Aaron Lipschitz. Erwin inadvertently turned around, exposing the telltale mark, then saw the look of stunned surprise on Aaron's face. It was now or never – he had to act quickly.

"Sure." He grabbed his towel and flicked it with all his might, catching Aaron across the eyes. His hands instinctively shot up to his face. Erwin's arm didn't drop until it was around the Jew's neck. He yanked down with enormous force; heard the neck break across his firm thigh muscles. Swiftly the German bundled the warm body into a seated toilet, leaving him lolling like a drunk against the partition.

After jamming the door with toilet paper to keep it closed, Erwin dressed rapidly then climbed through a window, slid down a short pipe, and walked around the building. After ensuring that he was neat and tidy, he entered the front door and sauntered up to the usual group, appearing to have come in from the outside. None of them had seen him in the squash court complex or in the changing rooms. The gentle giant looked round the bustling group amicably.

"Guten abend! Who's for a drink?"

Chapter 26

1947 - 1955

NEUSTADT

Hermann Schmidt became a Wirtschaftswunderkind, or economic miracle worker. Entrepreneurs like him, such as Heinz Nordhoff who single-handedly rebuilt Volkswagen, were credited with having stimulated the economic revival. A welcome relief from crushed morale under numbing defeat, they captured the public interest and won their adulation. Their achievements had a revitalising effect as Hermann, and others like him, set about rebuilding their factories in the dark days after the war and getting into production again. Before long, the Neustadt factory was restored and profitable. Serviceable sections were renovated. He was fortunate that the lift was useable after minor repairs.

The economy was teetering on the edge of national bankruptcy. It was a time to be bold or fold. Going for broke, Hermann came through. He financed his operation from an income derived from wine sales, Marshall Aid hand-outs and money borrowed against the mortgaged factory. The rest was hope and good luck.

Public demand in Germany and Europe for consumer goods was limitless and production a first priority. Every item produced could be sold to someone; coats were essential in winter. In those early days salesmanship was not a necessary talent. Factories were not even in competition as they were all under pressure to meet an insatiable demand.

To all intents and purpose, Western Germany's national inventory of capital and consumer goods had been wiped out. Those who had courage, climbed in early, survived and came out on top. Many became millionaires, like steel trader Willy Schlieker. Hermann would follow in time. His work flow methods and management skills, combined with generous tax concessions soon had the factory mortgage redeemed. As he now had property besides the family wine farm as playing chips in the game of economic roulette, Hermann decided to go for female fashions. With seven million surplus women, there was no limit on the horizon to a hungry market. In 1949 Hermann took the plunge and bought a second bomb damaged factory, which he rebuilt on much the same production model of his original.

"We need a modern image. Think, Ingrid. We need our new company's products to make an impact. I tell you what I thought of. Yanks call women 'birds'. What about 'Vogel Models' for Bird Fashions?"

"Great idea! Have a matchstick female logo!"

"That's it!" Hermann looked hard at Ingrid. "As managing director of Vogel will you accept Gerda Blom as your Production Manager? She knows the rag trade backwards."

"Yes, darling. She's good. I could use her skills, but she mustn't try to run the show or there'll be fireworks!"

"Ingrid. Bury your bloody pride for God's sake! We NEED Gerda to get into first spot in the market. Once there we can please ourselves."

Ingrid nodded. He was right. Hermann could see that Ingrid had accepted the truth that Gerda would be a great asset in her business.

"You know Ingrid, she has contacts in New York. We should try to get her over there. Pick up the latest fashions and production methods; get a head start in Europe. Then combined with your flair and individualism, build on and set the pace in Europe. We personally would never get into the States. But we need to know the latest factory methods to jump the market. What do you say?"

"Yes Hermann. I agree; you are quite right of course." During the American military occupation, Germans had learned a salutary lesson on just what it felt like to be subjected to racial discrimination. Even in ladies' hairdressing salons American women sat under segregated hairdryers. So out of favour were Germans, securing a passage to the United States would have been virtually impossible.

Hermann persuaded a US Air Force Colonel to fly Gerda Blom to New York to see her old mother. Hermann explained that Gerda, a Jewess, had been through a lot during the war and seeing her mother for three months would do her good. He would pay all her costs. He had helped rehabilitate her and employed her. The colonel was impressed. When Gerda spoke in Bronx slang he was satisfied she had lived there, and duly found her a seat on a transport plane to America.

Once in the Bronx, Gerda picked up the threads of her past, welcomed with open arms by the Jewish community. They failed to persuade her to stay in New

York.

"Opportunities lie in the new West Germany. I want to make my contribution to building a new nation." Coming from someone who had been subjected to diabolical persecution, they were astonished, but still helped her unstintingly. Gerda's calm attitude of "Well, I survived!" displayed a tenacity and acceptance of the destiny of their race. It made other Jews feel humble and proud of their heritage. She was swept along on a whirlwind course of modern rag trade methods.

On her return to Neustadt, Ingrid listened in awe to Gerda's descriptions.

"There are new cutting machines which can process between 50 and 100 pieces simultaneously. I have suppliers' names and addresses for equipment. Can we get Marshall Aid dollars to import them? Production is so fast." In detail Gerda explained the savings in material costs when meticulous planning was applied to obviate wastage in dresses, skirts, coats, and blouses under mass production. She further described the systems used for underwear manufacture, bras, panties, slips and foundation garments. Wire support work was an art in itself.

"I couldn't comment when I was there, Ingrid, but I was appalled by the poor standard of finishing. Inside seams raw and untidy. It would never do for us Germans." There was a pause, then they both looked at each other and burst out laughing. From that moment Ingrid accepted Gerda as a German and her attitude towards her changed completely. A good working relationship developed and they became a team.

Hermann decided to contain his business expansion in Neustadt where he and Ingrid lived together in a house. He bought two more factories in 1950 on a shoestring, hobbling together mortgage bonds and receipts to meet commitments. Heinz at the bank was tolerant and their underwear factory was launched at last.

Vogel took off like a bird. Demand was insatiable; their products sought after.

The June 1952 summer was hot and tiring. One Friday afternoon, after paying wages Ingrid looked exhausted.

"Come along. It is time to take a break. Drop everything – let's go to Berghof. You need a break. You look all in." Hermann laid his hand on Ingrid's shoulder.

"You can say that again. Yes let's go. We need to get away for a couple of days."

Once at Bacharach, Hermann called Ingrid over to him as he sat in an armchair, a bottle of chilled wine with two glasses by his side.

"Come here M.D. Sit on my knee." Ingrid obliged with a perky smile. "Yes sir! Three bags full sir!"

"I have been thinking about our future. I think it is time I made an honest woman of you. You're so involved with me anyway, it would be a job to get rid of you!" Ingrid gave him a playful shove. "Beast," she scolded jokingly as he ducked her blows. "But if that's your crazy way of proposing marriage to me, then I accept, provided…"

"Provided what?"

"You make love to me everyday," she teased, smothering him with kisses.

"What a pleasure," he responded with a broad grin. "Talking of which, are you too tired?" unzipping his fly playfully.

"Have you ever known me to be? Here's to us and our future," raising his glass. "To our first million," he toasted laughing.

"I didn't realise before, Hermann Schmidt, but I'm very fond of you." She kissed him with tenderness.

"Thank you. You are my woman too," he replied earnestly, pecking her red lips and patting her delightfully curved bottom.

Hermann invited Henri and Raoul to their wedding. Raoul's pretty wife Louise came along which pleased Ingrid. Henri however, that lecherous bastard, was a problem. She had telephoned Henri to tell him that their affair was over – they had just been ships passing in the night. She was now dedicating herself solely to Hermann, as his wife. Henri had completely accepted her virtuous statement.

When Henri arrived, tanned, handsome and gorgeous, his physique and sexy way of walking turned her knees to jelly. She was unable to keep her eyes off his thighs and muscled backside: her heart pounded like a schoolgirl with a crush. Guilt-laden, she was swept along by her devious scheming brain. Control evaporated, desire overwhelmed her. It was hopeless to deny that she had 'the hots' for him.

"Henri," she gazed at him, shaking slightly, "let me show you up to your room. I have a nice view for you." Hesitating, Henri nevertheless felt that as he was a guest he had no choice but to follow his hostess. Her hand was hot.

Once inside the room, Ingrid threw her arms around his neck, kissed him passionately, feeling him greedily, without any finesse.

Henri's eye twitched. "Are you mad?" he whispered incredulously, looking into her sparkling blue eyes. "It is the day before your wedding. If we get caught we've both had it with Hermann."

"Shush, Henri darling. I don't care. I want you NOW. Quickly – take me for the last time. PLEASE!" Ingrid quickly stepped out of her panties, grabbed his hand and put it between her legs. Henri, apprehensive, found his willpower weaken as Ingrid's skilful caresses aroused him, making him hard.

"We had better be quick then," he mumbled, unbuckling his belt.

"That was a lovely wedding present Henri. I'll treasure it," she whispered kissing him sweetly.

"You're mad," replied Henri, smacking her bottom on their way to join the others. Passion sated, Henri had been stunned by Ingrid's unbridled sexual lust. In retrospect he began to see her in a different light; as a bit of a whore. She was selfish, with no loyalty to Hermann, whom she would marry the very next day. His own weak reaction to the invitation began to disgust him; he chastised himself, feeling a combination of remorse and regret. 'Dangerous that one', he thought: best to leave her alone. A weak character, resolutions were not sustained for long with Henri.

Hermann and Ingrid were married and lived in their modest house in Neustadt. Ingrid gave birth to Franz, her resolve broken in the need to provide an heir to their developing fortune. It made sense that someone would inherit the burgeoning empire. She was now satisfied that she would be wealthy.

Hermann bought two more factories in 1952. In 1953 on a trip to the UK to buy lace in Nottingham for Ingrid's underwear factory, he accepted an invitation to visit Mansfield in the county, to see the latest methods in nylon hosiery manufacture. Nylon stockings were in great demand in West Germany.

"Do you know why they are called nylons?" his host enquired.

Hermann shook his head. "It is a combination of New York and London, NYLON, being a joint development venture in both cities. Now we can make stockings quite sheer, with or without a seam. Come, I'll show you around."

After the conducted tour Hermann had made up his mind there and then that he was going into nylon stocking production. He promptly persuaded a young textile engineer to join him on a contract basis for two years to set up a hosiery mill in Neustadt.

It became Hermann's third success story. By 1955, he had two hosiery mills and millions of dollars worth of property.

At Vogel, Ingrid realised shortages in a seller's market would not prevail indefinitely and organised a nucleus of saleswomen to market her products. Diversifying from the traditional 'team of salesmen' approach, she took a risk, determined to play her hunch that with the right incentive, girls would be better than men. She would provide all expenses and a retainer, generous commission on sales after a target on an escalating basis. Ingrid employed the loveliest looking girls she could enlist, who also identified with the company. Always frank, she told them. "We have excellent products. You want to live well. It is your choice. If you are not a success, there are plenty who want to be! Your own figure is part of your samples case. If no models are available, model the garments yourself: make that sale, use your talents."

In consequence few salesgirls from Vogel Mode had to break the door down. Business boomed, and the girls made their fortunes.

Chapter 27

1955

NEUSTADT

The nanny, Gizelda, brought in two-year-old Franz to see his parents before putting him to bed.

"Say 'Goodnight' to Mama and Papa." She looked at Hermann and then at her mistress, who smiled and nodded before she withdrew.

Hermann stretched his legs as he slumped down in his favourite lounge chair, exhausted. He had recently opened three chain store tailor shops, Gurtel und Hosentrager (Belt and Braces), which had been welcomed by the public and were an instant success.

"I can't cope. Like Nordhoff at Volkswagen and Grundig, it is too much success! The estate is going to pot. I can't afford the time to manage it properly."

"Well, what are you thinking of? You would never sell it, would you?"

"No. But I've been thinking about a consortium."

Ingrid looked at him inquisitively.

"I'm not mad, but this is my idea: ask Henri to manage and market our wine. He's an expert and a good friend to us."

Ingrid looked away for a second, recalling her recent rendezvous in Paris with him. "Yes. Good idea," she volunteered. It had endless possibilities.

"We need greater sales penetration in France. There is a good market there. I want Raoul to help handle the Paris side of France and we the east. What do you think?"

Ingrid had to think quickly. "Well I can't tell you what to do, but I want control of Vogel Fashions! What you do with tailoring, men's fashions and stockings is your affair. I'm still apprehensive about Raoul."

"Ingrid, you're crazy. That guy has such influence and knowledge of France he can get you in all over." Hermann leaned towards her enthusiastically. "Think. We want to go international. You're Managing Director. Use him to open doors. If it doesn't work out, you can tell him to drop Vogel Fashions. Would you agree to a six-month trial? No benefit; break! Will you go for it?"

"If I still have final say."

"Absolutely."

"A trial then, for six months." Ingrid could still have her sojourns to Paris. They were an important part of her life. She had female intuition about her husband. He was out of the office too often when she telephoned him. Then one day she telephoned the house and it took time for Gizelda to answer. Gizelda said she was washing some underwear and had to dry her hands. She sounded out of breath at the time, and the incident had Ingrid wondering. But could she throw stones? It bothered her so much she had to confront him.

"Hermann," she plucked up courage and began.

"Yes. What is it?" It sounded important to him.

"Something concerns me. Yet after all these years we've been together, I find it difficult to talk to you, probably because we're married, and are parents too."

"Come on. What is it? Tell me."

"Alright. I will. I've noticed the way Gizelda looks at you!" Ingrid looked straight into his eyes. "You're having it off with her aren't you?" Hermann was flabbergasted.

"No!" he blustered. "What nonsense! Whatever gave you that ridiculous idea?"

"Well know this! I am mistress in this house. If I find out she has been generous beyond the call of duty, she's OUT! O.U.T. OUT! Is that clear? Nanny or no nanny!"

Herman shook his head like a schoolboy who has been accused of dipping into the cookie jar.

"Ridiculous!" he repeated. To himself though he wondered how the hell she had guessed. When Ingrid went away to Paris, Gizelda slid between his sheets. There were other times too.

Ingrid knew it was not 'ridiculous': she knew him too well, knew how randy he was. They were a pair, after all.

"If you need to stray from time to time, let me know. I'LL arrange it, like I've always done. But don't try a fast one on me in our home! Now, I've said my piece. Let's drop the subject. We have always been good friends, let's not fall out. What about a drink?" she asked, still flushed. To herself, Ingrid thought, 'My God, what would he do if he ever found out about Henri and me? What would he do to ME? I won't give him up though. Henri's good medicine for me and my tensions'.

Chapter 28

SPRING 1960

HEIDELBERG

"**A**re you sure you couldn't find records on young Schmidt? I'll bet he was mixed up in it during the war!"

"I've told you," she said impatiently. "There was nothing on the strategic suppliers' list except for the bombed out factory, which went out of production in '44. Anyway the son would be too young to be involved in those days."

Adele brushed aside his comments as irrelevant.

"He has done bloody well for himself since! He is damned wealthy now," he insisted. Hermann's success as a Wirtschaftwunderkind had not gone unnoticed by Erwin, especially as Hermann was aspiring to become Mayor. Hermann was not aware of his silent friend, Adele Mathieu, who would never give him away.

Adele well remembered Gerda Blom's words, "Hermann is a gut man. If it vas not for him hidink me in der schloss, I vud be in zee gaz chambers." Gerda owed her life to Hermann who had hidden both Adele and her at Berghof, at considerable risk to himself. Adele was also aware Gerda had joined him and they were successful in business together. She would never betray them. Wherever possible Adele blocked any attempts by André to find cause to blackmail Hermann or expose him as a Nazi war criminal. She knew he qualified from her short experience there, using forced labour, but she knew from Gerda that the excesses and murder of the workers had been the work of his brutal father, Karl. They had been avenged when they threw Karl out of the top factory window. Hermann had been decent to the interns, especially to Gerda and herself as an employee. She owed him one. But she could not say the same for his mistress, Ingrid Penz. She was a first class Nazi bitch and Jew hater, throwing her weight about with the Jewish interns, many of whom she had smacked and brutalised.

Adele thought she was mentally deranged. Whilst at Berghof, she had heard stories from the Ukrainian maid, Natashya. Ingrid Penz was indeed a peculiar and spiteful woman. She was hated.

"I hear what you say Adele, but I smell money there. He's loaded. I'm convinced he was involved. Look, for God's sake it was inevitable that a uniform factory would employ Jewish slave labour in the wars. It was inevitable as concentration camp guards kept the best Jewish girls for sex until they were past it. If they didn't satisfy the guards; got too many 'no's' when they asked, their time was up. Cattle trucks to Belsen." The Jewess Sophie Gaston shuddered, vividly recalling the chilling devastating violation when raped by Arnaud Saint-Laurent. Her imagination drew fleeting horror pictures of a life condemned to such degrading pitiless treatment day in, day out.

"I just need the evidence, that's all."

Adele pulled herself together. "Shush now. You will tire yourself out. You don't have any evidence so don't get worked up about it. We've got plenty others to work on."

She forced her mind to switch off the horrors.

The Sophie Gaston in Adele Mathieu had other ambitions in life. Like her land. Maybe it was a dream, but one day she would prove her claim to her father's estate. In the two-year search at the Berlin Document Centre, Adele had found nothing to prove the theft and misappropriation of her deceased father's estate. She had even searched the inner sanctum. There was nothing.

In the first two months' employment at the Centre, Adele tried to show herself as a model clerk typist, ever ready to help and oblige. In 1952 the Centre was under the control of the occupying forces, as it was in the American Sector. She had been there for 10 weeks before she met the Lieutenant Colonel. More lawyer than soldier, it was his vocation to sift data and prepare documentation for tribunals at Nuremberg and elsewhere, indicting Nazi war criminals. The Centre had manual filing systems; computerisation would come in later decades.

Luck came her way when a senior secretary was suddenly rushed into hospital with appendicitis and Adele was asked to deputise. 'It's an ill wind… ' she thought. 'Here's my break. I'll grab her job'.

Adele was pleased Gerda Blom had insisted she learn to type in those idle days at Berghof. That expertise could pay off.

"I realise it is extremely short notice for you, but we have an urgent brief to prepare for Nuremberg. Do you feel up to it?" the suave 43-year-old American put to her.

"Oui, Monsieur. It would be a pleasure," she replied coquettishly, emphasising French-accented English.

"I'm told you are fluent in French, German and English; correct?"

"Oui, Monsieur," she smiled sweetly with a demure nod of her head. Her eyes found his for a moment, full of promise and intrigue. Laser telepathy crossed the gap as his grey eyes locked on hers for seconds to decipher her intentions.

They worked through for two days and nights. He was very impressed with her. Ten days passed as they busily worked together, conforming to every social convention. She was determined to play it cool and let him hunt. It would be so much more meaningful if it was his chase and conquest. However she saw no harm in lowering the obstacles a little. It would not be easy. She knew he was married, but he had to advance, not her. She would manipulate him once he thought he had conquered her. One day her sixth sense perceived he was studying her closely as she typed. It was early afternoon, hot and stuffy. Adele went to the ladies' cloakroom for a drink, after which she removed her bra. Later she walked over to the colonel's desk with papers in her hand.

"Monsieur, please. I have a small problem with this interpretation. This sentence please; is it a repeat of yesterday's?" she enquired, explaining her fictitious dilemma. It had an electrifying effect on her prey, his eyes popping as if magnetised, he ogled in wonder at the ample assets revealed under her thin blouse, clearly defined as naked truth. Close encounters had given her the opportunities to place a consoling hand on his on the pretext of some light-hearted quip.

Never too obvious or pushy; always promising the mysterious 'maybe', Adele had the half colonel in a tizzy. She could feel him watching her as she deliberately postured, showing off her long shapely legs. Then one day it happened. Adele was leaning forward at his desk to place a sheaf of papers on his blotter. She felt his hand caress the curve of her buttocks. Thinking quickly, instead of pulling away she rearranged the items, staying where she was. His hand slid down to her hem and touched her calf. Adele smiled acceptance and awaited the inevitable climb to paradise. This was the commencement of a sexual liaison which secured her a permanent post as his secretary. It was the first of numerous occasions when she knelt in the large executive chair facing the wrong way.

He was like putty in her hands, becoming dependent on her daily manipulations. Eventually she acquired keys and access to the inner sanctum where files on major Nazi criminal cases had been tabulated. She could find nothing on her land at Montmort amongst reams of indictments, where factories, businesses, farms estates, even shipping had been appropriated by the Nazi State, wrested from Jewish hands. Adele virtually had the run of the Centre, enabling her to become remarkably adept at stealing files and inventing cover up documentation in specific cases. She hoped that the day would come when she would be in a position to challenge Henri Saint-Laurent for her land; she was convinced of it.

Chapter 29

SUMMER 1960

HEIDELBERG

"Come on Andre! Race you to the top!" Adele challenged, putting her head down, surging forward in her jogging shoes to their Heidelberg house.

"You devil!" he laughed, watching her delightful bottom jiggling in tight shorts as she sped away on long legs. "I'll catch you! Then you know what!" Adele's laughter drifted down to Andre, who was already 15 paces behind her.

Both natural athletes, they engaged in some form of physical exertion every day. They enjoyed running and ran hard, legs pumping and hearts racing, reaching the gates almost simultaneously.

Adele turned. "There! Beat you!" she grabbed him, hot and sweaty, kissing him and pulled him inside the house with pent-up urgency.

"Come, let's shower. Then I'm ready for a hard day's work." Erwin never failed to be amazed at her energy as she worked an unrelenting 12-hour day. What a woman he had found in Adele.

Physically powerful and agile, Erwin Ehrhardt was a mental hermit. Over the years it had become easier to lead a double life. Adele saw a likeable, clever blackmailer, dedicated to tracing Nazis for his personal financial gain. If she had been able to see through his facade and discover the real Erwin, she would have run to eternity. 'I am a member of the Master Race', was his creed. His dedication to Hitler and the Nazi principles of rule by terror and kill for the system was deeply engrained. He had changed his philosophy when forced to accept the defeat of Hitler's Germany. 'I killed for the System; the System owes me!' was his reasoning.

Erwin burned with intense jealousy when recognising beneficiaries of the Nazi system. He demanded his share: it was his due, after all, as a member of the elite race. If he could not rule by force, fear and power he would rule by wealth; extort for wealth; kill for wealth. The power he found in the files; his benefactors, the Nazis who had escaped the Allied net of exposure and penalty. There were so many guilty; more had been missed than caught.

One such victim was Karl Fleischer, a successful motor dealer in Munich, known as Hans Frick. During the German Army retreat from Italian soil, Hauptstürmfuhrer Fleischer had systematically misdirected army stores of Mercedes Benz engine parts and spares into a cave complex near Lake Como. He added to these by appropriating Jewish assets from motor businesses to stock the cavernous warehouse. In post-war years, when parts for vehicles were scarce to non-existent, he had used his secret stolen stocks to provide capital for his eventual garage chain.

Erwin greeted him in Italian.

"Buon giorno! Come sta lei?"

The German with closely cropped grey hair flinched, taken completely by surprise. Even more so when Erwin presented him with an indictment – the murder of six Italians he had forced to work for him at Como.

"What do you think of that?"

"You can't prove anything!" came the smug retort. He had been cleared by Allied screening as serving an active military service with no evidence of criminal activities.

"And this?" Erwin produced a statement signed by a Corporal Linz. This testified to Fleischer shooting his driver, two Sturmtroopers and Linz, and leaving them for dead.

"Linz survived," Erwin informed him, half smiling. The previously smug face turned grey. "I know where he is. If he testifies in court, you're finished, Hauptsturmfuhrer!" Erwin sneered, mocking him. "I will need 10 percent of your profits for silence. Forever!" Erwin conspicuously rubbed index finger and thumb. Hate in his burning eyes, the bullet head nodded. Deal secured, Erwin returned to Linz.

"You get a pension from me. Attempt to find Fleischer and I'll kill you." Linz was convinced.

Leaving Linz in Nuremberg, Erwin walked past enormous pretentious buildings, the legacy of Hitler's dreams and favourite architect. Erwin's mind filled with the roll of drums, the massed thunder of 10 000 feet crashing down on the square in perfect unison. Involuntarily his back straightened, his step quickened to a smart march, head up, pride bursting from his chest. He could see the standard bearers, like Roman Legions, black swastikas, white circles, red drapes furling in the breeze. The unrestrained mighty roar of 100 000 throats shouting "Heil Hitler!" in adulation, Erwin in the proud and feared S.S. contingency.

Strains of the S.S. marching song rang in his ears:

> *"Clear the streets, the S.S. marches*
> *The storm-columns stand at the ready.*
> *They will take the road*
> *From tyranny to freedom.*
> *So we are ready to give our all*
> *As did our fathers before us.*
> *Let death be our battle companion.*
> *We are the Black Band."*

Adolf Hitler's ghost was there for a moment, on the stone dais, his eyes hypnotic, intense, glaring, comical under the military peaked cap.

"Deutschland uber Alles!" screamed the demented leader of millions.

"Heil HITLER!" roared back the mesmerised multitude.

To be an S.S. member of the Third Reich was to be above and beyond the ordinary laws of civilisation and society. It was belonging to what Himmler himself called an 'Order of Germanic clan'. The Third Reich could never have existed without the S.S. and the converse is probably true as well. The S.S. was used for criminal purposes; brutalities and killings in concentration camps, the administration of the slave labour program and ruthless murder of prisoners of war.

Part of the system was still working for Erwin Erhardt, but not quite as Der Fuhrer had intended in Mein Kampf.

Erwin had watched the progress of many successful men. One was Hermann Schmidt, a source of burning jealousy and frustration to Erwin.

'There has to be something to incriminate the bastard,' he thought of the Wunderkind. 'But what?'

Chapter 30

1960's:

THE ERA OF MINI SKIRTS, ROCK 'n ROLL AND THE BEATLES

The Consortium worked very well.

Raoul had enormous influence through his infinite connections and had opened up business opportunities for Hermann and Ingrid beyond their wildest dreams He masterminded a chain of boutiques established in most provincial towns in France. Europe was crying out for the vitality that Vogel Mode and Gurtel und Hosentrager boutiques offered. In 1963 Vogel Fashions was launched in Britain. Opening the first Chelsea boutique took Ingrid's mind off her inner conflict. She had been shattered emotionally.

In 1959 Henri had met a girl, Dominique, who looked strangely like his first old flame, Sophie. In fact, he was so completely taken by the French girl that he rebuffed his erstwhile mistress. Ingrid hated Dominique, who she thought was a conniving bitch. But who could blame her for chasing a man with a big yacht in Monte Carlo? Ingrid had learned that money did not bring the happiness she had expected. She consequently dabbled with a few gigolos and toy boys, but they could never replace Henri. She would keep trying. One day he would come back to her; she was convinced of it.

Henri had used his Nazi treasure spoils well, investing in two further wine estates near Montmort and Epernay. Raoul had made good sales in the US on Henri's behalf that had enabled him to buy a streamlined yacht. Henri's level of wine estate management was truly state of the art, and controlling the Berghof estate presented no problem for him. Champagne and wine distribution sales reached unprecedented heights. Exporting to Britain was the next step.

Raoul had long acted as a catalyst for others' ill-gotten gains and hidden treasures secured from the Nazis prior to their rapid withdrawal to the Fatherland. He unearthed the spoils stolen from the Louvre he had hidden with Henri, and exported them to the US, where he received a fortune for them. He also sold in Britain. Artworks were smuggled with stocks of clothing and in large pantechnicons of wine cases on cross channel ferries.

Hermann Schmidt had become a major West German industrialist; a multi-millionaire. Some politicians were making approaches to him and offering their hands. As a leading nylon stocking manufacturer in West Germany, his factories churned out fashion designs and creations in vast quantities every month to supply his chain of stores. Ingrid's Vogel Mode enjoyed outstanding success with her team of the original salesgirls, who went on to manage their own boutiques. Her fashion design team headed by Gerda Blom stayed ahead of the rat race.

The Consortium met quarterly in Paris at Raoul's spectacular premises near the Eiffel Tower, whose 300-metre high structure was a draw-card for wealthy Americans. Appropriately, the Paris Hilton was established at its base.

"Well that wraps it up for another quarter," said Hermann, stacking the account books. "What have you got lined up for us this time?" he glanced at Raoul, his expression avaricious.

"Wait and see. Madame Roget has got something special she tells me."

Henri enjoyed their quarterly meetings for the 'apres ski' as they termed their indulgence. "How the hell does she pick them up?"

"She heard there's a paedophile network in UNICEF. The supply comes at a price," Raoul replied.

Later on, outside what looked like any office block in Montmartre, he spoke a few words to the concierge who swung the grille gate open to admit them. The old Otis lift had seen better days. As the gate slammed, they whirred to the third floor, where Raoul tapped on one of the doors in the corridor. It opened into an office which boasted walls adorned with theatrical pictures. Raoul spoke quietly to the girl at the reception desk, who pressed a button. A bookcase swung open to reveal an aperture and she motioned to them to go through.

"Bon soir, Monsieur Montpelier. Bon soir Messieurs! Faites entrer les messieurs," Madame Roget instructed the pretty receptionist. She led the way into the discreetly lit inner salle decorated in red and gold, where scantily dressed girls lounged on chaise longues and cushioned seats. One patron was already engaged in playful pursuit, his hostess for the night pouring wine in his mouth. A second nuzzled his quarry's breasts.

"Drinks, Messieurs?" Madame Roget waved towards a dimly lit bar, serviced by a topless waitress whose hair was swept up in a fetching coiffure. She touched her nipples with long painted fingers, teasing them until they stood erect.

"Your drinks, Messieurs." Not for her the long grind. That was for the others.

A girl caught Henri's eye as he sipped cognac. Negligee swept aside, her palm caressed her abdomen seductively. It usually turned them on, she had found. She was desperate for a sale that night or there would be trouble. Bitterly she saw that he didn't want to react.

"This place once belonged to Madame Courtier," remarked Raoul. "She was a real bitch to the girls. Madame Roget took over, so it is better run now. The old bag was murdered, you know."

"Really? What happened?" Henri was vaguely interested. "A young Jewish girl I knew, Emilie Cohen, once worked here in the war. She was young and very profitable, so Courtier kept her from the Nazis. Emilie told me how Madame Courtier used to pinch and beat them, and that she was a sadist, a real beast, who treated the girls horribly. When Paris was liberated, the girls ganged up on her and went beserk. They dragged her to the abandoned Gestapo Headquarters and tortured her to death. Pulled her hair out, nails, gave her electric shock treatment and did a lot of damage with a heated metal rod. Emilie told me that blood was everywhere. There's some history here let me tell you."

After a few drinks, Madame Roget approached, diamond ringed hand elegantly extended to Raoul, blood red lips smiling.

"I have just what you boys will enjoy! Three perfect little girls for you," she whispered, her barely concealed voluminous breasts heaving. "Come!" She led them into a small delightfully furnished room, and clapped her hands. Three 16-year-old girls appeared at the summons.

"Look after them girls," she announced, beaming at the men. "Enjoy yourselves." She left the girls to their devices. They were well trained, and her clients would pay her a small fortune for the privilege she so generously offered to them.

Chapter 31

SUMMER 1961:

NEUSTADT

Eyes wide, distraught, white-knuckled, gulping air, Ingrid's beautiful model had to let it out. "Frau Schmidt… bitte…"

"What's the problem? Erika – tell me!"

"It's Grete. She's missing! She is not in her apartment – I have just been there. She is gone!"

"Since when?" Ingrid blurted out, sensing molecules of fear creeping along her arms. Erika was shaking, gorgeous grey eyes haunted by trepidation.

"I have not seen her for two days. I didn't mention it yesterday; I thought she'd been out partying and had slept in… "

"Really? Why, was she out on the tiles?"

"She met a guy at the Tuesday photo session. She was wearing that black see-through lace leotard at the time, you know, cut down to the cleavage – remember?"

"Yes. Yes I do. But why was he there? Do you know?"

From a magazine he said. He was doing an article on Vogel; also Gordel und Hosentrager. Convincing he was; knew some facts. He asked what it was like working for Vogel, and was really complimentary!"

"Is that so? What happened?"

"He couldn't keep his eyes off Grete, and sat quietly watching her More like ogling actually. Grete had recently broken up with Fritz, her boyfriend. She was really flaunting herself, and this big hunk of beefcake was like a rebound bombshell. He had a sexy short ginger beard and moustache; a handsome bastard. He was a real he-man alright. She obviously fancied him. He asked her to lunch and that was it! We could see him hovering around Grete, who lapped it up, the sexy monkey…" Erika smiled in recollection. "As she had finished with Fritz, it would not have been surprising if she shacked up for a one night stand and got a bit hungover – but that was Tuesday."

Erika's usual ready smile had disappeared. Genuine concern spread over the delightful oval face framed in a cascade of black curls. Ingrid picked up the nervous vibes.

"It could be serious. Do you know his name? Any ideas where she might have gone?"

"I don't even know his name. All I can tell you is that he's a smart dresser; a big powerful guy, looked extremely fit, a healthy type – you know what I mean! God knows where they went. To a hotel or motel maybe," Erika shrugged vaguely.

"Or his place perhaps, who knows. Sounds mysterious," suggested her blond employer, whose ample bosom and figure was still a match for her girls. In her forties, Ingrid was devastatingly beautiful.

"Let's get the Police onto it."

*****

Grete's escort was meticulous; he had done his homework. His ravishingly beautiful dining partner had been with Ingrid at Vogel since she was 19. Her face featured in fashion spreads, and her figure would rouse the dead. Grete was important in the Vogel heirarchy. She enjoyed their candlelight dinner. When the second bottle of Tassenheimer Riesling was nearly empty, his suggestion of a motel was accepted with a sultry yet cultured smile.

Rain beat on the windscreen as he booked into a motel near Landau. It would have been difficult for the proprietor to describe his guest's appearance beyond height and size. Collar up, trilby brim pulled over his eyes, the guest spoke with a Parisian accent.

"Sil vous plais – I would like a room at the end of the block. I snore myself, but I am a light sleeper. Ha ha!"

"Oui Monsieur, certainement! Chambre vingt, Monsieur."

He had seen them all. It was off season and glad to fill any room, he handed over the key, acknowledging the gratuity accompanying the payment with a nod of his head. A secretary? A neighbour? Who cared? The name, car registration and destination were probably all false anyway.

It was still raining and Erwin drove the car under the shelter overhang of Room 20, satisfied no one had seen the girl with him.

"Wait while I get the door open; it is still pouring down," he instructed. Despite the dark, it took only 30 seconds to open the door of Room 19 with his skeleton key. He turned the light on and returned to the car. "Right sweetheart; out this side and you won't get wet," he said, while helping Grete climb out. "Hold on to me." She was a little unsteady so he picked her up bodily, cradling her in his huge arms and carried her towards the bed. She clung round his neck sexily, kissing him. He laid her on the covers, then returned to the car and locked it. Quickly opening the door of Room 20 with his motel key he rumpled the bed, pulling back the blankets and sheets, then rolled up his shirt sleeve and wiped his arm on the sheets to transfer skin cells to the fabric. Finally, he rubbed the pillow vigorously on his hair and left it dented. After a quick look around, he closed the door and went out, turning out the light. The hired car remained parked outside Room 20 all night. Erwin was excited; convinced that this girl would know the background secrets of Hermann Schmidt's wartime past.

Back in Room 19 he undressed, watched by Grete, who was still happily tipsy. The big man took her clothes off and started to fondle her, much to her delight. She giggled. "Schnice!"

"Tell me about your boss," he began casually, circling her mound, sliding his fingers between her thighs. "Whash you want to know… " Her question was interrupted by a loud hiccup. "Pardon," giggled Grete, polite fingers to lips.

"You know… in the war. Schmidt had a factory in the war, right?"

"I don' know. Why?" came the dreamy response.

"Listen! Did he have a clothing factory in Neustadt during the war? Employed forced labour?" He spelt out his message clearly, raising his voice.

"Whatsh thish? Why you shouting at me?" She was clearly upset by his abrupt approach.

"LOOK! I want to know," he said harshly, grabbing her wrists, "and you'll bloody well tell me sooner or later!"

Shocked, Grete sobered up remarkably quickly. "My God! What is this? Who the hell ARE you?"

He pinned her arms back on the bed. "Never mind. You're a senior girl in Vogel; you have been with Ingrid Penz since she started. Don't give me a load of nonsense! You must know all about Hermann Schmidt."

"I'm not talking to YOU about my employer," she retorted. "She has been good to me. Who the hell are you anyway?"

Then she saw it – she had once been told about underarm marks. "NO! Oh God, you're S.S!" she blurted, not thinking. Aggression aroused him; he was fully erect. He climbed astride the lovely girl, forcing her legs apart and thrust into her with all his force, as far as he could go. When Grete shrieked he hit her hard.

"Shut up bitch! NOW TELL me. Did young Schmidt have a uniform factory in Neustadt in the war? Was he running the place?" He plunged into her again with all his might. "Tell me!"

"OOoww," she groaned. SMACK. Grete was sober.

"His father had a factory there I've been told."

"The SON! Hermann. Was he there in the war?" His lunge knocked the wind out of her. He deliberately hurt her. "Why are you raping me?" I thought you liked me," she sobbed.

"I like your information better! I'll rape you till you die unless you tell me all about him," he threatened, with another forceful thrust.

"But I don't know. I wasn't there! No one told me he had the factory. Ingrid never talked about the war or having a factory then. How can I know? I'll tell you anything to stop you raping me. Yes, he had the factory – are you satisfied? But who are you?" she quivered, terror showing in her eyes.

Did she know nothing, or was she holding out? He would make sure. There were ways and means to get people to talk. He lunged into her until he climaxed. She knew too much already, after recognising the scar left by the skin graft he had undergone to remove his Nazi number. It had not healed properly, and had left its mark.

"Me? I'm a Nazi torturer as you're about to see. Tell me about Hermann and it stops." Before she could scream in earnest he stuffed his handkerchief in her mouth. The 'bow' rarely failed. Erwin pulled down a curtain cord, then tied the scarf he had worn around his neck onto one end of the cord. Roughly turning Grete onto her face, he lashed her wrists and ankles behind her back with a loop around her chin, forcing her body to resemble a curved bow. This forced her head back, causing an excruciating pain in her neck. The slightest pressure on her feet increased the unbearable torture and made her limbs increasingly numb as she attempted to relieve the pressure in her throat. Grete gurgled with the pain, her saliva nearly choking her. He left her for 15 minutes.

"What can you tell me?" enquired Erwin casually, looking up from his paper. "I'll take out the hankie, but if you scream out I'll press down on your legs." She knew what that meant and kept quiet.

"I don't know anything about him. Nothing. I know nothing. Please, oh please, let me go."

She forgot and. screamed as he pressed down on her raised head, causing severe pain to shoot down her neck and spine.

"Nothing?"

She screamed again as he racked up the already excruciating tension of the delicately stretched bow.

"I'd tell you if I knew anything, but I don't! All I can tell you is that I started in 1952. Nothing else!" she cried.

He believed her. It was a pity.

"Alright. I believe you. I'll let you go," he said, untying the cord. Exhausted she rolled and stretched on the bed, rubbing her sore wrists, tears running down her once sweet face.

"You won't tell anyone about this little experience will you?" Erwin smiled sardonically down on her.

"Oh no! No!" she lied, shaking her burning sore neck.

"Good girl. I knew you wouldn't," he replied, grabbing a pillow and holding it over her face. He had no choice. She kicked for a while, then eventually became still.

*****

Needing water for his radiator, a motorist who had stopped at a ditch on the Strasbourg road reported finding the body of a partially dressed young woman. The police physician summoned to the scene diagnosed death from cardiac arrest. His report read, "Traces of fairly recent copulation. Bruising of wrists and ankles consistent with tight bindings. No evidence of strangulation in the normal sense, with a rope or the bare hands. There is however a strange mark under her chin, which is puzzling. The skin has not been lacerated, but is however inflamed. How? I am not sure. Perhaps the mark was caused by a silk scarf, or man's tie? The actual cause of death remains a mystery."

The Gendarmerie made systematic calls on hotels and motels in the vicinity, but in vain. "No sir. The man in Room 20 was alone, to my knowledge. No, I didn't actually see a woman with him. I'd say that he was a traveller. No, I saw nothing unusual."

"That figures. Our forensic people confirm that according to their tests only one person used that bed. Merci Monsieur," he replied, touching his kepi peak in a salute of dismissal.

Erika identified Grete's body. Still shocked, she told the police of her fears and described the big well-built man with a ginger beard and moustache who had been present that evening.

"Have you seen him before?"

"No. Only on that day."

"What makes you think he might have killed her?"

Erika paused. "I'm not sure. It is just that he appeared so unexpectedly and took her out to lunch," her voice was devoid of conviction.

The Inspector smiled.

"Really? Well a man answering your description, according to a statement by the owner, stayed at his motel. Forensic tests confirm this."

"Really? "Well, can't you.... "

"Only one person slept in that bed," he interrupted her. "No. It's not your man we are after! Hell, she was beautiful! Can you imagine any man sleeping alone if she was available? Maybe someone else picked her up later in the day."

Ingrid shared her fears with Hermann. Who was the mystery man? Hermann felt quite sick. The day of reckoning he had thought about in 1943 seemed closer at hand. Hermann was not stupid. Who the hell would kill a young kid in the business? He was certain that they were after him and Ingrid. But who? The Jews?

AUTUMN 1965:

PARIS, LISE DELORS

"Would you come with me to grandma's farm? For two weeks?" "I'd like that," Lise replied enthusiastically. But I don't know if they will let me."

Lise Delors had found her friend Jacques waiting for her after school, and they had walked home together.

"I'll get my folks to ask yours. If I ask your folks they will say 'No'. It sounds better from parents. There is no difference really, but I think it's harder for them to say 'No'." At 15 Jacques du Pont knew how adults thought.

His tactic worked, and they had two unforgettable weeks together on the farm. Once there, Lise confided, "Oh I'm so happy with you, Jacques. My parents never seem to have enough money to go away for a good holiday. It's the upkeep of the house. Papa has never been a successful architect, but they get by with my mother's teacher's salary."

Her father had met his future wife, Anne, at Nottingham University, where he had studied architecture. Anne spoke French like a native and was a capable teacher in both English and French. When they married, his pride as an architect made him promise her a house at St. Denis outside Paris. His wife had been paying for the privilege ever since. They had one child, Lise.

Lise at 13 was a credit to them academically. Brilliant at school she was always near the top of her class. But she was shy. An only child, she was timid and withdrawn at times, and had difficulty mixing with other pupils. She had one friend, Jacques, who was 18 months older than she and one class ahead of her. He understood her, could relate to her, making it easy for her to confide in him and talk to him about her problems.

They were strolling along the hedgerows before dinner one evening, batting midges away from their faces as they made their way back to the farmhouse, when Lise told him, "I can't talk to my mother like you do to yours. I've seen how you two get along, and the way she hugs you. You're like real friends, I can see that. With Mum and me it's different. We have never been close. She sees I do my homework properly, things like that, but she keeps a distance between us. She never talks to me woman to woman."

Jacques could see tears in her eye. "What about your father? How's he?"

"We get along fine, when he has the time." She shrugged.

"Did your mother never talk about," he paused, then rushed on, "babies? And periods and those things?"

"No." Lise looked as lost as an angel without wings.

"What! Your mother never explained it all to you? And she's a schoolteacher!" Lise felt nervous and deprived.

"Perhaps it's because she's English. Maybe she is too shy." Lise did not particularly want to defend her, but it came out. "She always seems to be so busy, rushing around all the time." She emphasised the word 'busy'.

"You will have to know sometime. It might as well be now. Do you want me to tell you about it?" Always practical was Jacques.

Self conscious, Lise timidly replied, "Yes. Please." Without embarrassment, Jacques told her. To her dying day she would always trust and respect him for that. She had a true friend.

She lay in the dark that night, vividly remembering how disturbed she had been at first when Jacques had explained the facts of life to her. She felt a strange resentment towards her mother. Two days later, when she had had time to think about the new information, they were again walking in the fields, when Lise put her hand on Jacques' forearm to stop his stride.

"Jacques. I don't know how to say this but… "

"What Lise? You can tell me." He was always reassuring.

"I'm embarrassed to ask. I want you to… you know, let me see you. I've never seen one. You told me about it, but… "

Jacques put his hands on her shoulders. "Are you sure now? I would never do anything to you, you can be sure of that, but if you really want to see me, I'll show you."

Her hazel eyes looked up at her tall friend. "Yes. I would like to see, please."

They didn't make love, that Jacques had promised, but now Lise knew what male organs looked like when aroused in earnest. Her eyes were riveted. She could not believe that something so big could go into what was such a small aperture. The prospect frightened her. Jacques reassured her that nature took care of everything.

Lise returned home with renewed confidence, speaking openly with her mother. Dispelling shyness and becoming more companionable at school, life opened up.

Disaster struck six months later. Her world fell apart when both her parents were killed in a car crash. At 14, Lise was shattered, compelled to live with her father's sister in the village of Chateau Thierry.

As mean as a peasant, the aunt neither wanted Lise nor the expense, making her feel like a burden and an intruder in their lives. However, the prospect of a share of her brother's inheritance persuaded the shrew to accept the obligation. The harridan had created a life of purgatory for her hen-pecked husband, a weasel at her beck and call. Devoid of any vestige of affection for him she devoted her attention to church matters and in particular to doing the 'Lord's command', as she liked to fool herself, with the local priest. He refused transfer.

Before school Lise had to sweep up and clean, then on her return, open boxes and stack goods in the general store. It was this time Lise dreaded the most.

Lise had a constant fear of being molested by her horrible uncle. It was the way in which he leered at her, making any pretext to get close to her and touch her. When it first happened she thought his steadying the stepladder to reach the high shelves was being helpful. Her initial smile of appreciation was misinterpreted as he contrived to devise such opportunities. Lise had to play a game of climbing high when he was engaged with customers, to avoid his detestable fondling.

She became increasingly frightened of him. Alone with him one afternoon, the store empty, her aunt away on her spiritual vocation and pursuits, Lise was unable to avoid noticing the bulge in her uncle's trousers. She had seen it before. Fear gripped her. Imagining the worst, she became terrified as he moved towards her. The vivid dread of disturbed nights returned when she panicked that one day he would force his lust upon her. Was he about to rape her? Lise rushed down the last three steps and turned to face the counter, thinking that it would possibly offer some form of protection. The lecherous man, out of control and burning with lust, came up behind her and cupped her tiny left breast, pushing into her buttocks, his right hand moving to her pelvis. Lise screamed. It startled him and she struggled free, running frantically out of the shop and down the street.

Gathering her strength, her determination to escape now formulated, she returned later. Lise said nothing to her aunt, judging it her best insurance against further torment by her beastly uncle until she escaped from the misery of her relatives.

She shuddered as she lay on her bed, tears rolling down her cheeks as she planned her escape. School holidays began in two days. On the last day of school she would walk the 18 kilometres to the main road near Montmirail and hitch a lift to Chalons sur Marne. She was certain that her friend Jacques du Pont would start his summer vacation at his grandmother's farm as they had last year. He went every year. She would gamble on it.

She knew he would help her somehow. It was through him she understood the dangers of staying.

She had to get away.

Geography had always been one of Lise's favourite subjects but she could not concentrate. She had her own geography in mind, and was leaving with no intention of returning. Tension built during the last morning lesson at the prospect of running away. Desertion takes a special kind of courage.

The lunch break bell sounded. This was it.

"Michelle," Lise grabbed an arm of a classmate in the next desk row. "I feel awful. It's my usual. I'll lie down for a bit."

"What a day to be sick! The last day too! I hope you soon feel better. See you later."

"Thanks. 'Bye."

The alibi would give Lise some leeway when the afternoon class reconvened. The teacher would hopefully think that she had gone home early, not well. It was the last day of term after all. Her aunt would not be aware she was not coming back until 16h00 or even later. By then she would be well on her way. No one she knew had seen her leave school.

Lise was clear of the village in a quarter of an hour. Still no one recognised her. Lise set a fast pace at first, only slowing down when she was some distance from school. At the sound of a car behind her, she quickly moved into the shadow of a tree and stood stock-still. A Peugeot 403 cruised by. She decided to change from her school clothes into the dress she had in her carpet bag. Five minutes later she heard the sound of a lorry coming towards her. This time she scampered behind a hedge. Lise knew hiding from traffic would slow her down but her plan to walk was sensible. She had tried to think as her aunt would. To Paris on the road through Montreuil would be her first guess, there to join Route 33 at La Fort. Not finding her on that road she would most probably turn back and try the eastern route to Epernay and Chalons or even north to Reims. Why would she go south on the Route 373? It might be her last choice. Lise was counting on it. She must not be spotted by anyone. There was plenty of time. Lise was convinced a lift could soon be traced by the Gendarmerie in a close community, and a wandering girl remembered. Once on the open road Route 33 she would risk hitching a lift to Chalons.

'Ouch! My feet hurt,' she said aloud. 'Oh, oh, another car!' Lise scrambled into a ditch as there was no cover. A Renault sped past.

'Time for a sandwich.' She had made them in the shop the previous night, and had also taken two tins of sardines because she could open them easily with their attached key. A swallow of water from her plastic bottle tasted like nectar on her parched tongue. 'That's better', she convinced herself, spirits high as she put the bottle back into her rucksack and set off once more to complete the last leg of the journey to Route 33.

Mud on her shoes, dress dishevelled, she was tired and footsore. So far she had not been discovered though so the discomfort was worth it.

'Not much further now. I can hear the traffic'. She looked at her watch: 15h40.

Chapter 33

JUNE 1966:

PARIS

Henri's introduction of Raoul to Hermann was the start of a good friendship. Through Raoul's expertise, Hermann raised capital from his paintings when he most needed it. To expand. He knew nothing of their value, relying instead on Raoul's advice on keeping certain works of art to appreciate.

A millionaire industrialist, Hermann decided to give half of the balance of his stock to Raoul. "Without you I would not be where I am today. Without you I would not know where to sell the bloody stuff. What to sell or keep. Raoul, you deserve it my boy. Say what we should do and I'll be with you."

Henri was wealthy. The champagne distribution company prospered and the vineyards produced good crops. Not in need of cash immediately, on Raoul's advice he waited for the sixties before selling some of his paintings. Raoul made a fortune for him. At 37, Henri decided to buy a yacht at Monte Carlo.

Raoul had three prosperous businesses, two in Paris and one in Strasbourg. He also had a very fat Swiss bank account in Basle. He had been a 'horse trader' all his life.

Three men. The mature survivors of the war, opportunists and successful in peacetime, they were wealthy people. They enjoyed a lifestyle in which sales of stolen objets d'art had been a major contributory factor to that wealth. All made possible by a time in history when Nazis had terrorised, persecuted and plundered the Jews. Dehumanised and murdered them, and systematically carried victims off to ghoulish extermination camps where belching crematoria destroyed all traces of their evil deeds and dispersed them on a sticky sweet stinking wind. They were backed by an army of bureaucrats and administrators, hell-bent on the destruction of an entire race of people. They did not consider them to be human; as far as they were concerned they were simply statistics in their ledgers. For those who survived, wealth brought the good times.

It was summer, 1966. After two carefree days in Paris, the three friends were in a mood of gay abandon. Raoul had pulled off an incredible deal with an American for their consortium, after negotiations had gone higher than they had hoped. That evening Raoul had arranged for three girls to join them at a splendid hotel. They had enjoyed a leisurely dinner and cabaret, drank a little too much wine and later struggled to fulfil their fantasies in bed. The girls thought this was hilarious. Rising late after a last fling with 'les filles de nuit' they had a champagne breakfast.

"We'll stay at La Verite. It is too far for Hermann to drive today in his delicate state of health!"

Laughing, they accepted Henri's invitation.

On Route 33 it was 16h00 when they were passing through Viels Maisons.

"We must be mad! We have just been to THE city of Les Femmes and didn't bring one with us!" Hermann was laughing. On the road their conversation had deteriorated into trivia and the normal subject of women. They also laughed about the exploits of the previous night. "Just thinking about them makes me feel randy," vouched Hermann. "It must be my second wind or something."

"Well I always say the value of a good painting is one thing, but the value of a good woman when you want one is priceless!"

"Quite so, quite so, Raoul," mocked Henri, laughing at him.

They were still laughing when a figure thumbing a lift came in sight. Hermann slowed. It was a young girl.

"Should we give her a lift?" As driver he thought he should ask his companions.

"Why not? Nice looking," said Raoul from the back seat.

Hermann pulled up past the T-junction and Henri leaned out. "Where are you heading Mademoiselle?"

"To Chalon, Monsieur."

"Get in. We can take you."

"Merci, Monsieur," the blond hitchhiker radiated innocence. Climbing into the back of the car she sank back onto the seat of the big Mercedes, weary from her long walk.

Raoul started looking at her and she became disturbed. Without taking his eyes from her he commented to his friends, "The value when you want one is priceless."

Henri and Hermann looked at each other simultaneously in the front seat. "You mean this one!" blurted Henri.

"Why not!" he nodded.

Henri turned round to look at their pretty passenger. In a flash she was Sophie to him. He broke into a wicked grin. "As you say, why not." Looking sideways at Hermann, he questioned, "Game?"

"Tell me where, that's all."

"First, no names, chaps! We can't go to my place."

"What about the old Jew's place," Raoul suggested.

"We can't. It's rented. People are there."

"Better tell me where to go! We will be driving all night," complained Hermann in good humour.

Lise sat trembling. She realised what she had run away from could happen right then!

"I know just the place. I can't go in to negotiate being a local. Go on 17 kilometres from our turning and right. I'll show you."

"Please Messieurs, please let me go!"

"Mon cheri! And miss the pleasure of our company. What a missed opportunity!" Raoul mocked her. She started to cry.

"When we get there," instructed Henri nodding at Raoul, "give the old bag two weeks rent. Then let us in the back. Affaires du coeur; shy you know. She'll leave us alone. Make her day!"

Hermann called over his shoulder. "There's a first aid container inside the back shelf. Put sticking plaster over her mouth. If she kicks up a fuss, belt her. Mademoiselle, if you don't give trouble, you won't get hurt," assured the German over his shoulder. "Arbeit macht frei."

Lise recognised French spoken by a German. The others were French. Bilingual, they slipped into German easily, joking.

She would try to remember everything. Stay calm she told herself.

Blindfolded, she counted slowly and in rhythm until the car stopped after the turn off. Lise shook with terror, gagged and blindfolded.

Raoul used his charm and eloquence on the old woman. The money sealed the agreement.

Once in the room, her ordeal began. The humiliation, pain and horror would haunt Lise for the rest of her life.

It was Hermann who joked, "Shall I go first or spin for it? I have poked plenty of virgins in my time, only in those days Ingrid held them down for me."

"Be our guest!" Henri smirked. "We'll have a drink," he said, looking at Raoul for approval.

"We should spin," said Raoul, "it would be fairer."

Nevertheless Hermann won the contest with Raoul second.

Only men with hearts of stone, immune to human suffering could have done to that 15 year old what they did. Brutes conditioned to view compassion as a weakness scorned. The quality had been systematically subjugated to non-existence.

Hermann stripped her and flung her on the bed, then threw himself on top of her, forcing his entry, and tearing her hymen. Lise cried out sharply in pain. He derived pleasure from the violation. In a state of dementia, eyes glazing, he muttered, "Take this, Jewish bitch," as he thrust into her. This was painful enough, but the subsequent violations built up to a level of such excruciating searing agony she was unable to contain her crying.

If the agony could be measured Lise found resistance caused the least pain.

As the blonde German exploded inside her she vowed one day she would kill him if it was the last thing she did.

Next was the suave dark-haired Frenchman. He had immaculately manicured nails and did not look as though he had done a day's hard work in his life. She thought that he was perhaps a playboy. She had seen them in Paris – the idle rich. Wasting no time he entered her. Lise choked on her saliva as she felt him penetrate higher inside her. He took so long she was terrified he would kill her. The pain was unbearable and she screamed out. After a long time he left her.

She remembered much later that she must have been only semi-conscious when the last Frenchman took her. He was huge and the hurt built inside her in piercing shrieking agony. Henri slapped her face. To him it was back in time with Sophie under him and she loved it. They all did. Yes, just like Sophie it was. Lise passed out.

After an eternity of Hell, the barbarism ceased. During three hours Lise had been raped twice by each of her persecutors.

As she lay in screaming agony, abdomen on fire, vagina stinging like a scalded wound, she vowed one day to find these animals and destroy them. She would hound them, expose and ruin the swines.

It became her life's obsession.

She was unable to walk; Raoul carried her to the car.

Outside Chalons sur Marne they put her down on the roadside and drove off to Montmort. Lise spat after them, cursing them to Hell.

What she had gained from the experience was her lost virginity, searing pain in her vagina and lower abdomen, ruined reproductive organs and recurring nightmares. In her hand she clutched a button, like a baby in a pram. She had ripped it from Raoul's barathea blazer when he carried her. She held onto it with the grip of a drunk on his last coin.

Lise lay crying, incapable of walking. Further along the road they had thrown out her rucksack as a last token of their disrespect.

Chapter 34

30 MINUTES LATER:

CHALONS ROAD

Lise had arrived on the outskirts of Chalons but her intended meeting with Jacques did not transpire.

Six cars passed and failed to stop. Then a Citroen swept by in the opposite lane, before slowing and turning around, stopping next to where she lay. Pierre Lavelle showed compassion for the dishevelled black-haired girl. Hazel eyes brimming with tears looked up at him, lips trembling. Her small mouth was complemented by a slim nose and oval chin in her narrow face. Tall and slim, possessing a neat figure, she looked older than her 15 years.

"Are you hurt? I'm a doctor. Can I help you?" Pierre asked anxiously. "I thought perhaps you had fallen from a bicycle. What happened?"

Lise cried again. "I was left here by some men," she sobbed.

Pierre was quick. Only 23 and a hospital intern, he correctly guessed the worst. "Did they attack you?" he blurted out.

"Ye-e-e-es!" she sobbed.

"Oh my God! Get in my car. Can you get up? Here, I'll help you," he offered, reaching to lift her. "Where do you live? Round here?"

"No," sniffed Lise. Then she explained her predicament and what had happened to her.

Pierre now had an awesome responsibility. His doctor's code of ethics did not allow him to desert her, but she had nowhere to go. It was then that he decided. "I'm going to Paris. Please climb on the back seat. I want to make a preliminary examination. If you can travel, then it would be better to get you into my hospital. We will be there inside three hours." He began his professional task. "Good. You are not bleeding much now. Try to relax; sleep if you can. We will soon be there."

"My bag, Monsieur. They threw it out."

Pierre walked up the road to fetch her sole possession. As he picked up the rucksack he could contain himself no longer and burst into tears. "The BASTARDS!" he choked.

On arrival at the hospital, Pierre telephoned his surgeon father. He told him what had happened to Lise, and explained his worst fears from the tear he had seen.

Eminent surgeon Cesar Lavelle came at once and made his examination. "How can we tell this young lady she may never be a mother? Those savages have robbed her of a woman's privilege to raise a family."

Pierre looked at his father. "She has no one! Now this. She lost her parents last year. Her relative is a real beast." Pierre looked at his father and the distinguished white-haired gentleman nodded. No words passed. "She can stay with us until she sorts out her young life."

"Papa. You are wonderful!" Pierre Lavalle meant it, clasping his father's shoulders between outstretched arms.

The surgeon did a fine job in the circumstances. Two weeks later Lise was installed in his splendid house, welcomed by his generous wife, Regine. The wealthy couple were very impressed with Lise, while the young girl was more than happy for them to be her temporary foster parents. A loving bond grew between them and they went through the official adoption procedure.

Lise excelled at school. Brilliant in geography, and coached in physics and science by a renowned foster father surgeon, fluent in English from her natural mother, Lise qualified with flying colours for university entrance to the Sorbonne. Under Regine's loving guidance, Lise developed the style and grace of a young lady and blossomed into a stunning beauty.

At 22 Lise graduated with a degree in Oceanography. It was 1974 and she applied for a situation in the Intergovernmental Oceanographic Commission of UNESCO in Paris, which she secured.

Up until this time, Lise had not had any involvements with men, shying away from many invitations from admiring and handsome suitors. Regine arranged for suitable partners for social affairs, balls and formal occasions and understood that Lise wished for no entanglement at this stage in her life. She did not realise just how deep her foster daughter's phobia about men was, thanks to her rapists.

Pierre had waited until Lise was well established in his father's home before tactfully broaching the subject of her dreadful ordeal.

"Lise, it will be painful to recall your ugly experience, but without your recollections it will be impossible to trace the animals who attacked you. If you can, write down the things you can recall. However small, write them down."

"I will, Pierre. Thank you. I can assure you the things I remember have been inside my head for months. I have nightmares every night."

"Tell them to me Lise and I'll put it all down. It's the start of our docket," he urged, bringing out his pad and pen.

"It was just after 16h00 on the last day of term. The big black Mercedes crawled to a stop. I accepted a lift to Chalons and sat in the back seat with a Frenchman. I remember him saying 'the value when you want one is priceless'. I thought about it a lot since. He had finely manicured nails. Who would talk like that? A dealer of some sort?

"He had dark hair, a moustache, deep set eyes, a parting on the right side, a square jaw. He was about 45, could be 40; horrible eyes! At one time I thought he was a playboy. He hurt me terribly! He went on and on. It was so horrible! He wore a blazer and I pulled a button off. Look." Lise fetched it for Pierre to see.

"Keep it safe!" he cautioned. "Anything else? Him specifically. Think now."

"Yes. The Frenchman in the front passenger seat told him to negotiate with the old bag for two weeks rent. He said, 'I can't negotiate being a local', and 'We can't go to my place'.

"Aha! Let's call him 'F 2'. You say he was a local?"

"Yes, because he also said 17 kilometres from the turning and right. They put a blindfold on me you see. Well from that right turn I counted 750 'thousands' in my mind."

"Excellent! So that means – at one second each, let me see," he said, calculating, "twelve and a half minutes. Were they going fast?"

"No, not really, but not slowly either."

"About 80, 100, say?"

"Then that would be approximately 16 to 21 kilometres. So we may be able to find the place. Tell me more about 'F 2'. Can you describe him?"

"Dark skinned, slender athletic build, not tall. He had a lean face, like a gypsy almost, and a black moustache, heavy, well-defined eyebrows, and yes, a narrow nose and pointed chin. What I remember most about him was his bedroom eyes, yet they were sometimes quite piercing. Mysterious, like he was guarding a secret. A weird guy. Seemed self opinionated – you know, a self-centred man. About 40 I would say. I have cause to remember him, well! He was so big, his thing I mean, and hurt me so much, I screamed. He slapped me, hard! He kept moaning about 'Sophie'. It was so strange… I thought he would kill me. I fainted with pain."

"Oh God!" commiserated Pierre.

"But it was the German! He was the bastard who raped me first. He was a

168

cruel demented man. Take that Jew bitch!" he screamed at me when he tore into me. "Oh, it was terrible!" Lise shuddered, grimaced, putting her head down. "He was the one who told the others to hit me if I caused a fuss. I was terrified! He was horrid! A beast!" Lise looked away from Pierre, embarrassed. "I don't think I can tell you."

"It's okay Lise, I am a doctor. You need to tell it to get it out of your system. What happened?"

"Well, he put his finger inside me. I cried out because he hurt me so. And then he said, 'Good. No one has been there before. You're going to like this, you bitch!' Then he raped me. I have never experienced such pain. I'm sure the swine got pleasure from my torture. I vowed I would kill him one day!"

"Describe him for me if can you."

"Fair hair, blue eyes, square-jawed; a real Kraut, around 40. He was the driver by the way. I am pretty sure it was his car. He wore glasses. Yes. I remember something else! 'Tell me where to go,' he said and 'F 1' asked, 'What about the old Jew's place?' Then F 2 said, 'No, it's rented. People there'."

"Oh! That is puzzling. I wonder what that was all about. We'll put it down anyway – it might make sense sometime."

Lise felt better to have related her experience, although psychologically she would live many years of torment from that dreadful ordeal.

SEVENTIES
*****
SEARCHING

Chapter 35

SPRING 1975:

PARIS

Lise picked up the receiver on the third ring.
"Guess who this is?" she heard through the earpiece.

Jacques! How nice to hear your voice. Where are you?"

She was excited.

"Paris, for a psychiatry conference. Any chance of my taking you out to dinner?"

"That would be marvellous. Thank you, I would love that."

Jacques could not believe his eyes as he surveyed the glorious creature waiting for him at the fashionable restaurant.

"Lise, you are BEAUTIFUL. My God, and I'm married. I should have waited… " He was laughing.

Lise blushed. She rushed on, "I'm established at Unesco Oceanographic and am enjoying every minute. I have been there six months," beamed the 23-year-old dark-haired beauty.

"And your love life? Not married yet I see. Some lucky fellow on the hook I bet?"

Lise looked embarrassed. Jacques picked it up in a flash. "Sorry. Said the wrong thing have I?"

No. But I'm not likely to marry."

"What? Why do you say that?"

Lise related her traumatic rape ordeal. Jacques listened attentively, not interrupting, allowing her to get it all out of her system. Like those times at school. "I may not be the world's greatest psychiatrist Lise, but I can recognise a problem when I see one. You've had an awful experience. It disturbs me that my dearest school friend has had to live with an ordeal such as this," said Jacques, taking in her peach-bloom skin, delicately chiselled nose and rosebud mouth, and the way she carried herself with such dignity on magnificent never-ending legs.

He also noticed her impeccable table manners as she began to eat.

"Lise you possess such vitality and intelligence, yet you have allowed that one unfortunate incident to block a natural emotional trait. Everyone should have someone to love and be loved by. It is the greatest treasure one can experience in a lifetime of ups and downs."

Lise's blue eyes were icy. "Men are all the same, want one thing. I'll make it on my own thank you."

"Oh dear, this could develop into an argument. Enough. Let's enjoy our dinner. Perhaps we can talk later. Tell me about your job, Lise."

Back on home ground, she sparkled.

"I'm being trained on submersibles at present. First it was the basic SCUBA, Self Contained Underwater Breathing Apparatus; tested in 1943 by Jacques Cousteau by the way. I've used one, which was scary at first. At shallow depths pure oxygen can be breathed, recycled through a carbon dioxide filter. Below eight metres or 25 feet, pure oxygen is toxic and has to be mixed with nitrogen or some inert gas. Air can be breathed safely to a depth of 65 metres or 200 feet. Below that nitrogen becomes toxic. So at great depths a mixture of oxygen and helium is breathed."

Lise paused to take another bite, then continued, "It is vital that we fully understand and have experience in the practicalities to operate effectively in the ocean. We have strict training to avoid being a burden through ignorance by ship crews on exploration cruises. We also have to know all about correct procedures in an emergency. Am I boring you?"

"Not at all Lise, it sounds fascinating. Please go on."

"I'm jumping a bit. You know the traditional 'hard hat' equipment; metal helmet, metal suit, weighted boots and watertight suit has not changed much for 100 years, only modified since a basic design by Siebe in 1837. The diver is supplied with air pumped through his suit from the surface and released through a valve in his helmet. As air pressure inside the helmet determines the pressure in his lungs, the pressure of air supplied must equal that of the water in which he is working, otherwise his breathing will be restricted by the higher pressure of the water on his chest."

Lise looked enquiringly at him. Jacques nodded, indicating that he was still with her.

"You've heard of the bends?"

"Yes. They sound awful. What causes it or them?"

"As the diver breathes air or gas mixture at the same pressure as the surrounding water, nitrogen or the inert gas in the breathing mixture becomes absorbed into the bloodstream. If the diver comes up rapidly there is no time for this gas to be expelled through the lungs in the usual way and bubbles form in the blood, impeding circulation. In mild cases this causes pains in the joints, known as the 'bends'. If it is severe it can render the diver unconscious or even be fatal. The deeper the dive, the longer the decompression time: this can be up to several days at great depths. There is an alternative. The diver may be saturated with inert gas for 24 hours in a pressurised chamber before a dive. He is then kept under pressure until he completes the work, with rests between short shifts in the pressurised chamber on the ship's deck. This avoids lengthy decompression periods every time a diver completes a spell of work. The advantage is the diver will not absorb any more inert gas and goes through one long decompression period, about one day for every 30 metres."

Lise took another mouthful, chewed, then resumed, "I am telling you this to explain why we need submersibles. They can go down to 10 000 feet, depending on design. Two or three men can live in relative comfort within a sphere two metres across and work for periods of eight hours. We use them for seabed surveys for geological, biological, archaeological, salvage and offshore oil exploration. Surprisingly they are relatively inexpensive and are very adaptable. The PISCES model is popular for work down to 2 000 feet."

She stopped, looked at him.

"You can imagine, Jacques, how the invention has opened up our scope.

"We also use the JIM, the atmospheric diving suit made of magnesium alloy which can go down to 1 500 hundred feet. A bathyscape or bathysphere, 'TRIESTE', was used off Italy in 1954 for a dive by Piccard to descend to a depth of 10 400 feet. His son Jacques went down 35 800 hundred feet in 'TRIESTE' in the Marianas Trench in the Pacific. So you see, we can access most quarters of the oceans.

"I find the work fascinating and can't wait to go on a big voyage one of these days."

"You have certainly carved out an interesting life for yourself," enthused Jacques.

He discussed her feelings towards men again and found he had started to make her think carefully about her attitude and its effect on her. "There are many, many more good men than bad in the world. To deprive yourself of love would be a tragedy. Put that ugly happening out of your mind. Don't waste your life."

"Jacques, I will think about what you have said and explained to me. I have been shown much love and compassion by Pierre, his mother and father. Thanks for your concern." Lise kissed him as they parted, still the wonderful friends they had always been. "It was a lovely evening. Thank you, Jacques."

"I would like to talk to you once more, Lise if you agree."

"Yes. I think I should. I feel better for having told you all about myself."

Jacques gave her additional therapy and Lise lost much of her phobia about men in general.

Pierre Lavalle had been through a rotten time with his wife. A real bitch to him, she was promiscuous; a proper tramp. Eventually he decided he had had enough and divorced her. At 30 he had at last escaped from the taunting embarrassment of being her doctor husband and cuckold.

Lise thought Pierre was a caring considerate gentleman who had shown generous compassion towards her in her distress. Lise was naturally concerned for him during the traumatic periods of misery with his wanton wife, and was glad to see his wife thrown out. Pierre deserved better.

Coming so soon after the earnest concern shown by Jacques for her wellbeing, Pierre and Lise were both looking for understanding companions. Without making positive moves, they gravitated into each other's orbit. For Lise it was a mixture of concern and joy for Pierre's freedom, mixed with gratitude for what he had done for her. Lise owed everything she had to Pierre. Through his caring and the persuasion of his parents she had the education to enjoy her engrossing work. She owed him a lot.

Pierre had been secretly in love with Lise since she first came into their lives. He had made strides with tracing her rapists, keeping a meticulous log of his findings.

One day he plucked up courage. "Lise, you have always meant so much to me. I am not a great catch I know, but if you would share my life and I yours, I would never interfere with your career in oceanography, which obviously means so much to you. I have learned that even a little love on occasion is worth any sacrifice. Lise, please marry me. I believe we would have a pleasant life together. Find happiness. We know each other very well and I love you very much. You would make me an extremely happy man if you would accept."

Lise gazed into Pierre's sad dark eyes, her own brimming with tears at his moving proposal.

"Dearest Pierre. My darling man, no one has been kinder than you. That I cannot deny. I believe you. Oh I believe you love me. I do believe that. But Pierre, at the moment I don't know if I love you. I am VERY fond of you. If I married you I would care for you. I always have. But can you accept that I may take time, maybe even years, before I fall in love with you? Can you accept that Pierre? I am being brutally honest, dearest Pierre, but I never want to hurt you."

"Oh, Lise. Yes. I accept you as you are, my sweet Lise."

"In that case my dear one, I accept your proposal. It could be fun, you and

I." Lise smiled lovingly.

They flew into each others arms and hugged and hugged like long lost brother and sister. For their relationship had developed this way, with tremendous respect on both sides. The loving would have to come slowly for Lise in the marital sense. Intelligent, they were confident their marriage had a good chance of success.

Their splendid society wedding was held in June 1975 at the Lavalle residence. Regine Lavalle shed tears of joy at the union, while Cesar was beside himself with pride. He loved them equally. Lise at 24 was ravishing, the true blushing bride, her dark eyebrows and eyelashes creating a mystique which had all the boys from the stag party jealous of their doctor friend's good fortune. Pierre knew there would be an awkward moment or two when they went to bed, while Lise was more apprehensive than she was prepared to admit. She even began to rue her decision to marry. But Pierre was marvellous.

"My darling, I know you will feel apprehensive. There is no way I would upset you, so please relax."

"Thank you Pierre. You really are a darling."

"Come angel. Just lie on the bed for a while," invited Pierre, curling his left arm under her, pulling her against his chest. They cuddled, gazed at one another, kissed.

"Happy?" he asked.

"Yes Pierre, I am. I am a lucky woman to have such a kind husband as you."

Pierre kissed her gently, then cautiously placed his right hand over her left breast, gently caressing. Lise felt relaxed and contented. Slowly he traced his hand over her body, her hips, thighs, down her long shapely legs.

"Ready to get undressed?" he asked quietly, with no urgency in his voice.

Momentary panic eventually subsided in Lise as she agreed. "Alright." She moved into the en suite bathroom, mentally pushing herself.

"I'll nip downstairs. Be back in 10 minutes," whispered Pierre diplomatically.

Lise was waiting in bed when he returned, bearing wine, a wine bucket, and two glasses. He poured. "To the loveliest woman in the world," he toasted, handing her a glass.

Feeling better, she patted the sheets, inviting him to join her in the bed, then motioned that he should link arms and drink together. "To my wonderful husband." She then put down her glass, took away his and turned to him. Making up her mind to act decisively she pulled aside her nightdress, exposing her white breast.

This would be the moment to conquer the fear she had nursed for eight years. Gingerly she put out her fingers to touch him.

He was intelligent enough not to go all the way on their first occasion There would be plenty of time for that if his introduction to loving sex was a success. Slowly he petted Lise, then decided to risk bringing her to a climax. Pierre gently manipulated Lise, enabling her to experience sexual ecstasy with a man for the first time. She was completely overwhelmed, gulping air, carried away by his skilful caressing, moaning blissfully as she reached a climax. She felt gloriously drained and relieved of stress.

Lise felt quite different. Here was a real man. A gentleman.

Recovering, Lise took hold of Pierre and gently massaged him to a climax, enthralled by his facial expressions. She thought that this loving really was quite pleasurable after all. Lise thought of Jacques' remark about wasted years. It was nice to be with someone who really loved you. She was sure of Pierre's love for her.

"My darling," he had whispered when she was stroking him, "only when you want to make love will we do it. Not before. You will know when my darling, and then it will be the moment."

Pierre was patient. Twelve nights later Lise intimated he should take her. Gentleness itself, Pierre slowly entered her with cautious tenderness. Lise had built up a confidence in her man, accepting him as her lover, forcing the pounding dread that beat in her head to dispel. The warmth of his loving tenderness soon melted her fear as they lay quite motionless for a time, absorbed in each other, kissing, reassuring, revelling in their union and eventually slowly moving in rhythm, breathing faster and more heavily with each stroke, their minds as one in a blissful retreat of pleasure and love.

The monkey was off her back at last. They made passionate love.

It was a good marriage, acceptance there that they could not have children. They were happy together but as in most affairs of the heart, one party loves whilst the other allows the other party to love them. Lise never experienced that earth-shattering, mind-bending, crazy ritual of being hopelessly in love. That was for Pierre, who would have died for her.

Lise respected him, liked him enormously, but never truly fell in love with him.

Chapter 36

MAY 1978:

MONTE CARLO

L ise revelled in motor racing. Invited to see the 1978 Grande Prix at Monte Carlo, she accepted with alacrity. Monsieur Duval, her Directeur, wielded a lot of influence.

"You'll have an opportunity to meet some of the racing drivers this evening after we have watched them practise. See who managed pole position." The reception was formal, although relaxed.

"Remember that red Ferrari you spotted? Seven? Well here's the driver. Rex, meet my protege, Lise Lavalle. She speaks fluent English, old boy! Lise, meet Rex Trent." Duval smiled at the man.

Rex had a grip like a vice as he grasped her fragile hand in sincere greeting. He couldn't keep his eyes off the apparition.

"Very pleased to meet you. Afraid my French is not too good. Find these receptions more taxing than the race," he smiled. His blue eyes held Lise's attention. They wouldn't leave her, penetrating like laser beams into her very soul. She felt weak at the knees, as if the handsome man was reading her like a teleprompt. With conscious effort she tore away her eyes to gaze at the babbling gathering around them.

"Have you been racing long?" she responded weakly, for some reason feeling trapped and embarrassed under his rapturous scrutiny. She had no reason to be, delightfully dressed as she was in a single-breasted linen jacket in lemon with white stripes and matching skirt, with round earrings her only adornment. The Englishman's strong face and tousled short blonde hair conveyed individualism and strength of character.

"Started as a youngster actually. Used to go to Mallory Park to watch motorcycles; then later on to Brands Hatch for cars. Got involved and found a sponsor eventually, so here I am after a long battle from my early days in Nottingham."

"Nottingham! My mother was born there!" burst out Lise. "She taught at the University, which is where she met my father. What did your folks do?" she enquired, advancing towards him unconsciously.

"Hosiery. Dad had mills in Beeston and Mansfield. Stockings are all the rage these days. The only way I was able to get into racing was with an independent income, and I am grateful to my father for making it possible for me to go for the life I enjoy."

Lise felt pleased for him. Rex seemed so – she couldn't find the word… honest, to her. The boy next door syndrome. Rex did something to her metabolism; disturbed her like no other man had done before. At the racing next day, Lise felt her whole being stretched out, urging this man to win. From her vantage point near the Casino, her heart missed a beat if he appeared a few seconds late from the normal hair-raising one-and-a-half minute circuit. The toll on cars in the shorter 78-lap race was horrendous, with only a third crossing the finishing line. Rex came in fifth. Even if he had won she could not have had more admiration for him. She trembled with joy.

'This is crazy', she told herself, 'but I must see him'.

"You were magnificent! What a dangerous circuit. The tunnel frightens me to death," she gasped like a teenager to a pop idol, eyes as big as saucers.

"Wow! Slow down now. I didn't do that well. But I survived. I suppose that's something." Rex looked at her and with riveting candour whispered, "You are pretty magnificent yourself."

The love in his eyes was unmistakable; his soul transparent. Lise blushed. She felt an inescapable pull into his orbit. He wanted her; the chemistry was there. Nothing ugly, only genuine desire for her. That first look, that long 45-second, seemingly 45-minute look, had them both hooked. Rex had fallen in love with her.

During the season Lise found herself attending most European Grand Prix race venues to see her 'hero'. Pierre had no inkling of her underlying motive in watching the events. Self-deception allowed Lise to suppress any of the guilt she felt. She was determined to keep her emotions under control by not allowing any meaningful relationship to develop, but she secretly enjoyed his adoration. Rex Trent had made up his mind that he would pursue Lise at every opportunity, married or not.

Lise was frank. "I can never leave Pierre. That would destroy him. I could never do that. I know I am attracted to you," she at last admitted. "You've made your feelings for me very clear, Rex. It would kill Pierre if I left him. I couldn't do that. Please understand. We can still be friends can't we?"

"Of course," he accepted reluctantly. There was no one else for him. Perhaps a few distractions 'to slake the urges', but nothing serious. Rex had set his sights on Lise. He longed to touch the delicate perfection of her cheeks, run his fingers through her gorgeous hair. Her bewitching eyes had captured his imagination and he longed to kiss those exquisite lips.

One day.

Chapter 37

1979:

PARIS

"I don't want to talk about it. Forget it! Understand? Forget it." Lise would never discuss the rape incident with anyone and the matter was studiously avoided. She went through a transition period after speaking to Jacques and seemed more settled. Lise was determined to make her marriage work. It was successful in the beginning, but she never truly loved Pierre. She owed him a lot, was fond of him, but that was the full extent of her affection for him. True love evaded her.

Two years had passed happily enough although her work came first. Then unhappily she felt her initial enthusiasm wane. They avoided fights but there were no fireworks either, their relationship becoming rather strained and brittle. When Pierre made advances for conjugal bliss, Lise submitted more as a duty than a commitment to mutual satisfaction. Her increasingly frequent excuses became tiresome for Pierre, who found sleeping next to such a beauty and having no physical contact frustrating. Pierre did not force the issue, knowing such action could be disastrous for their relationship. He remained patient.

Eventually he invited Jacques to stay, and found an opportunity to explain their problem. Jacques drew Lise aside. "I never wanted to suggest this before, but I believe you have a deep-seated problem relating to the rape experience. My advice is for you and Pierre to try and find those bastards. Even if you fail, I'm convinced that sharing what has become a major problem in your life will be good for your marriage. I think you have issues that need to be sorted out in order for you to have some peace. I have always been your friend. Please listen to me."

His advice was like a catalyst. The purpose acted as a bond and they tackled the situation as a team. They both felt happier with each other.

Pierre suggested a methodical approach, so their first step was to drive to the spot where Lise had accepted the lift from her molesters.

"Sit in the back seat and try to visualise where you went that day. Blindfold yourself."

Pierre drove too slowly the first time, wandering aimlessly. He turned back.

"You told me the second Frenchman, 'F 2' had said, 'Seventeen kilometres from our turning and right', is that correct? Well his turning could be before or after your pick-up point."

"No. It must be after. I'll tell you why. He became nervous that they might turn in on the way. It was the way he said it. 'We can't go to my place'. Full of anxiety."

Pierre had an idea. "Let's find a right turn off the Chalons road 17 kilometres from another road. See how many there are." He studied the map. "Seventeen kilometres from Champaubert there is a road crossing to the right just before Bergeres, leading to Fere-Champenoise. It looks about 15 kilometres from the road. Should we try?"

"Why not? At the turn off I'll put on the blindfold and count."

At Fere-Champenoise, Lise had counted to 510. She took off the blindfold. "How fast were we going?"

"One hundred – 80 is like crawling. I think it must be further on, you know. But which way? That's the problem. Let's try Connantre, about six kilometres further. Blindfold on! Count!" Lise counted to 750 by the time they reached the village.

"Let's look around," suggested Pierre as they slowly motored through. They turned round and came back, when they noticed a pension.

"Could be! Their Mercedes drove over some gravel behind the building. It was difficult to walk on, I remember."

Pierre's car tyres crunched on gravel in the backyard. When he rang the bell a middle-aged shrew in a pinafore answered the door. He smelt cabbage.

"Want a room?" she asked, sniffing with a cold.

"No, but I would like a word with you. Can I come in?" Reluctantly she let him in.

"Monsieur. What is it? This is a respectable house you know!"

"I am sure it is. I am not from the police. But I have a matter I am anxious to clear up. I have to ask you if you remember an incident a long time ago in the summer of 1966 in June, the day the schools closed up at term-end. Three men came here Madam, to this pension. They brought a young girl with them. A Frenchman, a Parisian, paid you two weeks rent for a few hours. Perhaps you remember that, do you?"

"Who are you?" The woman was clearly disturbed. "What do you want with me? I run a proper house, I do!"

"Calm down Madam. All I want to know is if this was the case. You have done nothing wrong. If he leaves early, why should you worry? Eh?"

The old bag relaxed, good argument. She became more helpful.

"Yes. It is true. A man came in a black Mercedes. A big car. I didn't see the others," she lied. Why say she peeped up the stairs? "He was about 40, dark hair and had a smart black blazer on."

"Yes, that's him. Fits her description. So at last I know where it happened."

"What happened?" She was anxious now.

"The girl was molested. Raped. Repeatedly. Did you hear anything?"

"No," she lied again. Cries of lovemaking were commonplace in the establishment. That's why they came this far out.

"If you can help me, I'll see no charges are brought against you. Will you cooperate?"

"If I can, Monsieur." She was shaking. Others came here with young girls, mistresses, lovers. She didn't want a local scandal. Her income was at stake.

"Do you know of an old Jew's wine farm somewhere off the Chalons road? It's rented out now I understand. I know it's not much to go on, but does it mean anything?"

"Well the Nazis dispossessed the Jews during Occupation. There must have been a number of Jewish vignerons. There was a Mannie Gaston, of Herod's nation," wrinkling her nose in disdain for such a heritage, "who had a place near Montmort before the war. I don't know what happened to him. My mother lived at Viney. That's why I know."

"Thank you. You have been a help to me. Listen carefully. Do not let anyone be aware that I have spoken to you; agree? I will keep quiet too." She nodded, relieved. She would keep very quiet. Pierre put two large notes in her palm which made her smile for the first time.

Tracing back they found the turning to Montmort and drove slowly around. The main estate was 'La Verite', where they saw a sign with an invitation to visit the cellars and War Museum. They decided to stop.

"Just in case, stay in the car out of sight. I will take a look and ask a few questions." Pierre was back in 10 minutes.

"Closed up. It's too late today. Let's go to Epernay; see the Land Registry." They found nothing entered for Gaston. They had no success at Reims either.

"They've never heard of a Mannie Gaston and the clerk tells me that he has no deeds registered in his name. Funny. That old bag seemed so sure. We'll come back again. As for now, it's back to Paris. I'll try the Central Land Registry."

*****

Pierre completed a Deeds Office search application in the Paris Registry. The elderly senior clerk condescended to acknowledge him.

"I'm trying to trace a Jew who owned land in Montmort. Name of Gaston." Pierre began.

Anti-semitic disdain was glaringly obvious, judging by his immediate reaction. Pierre went on. Disdain for disdain. "I found an estate, 'La Verite'. I have reason to believe Gaston's land was near there."

"This land here," he pointed at the grid map, "there, 1 200 hectares. Name of Dupont. No record of change since '29. No new registration. Can't help you further. Certainly no Gaston," glaring over his glasses for the final touch. Emile Laconte kept his voice under control although the mention of 'La Verite' had immediately set his mind racing. His wartime collaborator friend Raoul Montpelier had his friend Henri staying there. Who was this man? He would find out.

"So perhaps Gaston was in another village. Things changed a lot during the war. I will take Monsieur's name and contact address and number. If I find anything I can let you know."

"Lavalle. Pierre. Doctor. My card. If you find anything at all, it would help me."

"In what way Monsieur?" trying not to seem too anxious to know.

"To trace a property there, that's all. Not for me, but to establish a landmark in the village."

"Oh, I see!" he smiled weakly. "Bon soir."

*****

"Raoul. Emile here! Think you should know something. A Doctor Pierre Lavalle, yes Lavalle, been here asking about property in Montmort – wine estate of some cursed Jew. Gaston, he said the name was. He mentioned 'La Verite', your pal's place. Thought you should hear that he's been poking about in the Registry. No. Not at all, a pleasure. Yes, next time. A drink? Yes, bye." He was smiling. He knew Raoul would fix him up with a nice girl if the information was of any importance.

Being a good friend. Raoul immediately telephoned Henri. "Suggest you get here quick Henri. We'll deal with this bastard. I have a sneaking suspicion this guy is on to something not good for us! Come to Paris! Quickly!"

"I'll be there tomorrow morning."

*****

"So Lise, I've still had no luck with the Gaston property. I think the old woman got it all wrong. I'm on night duty. See you tomorrow." He kissed her goodbye, and she smiled sweetly.

A young Belgian girl was brought into Pierre's office at the hospital at 13h00 in the morning.

"This girl is asking to stay here, Doctor. Has no address. What do we do?" the admission nurse asked, sweeping hair from her face, obviously flustered by the unusual request.

"Let me speak to her. You go nurse. Thank you." Looking at the youngster, "Sit down. What is your name?"

"Hilaire, Monsieur," near to tears.

"Now what can we do for you, young lady?"

"I want to stay here. I've run away from a brothel."

"You have WHAT?" Pierre couldn't believe his ears. She was barely 16, such a pathetic waif. "Where is the place?" The young Belgian described offices in Montmort fronting as a theatrical agency. Behind the facade was a very active brothel.

"Me, a French girl from Marseille and a Yugoslav girl my age who can't speak much French, have been kept there for six months. The woman didn't lock the back door this evening and I ran away. I ran and ran. I saw the hospital and came in. Please don't send me back," she pleaded.

"No, Hilaire. First a nice bath and then I'll examine you. Put you to bed. We'll get the police on this tomorrow. The woman forces you to have sex with men, correct?"

"Oh yes. We know what to do, or we get smacked. She brings men who want young girls. Pay a lot of money they tell us."

Pierre was disgusted. "Can you describe any of the men?"

"Well, men come every day. Different men. One is a regular with me. An old guy. But I remember last week three men came together. Two Frenchmen and a German who took me." Hilaire described the three men, who sounded very similar to those who had raped Lise. His heart pounded.

"Tell me more about these men. What did they say to you?"

"Madame put us in a special back salon with posh furniture and snacks and drinks on a sideboard. They made us take our clothes off and walk round so they could look at us. Then we sat on their knees and fed them bits to eat. They got undressed and we played with them; all kinds of things, giving them drinks and that. After that they took us on the beds. They talked to us too. A French chap talked about paintings; canvases he called them."

Stunned, Pierre remembered Lise, and her mention of an art dealer. It seemed too good to be true.

"Do you know any names?"

Her reply brought a sardonic smile to his face.

"Napoleon, Bismarck and Rasputin."

'Cautious… and well they might be', he thought.

"One last thing. Not pleasant to ask, but it is important. The Frenchman who you said had a dark complexion; has he a long, shall we call it, instrument?"

"Yes. That's right! He hurt the Yugo. She cried."

"Thank you. Now, a nice bath for you, Hilaire."

*****

Pierre knew only a few art dealers. The subject did not interest him. But he did remember a display in the window of one exclusive salon near the Eiffel Tower: you couldn't miss it. He drove there, deciding to speak to the police later. Outside the delightful salon, with RAOUL MONTPELIER gilded on the exterior, he saw an ex-army beggar with one leg, on crutches.

"Good day to you. If this is your usual pitch, can you tell me anything about the owner of this shop? I've been recommended to a place, but I can't be sure if this is the correct shop," he informed the beggar, handing over a bank note. The old soldier looked awry at him.

"He's alright is the Governor. Gives me a few francs to keep me going. Clothes too. Gave me this blazer some time ago. Got a good business he has." Pierre looked at the black barathea blazer and as he glanced at the row of medals displayed on the pocket, his eye caught sight of a hole where a button had been pulled out of the cloth, spoiling the garment. This was it! Confirmation; descriptions all fitted.

"Merci beaucoup!" he replied hastily, slipping his informer another 10 francs. In a rush he telephoned Lise. "I think I've found the owner of your button! Near the Eiffel Tower. Tell you later!"

Pierre's rage got the better of his intelligence; commonsense would have been to regroup and bring resources. Inform the police at least. Instead Pierre barged into the shop full of fire.

"I want to see Montpelier!"

The saleslady, shocked by his approach, disappeared and returned. "Come this way Monsieur, sil vous plais." Pierre went into the back office of the palatial display salons.

"My name is Lavalle," he barked, glaring at Raoul, who jumped. He had expected that he would have had to track this man down instead. Here he was in person.

"Mais oui Monsieur! What can I do for you?" regaining his composure.

"I have unearthed your dirty little scheme with children for one thing! More important to me, I am about to take you apart – you and your filthy colleagues, for the RAPE of my wife! I have all the proof I need to nail the three of you rats. It will be a pleasure, you BASTARDS!!! Remember the Chalons road in June '66? You are a bunch of swine!"

The vision flooded back into Raoul's mind.

"Rather unfortunate that! It was not a good idea! Sorry about the girl; now your wife obviously. Perhaps we can make some form of… compensation, even at this late stage? Cash restitution?" Raoul said it, but in no way did he mean it, moving towards the cocktail cabinet.

"NO. Gutter swine like you must be exposed!" Pierre spat out.

"Come. Have a drink! Let's talk it over," Raoul appeared to wheedle his point with the doctor, moving into his plan.

"NO! I don't want a drink with scum like you!"

"Mind if I do?"

"What the hell," retorted Pierre, turning away in annoyed defiance, avoiding the invitation with hostility. Precisely what Raoul had anticipated as, grasping a heavy glass decanter by the neck he brought it down with a vicious crash on Pierre's head, knocking him senseless.

Raoul then dragged him down cellar steps into his strong-room. He rushed inside to check the one ventilation panel was in an open position, then slammed the door and locked it. Picking up a metal canister like a scuba diver's bottle from behind a small safe, he ran hastily upstairs to the fan motor room and opened the panel of the air chute supplying the safe below. Cautiously he arranged the canister inside the air chute, connected the nozzle to a rubber hose, and then dropped the other end of the tubing down to the safe's air inlet. Satisfied, he turned the tap, releasing a quiet hiss as Zyklon gas flowed through the hose. He then quickly slammed the chute panel closed and turned the air pump on again, knowing any surplus gas would pass harmlessly into the open air above Paris. Tonight he would see what effect Zyklon gas had on the Jews in the gas chambers. The S.S. Colonel had told him that a canister might come in very handy one day, as it left no marks.

When Henri arrived at lunchtime Raoul quietly related the events. "So now we have a body to get rid of this evening. That bastard had us completely! I had to do it!! He would have nailed us for that girl we screwed near your place. Remember? What – some 12 years ago! He also found out about Madame Roget's place. Anyway, I've gassed him. No gunshot, bullet wound and slug to trace. Gave him a crack on the head with a decanter, but that could be anything; a fall. We'll dump him in the Seine later. Fake it like a suicide. I just had to get rid of him," throwing his hands up in Gallic fashion to secure the seal of approval from his accomplice.

"Quite so. Quick thinking," Henri twitched nervously.

"We'll soon get rid of his body. Better in the river I agree than some forest.

Messy that. In the river it could look like suicide."

Henri agreed, twitching again.

Raoul reversed the air intake for an hour, then opened the safe. The corpse lay in a grotesquely twisted position.

"He must have come round before the gas killed him," observed Raoul. "Look, his fingers have been clawing at the door before he eventually went under. Ghastly sight isn't it?" he commented, smiling cruelly at his friend.

They wrapped the body in a Persian rug, then quietly went out and loaded it into the boot of the Citroen. They set off in the late evening. As Paris teems by day and night, they had to wait for a safe moment to heave the body into the inky waters. It splashed momentarily, then disappeared. They stole away like thieves in the night.

"Let's have a drink," suggested the Parisian, slipping behind the wheel.

Chapter 38

1979:

PARIS

"Pulled him out of the Seine they did!"

Hilaire was shaken when she heard about Doctor Lavalle. She had been relying on him.

"Know him?" quizzed the plump Matron.

"Not well Ma'am, but he was kind to me at the hospital." There were tears in the girl's eyes.

"A tragedy. Could I meet her? Perhaps I can talk nicely to her." The waif's sincerity was touching.

"I'm sure we can arrange that," a chubby hand on her shoulder reassured her.

Hilaire related her escape story to Lise. "I told Doctor about the three men who visited Madam Roget's together. Sounded like the men who attacked you, he said. Wanted names, but I didn't know them."

Lise's face was distraught. "I'd dearly like to find out their names. Think that Roget woman would know? I'd like to fix the swine!"

"Did your husband tell you about me… and the men, before he…. " her voice trailed off.

"No, but he called and said he'd found the owner of the button! I tore it off the Frenchman's blazer. All three raped me, you know." Lise paused. "Pierre was murdered. I'm convinced of it! He'd NEVER commit suicide! They must have been responsible. Perhaps Pierre found out too much," she said with conviction.

"If you have nowhere to go you can stay with me. The Lavalle family did the same for me. They were very good to me. They even let me stay with them and brought me up. I married Pierre years later," Lise explained.

"Oh thank you Ma'am, you are so kind. I'd like to help you find those names, but I'll never go back to Madam Roget's place!" There was stark terror in her grey eyes.

"Fortunately I have a good friend I can rely on to help. I'll ask Rex to listen to your story. Pierre died before talking to the Police."

Rex called at the inn Pierre had located, where the theatrical receptionist created enough diversion and delay for the Roget establishment to hastily assume an air of respectability. Madam appeared, believing Rex to be from the Prefecture. He perceived apprehension in her defiant face.

"I'll come to the point. I have enough information on you to put you away Madam. However I will trace information and leave you alone." Rex looked the middle-aged woman straight in the eyes. There was an understanding. She would weigh up his proposition.

"What do you want to know?" she ventured.

"Names! The names of the three men who come and visit you together for young girls. Don't deny it! I've got proof. It's up to you... otherwise I've got information to close you down. I've nothing to lose. You on the other hand... " shrugging his shoulders.

Madam Roget saw her chance of a compromise. "Do I get off the hook if I tell you that I know only one? He brings the others. I don't ask questions. They all lie anyway."

"Better than nothing. Well?" lifting his chin.

"His name's Montpelier."

"Telephone number? Address?"

"Don't be mad!" she scoffed, "do you think anyone would give me their details! He always phones first when he wants something." She touched her bun with her fingers, bosom thrust forward. If nothing else, she was a professional through and through.

"What does he do? Profession?" His eyes bored through her.

"I think he's in art, or keen on it. He commented on my salon canvases. Promised to donate one. I have yet to see it," as an afterthought.

"Are they coming again soon?"

"He hasn't been in touch recently. No."

"Where do they stay in Paris?"

"I really don't know." She was lying. Rex sensed it.

"Well in that case we'll call it..."

"The Ritz," she blurted out.

"That's better. Alright – I'll keep my side of the bargain, but kidnapping young kids carries dire penalties. Think about it."

Madam Roget was visibly shaken by the intruder's knowledge. As the door closed behind him, she telephoned Raoul Montpelier. "Don't come here again! There's a man been here asking questions. I told him nothing. If you want something I'll send to a hotel. Anywhere, even the Ritz, but not here!"

Rex Trent was not without his connections. At the Ritz he was able to examine the hotel registers over some years. A laborious process but he picked up a pattern where the names of two people appeared together on the same night at approximately three monthly intervals. H. Saint-Laurent and H. Schmidt. Rex jotted down their addresses. A big note to the commissionaire had their descriptions. They fitted.

'Got you, you bastards,' he whispered to himself. 'Now for some detailed research'.

Rex asked Lise to tell him everything she had learned from her research with Pierre, including their rape scene visit to the pension. Rex disregarded any promises given by gentle Pierre to the old shrew.

"I'm after those three bastards and when I do find them and identify them, you will be subpoenaed to testify they came here."

"But the man said if I told him, he would leave me out of it. My reputation, Monsieur. My business… "

"Tough on you, old bag! Time to start paying for your ill-gotten gains, Madame Farrasse. Think! You could be famous."

The old witch was clearly very disturbed.

"Don't run away! I'll find you. Or the police will. See you again someday," he took his leave with a mocking salute.

She slammed the door behind him and was uncharacteristically rude to a client who settled his bill a few minutes later, his flushed secretary clinging to him.

'Now to find them', thought Rex as he drove away.

Chapter 39

NOVEMBER 1980, SUNDAY 23

Sombre-faced television newsreaders throughout the world described the horrific disaster of that day in southern Italy. "Human tragedy of monstrous proportions has occurred today following a gigantic earthquake in southern Italy."

Observers described the disaster as the work of the Devil, not an act of God.

"For two terrifying minutes land was pulled like a carpet from under millions of Italians as eastern Italy was jerked towards Yugoslavia. Seventeen villages have been completely devastated by the epic earthquake. Reports coming in estimate 5 000 people have lost their lives in a hideous cauldron of destruction. Our reporter at the scene described the horror of crushed, mangled, screaming people, some buried alive under falling buildings. Thousands have suffered hideous injuries and disfigurement. Official estimates estimate that about 400 000 people have been left homeless, and that survivors are fleeing to Naples for refuge and a new beginning. Many are destitute; for them it will be a struggle for existence.

"The Herculean task of rescue units has been hindered by fallen rubble and huge cracks in roads have cut off water supplies. Communications are virtually non-existent. Helicopters are flying in to render assistance, and four wheel drive vehicles are being commandeered by the authorities. The whole world feels compassion for the terrible suffering of these villagers. Disaster fund organisations are doing splendid practical relief work to alleviate their suffering..."

The tragedy filled television screens for days.

To avert the possibility of a second such appalling disaster and loss of human life, relevant authorities decided that an urgent examination was vital to determine the cause of the tragic quake and try to ascertain whether any further activity was imminent. Steps had been taken in America to monitor the San Andreas Fault by seismographic measurement in order to warn San Francisco of the threat of annihilation by earthquake. There was concern for a possible recurrence at Naples, as it was situated near the centre of the world's most hazardous volcanic areas on earth – the Phlegraean Fields. Urgent investigation was deemed imperative to avoid catastrophic loss of life in that teeming city of some one and a quarter million inhabitants.

The Grande Prix racing season was over. Rex Trent had a code to live by. 'The best way to predict the future is to create it'.

Determined that Lise would be his woman one day, Rex talked his wealthy father into leading the sponsorship of a group of businessmen to assist in the investigation of the causes of the Italian disaster. The event had made newspaper and newsreel headlines throughout the world with television coverage portraying the event. What better time for major companies to get advertising exposure through their combined talents in the hope of averting a second dreadful recurrence? With studied self interest Rex got them to agree and cobbled together the required support, promising indirect advertising whilst television crews covered the expedition.

"So you see Lise, we can offer the financial resources whilst you and the Institute have the skills. Will they accept our contribution?" He was confident the offer would not be refused. The Institute promoted Lise to head the scientific investigation and offered the valuable assistance of. seismographic equipment and a submersible vessel.

At Monte Carlo, Rex made enquiries at a ship broker for a large vessel to be hired at short notice, explaining the purpose of the voyage. The bearded suntanned seafarer stubbed out his Gauloise cigarette, pointing at his list with a tobacco stained index finger. He stopped at one name. "'Le Champagne' is a splendid yacht but still out on contract. There's this 'Meridian'; 120 metres. It is moored in the harbour. There is a captain and skeleton crew on board. It has just come in from the Greek Islands. Two months you want her, right?"

"That's right. It sounds fine. Can we go and see her?"

"Certainly. Follow me."

They climbed into a motorboat and set off through the moorings. Rex looked up and saw 'Le Champagne'. The glistening white yacht was indeed magnificent.

"Yeah! That's the yacht I mentioned. Owner is Saint-Laurent, a multi-millionaire in the champagne industry. He hired it out to some friends."

They reached 'Meridian', an impressive vessel. Rex climbed the companion way to be greeted by Captain Tanriant.

"Welcome on board." They shook hands.

"Thank you. We need a boat to sail to Naples. We are doing some scientific surveys; diving to examine the ocean floor for movements. We will be taking diving equipment, scientific instruments and a submersible too. Can you handle that?"

"No problem. We have davits port and starboard, which we used previously when searching wrecks. No problem, really. How many in your party?"

"Ten. Can you accommodate them?"

"Certainly. When would you want to sail? We have supplies except for fresh vegetables and water, and can be ready at 24 hours notice."

"Splendid. It looks like a fine boat. I will negotiate with the owners for sailing in maybe two weeks. You will hear from Monsieur Guirlande in due course," he concluded, nodding at the agent.

They returned to shore and made arrangements.

Chapter 40

DECEMBER 1980:

ON BOARD 'MERIDIAN'

Lise had been badly shaken when Pierre was murdered in 1979. Despite the official police theory of suicide she was convinced he had been murdered. By whom she did not know: there had been no proof, no evidence. Just his cryptic telephone conversation, then his drowned body washed up in the Seine.

For more than a year Lise was prone to momentary lapses of melancholy solitude and self-recrimination. His last words had meant nothing to her. Rex was going to do his best to release her from this self-appointed prison sentence of guilt. In her tortuous state he knew there was limited prospect of switching her emotions in his favour. The chains had to be broken and he slowly worked on her.

"A sense of guilt won't bring Pierre back. You must go on with your life. He would want that. It has been a shock, but brooding won't help, Lise." He offered practical comforting truths.

"Perhaps you're right, Rex. I can't help thinking though that a good man would be alive today but for me."

"Now that is nonsense Lise! Pierre did what was right at the time. You must close that chapter. We've got a tremendous challenge. Concentrate on that."

Lise nodded at this gentle loving man's words. She knew he adored her, and that he was thinking of her, not himself.

Two hectic weeks of preparation for the expedition helped to dispel her erratic moods of depression.

The 'Meridian' ploughed through calm moonlit seas, destined for Naples. Lise and Rex sat in deep relaxing chairs, glasses of cognac in their hands. The tiny ship's lounge was comfortable and intimate. Rex had a serious expression on his face when he spoke.

"We have been rushing about setting up this voyage, but for the life of me I don't know what we will be looking for in the sea. Tell me about it. I'd feel less dumb if I knew what was going on." Rex smiled at her. "What makes earthquakes, landfalls and so on."

"Sure Rex, it would be a pleasure," responded Lise, eyes sparkling. This was her subject. "We'll start at the beginning. Think of the world as an egg. The core, intensely hot, is the yolk, 3 500 kilometres across; the egg shell is the Earth's crust, 50 kilometres thick, with the white of the egg representing the mantle 3 000 kilometres to the core. Got it?"

"I'm with you, go on."

"Let me first explain our understanding of the Mediterranean, which in Latin means 'sea in the middle of the land,' by the way. It has been moulded by the vice-like pressure of colliding continents. It consists of a chain of basins, 3 750 kilometres in length, and 1 100 kilometres at its maximum width. It has fascinating formations created by the forces of plate tectonics. Geologists believe that about 200 million years ago a single land mass was perched above the Earth's molten interior. This began to split up into continental plates. Between the Eurasian and African plates was a vast sea called Tethys. Then Africa shunted north and the plates closed like jaws, enclosing the ancient Tethys Sea, part of which remains today as the Black Sea, and a new sea developed which eventually became the Mediterranean. More pressure was applied in continental plate shift or drift as the jaws tightened even more. There was nowhere for the African plate to go except for underneath the Eurasian plate. As it began submerging pieces split away from North Africa. One chunk became Italy, which was jammed into Europe, causing the Alps to emerge. As the plates continued to collide in continental drift, both Corsica and Sardinia were pulled away from France and Spain. These two continents are still colliding head on in the western Mediterranean."

Pausing, Lise took a sip of her cognac.

"Along the plate boundaries near Sicily, a cluster of volcanoes grew. You know I'm sure of Stromboli off the toe of Italy, Vulcano just north of Sicily and Etna at the eastern end of Sicily. These are fed from lava deep within the Earth. These plates continue to jostle each other and when this happens, Italy is rocked by earthquakes. During the Mediterranean evolution, geologists believe a connection to the Indian Ocean was cut off and Europe and Africa ground together at Gibraltar. Core samples have been taken from the seabed showing salt deposits two kilometres thick. This means that about six million years ago all aquatic life became extinct. Coastal rivers cut deep gorges as they plunged towards the basin bottom. Fossils retrieved show a return of marine creatures half a million years later. It was perhaps an earthquake or maybe the Atlantic rising which breached the dam at Gibraltar. It today took about a century for the Med as we know it today to fill up with flood waters."

"Incredible! Tell me, what makes a volcano erupt?"

"Any idea?" she was smiling at him.

"Not really. Explosion underground I suppose."

"A volcano probably begins as a crack in the Earth's crust. The cracking is caused by shifting white-hot putty-like rocks which have melted, forming a molten mass 30 to 50 kilometres beneath the Earth's surface called magma. There is another force, gas, made from steam formed by contact of water with the super heated magma. We still don't know where the water comes from – it is one of the unsolved problems of volcanology. It probably seeps down from the Earth's surface. Water is the trigger, the active agent of volcanic eruption. When it meets magma, steam expands 1 000 times, forcing the gas-charged magma upwards, through vents or chimneys to the surface. It can be a slow process, not always violent. What happens is this. In a chimney for example, some magma cools down after a period of activity and sets into a hard mass. It forms a plug, like an oversized cannon ball jammed in a cannon's barrel. The gas force builds up and up until it eventually overcomes the plug's resistance and explodes in volcanic eruption. Once open, the magma flies out until all the force is spent and it settles down again – and so on in an active volcano."

"Amazing! And Vesuvius? Is that still active?"

"Vesuvius has a history as a killer. The most infamous eruption was in 79AD, at lunch-time on August 24 to be exact. It blew an H-bomb like mushroom cloud of cinders and ash over Pompeii, covering it with showers of dust and pumice rocks, in some places 10 metres deep and more. It blew again in 473, then in 1631 and in 1906, each time erupting with catastrophic violence, killing the farmers and vine growers who inhabited its slopes. You would think they would learn from history, but they continue to risk their lives. Vesuvius also poured out gentle lava streams which made the soil rich and fertile, drawing farmers to the slopes. Diabolical really. The last eruption was in 1944; mercifully not catastrophic this time. So what we're looking for is evidence of cracks in the seabed where there may be clues that blobs of magma oozed through. If we find some we can date test how recent this was, and assume that water seeped into the system. Too much would send the area into convulsions. Great plates of land can start to skid, creating an earthquake as it heaves up to compensate for the massive force build-up. Like a giant taking a deep breath! Pozzuoli could be our clue'."

"Where?"

"It is a town 10 kilometres west of Naples in the Gulf of Pozzuoli, near the centre of the world's most hazardous volcanic areas. These go by the name of the Phlegraean Fields. Thirty-six thousand years ago there was a huge explosion which blew open a caldera 12 kilometres across. Then 17 000 years ago there was another explosion which filled in most of the Gulf, depositing a layer of ash. Naples was built on this.

"The town of Pozzuoli is rising. Between 1969 and 1972 it rose two metres. It's going up and. down actually, which indicates magma is accumulating again. Like a volcanic trampoline. The loading dock is now 20 metres from the water's edge! Fishermen at one time dragged their boats up there, but in 1969 the Earth started rising. Apparently it happened once before in 1538, just before a new volcano erupted. The accumulating magma could be the indicator for an explosion which could bury Naples under 100 metres of ash. That, my dear Rex, is what it is all about," Lise grinned at him again.

"Frightening! Incredible but frightening." Rex looked steadily at her; intensely. "I do admire you. You are very clever, Lise." Rex put out his hand to take her slim fingers in his. Lise felt an electric shock run through her at his touch. A gentle smile showed her appreciation of his comment. Her thumb on his knuckles told it all.

Rex gently pulled her up from her chair. "Let's take a stroll on the deck. It's a lovely evening." He arranged her fluffy woollen cardigan on her shoulders.

"Okay. I hope it's not too cold and windy," she said, smiling her thanks.

They stood together, staring at the play of silver moonlight dancing on the water; the sea parting and merging in a turbulent path behind the boat. Rex stood closely behind Lise at the rail, hoping to keep the chill away.

"The sea is beautiful, don't you think?" she breathed over her shoulder.

"Yes, but not nearly as beautiful as you." Rex turned her towards him, bent his head and kissed her. Lise's left hand slowly moved up to encircle his neck, followed by her right, then she kissed him fully, hungrily, on his mouth. Rex hugged her close, felt her soft breasts on his chest.

"Oh my darling, I love you so much," he murmured against her cheek.

It was the way he said it. Lise had heard the words from Pierre in an endless stream, but it was only now that these words had a magic all of their own. For the first time in her life Lise felt the true power of love. Muddled, confused, elated, ecstatic, her emotions spun out of control. Rex had been so gracious, so caring and understanding. When she had met him in Monte Carlo she had gone weak at the knees; that had been two years ago. Now she could not help herself. Lise wanted him; wanted to love him. To be loved.

"Hold me tight!" She was trembling. "I love you too, Rex. Yes, oh yes. I love you – my darling Rex." She kissed him, pulled him to her.

In Lise's cabin they undressed, eyes fixed on each other.

Lise slid between the sheets. "Take me, darling, take me," she commanded, eyes sparkling, lost in a whirl of loving confusion, at last experiencing the topsy turvy world of true love. With tender patience Rex lowered himself gently and slowly, forging a link between them as they clung to each other, merging in a bond of loving pleasure in their new world. Lise had found peace and love.

Chapter 41

NAPLES

The Italian authorities were very helpful to Lise. A meeting was organised in Naples where Lise met the five Italian volcanologists assigned to the task from the Academy of Sciences: two Frenchmen, a Yugoslavian expert and two Americans who had assisted with land research on this project. The team represented a formidable concentration of knowledge and experience on the subject of volcanic and earthquake research. The senior Italian professor spoke.

"Colleagues, our objective is to establish within reasonable doubt, any evidence to support the contention that further volcanic activities and earthquake tremors are imminent in the Naples area. Is a new volcano about to be reborn? We must first look at Pozzuoli. It was an ancient trading station in the Roman Empire. Archaeological finds tell us that wealthy members of the Italian aristocracy lived there. Since these times the market has been submerged by water. In 1972 we measured a rise of two metres over three years. Fishermen reported seeing bubbles rising from the sea floor. Minor volcanoes are still active in the 'Sulphur Earth' and it was not for nothing Vesuvius became the inspiration for Dante's Inferno."

He paused to smile at his audience.

"The last time, back in 1538, look at what happened. The earth rose 120 metres in four days. Are these the birth pangs of a new volcano? Since this earthquake the population of Pozzuoli has lived in tents. It is a ghost town at night. Few people dare to stay there. We discourage their presence until things stabilise. In Naples, 80 streets remain closed. We were forced to evacuate

100 000 people from condemned apartments, even evict tenants. Buildings were trussed by scaffolding extending over the streets. They probably remain like these, especially in the old Spanish Quarter. Thousands are homeless. The rise of Pozzuoli indicates magma is accumulating again. An eruption like the one 17 000 years ago could bury Naples. Signora, Gentlemen. If we are not prepared, a tragedy of enormous magnitude is possible. I would go so far as to say probable. We rely on your skills."

A senior American spoke. "Our land studies enabled us to establish a shock pattern. We have established a fault line along the drift."

A huge relief map model had been constructed which clearly demonstrated the effect of the recent earthquake and landslide. The American's pointer followed his clipped speech.

"From our findings the fault lines have been extrapolated into the sea which would indicate where we would expect to find some seabed evidence of distortion. This is where we anticipate Lise and her team of oceanographers to lend their talents."

Lise spread the IBCM, the International Bathymetric Chart of the Mediterranean, on the table, obtained by courtesy of the Intergovernmental Oceanographic Commission of UNESCO, Paris. She drew pencil lines and crosses.

"This is where I suggest we make our initial follow up on your seismographic readings. Follow a systematic search pattern of the seabed. We hope to find extraordinary distortion. Rather like looking for a needle in a haystack, but at least we know which haystack in the field!" They all smiled at her comment, nodding.

The line Lise had drawn extended through the Island of Ischia.

"As you see gentlemen, the chart gives a graphic representation of the sea floor." Her slim index finger traced her commentary.

"A continental shelf runs along the western seaboard of Italy about 20, in parts 30, kilometres wide to the edge. It then drops steeply into ragged valleys, producing the Tyrrhenian Basin. In the centre the seabed is deepest, about 3 400 metres. It is dotted with seamounts; Narchi, Vavilov, Poseidone, Cornaglia. Here is the Stromboli Canyon where the toe of Italy almost meets Sicily and the Cefalu Basin." Her finger moved south of Naples to Salerno. "The Salerno Valley is sculpted from the land mass forming the Gulf of Salerno, leaving Sorrento and the almost barren rocks of the Isle of Capri on the cliff edge, forming a southern bluff to the Bay of Naples. The Bay remains part of the continental shelf where the northern perimeter edge turns round the Isle of Ischia. Further north a basin is scalloped out following the land outline of the Gulf of Gaeta. In the centre of this relatively shallow basin is a huge knoll or plateau, much like a hub in a giant half cartwheel. Westwards the crust falls away in precipitous valleys to the basin floor in very deep waters. We will research inside a radius of 80 kilometres from Pozzuoli."

"Thank you Signora. Bill Straffen here from San Francisco will be with you to decipher their readings and make further interpretations if necessary. We all wish you the best of luck."

*****

"Young lady, I know you have a lot to think about, but before you get too involved I would like to take you to the most romantic place in the world; Sorrento!"

"Not now, I must get organised. Then I promise you can take me for dinner this evening. How's that?"

"Done!"

Overlooking the Bay of Sorrento, the moonlight was perfect, the wine delightful and the food delicious.

"Happy, love?" Rex asked.

"Yes darling. You're wonderful to me." She wrinkled her nose at him, "I love you, Rex Trent."

"Enough to let me down in your submersible?" He made a playful duck as if she was about to aim a plate at him.

"If you are good! We will see," she teased.

"Oh I'm good alright, even if I have to put my modesty behind me," he quipped, laughing at her, rocking back on his chair.

For the first time Lise could joke about these things. "You can say that again!" she responded, rolling her eyes wistfully, and blowing a kiss.

Rocking forwards, Rex put his large hand on hers. "1 love you," was all he said as they watched the silver threads of moonlight on the bay waters. It was a happiness all of their own.

Lise broke their temporary silence.

"The good people of Pozzuoli have a religious ceremony every year. The dry, solidified blood of their Saint Sebastiano, who encouraged the people to rebuild their town after a disaster long ago, is kept in a glass phial and exhibited by the priests in church. If the blood liquifies on the day, the population will be safe for the following year. It appears to work with uncanny accuracy. When the blood fails to liquify, disaster occurs."

"Well I know what makes my blood liquid – and racing!" Rex squeezed her hand as they got up to leave.

"You're naughty!" Lise nudged him, cuddling into his strong arms.

Chapter 42

POZZUOLI, UNDER WATER SEARCH

A series of repetitive tests conducted on the seabed kept the crew busy with routine duties and tired at day's end. They were using a Pisces submersible, a popular commercial machine used for oil exploration and seabed surveys. It could be used for observation only, having no lock-out facility for divers to leave and return. The Pisces, which has been used in experimental rescue operations from submarines, normally carries two men and can descend to depths of 2 000 feet. Lise had considered the lock-out advantages of the lighter Sea Link with an acrylic observation dome, but thought the 1 500 feet limitation might prove restrictive in these waters.

The divers scanned the seabed for bubbles reported by Pozzuoli fishermen, and hearts on board beat faster as intercom crackle came through from the black depths. Lise could visualise the young Frenchman, Paul, so tall to be cramped in there, typically Gallic in looks with his black five o'clock shadow and bedroom eyes, as his voice spluttered through the speaker.

"Magnifique! Zehr are zee bubbles… we 'ave bubbles. Eet looks like new magma. Oui! More, 'ow you say, blobs of zee new magma."

His partner announced, "Dropping… anchor to seabed. Releasing marker."

An orange balloon suddenly bobbed on the surface. A small boat was lowered and a gaff hook soon retrieved the balloon and trailing wire. A buoy was secured to the wire and once anchored to the seabed, the measuring devices could be lowered and recovered from the cable. These instruments would measure uplift of the sea floor and changing water temperatures. On shore a 24-hour watch would be maintained, monitoring information for deciphering their import.

After four days out, Rex went down for his first time.

"Well, what did you think of it down there?" asked Lise, thrilled when he reappeared from the metal pod, tired but happy.

"What a fascinating world! Incredible is the only way I can describe it. No wonder you are so taken by your research."

"Tomorrow we are going into the Gulf of Gaeta in line with Ischia. Did I tell you Ischia is itself an extinct volcano? Our plan is to see if we can find evidence of fault lines extending from the land fissures and parallel to the cracks we have just found in the seabed. If we can find similar activity, we will lower more instruments to get a fix on the magnitude of sea-floor shift and temperature variances. Then the professors can stay on vigil and get their seismographic data and make their decisions. Let's hope we are in luck."

The next day, in position off Ischia, the familiar rhythmic ping of sonar was ever present in their ears. After a time they didn't even notice it.

"It's strange Rex, but water is a difficult medium in which to transfer messages. Sound is the most effective: we have copied this method from dolphins and whales. Your Asdic people did a lot of research from 1925. Asdic stands for Anti-Submarine Devices Investigation Committee. By sending out sound waves, we wait for the bounce back and from the instrument we can reasonably accurately define depth by time delay."

Lise had just completed her explanation when a huge commotion broke out in the sonar room below. They went down to investigate. The answering ping echoed back with a distinctly different sound and speed.

"There's something down there – perhaps it is a wreck!"

"I hope it's not a mine." The bosun's pessimistic remark caused some consternation. "A lot went down here in the war you know, before the Italians gave in."

Cautiously 'Meridian' moved closer to the source. When they were almost right at their target, the ping and response were almost continuous. The captain called out, "I reckon we're on top of whatever it is. You people going under to see?"

"Yes," replied Lise. "Prepare to launch. This time I'm going down."

Natural light soon faded as the Pisces descended, its light probing the depths. The thought of a mine gave Rex goose pimples. On deck he was more nervous about Lise's safety than he was racing round the hair-raising bends of Monte Carlo. The mystery object could conceivably be a dreaded mine. If it was, and was still active, the submersible would be pulverised on contact.

Lise felt confident that it was not a mine; more likely a wreck, as they had picked it up some distance from the actual site. Was it on the deep sea bed or on the knoll or plateau in the Gulf of Gaeta? Her calculations made her suspect the second option, and she wondered if she would prove to be correct.

"We've bottomed," the pilot called to her. He put the machine in slow forward, peering in the limited light beam. After repeated turns, he could detect only gloom.

"Must be here somewhere, unless it's so covered over we can't see whatever it is." Cautiously he edged on; slowly. Nothing.

"Carry on," instructed Lise, "then come back round in a sweep." She felt perspiration trickle down from her armpits in the tension and sticky heat of their confined space.

The nose turned and the spotlight picked out a dark shape. It was unmistakable now. A bow shape; unusual but familiar all the same.

"Philippe! It's a submarine! Can you believe it!" Lise's voice was shrill with excitement. She rubbed the tiny porthole.

"Fantastic! I'll edge a bit closer," came the reply, breathless with their stunning discovery. Philippe cautiously closed the distance. They could see it more clearly now; pick out the conning tower precisely amidships.

"It doesn't look very big to me, Philippe. I always thought submarines were enormous things."

"That's what I was going to say. I'll go along slowly… start at the stern and see if we can guess the length."

"I would say not more than 40 metres, maybe less, what do you think, Philippe?"

"Right. Look Lise, see that bow shape… its pointed, with a broad chisel profile. Wonder whose it was? Italian, British, German, Yankee even. Look there! See that rip in the top decking. See that mangled metal? Looks like a depth charge perhaps, but it's localised… more like mine damage."

"I wish we had lock-out facility. Still we can use a Perry chamber and go down to investigate properly. Two hundred and seventeen metres," Lise recorded. "Is that a cross? On the tower and a U?"

"I'll drop an anchor off and send a balloon to the surface, otherwise we might not find it again," commented Philippe, initiating the necessary procedure.

"Philippe, won't they be excited on top!" breathed Lise. "We'll keep them in suspense, OK?"

He grinned back. "I was with National Geographic once. They have a team in Greece looking over a sunken galleon off shore. Don't you think we could borrow their Sea Link to have a look in the sub? It's not too deep. The National Geographic boys are great – I'm sure they'd help us."

"We'll see. Let's get up again."

On deck there was a buzz of excitement when the orange balloon bobbed out of the sea. When Lise emerged, Rex hugged her tight, much to everyone's amusement.

"So what's the big secret? Why didn't you tell us over the intercom?" he enquired, holding her slender arms in his big hands, grinning at her.

"Surprise, surprise!" She turned, looking and smiling at Philippe. "We have found the long-lost submarine of World War Two!"

Amid the babble of excited questions and speculation, Lise could not have appreciated the accuracy of her jest.

Chapter 43

DECEMBER 1980:

HEIDELBERG

"Guten abend Herr Beckenbauer;" the waiter greeted his regular obsequiously, placing a drink at his table.

"Danke," acknowledged the middle-aged gentleman who sat gazing across the Neckar at the magnificent panorama of Heidelberg Castle and town. Dressed in an immaculate mohair suit, he was distinguished, with almost white-blonde hair. Most evenings he popped in to Zur Philosophenhohe Restaurant, halfway up the mountain side, a short distance from his home in Philosophen Weg. It required matching wealth to enjoy domicile in one of West Germany's most pleasing prospects. Prosperity oozed from its residents. Not bad, seeing that he had started with nothing.

The man's business had grown well in 25 years from a stock of stolen files, accomplished at a rate of some 100 a week over a two-year period. Adele Mathieu had done a fantastic job. Before it got too close for comfort, putting his faithful friend in jeopardy, Erwin had pulled out from Berlin. The familiar old window cleaner had been missed at the Document Centre; they had probably thought that the poor fellow had died.

Erwin had chosen Heidelberg as the nerve centre for their blackmail racket. Blackmail required methodical plotting, to say nothing about the extensive employment of disguises. Success had not been easy, fraught with risk and danger. Sophie had proved a willing, enterprising accomplice in her man's nefarious schemes, especially working on collaborators in France. Both had endured nerve-racking narrow escapes. Erwin had lost none of his skills, silencing five objectors over the years. In their 25-year partnership as Andre and Adele they had formed a deadly blackmail combination of elite Nazi killer and reticent Jewess, each cocooned and unaware of their partner's true identity. As Nazi connections in South America diminished in power, Erwin held all the aces. He had found that wealthy ex-Nazis with political aspirations were easy meat; protective of their image.

Adele (alias Sophie) went in as bait, often free with her charms. She liked the time when she could smile sweetly at them and say, "Have your last look, you fool," as the moment of truth dawned on their victim, who had to face either compliance or exposure and probable ruin. It made them look at her seductive body in a completely different light.

The team enjoyed the fruits of their crooked labours in wealthy style as the respectable Beckenbauers, which is the name they had assumed.

A jangling signature tune heralded the TV news, making heads swivel in the direction of the corner set.

Stunned silence gripped Erwin Ehrhardt, who sat gazing in stunned disbelief at the newsreel coverage. TV crewmen had found the rare coverage needed to spark public interest in the sponsored sea-bed search off Italy, which succeeded in adding a whole new slant to a fickle flagging audience. The advertising men were delighted. The discovery of a submarine was causing all kinds of wild speculation. The mystery submarine was described only as small: official identification would have to wait until formal investigations had been completed. Reporters thrust microphones in crewmen's faces. "Will you bring her up?" "Get inside?"

Erwin forced himself to remain calm. Could this be THE sub? Think rationally now – many submarines had been sunk off the Italian west coast in the period leading up to the Allies' Anzio beach landings in January 1944 and prior to capturing Rome on June 4, 1944. The newsreader had said a small submarine, and the U793 had been a small one. It had not achieved rendezvous with the larger Electro-boat off Ischia according to Heinrich Muller. He swore under his breath. It had to be! The coincidence of these points persuaded him of the distinct probability. 'If I can only get those canisters! Hell! I'll clean up', he thought, breaking out into a cold sweat. In his excitement to rush home and tell Adele, he forgot to pay the waiter.

Cheeks flushed, he bellowed through his front door.

"Adele! Get packed! We're going to Naples. Did you see that newsflash on TV on the submarine discovery off Ischia?"

"Yes. Why Andre?" her face was serenely beautiful, possessing an ageless attraction that few people can lay claim to. Her trim figure and stunning legs were the epitome of gracious loveliness and certainly gave the lie to middle age. This was his woman. His eyes flashed. "Canisters! Worth a fortune, names; BIG names, Adele. I'm sure that's the one. They say a small submarine. There aren't many! I will tell you on the way. This could be it, girl! The BIG one we've been waiting for! We leave within the hour," as he rushed up the stairs two at a time to pack. He would think on his feet – he had no plan beyond getting on site.

Chapter 44

SEARCH CONTINUES

Lise's directeur had enormous influence. An appeal to the right quarters received ready assistance from the US Navy, in the form of their DSRV 1. The 37-ton 50 feet long Deep Submergence Rescue Vehicle had been designed for rescuing 24 crewmen at a time from a sunken submarine, by mating with the vessel's escape hatch. To enter a submarine on the seafloor needed experts, particularly if a jammed hatch required a cutting torch. The DSRV descended with the pilot, two crew members, Lise, Rex and their American companion. Manoeuvring slowly alongside the small submarine, the crew peered up at the barnacled hull.

"See that top decking! It has been ripped upwards… an explosion from the side or bottom up. Looks more like mine damage than a depth charge." The crewman's colleague agreed.

"Okay, Theo. Take her on top. Let's see if we can get into this beauty."

In the pilot's skilful hands the DSRV hovered over the submarine.

"Where's the goddam escape hatch? If we can't locate it we may have to jerry rig round the conning tower. When they said it was small I guessed we might have this problem. HELL! There it is!"

They closed in on the forward hatch with extreme care. Secured at last, and satisfied it was water-tight, they tapped the outer lid clear of crustaceans. But the burly crewmen could not get the wheel to move – it was as though it was welded in place. Fortunately Marvin, who was in charge, had infinite patience.

"I don't want to cut it if we can open her up. Try the torch to ease it, then we'll try a crowbar on it." They tried and wrenched, heaved and pulled until it eventually gave. Once free they wrenched back and forth to draw the inner bars, then eased the lid open with the crowbar. Whoosh! It was open. Air pressure in the DSRV was expected to compensate water pressure in what they thought was a waterlogged submarine. What transpired next literally took their breath away. As the hatch lid tore free, an obnoxious wave of putrid air engulfed them. Frantically hands flew to their noses to shield them from the vile stench. Captain Marvin Serle grabbed an aqualung and scuba outfit.

"I'm going in to see what is down there. I need this to breathe." Rex held his arm.

"Marvin, let me go down. If there is a problem, poison gas or whatever, we need you in charge, not stuck down there! I'm fit. Let me go." Marvin nodded his head at his logic.

Rex wriggled into the scuba harness and eased himself through the aperture backwards, feeling for ladder rungs under his feet, one by one. His light, strapped on his forehead, grew dimmer as he disappeared below. Lise wanted to shout, "What can you see Rex?" but restrained herself. The others felt the same way, although no one spoke in the electrically-charged silence. They peered after the now faint dancing light below; heard his steps on metal decking. Rex felt for the floor, tentatively seeking reassurance with his right foot before releasing his left from the comparative safety of the last rung. Solid. OK, so left foot down. His light picked up the myriad dials and pipes of the forward control room. He turned slowly, desperately unsure of himself in the alien environment.

The sight caught him completely off guard. His immediate reaction was to scream in terror, but he was prevented from doing so by the scuba mouthpiece. He had seen a ghost. A ghost in the flesh… if you could call it that. His hands tightened on the ladder rungs until his knuckles were white. Every atom in his being screamed at him to propel his body the hell out of there! His flesh crawled.

Slumped over the trimming wheel a sailor's wizened fingers were locked in rigor mortis, the snarl on the wrinkled skin stretched like a mask over the scalp an indelible stamp of the cyanide pill that had struck the death blow. Rex choked on the bile in his throat. It was a scene from a Hollywood horror movie. Stark terror had him in its icy grip for seconds stretching into an eternity. At last he could move again as the shockwaves dissipated. For a man who had witnessed and experienced many terrifying moments on Grande Prix race-tracks around the world, what he had seen in this watery grave would have turned a cement mixer, not only his stomach. Rex choked back the urge to retch violently.

Strong-minded, Rex managed to push the horror aside, determined to complete his search.

The commander he found slumped over his tiny wardroom table, a Mauser pistol still in his shrivelled right hand whilst his left hand rested on the ship's log, guarding it to the end of time.

The pistol had been placed at his right temple, the bullet passing through his skull and out the other side, tearing a jagged exit. Turning, Rex imagined the trajectory of the bullet and saw where it had expended its force on the wardroom bulkhead before falling spent to the floor.

By a quirk of fate, the doomed U793 had remained hermetically sealed. The meticulously constructed U-boat had not ruptured – the superficial damage had been limited to the hull. Air had continued to be scrubbed until fuel had petered out. Incarcerated in their tomb, the men were sealed in a watertight pocket of air. Some of the bodies strewn around the control room were fully clothed. Their skin had shrivelled and clung to skulls like Egyptian mummies, grotesque on first appearance. There was a gooey mess on the floor. A wave of nausea hit him as his mind speculated on its origin. He fought back the sickening involuntary contractions in his throat, and turned his light in the direction of the forward end of the control room.

It was like the Devil's workshop, faces twisted in agony as the searing agony of cyanide robbed them of their breath and lives. Rex knew the drill; he had read about the practice. His initial revulsion subsided as a wave of compassion registered the hopelessness faced by men when disaster suddenly struck under the sea. Those brave submariners. 'Would I be any better or different if it had happened to me?' he asked himself.

Rex returned to the wardroom. Anything valuable on board would surely have been entrusted to the U-boat Commander. Feeling almost guilty, he fumbled in the Commander's pockets for keys. There was one, which he thought would most probably have been for the locker cum safe. It fitted; the safe door opened. Ignoring ammunition and cash, Rex pulled out two round tubular canisters, carefully sealed. He was sorely tempted to tear them open, but his conscience told him that it was not his right to do so. That right belonged to Lise. It was her expedition, her decision, so he left them on the table. Lifting a sleeve, he pulled the ship's log book from beneath the author's fingers. Rex scanned the last words penned in neat Gothic script by Commander Muller before he had ended his life, but his knowledge of German was too limited to make out any of the words.

Returning to the same area of the control room he discovered the horrendous death of the sailor whose jammed leg had broken between two pipes. Rex cringed at the thought of the man's last agonising moments before the other members of crew had administered the death-relieving pill. Beneath his body were loosened decking plates. Peering below he saw a canister similar to the two in the wardroom. Pulling the corpse aside, and scraping his hand, Rex pulled the deck sheeting further open and saw what seemed to be at least another dozen, if not more. He took one with him.

The forward bulkhead watertight door was closed. There was no way he would touch that door. It may be flooded up in the forward torpedo room. Perhaps that door sealed the mummified corpses from a watery grave.

Rex decided to go back to the surface and report his findings. He gathered the ship's log book, the three canisters and started to climb up the escape hatch.

"Lise, we may have hit the jackpot!" he called out, looking up from one of the lists from the three canisters.

"What do you mean?" Lise looked over Rex's shoulder at the micro-fische screen.

"A Hermann Schmidt listed here. Uniform manufacturer. I know a Hermann Schmidt!"

"You do! How?"

"A man by that name visited father's stocking factories in Nottingham. When he left, he took some of the workers back to Germany to set up there. He became a big shot; President of West German Stocking Manufacturers, has a line of shops for men's wear, on the Advisory Council for ECC, and so on. He was even Mayor of Neustadt at one time. Imagine if this is the same man! Schmidt is a common name, but what if it's the same H. Schmidt that appears in the Ritz register? Same age group! If it's him, we've got him! War criminal – employing slave labour – it's all here, look. I'll get a press photo and see if I can recognise him.

Lise was tight-lipped with determination. "All I want is revenge. I'll destroy him like he did me! Put the swine away, sooner the better! It goes for all of them."

Chapter 45

SPRING 1981:

NAPLES

Rumours were rife in Naples, hotel bars and coffee shops buzzing with speculation. It was no secret that some mysterious canisters had been landed. What was in them was prompting all kinds of wild rumours and endless speculation. Erwin Ehrhardt knew.

He tracked the Italian sailor down the gang-plank of the support ship with his powerful binoculars. He had been seconded to assist in the seabed search. He kept watch as he made his way to a sleazy hotel bar across from the warren of dockland quays and wharfs.

The Italian-speaking German drank a cold lager in a corner while keeping an eye on his prey. Almost catching Erwin off guard, sea-man Valgimigli finished his vino and walked out into the night, senses dulled by tiredness and three large glasses of chianti. Even so, he could sense that he was being followed as he strolled home. He stopped abruptly and turned around quickly like a startled buck. He stood still a moment, but saw nothing.

His predictable path was right angled, around a warehouse corner. Erwin sprinted on rubber-soled feet like a cheetah. He was through the quayside shed in 37 seconds, waiting for the Italian to pass through the far entrance. Breath controlled, Erwin started counting down the approaching sailor's steps until he drew level. Then he pounced. A brief cry was barely audible as Erwin tightened the garrotte around his neck before dragging him inside. Completely winded, the sailor had no fight left when the noose was released. Erwin's right arm flew round the Italian's neck in a half Nelson, while a sharp knee jab in the base of his spine dissuaded any heroic tactics on his victim's part to go for Erwin's groin.

"Dov'e pacco? Where is the cassette?" Erwin snarled.

"Don't knowt. No sapendo. Aaggh!"

"Dove porco?" A steel belted forearm was crushing the hapless character's throat.

"Aaggh." The pressure eased. "She – Laavalle... has them... Hotel – Luciano!" hands desperately clutching the merciless arm. The arm squeezed a moment, then relaxed. The sailor staggered forward dazed, when a stiff hand chop behind the neck felled him like an elm tree. Kneeling down, the big German pressed two clenched index finger knuckles into the man's windpipe. His eyes popped wide open, his life expiring in a rasping gargle. Erwin dragged the body behind some packing cases and left.

*****

As she entered the Luciano Hotel, Adele was dressed to kill and felt like a million dollars. The Adele in Sophie knew what effect it would have. She had done it so often. A half smile; almond eyes full of promise, eyebrows arched, tip of her tongue peeking out between her lips, revealing a glimpse of perfect white teeth. A slight twist of her head accentuated her finely sculpted retrousse nose; such classic features.

The male receptionist was mentally pulverised. He had pinched bottoms, been slapped, but no wealthy woman had actually visually raped him at the Reception desk. And this one was gorgeous. Trembling uncontrollably he handed over the key, knocking the pen off its stand, miscalculating a distance he utilised daily. Adele closed manicured red-tipped fingers lingeringly on his hand and with a dazzling smile whispered, "I want to know something. In the hotel you have one Madame Lavalle staying with you. What is her room number?" Her fingers released their gentle pressure. "Well?"

"Er. This is difficult for me. We are asked not to divulge any information – security you know, especially this one, but... " Adele took her hand away.

"Room 407."

"That's better. But not a word to ANYONE, hmmm? My husband might decide to kill you."

*****

Strong fingers gripped scaffolding poles as Erwin's huge frame swung into space from Adele's second-floor room window.

"Be careful Andre," whispered his woman.

They planned to raid Room 407 by unconventional means after Adele had spotted a guard seated on duty outside the door. Undeterred, they calculated the windows corresponding to 407 in relation to their own.

A legacy of the earthquake, repairing cracks in the walls was underway and scaffolding covered one side of the hotel. Erwin calculated he needed to ascend nine stages of scaffolding and 17 to the right to be able to break in level to room 407. The gaps seemed greater than their prior assessment from across the street.

'I must keep count', he thought, edging sideways like Spiderman. A glance down confirmed a slip would be fatal. His circus training had taught him to contain any fear of heights. He was not nervous. Holding tight, with the muscles in his forearms stretched to capacity, his plimsoll-clad insteps gripped an upright to shin up to the next staging. Progress was slow but sure. That was the secret they had taught him. One more stretch sideways and sweating, he was there. He reached into his black hip pouch and withdrew a flat screwdriver, then carefully tried to prise open the lower sash window. It wouldn't budge; it was locked. They were old fashioned sash windows; he saw the catch secured the two window halves. Feeling behind him again he retrieved a thin stainless steel blade which he inserted between the frames. Hooking his left arm over a horizontal scaffolding pole and withdrawing a rubber mallet from its belt frog on his waist, he gave the latch a sharp tap. It shot across, making the window rattle. He froze momentarily, then ducked away from the window and waited. When he did not hear anything, he cautiously peered over the window sill. All clear. His right leg swung up and over the ledge; his hand pushed up the window; hip over and his body was inside.

An experienced cat burglar, his search was systematic and skilful. No haphazard tugging open drawers and scattering contents like an amateur. Maintaining silence, he had practised in their own suite, believing the rooms would be similar, guessing where he would have hidden the canisters. Not being small, there were limited options. The air conditioning ducting drew a blank.

Erwin moved into the bathroom, opened the cupboard under the vanity unit and stretched his arm to feel behind the sink pipes. His fingers closed on a metal tube. Bingo! A jiggle and it was loose in his hand, the seal already broken. Trembling, his fingers delved inside and pulled out a coil of plastic micro-fische slides. As the writing was impossible to read in detail he used a magnifying glass from his kit and was able to decipher the larger header letters and numbers. Adele had told him which series she thought would be used, and he managed to find a section of these. Four slides. This was it. Pulling a standard lamp into the bathroom, he carefully closed the door and threw towels on the floor at the bottom to prevent light showing underneath. He placed the four slides flat on a white towel, switched from torch light to lamp, set his spy camera at close range and shot a series of flash exposures. Super magnification would reveal the contents later.

Taking one last flip through he spotted a micro-fische with the heading, 'Grenze Niete Montmort'. He took a shot and closed up.

Job completed he carefully retraced his actions. The gold canisters were somewhere else. He was not interested at this stage after being lucky with the one canister he had found. Secrecy and surprise were the elements in the game of extortion. Some people would not know what had hit them. Or from whence it had come.

Super cautious, window locked behind him, Erwin returned as Spiderman to Adele on the second floor where she pulled him in.

*****

"That's strange."

"What is?"

"I am sure I put the lock on this window, but it's unlocked. Look," pushing the catch across.

"Think someone would get in through the window Lise!" Rex was laughing. "There's scaffolding, but no planks and ladders. It would take a brave guy to climb four stories on open scaffolding poles."

"Call it women's intuition if you like, but I think someone's been in here." She was adamant.

Rex took her seriously now. "How? What makes you think that? I'll check the gold canister," he remarked, climbing on a chair to a top built-in cupboard. He reached up to shift the ceiling board he had cut and prised loose the day before. "Phew… it is still there. You gave me a fright. Besides, who would get past the guard?"

"This standard lamp didn't work when I pulled the cord – when I looked closer I saw that the plug was not pushed into the wall socket far enough. It's fine now that I have pushed it in properly."

"So what?"

"It worked perfectly well last night."

Rex had no answer for her logic. In the bathroom he felt behind the pipe. "The canister is still there. The next day is Monday: we can put them in a bank vault. Use their micro-fische screens too to find out what the slides are all about. Anyway, if someone has been in to clean up when we asked them not to, nothing seems to be missing. Are any of your clothes gone; your handbag?"

Lise shook her head.

"So not to worry. Let's eat – I'm starved."

"And then, lover?"

"Need you ask?"

Lise laughed at his sparkling eyes, nodding in good spirits to the guard as hand-in-hand, they strolled to dinner.

*****

Luigi Contellini was a man Erwin could trust. Luigi had provided shelter for him in 1943, and had then introduced him to the circus.

"So there you are my good friend. I think I have made them big enough. Any more, tell me," Luigi smiled with professional pride. Mafioso from many countries placed their trust in Luigi Contellini, the best man in the photographic industry. He had never tried to double-cross anyone; the fact that he was still alive was a testament to his fidelity amongst thieves.

"If I strike it lucky you get a good cut, Luigi!"

Luigi waved his hand in dismissal. "Any time for an old friend. You've given me enough. But… " the old Italian grinned, "we grow old and a pension we need someday!"

Erwin nodded and smiled at his friend's humour. "Just wait," he exclaimed, waving farewell.

Returning to their Florence hotel room, the big German displayed his blown-up photographs with the panache of a casino croupier.

"How's that?"

Adele felt beads of sweat form on her upper lip through acute anxiety at the sight of one of the frames. She hoped Andre hadn't noticed her involuntary gulp of air. She worried that like her, he would spot it. When she had given Andre serial numbers and codes, she anticipated that he would find names of Nazis in armament production, as the industry employed Jewish and Slav forced labour in thousands. She had been correct, but had thought it would have been sufficient information to sate his appetite. A collection of assorted standard wartime items from various support industries, ranging from shoe polish, toothbrushes, mess tins and water bottles to badges, webbing, underwear and helmets was also ranged on the table. All these manufacturers had presumably profited from the war and it was the compilers' intention to make them share their spoils after war had ended.

Erwin eventually read an entry under the heading of 'Uniforms'.

Uniforms— Neustadt Factory Luftwaffe.

North Western Zone	
S.S. Regiment South West Zone	High quality and
S.S. Gestapo South West	officers' class uniforms.
Reichmarschall H.Goering	Dress uniforms

SCHMIDT, Karl		Party Member '34
SCHMIDT, Hermann (Son)		Party Member

Civilian Local	327	312 female
Metz Conc. Camp	563	Jewish female
R.M. Himmler policy	10	Ukrainian female

March 31, 1943.

"I have the bastard at last. I knew I'd get him one day!" gloated Erwin.

Adele felt sick. The last thing she had wanted was to have betrayed Hermann as a Nazi war criminal. She pinched her cheeks to bring colour back.

"We fly back to Naples immediately. Pack your things. They're diving tomorrow and I've organised a reception committee. Good to have friends."

Erwin had told Luigi about the seabed search for the submarine and the gold treasure he had put on board in '43. The tip-off from Luigi had the Naples Camorra organised with a raiding party in a matter of hours. Erwin would direct them.

Adele felt real concern for Andre's safety. Hermann's exposure also gnawed at her intestines. Whenever Adele felt worried or distressed she grabbed her silver-plated weights and began pumping; left hand up, down, right hand up, down; then arms stretched down in front of her, she swung the glistening metal bars apart and out to the side and back to the centre.

She normally performed this before a mirror, imagining her muscles tightening, firming and maintaining the shape of her voluptuous breasts. She believed that a daily exercise routine like this turned adversity into good; it also calmed her nerves.

EIGHTIES
*****
TRIAL AND ERRORS

Chapter 46

APRIL 1981:

EIFFEL TOWER, PARIS

All the silver-haired woman could recall later was the squeal of brakes, a thump on her elbow spinning her to the ground, followed by a loud bang before she hit the pavement. It happened so fast.

Riding on the pavement, the wing mirror of the Peugeot had caught her arm before the car went crashing into a fire hydrant near the Eiffel Tower. It was evasive action, swerving to miss a maniac taxi driver. The middle-aged woman did not have a chance as the car careered past her, spinning her slim figure like a top to the ground where she lay in stunned shock.

A young girl screamed. "Quick! A coat someone! Keep her warm!"

In moments a stooped war veteran with a wooden leg was at her side, holding out an old black blazer in his mitten-covered hand. Grabbing it without ceremony, Hilaire wrapped up the woman, while shouting out to bystanders to call an ambulance. The one-legged ex-serviceman hobbled away, leaning on his walking stick. Siren blaring, an ambulance sped up.

"I'm going with her," shouted the girl.

"Do you know the injured woman?" barked the stretcher attendant abruptly.

"Oui! Madame Vallet," she lied, thinking up a name in a flash as she climbed into the back. In moments the Eiffel Tower starting receding in the rear window as they sped towards the nearest hospital.

*****

Hilaire looked back at the Eiffel Tower to get her bearings. "It was about here I'd say the car went up the curb," she told Rex, pointing to indicate where Rachael had been knocked over.

"What happened to the veteran?"

"I can't say – I jumped in the ambulance. "He just disappeared."

"We have to find him somehow. Lise's button came from that blazer."

"Who gave it to HIM! Let's take a stroll."

They walked passed the Hilton Hotel when a palatial art salon came into view. Rex read 'Montpelier: Objets D'Art.'

"Well what do you know! Looks affluent, I'll say that."

Hilaire drew in her breath in surprise. "That's him!" she whispered, pointing. "The old man with a wooden leg!" Rex approached the army veteran. After a brief discussion and a generous exchange of banknotes Rex extracted the same information gleaned by Pierre.

"Do you remember this man?" he enquired, showing the veteran a photograph of Pierre. Rheumy eyes peered at it.

"Ahh, oui Monsieur!" chomping his jowls.

"Merci."

Rex sauntered into the antique and art salon and walked up to a middle-aged woman.

"Manageress?" he enquired.

"Oui. Bonjour Monsieur. Can I help?"

With a suave wave Rex briefly flashed a wallet containing his racing driver's card. It looked impressive.

"Interpol! We are looking for this man," he informed her, showing her Pierre's photograph. "We have reason to believe he came here in the summer of 1979. Do you remember him?" Rex rushed on. "Cooperate, and you won't be involved. Hide information and you'll be implicated." He was a tiger about to pounce.

The woman was scared. Darting one look at the picture she recognised the face. In shocked reaction she broke wind. "Pardon!" Then nodded. "Oui!"

"What did he want?" He looked fierce, staring her down.

"He wanted to speak with Monsieur Montpelier. I didn't deal with him."

"Fair enough. Thank you." He took one of her business cards from a holder on her desk.

"Don't mention my visit to ANYONE! Do you understand?" he rapped, doom glinting in his eyes.

"Oui, Monsieur." She was a mouse as Rex departed with a bounce in his step. He had positive identification.

Chapter 47

PENDING TRIAL

L ise was bubbling with excitement.

"Hey Rex! We've got the Assize Court. Isn't that fantastic?"

"Slow down," he responded, waving his hand. "What's so great about that?"

"Well normally a case goes to a tribunaux de grande for instance, but major crimes can be brought directly to the Assize Court, without first having to go to an inferior court. Only then does the Assize Court have a jury. In criminal cases an examining magistrate examines the case to see whether trial is warranted. That's why when an accused person comes before a regular court a formidable array of facts is already assembled against him. This is probably why people think that in French courts the accused are guilty until proven innocent! It's not so. The State has to prove the guilt of the accused. The magistrate says that we have a strong case, that we are serving France in regard to war crime activities we have disclosed!"

Rex hugged her. "It's all coming together."

Chapter 48

THE ASSIZE COURT, PARIS

The Court settled down as the judge took his seat and rapped on the stand with his gavel.

"This Assize Court is convened to try three men standing in the dock. Members of the Jury will hear evidence brought before the Court. Guilt or innocence will be assessed on the balance of probability according to the evidence of witnesses and proof presented. Judgement will be made on the findings of the Jury.

"Raoul Montpelier, Henri Saint-Laurent, Hermann Schmidt. You are jointly charged with the abduction and gang rape of Lise Lavalle in the summer of 1966. How do you plead?"

"Not guilty," they repeated in turn.

"Raoul Montpelier, you are charged with collaboration with the Nazi regime and undue enrichment of a business practice in reward for your services during the Occupation of France. How do you plead?"

"Not guilty."

"Not guilty WHAT?"

"Sorry. Not guilty, Your Honour."

"Henri Saint-Laurent, you are charged with collaboration with the Nazi regime, using Jewish internees from concentration camps as forced labour and becoming unduly enriched by the appropriation of land adjacent to your estate without due right, as a gratuity from the Nazi regime for favours given to the Occupying Power. How do you plead?"

"Not guilty, Your Honour."

"Hermann Schmidt, you are charged with providing material assistance in the form of clothing goods manufactured for the enemies of the Republic of France for the express purpose of waging war against the Republic of France and its allies, as well as using female Jewish internees from concentration camps as forced labour in the period between 1941 and 1943. How do you plead?"

"Not guilty, Your Honour."

The judge nodded, gavelled again. "Prosecution will present its case," and settled back in his huge chair.

"Members of the Jury, in our opening address the Prosecution charges Hermann Schmidt, Henri Saint-Laurent and Raoul Montpelier collectively for the abduction and gang rape of Lise Lavalle nee Delors and for crimes against the Republic of France.

"The three men arraigned before this Court are well known, respected men in society, considered doyens in their respective fields and each eminently successful in these pursuits.

"Hermann Schmidt is an advisor to the Bonn Government on the textile industry and heads a conglomerate of clothing and stocking manufacturing companies and chain stores. He is an economics advisor to the European Common Market.

"Henri Saint-Laurent is the President of La Verite Champagne and Wine Distribution Company. He has held high office in the Guild of Vignerons. He is the owner of La Verite champagne estate which produces champagne which is served in the top restaurants of the civilised world. He controls and manages champagne vineyards of the highest repute.

"Raoul Montpelier is a most successful art dealer in Paris, a man whose favourable opinion of an objet d'art can spell great value. This man is respected for his knowledge by people of wealth and eminence throughout the continent and the United States of America.

"The accused are all immensely wealthy men held in high esteem. Yet they are charged before this Tribunal for the abduction and heinous rape of Lise Lavalle, an innocent 15-year-old girl at the time.

"After many years of investigation and dogged determination, Lise has traced her rapists and charged them before this Court. In so doing, their murky backgrounds have now been exposed to light. Far from beacons of virtue in their respective communities, they appear to be bereft of decency and have led lives of depravity that would disgust the average citizen. We intend to prove to this Court that the three charged have one Common Denominator. They are rapists and child molesters. We intend to prove that Montpelier and Saint-Laurent were guilty of cooperation with the enemies of France during the War. Further Schmidt and Saint-Laurent used forced labour from concentration camps. They are charged as War Criminals acting against the Republic of France during the

Second World War."

The Prosecutor moved from the Jury benches and stood in the centre of the Court.

"Prosecution calls the Plaintiff, Lise Lavalle."

The moment of revenge Lise had planned all those years was here. NOW. Nervous, yet prepared to reap her revenge, Lise faced him.

"Do you identify the three accused? Lise nodded. "Yes, I do," pointing to them in the dock.

"I was 15. I had lost both parents in an accident and was running away from my aunt and uncle who ill treated me. I thumbed a lift, trying to get to my friend in Chalons. A large black Mercedes Benz stopped."

Pointing to Henri, "Saint-Laurent said, 'Get in. We can take you'. Once in the car they started planning to abduct and rape me. I was terrified.

"They agreed not to use their proper names. I was blindfolded and they put sticking plaster over my mouth. They drove some distance.

"Montpelier," pointing at him, "negotiated with the pension owner, then I was hustled upstairs to a room and my blindfold removed. They said if I screamed they would beat me and replace the plaster. Schmidt removed the sticking plaster," indicating the third accused with a nod of her head, "then stripped me. He turned me slowly around, fondling me. I shuddered but was terrified to scream out due to their threat. 'Look what we have here', he said and the others grinned. Then Montpelier said, 'See? I always fix you guys up with quality'. And they all laughed.

"Schmidt asked the others, 'Shall I go first or should we spin for it? Stuck plenty virgins in my time. In those days Ingrid held them down for me'. They agreed to spin," looking at the three.

"Schmidt won, threw me on the bed, held my arms back and violated me first. He thrust into me like an animal. He was demented, muttering 'Take that Jew bitch', as he raped me. He was sadistic. The more I cried, the more he hurt me, grinning. Next Saint-Laurent lunged into me. He seemed convinced that I was actually enjoying the whole experience judging by what he said at the time. I couldn't believe that a person could be so callous, then I realised the man thought he was doing ME a favour. Then Montpelier came at me. The pain was excruciating. I was sore beyond belief; my insides on fire." Lise's lips trembled.

"My abdomen was so swollen I was terrified. I thought the entrance to my vagina would tear and I'd bleed to death. I thought they would kill me unless they stopped," she whispered, shaking.

"After a time they came at me again. I passed out with the pain. Eventually, half crazy with agony, I was blindfolded and gagged once more. Montpelier carried me to the car. They drove for a time, then removed the plaster and blindfold before dumping me at the side of the Chalons road. They threw my bag out after me."

The gasps in the Court died down, then the Prosecutor addressed Lise.

"We have your statement that these men raped you," there was disgust in his voice, "but have you any proof to offer the Court?"

Lise nodded, pointing to the table in front of the judge's bench.

"That button I tore from Montpelier's blazer when he carried me to the car."

"Has that button remained in your possession ever since, until you handed it to the examining Magistrate during his preliminary investigation?"

"Yes, Monsieur."

"If it please the Court, we ask that the exhibit be listed in proceedings and accepted as evidence. We will prove the identity of the owner in due course. After your horrific experience," the Prosecutor continued, "were you left with any lasting effects?"

"Yes. I was left with a dread of sexual activity and a horror of the smell of semen. It took me many years to accept a normal lifestyle. But above all, that attack robbed me of the ability to have children."

A ripple ran through the packed courtroom.

"You may stand down. We call Jacques du Pont to the witness stand. He is a qualified psychiatrist."

Jacques testified to treating Lise for the traumatic effects of the gang rape and that he had assisted in Lise's rehabilitation to enable her to marry Pierre.

"Monsieur du Pont, did you see that button in her possession?"

"Oui, Monsieur."

"Merci Monsieur, you may stand down."

Chapter 49

ASSIZE COURT

The Defence attorney took centre stage.

"Members of the Jury. You have heard disparaging indictments against the distinguished men in the dock. In defence we contend it is a case of mistaken identity. The defendants deny their presence or participation in the alleged scandal. The State must prove their identity and complicity in the alleged rape, beyond doubt. I recall the plaintiff, Lise Lavalle to the stand. "Madame Lavalle, you allege these men raped you. What shred of evidence can prove your claim? A button!" derision in his voice. "You can pick up a button anywhere!" throwing his hands wide in disbelief.

"Sir, the button came from Montpelier's blazer. We have traced ownership of the blazer back to Montpelier. The blazer too has come into my possession – by accident!"

A rumble spread through the courtroom as the old blazer was produced.

"You will have to convince the jury that this… garment was not picked off a rubbish dump! You may stand down."

Prosecution attorney called Hilaire, and proceeded to ask her to describe events in the brothel frequented by the three and her subsequent escape, and then relate her involvement in the older woman's accident near the Hilton.

"Did you receive the jacket from a bystander?"

"Yes. That war veteran over there," pointing. "I used it to keep the lady warm until the ambulance arrived. At the hospital they gave it to me to take away."

The old one-legged ex-serviceman was called by Prosecution. He testified giving the blazer to Hilaire and receiving it from Raoul Montpelier many years before. Prosecution counsel elucidated. "Forensic tests have been concluded; here is the report Your Honour. Minute cloth fragments attached to the button thread have been found. The tear has been identified under magnification as being a perfect match. The material is barathea, identical in age and quality. We submit it as evidence." The blazer was placed on the bench.

The Prosecutor looked pompous, fully aware that he was on firm ground.

"Gerda Blom, tell the Court in what circumstances you worked at the Schmidt factory in Neustadt and when."

Gerda cleared her throat, "I vas interned at Metz concentration camp in 1941. Zee S.S. selected Jewesses mit experience in clothing industry. I vas in New York before zee war, in vat vee call zee rag trade. Vee ver transported to Schmidt's factory in 1941."

"What did you do there?"

"Karl Schmidt see I know rag trade. Made me forewoman over internees. I vurk there until zee bombing in late 1943."

"How many Jewish female internees were in forced labour at the factory?"

"About 500. Ja," nodding.

"Who was the factory Manager?"

"Herr Schmidt. Hermann Schmidt," she muttered with her eyes downcast.

"Really! So Hermann Schmidt used slave labour from France to operate his factory! Uniforms I believe. Is that correct?"

"Ja. Zat is correct."

"What kind of uniforms?"

"Luftwaffe, S.S. and Gestapo."

"Uniforms for the S.S, Gestapo and Luftwaffe, made by the slave labour of citizens of France, for the oppressors of the people of France and Europe!" The Prosecutor raised his nose haughtily, awaiting her response.

"Oui Monsieur," Gerda acknowledged quietly.

"If the girls did something wrong, were they punished?"

"Oui Monsieur."

"How? Tell the Court."

"Sometimes beaten, sometimes raped," Gerda said slowly.

Gleefully now he pressed on

"So during that time at the factory young defenceless girls under the diabolical control of Schmidt," he spat the words out, nodding in derision at Hermann, "were raped for contravening some stupid instruction or other! Is that correct?" leaning fiercely towards her.

Gerda drew back defensively which she immediately regretted. Regaining her composure she admitted, "It happened on a limited number of occasions. But… "

"No further questions," wheeling away to his seat. "Your witness."

The Defence attorney approached Gerda Blom and smiled. "By the examination of the Prosecution we would be led to believe that Hermann Schmidt was a violent rapist amongst a host of innocents! Miss Blom, by your own experience would you give the Court your opinion or assessment of Hermann Schmidt? Remember you are on oath!"

"Herr Hermann Schmidt is a gut man. In zee vor it vos his fader, Karl Schmidt who vas zee brute. He beat zee Jewish factory girls. Raped zem. Zen von day, ven I vos forewoman, zee Jewish girls push zat beast Karl Schmidt through zee top factory vindose. Hermann not tell Gestapo or everyvon vould haf been dead. Hermann Schmidt look after girls vell. Ven factory bombed out, he took me to Berghof Schloss to hide from Gestapo. He took risk to save mein life! He is gut man. I vurk for him after zee vor. Been kut to me, Ja! Gut man."

"Have you worked for him all the time since the war?"

"Ja. Zen also viv Ingrid Penz who now is Frau Schmidt – in Vogel Mode. Ja."

"Was Ingrid Schmidt, nee Penz, also good to you?"

"Vonce I vurk viv her, she OK."

"Before that? Difficult?"

"Sometime," Gerda breathed with a weak smile to hide her embarrassment.

"In your opinion did she have an influence over Hermann Schmidt?"

"Ja, I t'ink so…" she nodded in deep thought.

"Do you think she influenced him to do what you would not expect of him?" The Defence scowled.

"Ja, maybe so," casting her eyes down.

"ENOUGH to persuade him to rape errant, defiant Jewish girls as there was no other form of discipline available?" his voice clear as mountain water.

Gerda was scared. "Ja. I zink zat is so. She very strong villed voman."

"Thank you. You may stand down," beaming at Gerda.

Natashya Gobishov seemed agitated in the witness box; scared at first, but slowly plucking up courage.

" …and two truck come first time. Then one week more came again… two trucks, brink thinks to castle."

"What did they bring?" asked the Prosecutor.

"Crates. Some beeg, some small. Put in cellars. Brink two Ukrainian kirls; my age. Then finish, go walk in evenink to Rhine. Two kirls no come back castle. Penz bitch say put kirls on train Neustadt to. Don' believe! She say she and Herr Schmidt drive trucks; to leave at Wiesbaden next day. Why no take kirls am think," shaking her head. "Why train?"

"How can you substantiate what you say? They deny bringing Ukrainian girls to Berghof Schloss," lapsing into her style for clarity.

"He say girls no come schloss."

The servant girl drew herself up to full height. "I steal camera from Nazi," she spat symbolically. "Take pictures; two kirls carry crate. See! And Penz bitch in uniform," handing the photographs to the Prosecutor who presented them with relish to prove her point to the bench. A buzz rippled through the courtroom.

"SILENCE!" Bang! went the gavel.

"Exhibits for recording, Your Honour." They were accepted.

Natashya explained why she had said nothing before. She had no hope of work in Russian-held territory and had asked to stay on at the castle as maid. She couldn't cause any trouble and get dismissed.

"The photographs show the girls at the castle but they hardly substantiate your implication that something bad happened to them."

"I think Penz bitch kill kirls!."

"Why do you say that?"

"Talk boatman on Rhine. Say Herr Schmidt, Penz, two kirls go in boat. Not see kirls come back. Boatman say sometime hear 'plop, plop'," she nodded. "Not see kirls akain."

"Thank you. No further questions."

Defence attorney for Hermann Schmidt approached the witness.

"Natashya. Herr Schmidt continued to employ you after the war. Correct?"

"Ja .."

"You were free to leave. But you chose to stay and work for him. Correct?"

"Ja, Monsieur."

"So do you consider Herr Schmidt to be a good or a bad man?" looking straight at her.

"He vas a kut man. Still iss. Keep me and two peoples safe at castle. One, she there – Gerda Blom."

"In your testimony to the Prosecution you constantly referred to Frau Schmidt as 'Penz bitch'."

Natashya rushed in. "She," pointing impudently with outstretched arm at Ingrid, "she bitch! No gut bitch!" she spat again.

The court was deadly quiet.

The Defence attorney drew in breath with a rasp, "Why do you say that?"

"She bad influence on Hermann Schmidt. She take over, ver' bad. Three kirls, me stay at castle. Me housekirl, cook, maid, karten kirl. When Nazi officer come castle, Penz bitch make kirls play with men." There was a buzz in the Court. "Jik jik all time. She push kirl, smack face sometime. Men too much drunk, kirls all over floor, seats, anywhere. Ingrid laugh. Slap kirl on bum. Skeem, shout at kirl."

"Scream! Why?"

"Watch men. Say not do right. BITCH! No kut bitch!" she spat again.

"She forced you all into sexual acts with the Nazi officers?"

"Ja, or smack, kick kirl. Watch men, kirl – Ugh!"

"Do you believe she influenced the defendant Schmidt to allow this to go on?"

"Ja. She control him zumhow."

"If you refused?"

"Too frightened what they would do to us." She paused for effect then uninvited offered, "One day after the war, Penz went off with that man," pointing to Henri, "Monsieur Saint-Laurent."

There was a babble of excitement in the gallery. "SILENCE". Bang went the gavel. At this statement, Hermann swivelled like a shot rabbit to look at Henri who averted his gaze.

"Did the accused Saint-Laurent stay at the castle?"

"Ja."

"Did YOU sleep with him?"

Natashya hesitated a few moments, "Ja."

"So morals generally were pretty loose in the castle – even when you had your freedom to leave the place. If there was willing cooperation later, then one can only assume that there was a measure of cooperation in the early days, for if not you would have galloped away at the first opportunity! The Defence contends that in war time and under stress, normal mores of society change. Herr Schmidt seems more sinned against than sinning. No more questions."

Defence counsel stood up. "I will convince this Court that Hermann Schmidt acted under orders of the Nazi regime at the factory; he was not responsible, it was the system.

Hermann Schmidt, be upstanding.

"Herr Schmidt, whilst in your capacity as factory manager working for your father, Karl, and employing Jewesses from concentration camps, do you have anything to say in mitigation of the charges brought against you?"

"Our factory was commandeered for war production by the Nazi authorities. We had no option. In terms of policy, we had to accept Jewish camp internees in our labour force. I quote from a policy document drawn by Pohl's deputy, S.S. Obersturmbannfuhrer Hermann Mauren.

'With a decentralisation distribution of the concentration camp labour force, a technically more expedient use of their manpower, along with better nourishment and more sensible lodging, would be possible. With the food that our factory directors continue to supply to their labour force in spite of all obstacles, and with generally decent and humane treatment, both the Jewesses and the concentration camp inmates work well and will do anything to keep from being sent back to the concentration camps'."

Hermann looked up from his paper. "The Jewesses worked 250 hours each month. We provided decent accommodation and working conditions. What food was provided by the authorities we served up in hygienic conditions in equal proportions to the labour force."

"Herr Schmidt. Would you say the people under your control were infinitely better off working for you than languishing in concentration camps?"

"Definitely, Sir!"

"Thank you. No further questions," looking at Prosecuting counsel. The latter walked slowly up to Hermann.

"The information retrieved from the submarine by the plaintiff has established beyond any doubt your complicity in producing war materials for the enemies of France. After your father was murdered you were in absolute control of the factory at Neustadt?"

"Yes, Sir."

"In your capacity as Manager/Owner, you were responsible for discipline?" he paused for effect, "or was it Ingrid Penz?"

"I was responsible, Sir." Hermann replied quietly.

"Did you rape Jewish internees?" almost matter of fact.

"Well I must expla..."

"Answer the QUESTION! DID you or did you not rape defenceless Jewesses at your factory? YES or no!"

"Yes."

"Members of the Jury, let us not lose sight of the fact that Pohl and Maurer were subservient to the wishes of Himmler. Himmler strove to impress people everywhere with the importance of his title, Reichsfuhrer S.S. and Chief of the German Police or GESTAPO, and with the flashy uniforms of the men surrounding him. The terror men. Schmidt made those uniforms. Himmler mixed with princes and counts too, but controlled murder and torture, using brutal thugs. He told Hitler that he preferred using criminals as guards for the camp prisoners. Hitler thought it was a good idea as they would be pitiless and make sure of order and discipline to avoid losing their jobs. Rule by terror!

"Himmler had an utterly insignificant personality, but in some inexplicable manner, he had risen to a high position. But his personality was strong, represented by the power concentrated in him: the control over life and death, and the spying by the Gestapo and the Security Service. It was Himmler's aim to create the Master Race of Hitler's dreams, some five or six million slaves working for the German elite.

"Members of the Jury, Schmidt participated in this Grand Plan and would have you believe the poor wretches in his control were dealt with in humane conditions! He has admitted that he RAPED them!" Turning with a sarcastic sneer to Hermann, "would you care to describe to the Court just how you dispensed your humane reprimands?"

Hermann shook his head.

"I thought not! Sit down. Prosecution calls Margot Sautet."

Ingrid drew in her breath, one hand covering her mouth.

Still dark-haired, but now streaked with grey, a thin woman ascended the witness box, sat and took the oath.

"Madame Sautet, you were engaged at the Schmidt factory in Neustadt. Please tell the Court of your experiences there."

"I am Jewish and was interned with my brother and parents at Metz. My parents were deprived of their furniture business and eventually exterminated. Some 65 000 Jews were murdered in France. The Nazis were particularly cruel to Jewish children. I was 12 when they tortured my brother to death. At 13, they made him carry buckets of water until he dropped, then they clubbed him. He died. They sent me at 13 to Neustadt to sweep factory floors.

"One day Ingrid Penz grabbed me by my collar and hauled me off to the office, saying I had not swept up properly for days. I was half-starved and had been caught eating a crust of bread one of the older women had saved for me.

In the office Penz screamed at me to strip. Trembling in terror, she made me climb on the big desk top; pushed me to lie on my back. She grabbed my left wrist, lashed a cloth thong round it and tied it to my left ankle. She did the same with my right wrist and ankle, tying them very tight. I was witless with terror. I had heard shrieks before from other young girls who had been taken in there. Now I was to experience it myself. My buttocks on the desk edge, Schmidt pushed my legs wide apart and pulled them up around his hips. He thrust up inside me. I screamed like I have never screamed in my life! Fraulein Penz laughed at me as she held my head back. After a time he exploded. I was unfastened and sent away. It happened to me once more, but this time I was simply pushed across the desk face down and he assaulted me from behind. Penz held my hands across the desk. A lot of young girls in the factory were raped by him. He had a fetish for young girls, but she was the pervert. A sadist! She used to manipulate him in front of us and get him ready to rape us. It was terrifying!

"We Jews were expendable, just sex toys. They could have killed us if they had wanted to. Penz was beastly to us. She put him up to it mostly." A rumble echoed through the courtroom.

"I escaped from the factory on the night it was bombed out. I had hidden in the cellars. I heard a bang; like a gun shot, and then the air raid siren screeching. I ran and ran."

Ingrid was white. Had Sautet seen the S.S. man's corpse? Margot Sautet stepped down. Ingrid breathed a sigh of relief and squeezed her trembling hands to stop them shaking. 'Stop it', she told herself. Then as a diversion she looked at Henri. As Ingrid's blue eyes rested on Henri, so aristocratic looking and ridiculously out of place seated in the dock, she felt a pang of compassion and a tear trickled down her cheek. Her son's hand consoled her, imagining it was concern for his father. Ingrid squeezed his hand. 'Silly young man', she thought, trying to hide her guilt from herself. Even now she still had the hots for Henri. 'Oh why! Why did the stupid lovely man marry that awful Dominique bitch! Look what good it did him. Some support she was!' Ingrid recalled that morning's headlines.

'Scandal rocks marriage. Wealthy socialite renounces War Criminal husband. Dominique, wife of Henri Saint-Laurent to desert millionaire champagne tycoon. Divorce action instituted on grounds of non-disclosure of criminal past. La Verite shares crash on Bourse.'

Aristocratic spoilt bitch! Ingrid stewed. She thought of those magical love-filled hours they had shared at Berghof; those nights of erotic abandon in Paris when she had stood on her head to satisfy him. And now that toffee-nosed bitch would get a divorce settlement of millions! Henri was pretty sure to be convicted. Oh why did he stop seeing her? She should have insisted, been more persistent. Ingrid decided she would wait for him. She reflected on her life these days with Hermann. It was not the fun it had been in the war. They had grown too used to each other, and the magic had been lost some time ago. There was no more 'joie de vivre'. She was also certain Hermann would be convicted as a war criminal too. Ingrid wanted her freedom again. She would continue to run the companies whilst he was inside. Financially independent with Vogel Fashions, she would divorce him before he got out. Then she would go to Henri. Ingrid had decided.

Across the courtroom, with a black veil concealing her identity, beautiful sensitive eyes had been studying Ingrid. Sophie knew that Ingrid was a witch. When she saw the look on her face, it was the first time Sophie had seen a vestige of compassion on her features. And the vulture was looking directly at HENRI, not Hermann. Now how about that!

Sophie's mind started to work overtime.

"Prosecution calls Ingrid Schmidt."

Immaculately dressed in a lemon two-piece suit, Ingrid looked confident, although she was churning and shaking inside.

"You have heard testimony of events which allegedly occurred during the war before you were married to Hermann Schmidt. As Fraulein Penz you were in the paid employment of Herr Schmidt. Is that so?"

"Ja," nodding respectfully. "Ja, Mein Herr."

"Some allegations of a despicable nature have been heard concerning your mutual conduct with your then employer. You are not being asked to testify against your husband, but the Court wishes to establish the veracity of those statements and in so doing asks you to corroborate or refute the evidence presented to this Court." He cleared his throat. "Did you bring errant Jewish female internees before Herr Schmidt for punishment?"

"Ja," she muttered quietly.

"We have heard in the Plaintiff's testimony that Hermann Schmidt boasted to his co-accused that 'Ingrid held them down for me' when he allegedly raped young internees. Do you accept that statement as accurate? Is that correct?" The words were spoken quietly without emotion. He looked at Ingrid for a reply.

Ingrid dabbed a lace handkerchief to her nose, tried to speak; faltered, then began again. "The circumstances were... "

"Please answer yes or no!" His tone was iceberg hard.

Ingrid shuffled. "Ye... yes," looking down.

"You were employed by Herr Schmidt and you received instructions from him. Is that correct?"

"It is so," she whispered, shaking.

"He was the manager and set the rules?"

"Yes."

"He was absolutely responsible for what transpired in the factory; including discipline?"

"The Defence would have us believe that YOU had an influence over him! You are not on trial. HE is! He was the rapist. We contend he developed his abominable sexual tendencies and forms of abuse at an early age, which he practised on defenceless young girls. Testimony of orgiastic arrangements at Berghof fits the degenerate mould. Prosecution is unable to pursue the matter of the alleged missing Ukrainian girls for want of proven evidence. However, it conforms to the scheming devious lifestyle we have come to associate with Hermann Schmidt. No further questions."

Defence attorney thought quickly. Natashya's connection between Ingrid and Henri had been ignored by Prosecution, presumably to focus venom on Hermann. To take up the matter might turn Ingrid into a hostile witness. He would ignore it for now.

"Frau Schmidt, as Ingrid Penz at the factory, were you popular with the workers?"

Prosecution jumped up. "Objection. Irrelevant! Frau Schmidt is not on trial here!"

"Your Honour. I contend that it is relevant and with your indulgence will prove my point."

"Proceed. Objection overruled."

"Well, Fraulein Penz? We speak of those days."

"I was not popular. No." Ingrid was stiff; precise. "I was strongly supportive of management in difficult conditions."

"Really! In your role as secretary did you see yourself as something of a disciplinarian too? Is that what you mean?'"

Ingrid became even stiffer. "Hermann was too soft."

"Please answer Yes or No."

"Yes! Karl his father was a strong man until he... he was MURDERED! If the Gestapo had known," rushing her speech now, "the culprits would have been SHOT!" Her Nazi indoctrination was showing through. "We had to maintain discipline to keep control. These were prisoners entrusted to our care remember!" she reasoned.

"You made suggestions?" his tone matter of fact.

"Yes. Hermann needed support."

You respected him? Enough to stay with him, marry him and build a successful business. Correct?"

"Absolutely."

"Gerda Blom says he was a 'good man'. Do you agree with her?"

"Yes I do."

"So does Natashya Gobishov! Then I put it to you Frau Schmidt that in your capacity as secretary, and mistress to him, you influenced Herr Schmidt and the disparaging evidence we have heard was caused by your recommendations on disciplinary procedure! You may stand down."

His point, however weak, had been corroborated by Natashya Gobishov.

"The Court will adjourn," announced the Judge.

Chapter 50

EARLY EVENING,

PARIS

Her taxi driver found the address easily. It was 20h00. Sophie looked at her reflection in the polished shining brass plaque by the door, which bore the name, Charles Poirot, Judge.

Marble steps and a heavily moulded oak door boasted upper middle class. Sophie pressed the bell. In the short wait she twice resisted turning on her heels; something kept her riveted to the spot. She must be crazy! But she had to save Henri. Damn him! The darling.

A prim young white-capped maid in a long-sleeved black dress trimmed with white collar and cuffs swung open the door. Black stockings and sensible shoes completed her decorous image of modern gentility in bourgeois Parisian service.

Ritual introductions completed, Sophie sank back into the luxurious embrace of a shiny leather chair, surrounded by a library of legal tomes ensconced in glass-faced shelving. The electronic security lock brought the study into the modern world.

"So Judge Poirot, whilst we cannot choose our parents, we should not be held responsible for the sins of our fathers. In those occupation days, as a senior magistrate in the Vichy Government, your father, Cesar, could hardly be termed benign when it came to depriving Jews of their businesses and property!" smiling at him.

"You forget, Madame that the judiciary had to go along with the system and follow the groundswell of public opinion to survive. Father was a good caring family man. He had no option." He was not annoyed, but spoke firmly.

Sophie smiled; opening a folder she spread out papers. "Review the decisions reached on these cases Judge Poirot, and tell me THAT was dispensing justice! Oh yes, these are genuine enough. They came from the Archives in Berlin. I thought one day I might need a good judge on my side and that day has arrived!

"Look Judge, I don't wish to prejudice the present case. We could both be on the same side. Have common ground in both wanting to see justice prevail, and a fair trial. But what appears on the surface is sometimes not the fair picture! Isn't that how you view your father's cases in retrospect?" Sophie looked at him with her chin raised in defiance.

Judge Poirot nodded slightly, tongue touching his top lip. "What you say makes sense. What do you want from me?" aware that public disclosure of her information would be embarrassing to his career to say the least, not to mention his upright standing in the community. People enjoy sneering at a successful man.

"Henri Saint-Laurent faces terrible penalties for conviction of war crimes if the Prosecution makes it stick. But Judge, it was his FATHER, not him! When you sum up Judge, I'm asking you to make the jury see the fundamental difference in responsibility. I couldn't bear to see him go down for a long stretch for his bastard of a father. That swine raped me. Henri is a good man. I want to save him. We were lovers once, Judge. I'll always love him!"

"Then you would have to testify to his non-conformance in collaboration. The Defence can build on that testimony and build some protection. I will sum up in all fairness, but I do take your point! Not a problem if it has been properly sworn in Court and adequately argued by Counsel," he replied, eyes narrowing, teeth clenched, scheming an acceptable compromise for her demands.

"I'm afraid it's not that easy! If I go on the witness stand as Sophie Gaston, I'll be in real danger."

"Why?" genuinely puzzled.

"I've lived a total lie for 30 years. It became a habit to live as Adele Mathieu and this became self-confirmed truth as years passed. I have a problem though, a major one. When my common-law husband, Andre, sees me on the stand and I blow my background, the disclosure means I've deceived him for 25 years as Adele. I'm a Jewess Judge, but he doesn't know that. He thinks I'm a French girl. My cover is then blown and I'd be of no use for further extortion work for him. Besides I've seen the slides taken from the submarine and obtained proof about the land next to La Verite belonging to my father. I want my land back! I'm fed up with skulking round Europe. But settled I'll be no use to Andre any more. He'll feel betrayed and cheated. If I go on that witness stand my days could be numbered."

Sophie was serious; there was no denying the sincerity of her message. It was plain truth. "I'd much prefer to keep a low profile and then disappear and leave him and then eventually take up my land."

"But you'll have to go on the stand to prove your rights to the land, so there is no escaping your exposure, Sophie. This Andre you've stayed with all these years. What's his background? Where's he from?" his eyes piercing, analytical.

"You know, I'm not sure. His father was in wine on the Rhine. A salesman. But I don't know much except our life blackmailing ex-Nazis."

"So what do you really know about his past? Nothing! If he didn't know your story... are you sure about his? If he knows so much about the Nazis, chances are HE was one himself! Thought about that?"

Shock registered on Sophie's ashen face. She had seen him kill.

"No! But you could be right! He speaks French, German, Italian, and some English. He has been all over the place. How? When there was a war on? Only the army had free travel access. He has a scar under his armpit – he told me he had an accident with a wine barrel, as a boy. My God! It could be... his old mark. What shall I do? He'll kill me!"

"Wait! You're speculating, getting carried away." He was laughing at her. "Let's find out for sure first. You're jumping to conclusions. Do you have a photograph of him? When he was young, I mean."

"Do you know that I have! He's a master of disguise; has four passports. He sent me to Florence once to fix up a bogus passport for him with a fence friend of his. I've kept a photo as a memento of the days when he could screw me three times a night and still come up smiling!" Sophie's long fingers touched her nose, half masking her impish grin.

Poirot threw his head back laughing, "That's better. At least you haven't lost your sense of humour."

"Oh no, Judge Charles Poirot! I take my sex very seriously, which you may find out!" She was smiling coquettishly. "Five minutes ago I was thinking how I'd like to seduce you, but the latest thoughts have put me right off my greens!" She rose to get her handbag.

"You're outrageous!" he laughed, shaking his head. "I like you Sophie Gaston. You're fresh air in this stuffy judicial library, you really are!"

It was then he began to confirm his original suspicion. As her body moved, clad in a clingy second skin of knitwear from neck to upper knee, try as he might without staring, he could not perceive the slightest ripple or bulge in her sleek contours. Sophie turned away from him deliberately, conscious of the tantalising effect she would have on him as she pushed out her left leg slightly to emphasise the smooth curves of thigh, bottom and hip. He was positive; she was not wearing any panties. His tongue felt like wrung-out chamois leather as he tried to speak.

The judge ran his left hand through grey locks. "We have some pressing things to sort out my girl," he said hoarsely, as she handed him the old passport size photograph from her inner purse pocket.

"Fortunately I have resources available to me through the Police archives and Interpol if necessary. I think I can find out if he was in fact a Nazi Party member. This Andre must have made many enemies through his blackmail racket! Any suggestions? Someone with the guts to rat on him and confirm he was an active Nazi?"

"I know of a motor dealer near Munich – he is very successful. Andre's made a fortune out of him! He has bled the poor bastard for years. He is known as Hans Frick, but in Andre's files his real name's Karl Fleischer. Andre told me Fleischer would never risk marriage in case he was found out at the Registry. He had two girl friends – they used to sleep three in a bed apparently. In his view if they wanted to leave the good life they could go! No divorce – no alimony! He runs a large motor dealership. I got my Mercedes 380 SE from him for nothing! Figures eh? He must HATE Andre."

"Exactly! We'll put some pressure on him. If he helps he's eventually off the hook. I'll get them to go through the S.S. archives for Fleischer. He could have been involved in the death camps. Plenty of them managed to get away and are still living under different identities. Many records were destroyed, but some still exist. You never know, we may be lucky. If he won't cooperate, then we'll roast Fleischer alias Frick on some income tax evasion charge. Get out of him what he knows about your private stud of these past 25 years!" he teased.

Sophie pouted. "Don't be like that!" then broke into peels of laughter. "I feel better for knowing where I stand! I'll carry on as normal, but once I've testified I'll have to go undercover. It will be over for me if he finds me – I have no illusions about that. Whatever I do though, this court case will expose me. I've no way to avoid being found out for me to establish my rights to father's land." Sophie slumped back in the huge chair and carelessly allowed her hem to ride high on her thighs.

As if lost in thought she raised a knee, resting her shoeless heel on the chair edge. Her inner thigh became visible and… was it what he thought?

The judge's eyes were like magnets with tunnel vision. Sophie's smile was soft and gentle, her voice barely a whisper as she looked at him.

"Would you like some company, Charles? Special company?" She was pure seduction.

"Oh yes," he breathed, "I would indeed!"

"I can be yours anytime Charles, if you help me," she cooed. "You will help me, won't you darling?"

"Of course I… I will, oh yes, yes," he burbled.

She had him, in more ways than one.

Chapter 51

ASSIZE COURT

The Prosecutor was on his feet.

"The accused Saint-Laurent – be upstanding! You sir are from an aristocratic family background; your Grandfather was a Baron with a chateau at Zellenberg. Correct?"

"Yes Sir."

"During the war years you worked with your father on the wine estate, La Verite and used forced concentration camp labour. Is that correct?"

"Yes Sir. My father Arnaud was compelled to p... "

"WAIT! Let me finish. We have evidence from documentation retrieved from the submarine that your estate had contracts to provide champagne to the Nazis. Well?"

"We were compelled to provide champagne for the Occupying Power. Labour was allocated to the estate, to work the land. We had no choice; it was policy. We housed them as best we could and fed them properly, using them for reasonable hours."

"Did your father have Nazi friends?"

"Yes Sir. He did."

"When the Nazis called, is it true that your female internees were called upon to supply sexual favours for these friends?" Counsel looked straight at Henri.

"It is true."

"Is it also true that you had a 15-year-old 'play girl' for your personal gratification? You were 20 at the time."

"Yes Sir."

"When you developed your interest in young girls, no doubt. Your father had no objections because he raped internee women himself. Is that right?"

"Yes Sir"

"And his Nazi friends?"

"Yes Sir."

"We learn that canvases stolen by Raoul Montpelier were stored for him in your cellars and later removed to Zellenberg chateau. In return for that favour, Montpelier used his considerable influence with the Nazi powers to deprive the Gaston family of their adjacent wine estate and give it to you!" Prosecution attorney stared at Henri for a moment before continuing. "Don't deny it! From the submarine documentation we see the Gaston deeds were kept by the Nazis – presumably to extort favours – and that they issued Mannie Gaston with a receipt."

"It was policy," Henri insisted, "to deprive all Jewish owners of estates and we were told we could incorporate these lands with our estate, provided we continued to farm the land. It was common policy in those days. Businesses of every description were taken from Jewish owners and given to Frenchmen."

"Indeed! But for collaboration on a major scale your family inheritance was unduly enriched to an enormous extent by your Nazi masters! As if that was not enough, they made certain of no future claim by ensuring Mannie and Rosie Gaston were exterminated in Auschwitz. Is it also true you provided 'private stock' for Reichsmarshall Goering?"

"Yes Sir, we did."

"Is it true that truck loads of champagne went regularly to Paris to Nazi Headquarters there?"

"Correct."

"Indeed! Prosecution perceives a very cosy collaboration occurred with the Nazi Occupying Powers and the Jury will draw their conclusion as to the reason for the Gaston estate being incorporated into La Verite! It was war booty from persecuted Jews for traitorous favours received! And yet you repaid your benefactors by handling stolen paintings stolen from your Nazi friends! A pity they didn't find out! It would have saved an innocent girl from… "

"Objection! Speculation! Irrelevant!"

"Sustained! Strike that last comment from the records. The Jury will disregard the remark."

"In conclusion, Henri Saint-Laurent, you have been proved to have a distinct liking for young underage girls – from an early age. Your conduct and that of your father was traitorous to France. You have been shown to be completely untrustworthy, even to pursuing criminal acts. We move that the portion of the wine estates which previously constituted the lands belonging to Mannie

Gaston, should be immediately wrested from your control and be vested in the State. Thereafter diligent search will be conducted to trace relatives of the Gaston family – so that the lands can be restored to their rightful owners."

As if in the routine of a golf practice swing, Defence counsel stood, adjusting the front of his gown between thumbs and fingers, lifting and releasing the folds before speaking.

"Saint-Laurent, prior to the adverse publicity of this case you were President of the Wine Guild until stripped of office in disgrace. La Verite champagne has also been subjected to bad publicity and a dramatic fall in sales! Is that so?"

"Yes Sir."

"We put it to the Jury that there are a number of mitigating circumstances to take into account." Counsel approached the Jury and stuck his right thumb in the lapel, holding the cloth in clenched fist.

"Henri was not in charge of La Verite during the war years but inherited the huge responsibility at 27 in 1949, when his father was murdered by felons unknown. The load was heavy on his young shoulders. Turning to his wartime acquaintance, Raoul, Henri believed his new friend to be a resourceful and successful man. After all Raoul had secured the Gaston estate for his family and pulled off the stolen canvases scam. Raoul had a strong influence on him. When Henri then introduced his old Heidelberg University friend Hermann, to Raoul, they became a trio. Henri owed much of his success to Raoul's marketing influence and expertise, as did Hermann. It was a great consortium." Counsel paused and hitched his gown.

"Saint-Laurent, why did you participate in the rape of Lise Lavalle?"

"Sir, I like women, but I'm not obsessed with young girls. It is not a natural desire. I got swept along with my friends and have deep remorse for my taking part in the rape incident." He sounded convincing.

"During the war did you once have a friendship with the daughter of Mannie Gaston?"

There was a gasp in the courtroom, while Henri was obviously startled that this information had come into Defence's possession.

"Yes sir. Sophie Gaston and I were friends. Mannie was keen that we should marry one day. My father would hear none of it. Our family hid her from the Nazis as a maid in our house."

"When did she leave?"

"She ran away in the summer of 1943."

"Why did she do that?"

"My father raped her."

The courtroom erupted.

"SILENCE in Court."

"Defence calls Sophie Gaston!"

Sophie mounted the witness stand and sat, crossing her sheer stocking-encased legs and placing her palms together in her lap. Her countenance was serene; five pearl strings, tightly wound, adorned her graceful neck, in sharp contrast to her short black tight dress, cut square and high, just below her collar bones A neat close hair style exposed two large pearl earrings. Sophie Gaston, alias Adele Mathieu, was strikingly beautiful, with the relaxed composure of a contessa.

Five people were in a state of shock, mouths wide open; Henri, Ingrid, Gerda, Natashya and especially Hermann. Sophie's heart went out to him. That lovely man did not deserve to be in this predicament. She felt proud of him, sitting up straight in the dock. He was a gentleman; a successful man who had provided employment to thousands through his industry and skill. But Sophie was prejudiced. Hermann had saved her life. She caught his eye. In a second she had communicated by sign language, placing fingertips of both hands on her breast bone to indicate 'me', at the same time slightly shaking her head. Her message, 'It wasn't me who betrayed you'.

The German replied with a slight downward drop of his head to acknowledge, 'No I knew you would never do that to me'.

Sophie felt a tear well up in her eye. She brushed it away, trying not to attract attention. Sophie had wanted him so much and this Frenchwoman was trying him for rape.

Deprived of men, Sophie's insatiable appetite had created demands for relieving her pangs. Hermann was the only man available at Berghof. Sophie struggled with herself, fantasising about the image of Hermann and her locked in each other's arms. Eventually she threw caution to the wind. It was to seek satisfaction from the burning desire which had pursued her since her first experiences at school.

She remembered that first time as if it was yesterday. She had made her intentions obvious to him by appearing at her bedroom door when Hermann was passing by, with a bath towel loosely draped about her. Contriving to register surprise, she caused the towel to open wide, exposing her gorgeous silky white body to his startled gaze. Her tempting mischievous smile had done the rest.

"Would you like me?" she had whispered, tongue playing on her lower lip. Hermann grunted his willing assent and her skills cemented their relationship.

Adele, as she was known to Hermann then, risked their very existence.

They had played a dangerous game in those days at Berghof. Sophie, masquerading as Adele Mathieu had been surrounded by danger. Natashya and Sophie soon realised: they too had wanted Hermann. Slim chance she had, but any sign of interest or competition shown by Sophie would have invited disaster.

Gerda Blom, her lesbian butch, to whom she was indebted for her sanctuary, was exceedingly jealous. So jealous, when Sophie ran away to join Andre, it had been a clean and final break. No farewells. Gerda's anger would have been unpredictable had she discovered Sophie's amorous exploits with Hermann. However the most dangerous had been Ingrid Penz. Sophie knew she was a vicious woman. Any clue that Sophie had enjoyed a relationship with Hermann would have meant exposure to the Nazis and extermination. Circumstances made their forbidden fruit all the more exciting, causing them to invent a sign system and message codes with household items, to arrange treasured moments of sexual pleasure.

Berghof Schloss was large and Sophie had walked extensively, investigating suitable places for them to meet. They had been good for each other in those days, both accepting that there could never be a future in their relationship. It was simply sexual thrills and nothing more. Hermann would never have known so many variations on a theme unless he had met Adele.

The most supreme irony of all was that there in the dock beside him, on the same charge, stood Henri Saint-Laurent, the first of her conquests on the bank of the stream separating their parent's wine estates, under the poplar trees. Sophie still had a soft spot for Henri, even now. She wondered if he would feel the same way about her when she got her land back from him!

Sophie's eyes went back to Hermann as she brushed away a second tear. They had enjoyed great days together. Poor Hermann, the darling; but that was long ago. Forget it; it's gone.

Her thoughts were now concentrated on Henri. At last her finest hour would soon materialise.

"Madame, tell the Court in your own words what you know about the accused persons Schmidt and Saint-Laurent."

Sophie's lips broke into a smile. "Hermann is not the dreadful person he has been painted to be! At great risk to himself he protected Gerda Blom and me, two Jewesses from the Gestapo. After the war I disappeared, leaving no trace, to start a new life. Hermann was strongly influenced by Ingrid Penz and together with his Hitler Youth upbringing, could slip into the facade of the Master Race with all its arrogance, when in truth his intellect rejected it as myth! He once confided in me that as compulsory reading he had ploughed through Hitler's 'Mein Kampf' (My Struggle) and found it inept, half-baked and untrue! Hermann undoubtedly had a conscience about the horrendous acts perpetrated in Hitler's Germany. He once told me of his fears of the dreadful retribution the world would visit on the German people when defeated! But he, like the rest, was caught up in a vortex and he carried on in fanatical desperation, delaying the awful day of reckoning until the factory was bombed out of production. Saving two Jewesses from systematic extermination was his rebellious reaction to the Nazi regime, not an insurance policy. He did it in spite of charges against his sanity by Ingrid Penz. She is a wicked woman, perfidious and pitiless. Being a little older than he was, she imposed her influence over him to satisfy her own perverted depravity and bestiality. She was able to persuade him to perform sexual excesses that he would otherwise not have contemplated. She derived perverted pleasure in observing sexual acts. It was talked about in the factory. It was common knowledge. Many of the young girls had seen her manipulate him, as you have heard in testimony.

"Hermann was an intellectual caught up in a period of history when cruelty, perversion and depravity were part of the system. He was basically a good man immersed in surrounding evil and confused as to his mode of conduct. Hermann Schmidt was not an evil man at heart."

Sophie paused and took a sip of water, then continued.

"I grew up on the wine estate next to Henri and became his friend. Henri is a weak character who was dominated by his overbearing father; he feared him and could not stand up to him.

His father Arnaud, was the evil one and like Hermann's father Karl, welcomed the power that Hitler's Germany represented. He exploited his Germanic heritage to the greatest advantage. Both sons were swept into the power system, taught crazy distorted values, despicable in normal civilised countries. They were steeped in hatred for the Jews to be on the winning side and were persuaded that it was expedient to go along with the Nazi system of terror and brutality. 'Might is right' they were taught."

Sophie looked at the jury members, eyes ranging over their faces to register her sincerity.

"I have made love with this man when he was young. Henri was as tender as any girl could wish for. But according to the diabolical regime which conquered our land, I was born on the wrong side of the tracks. I was born a Jew! Classed as vermin! We Jews were despised, harassed, persecuted, tortured, raped and exterminated throughout Europe. When the chips were down, there was no one to help us, nowhere to go. Henri's father broke his pledge to my father to save me. Instead he raped me. I ran away. Ironically his German friend, Hermann saved my life." Sophie paused as a murmur went around the courtroom.

"By good fortune I found out that a receipt had been given to my father when the Nazis took his property deeds. They probably gave him the receipt in mockery, having no value but satisfying their Teutonic methodology. I knew where my father would keep such an important document of proof. The number seven is important to Jews. The seventh step on our estate house cellar steps had a loose tread. Only father, my mother and I knew that some gold coins were kept there for emergency. I could imagine nowhere else he would have put his proof. I broke into the house and retrieved it. Here it is!"

In a brief babble of excitement Defence counsel offered the receipt as evidence. "SILENCE in court." The gavel fell.

Chapter 52

ASSIZE COURT

"Emilie Cohen to the witness stand."

Emilie was still an attractive woman. Her long shapely legs, trim figure and pretty face, flowing black hair artfully arranged to fall in organised profusion over her shoulders, made her look younger than her 51 years. Earlier years as a prostitute had miraculously not taken their toll in an aged face or broken spirit. Her eyes still sparkled with mischief. Prosecution smiled briefly at the openly provocative but vivacious witness.

"Tell the Court of your personal experience with Raoul Montpelier."

"The first time I met Raoul was in his flat in April 1942. Madam Courtier threw me through his door to service a colonel friend of his. I was desperate not to return to that horrible woman in her filthy brothel. I begged Raoul to let me stay. I slept with him. I did everything I could to please him."

"How old were you at the time?"

"Twelve, Monsieur. I turned 13 in September '42. He bought me from Courtier for two paintings."

Shocked whispers reverberated through the public gallery. A gavel fell.

"Did he ill treat you during that time? Did he beat you? Hurt you at all?"

"No. Well, he was infatuated with me."

"Would you say he was obsessed with you?"

"Oh yes he was! He even resented his Nazi friends having me in the end. But he had no option in order to avoid 'Rassenschande.' They were all in it together – he had to share me, you see. It would have been too dangerous for him to be seen to be other than a bully and me a plaything. I once saw him trembling with rage when a Nazi officer wouldn't leave me alone."

A titter echoed around the court. The Judge gavelled. "Silence in Court!" he bellowed. "Counsel, I fail to see where your witness's testimony is getting us; if anywhere!"

"Your Honour, from Madamoiselle Cohen's testimony we have established Montpelier's collaboration with Nazis and that the accused had a deep-rooted sexual desire for young girls. As such he was likely to take advantage if a situation presented itself. Prosecution contends such an opportunity arose in the company of his dubious colleagues who shared a similar penchant for sex with underage immature girls Together they perpetrated the abduction and gang rape of Lise Lavalle to satisfy their wanton lust.

"Your Honour, Madamoiselle Cohen has testified Montpelier bought her for two paintings." He signalled to the Court bailiff to remove a cloth covering two canvases.

"Do you recognise these paintings?" looking at Emilie.

"Oui Monsieur. Those were given to Madam Courtier by Raoul to buy my release. They hung in the brothel."

"Thank you. Your Honour, they were removed by the Police from the brothel where they have hung ever since. We request these exhibits be accepted as evidence." The Judge nodded assent.

"Do you know who the artists were?"

"Non monsieur," smiling her ignorance.

"Very well. Thank you. Your Honour, we call upon an expert in the world of art to identify them for us." The Judge nodded; Emilie stood down.

"Madame Garratt, you are a senior assistant in the Salon Objet D'Art of Raoul Montpelier; correct?"

"Oui, Monsieur."

"How long have you been with him?"

"Thirty-two years, Monsieur."

"In your professional opinion who were the artists responsible for these paintings, please? Examine them again, be absolutely sure!"

The grey-haired, well groomed woman looked carefully and returned to the stand. "The artists were Klee and Miro."

"Members of the Jury, Klee and Miro, together with Leger, Picasso, Max Ernst, Mane-Katz, Masson, Picabia and Kissling were Jewish artists despised by the Nazis. Their paintings were earmarked for collection and systematic destruction. Their works would become extinct. Some 600 canvases were recorded in typical Teutonic bureaucracy and filed, before the offending works of art were burned to ashes in the courtyard of the Louvre. Your Honour, here is the record of the destroyed canvases. It came from the Berlin Archives of Jewish Affairs. The question is how did those two canvases," pointing, "come into Montpelier's possession?" Prosecution paused for effect.

"Madame Garratt, you have assisted in this investigation. Please testify to the Court how many canvases of the aforementioned Jewish artists have been sold over the years through your salon!"

"We have identified 207, Monsieur," she replied timidly, terrified of the consequences of her disclosure.

"Your Honour, Members of the Jury. The accused Montpelier gave away those two paintings and our investigations have traced ownership from sales through his salon of no less than 207 canvases that records state were destroyed by fire! Madame Garratt, remember you are still under oath. Do you recall a Doctor Lavalle calling at your salon in the summer of 1979?"

"Yes, Sir. He was rude and pushed past me saying, 'I want to see Montpelier!'"

"Did you hear an argument? Raised voices perhaps?"

"Yes. Doctor Lavalle was shouting and abusive."

"Think carefully before you answer. DID you SEE Doctor Lavalle LEAVE the premises?"

"Non Monsieur," she replied, looking straight ahead of her.

"Your Honour, Doctor Lavalle was pulled from the Seine; drowned. You may stand down," as the buzz of excitement subsided.

"We call Raoul Montpelier to the stand. Montpelier, in your anxiety to secure and seduce Emilie Cohen as a sex slave, you took a chance with two paintings in your possession. There were no records as far as you knew. In your mind no one would connect you with those paintings. Furthermore the Allies would probably overrun Paris anyway! We contend that you pulled off a gigantic fraud under the noses of, and against, your Nazi paymasters! You stole perhaps 400, 500 or even 600 canvases, replacing them with inferior paintings of little value, which were later destroyed outside the Louvre. There can be no other logical explanation. You selectively sold those rare paintings after the war, making yourself many millions! That is what happened, is it not?" Raoul lifted his head up, resigned defeat on his face.

"Oui. Oui, Monsieur."

"We have the testimony of Saint-Laurent but you will confirm to the Court where you hid this enormous hoard."

Raoul raised his eyes to the ceiling, took a deep breath, "In La Verite cellars and later in Henri's chateau at Zellenberg."

The gavel fell twice and silence settled over the court. The Prosecuting Attorney established the entire conspiracy and consortium in detail, referring to the enormous collation of evidence prepared for the Assize Court. Spinning round to face the Jury, Prosecution counsel explained. "In addressing the specific case against Raoul Montpelier we ask you to consider certain unexplained events in conjunction with evidence presented. We have led evidence that Doctor Lavall visited Montpelier; a heated row ensued and although he had entered the salon from the front door, the witness Madame Garratt has testified that she did not see him leave! Doesn't that strike you as odd? Doctor Lavalle had never been there before. It is unlikely that he would leave by a back door! NO! He was certainly no friend of Montpelier's.

"Madame Garratt, a faithful servant for all those years, would not desert the showroom and leave no one to attend to clients when she knew her employer was involved in a blistering row – for whatever reason. It is simply not logical! Madame Garratt was in the showroom and Doctor Lavalle never came out again!

"Members of the Jury, two days later the body of the doctor was washed up on the banks of the Seine! The reason for his going to see Montpelier was that he had got so far with his investigations that he called his wife Lise and excitedly told her that he had found the owner of her button. Does that sound like the act of a person about to commit suicide, as the Police report would have us believe? We speculate that Doctor Lavalle, however foolish his action may have been, stormed into Montpelier's salon and accused him of his crime. Rape. Montpelier panicked and killed him. How he accomplished this has not been proven as the body was not punctured by bullet or knife – although the skull had been subjected to a blow sufficient to cause concussion and rupture of the membranes of the skull.

"We call Doctor Perot to lead evidence of his findings."

"Commensurate with suffocation by submersion, or drowning, the lungs become polluted by noxious water content. We have had experience with suicides in the Seine. In this instance my colleagues and I were unable to explain the rapid deterioration of the lungs in so short a period of immersion, assessed on the skin discolouration and so on. The lungs released an odious green slimy liquid. We suggest possibly the man was gassed to death, but laboratory tests cannot identify the type. A colleague, well read on the subject of gases, believe it was Zyklon, used in extermination camps."

The court was in an uproar.

"SILENCE." Bang, bang. "Silence in Court!" Normality resumed.

"Thank you Doctor Perot. You may stand down."

Prosecution attorney walked up to the Jury benches. "What we have here is a man who was so integrated with the Nazi regime during the occupation that he abandoned normal restraints of civilised conduct. Whilst we cannot prove Montpelier poisoned or gassed Doctor Lavalle, it is probable that he, of all people, could have come into possession of such a vile means of extermination. He could have got Zyklon gas from his Nazi paymasters for services rendered. He would strenuously deny it so we will not press the issue!

"Instead we call on a witness who can relate for you the life Montpelier led during the occupation of Paris. On the balance of probability you will decide your opinion of Raoul Montpelier and whether or not he would be likely to liquidate any opposition.

"Prosecution calls – Rachael Goldberg!"

Raoul clutched at his chest in total shock.

Rachael mounted the stand and sat down, cleared her throat after taking the oath and began.

"Raoul's father, Edouard, was apprenticed to my father. He was jealous of success. As a Nazi collaborator, Raoul raped me in my father's house. I was 19 at the time and he would just walk in, throw me on the bed and rape me. There was nothing I could do under threat of my parent's deportation." Tired eyes glanced for moral support at the Prosecution counsel. He nodded that she should continue their agreed revelation.

"Every moment Raoul Montpelier humiliated me. On some days he made me wear a dog collar and led me round naked on a leash, kicking me on the behind. Sometimes so hard I fell on the floor and then I would get another good kick. During the last six months he acquired drugs which enabled him to perform intercourse for extended periods. To him I was an object: a sex slave. He continued to rape me at will, and forced me to service Nazi officers' friends. There were many.

"He arranged to have my parents arrested in 1942 and sent to Drancy Prison. I never saw them again. They probably went to Buchenwald or Auschwitz. His father Edouard and he took over our family business. It was an arranged reward from the Nazis for collaboration.

"He then had me sent to Madam Courtier's brothel to service Nazi acquaintances and collaborators. He said he'd trained me and that I was good at it. It was forced sex, day and night. Sometimes I could not sleep for 24 hours.

"In 1943 Hauptsturmfuhrer Alois Brunner came to Paris and Raoul wanted me dead. I was an embarrassing link to his past deeds and still the rightful owner of our former family business. He wanted to make sure I was dead so that no traces could be found, in order to avoid any charge of conducting a 'special' relationship with me. He could have been in trouble as he had made no secret of his relationship with me. Furthermore he was at that stage living with a 12-year-old, Emilie Cohen. He didn't need me anymore; only dead.

"The police raided Madam Courtier's brothel; I'm sure he arranged it. I was arrested and also thrown into Drancy Prison. There Bruckler, a known sadist, raped me and many others too. Then Brunner heard about my talents and he wanted me for himself! Brunner had me sent secretly to a hotel. From there, when he was exhausted and asleep, I escaped down a fire escape.

"It was extremely dangerous in those days to be a Jew. Deportation and extermination had been stepped up. I decided to stick close to a railway track leading out of Paris. I knew strategic installations would be guarded, but it was even more dangerous to be on the roads with no papers. I scrambled along railway embankments at night until I got to the outskirts. The first day on the run I slept inside a railway coal bunker. I was starving hungry. I staggered along for a second night. Exhausted, I came to some school grounds. At the rear was a pig sty complex. The school reared pigs from hotel scraps. Desperate, I picked amongst scraps and chewed some bran meal. I found a tap for water. During the night I hid in a pig sty. Next day a man and some children came to feed the pigs, but I survived the stench and remained undiscovered.

"Desperate now, knowing I would die if I continued to stay in such conditions, but realising that I was probably safer from the Gestapo there than anywhere else, I took a calculated risk. I cleaned up as best I could, moved with caution away from the complex and waited for the man to arrive the next day. He was surprised but not as startled if I had appeared from a pig sty! He looked around 40, with a bad limp – he was probably a disabled soldier. 'Please Monsieur, I want work,' I approached him. 'Any work, even in the pig sties.'"

"He was taken aback. 'There's no work here', he told me. 'There is only enough for me'."

"Taking a gamble, I moved towards him. 'I'm desperate. My husband beats me. I have to get away. Please give me some food. I will give you sex if you help me.'" By this time I had made my intentions blatantly obvious.

"I was fortunate: he was a good Frenchman. He guessed I was a runaway Jew. With a grin on his face he said, 'I will help you and I don't need sex in payment. You are lucky my girl. I'm with the Resistance'. He housed me in a tool shed and brought me food every day. In return I helped him in the sties. Etienne was my only connection with the human race until liberation. In the winter when the nights were dark early he used to smuggle me into his home. I owe my life to him. Caught, I would have been dead.

"After the war, I returned to Montmartre with nothing. My only option was to return to prostitution. I found Emilie Cohen again who had been captive with me in Madam Courtier's brothel.

"We set up as 'working girls' in a room together. I told her I was determined to get back into the objets d'art business like my father. So we scrimped and saved.

"In 1949 we opened our single window antique shop, augmenting our living as prostitutes. Our new business grew until it could eventually support us.

"I was too frightened to tackle Raoul Montpelier and try to prove ownership of father's former business. I knew Raoul would have me murdered. It would not be the first time he had tried. I knew him as a powerful and dangerous man and decided to keep out of sight. He terrified me.

"One day I went back to look at father's old business premises, but kept a low profile. Then a car knocked me down and through that freak accident, I met Hilaire. This led to this Court, all because of an old blazer with a missing button which was used to cover me."

"Have you any proof that you are indeed THE Rachael Goldberg, daughter of Hymie Goldberg who was dispossessed illegally of his objets d'art business and of which you are the rightful heir?"

The grey-haired, dignified woman made no reply. Instead she removed the jacket of her two piece suit and rolled up her blouse sleeve, revealing a small tattooed number.

"P42743," droned the Court bailiff.

Prosecution counsel read out, "Drancy Prison Paris, April 22, 1943. Number P42743 Rachael Goldberg – Jude. Lager Dachau," and closed the prison record book. Defence shook his head.

There was deathly silence in the Court as she stepped down.

Chapter 53

ASSIZE COURT

Confident, in for the kill, Prosecution Counsel's final address at the start of the day's proceedings was brief.

"Indisputable evidence has been presented to you proving the indictment of the accused in the conspiratorial abduction and rape of Lise Lavalle. There can be no doubt in your minds as to their dastardly treatment of that defenceless girl of 15.

"Society demands that they be punished. Your verdict will ensure that this process is put into effect.

"Their traitorous conduct against the Republic of France has been amply illustrated and proven. Indisputable evidence from German records found in the submarine has exposed their evil involvement with the enemies of France. Individuals have testified to their obnoxious misdeeds. You have heard enough testimony to reach your conviction to put these villains away for a long time. We look for your recommendations for suitable recompense for the victims of their malpractices.

"Your judgement will determine if justice is to be done, Members of the Jury. We, the citizens of France, expect a verdict of Guilty.

"Prosecution rests its case, Your Honour."

With a swirl of his gown he turned and sat down.

Defence Counsel hitched his gown. "Members of the Jury, in presenting our final address, Defence is not distracted from the earliest contention of mistaken identity. The arguments levelled against the defendants have been pure fabrications. Let me elucidate.

"Lise Lavalle may have regrettably suffered a gross humiliation by some parties unknown. However, she saw an opportunity to make a claim against three wealthy men of title and position after hearing from a child prostitute that they happened to frequent the place where this child herself was available.

"We have had presented before us, as vital evidence, a button and a blazer! One can pick up an old blazer from any second-hand clothing shop, tear off a button and fabricate the story we have heard. Of course the forensic tests prove the button came from the blazer. So what!

"The poor old veteran, given a goodly consideration which would ease the burdens of his miserable life, could be relied upon to testify to its origin! Likewise the pension owner could be persuaded to identify one of them, for sufficient inducement. The testimony of Hilaire is ludicrous! What validity can be placed on its relevance in this case? What three men do in Paris on a night out has nothing to do with the case! Or whether or not they stayed at the Ritz Hotel! If they could afford it, why not? What is so suspicious about that?

"Allegations that Montpelier murdered Doctor Lavalle is pure fantasy. Crime novel stuff! There is no substantial evidence to back such claims – it is mere speculation. Madame Garratt did not see the doctor leave!" he scoffed. "Members of the Jury, just what does that prove? Could you reasonably expect her to watch every single person enter and leave the salon?

"My clients grew up during wartime, when, as Sophie Gaston pointed out, morals and attitudes were very different from those in normal peacetime conditions. War is a stressful time!

"Defence contends that Hermann Schmidt was a better factory manager than his father and looked after his people well. He inherited the responsibility and fulfilled his obligations better than his father, even though the son had less experience. He did his best in difficult circumstances. We have the testimony of Gerda Blom on that score. He was a humane person. Gerda, Natashya, Sophie and Ingrid agree on that unanimously! He saved the lives of two here from certain death at the hands of the Gestapo. Is that the act of a fiend?

"It is incongruous that he be found guilty of the alleged crimes.

"Henri Saint-Laurent was still a youth during the war. He cannot be held responsible or even share blame for the collaboration of his father, Arnaud. Whilst Henri was working at La Verite he was under the control of his father and not in a position to take decisions. He cannot therefore be considered a war criminal, accused of employing forced labour or for collaboration by supplying champagne to the Germans. It was his father's contract, not his!

"He is not guilty!"

He paused to let his message sink in, then continued.

"Raoul Montpelier was apprenticed to his father, following in his father's profession. By nature of his position he was under his father's influence and direction. He did as he was told.

"We have testimony of one Rachael Goldberg who says the FATHER, EDOUARD, not Raoul, was jealous of her father! HERE, Members of the Jury lies the KERNEL of the allegation and bitterness against my client. It is a grudge; a longstanding family feud. It was an opportunity to vent revenge against the Montpelier family. If she was rightful owner of the property and business, why did she wait until now to claim that right?

"Rachael Goldberg alleges Raoul engineered the deportation of her parents! Can you really believe he would have had such influence with the Germans? Such a young man? It would be more logical to assume that Montpelier Senior would have been able to lever this concession with the authorities! It was he who procured the business! But such a youngster! How can you believe that? She alleges Raoul did the same to her, without a vestige of proof. I put it to you that this is a figment of her imagination and, to put no finer point on it, a pack of lies to discredit the Montpelier family."

With a melodramatic swish of his gown, he spun round to address the jury.

"Members of the Jury, we the Defence contend Prosecuting Counsel has failed to prove the heinous charges against my clients. We move the charges be dismissed and defendants released with costs. My clients have suffered defamation of character and public humiliation. Defence presses for substantial damages to be awarded in partial restitution for the wrongful actions brought against them for unsubstantiated misdemeanours. If you wish to see justice prevail this day, you will bring in a verdict of Not Guilty.

"Defence rests, Your Honour."

The Judge gavelled.

"It is time for me to sum up the evidence, testimonies and arguments put by both Counsels.

"The Law requires you, under your elected foreman, to decide beyond reasonable doubt, the guilt of the accused. If you cannot hold that conviction, then you must bring in a verdict of Not Guilty.

"What we look at here are the issues of Law, not emotion. Was a crime committed – or was it not? The various testimonies should assist you to make an assessment and come to a conclusion based on the events that actually took place. When you have weighed up these facts and decided on the most probable occurrence, on that you will base your verdict." He reached for a glass of water.

"Consider. Collective abduction and rape of Lise. Plaintiff identifies the three accused on trial. Pension owner identified Raoul Montpelier. Plaintiff tore off a button. Jacques, the psychiatrist who treated her for rape trauma, saw the button in her possession. Forensic tests show the button and blazer match. The veteran soldier testifies the blazer came from Raoul.

"Hilaire related their nocturnal habits in Paris with young girls at the brothel. It was established they stayed at the Ritz Hotel on regular occasions. Testimonies that all three had a liking for young girls. Testimony of past history of rape incidents by Raoul and Hermann.

"Defence Counsel contends mistaken identity, with blazer and button a fabrication. Set up. Object, to win damages from wealthy men. Question to ask yourselves… would a respectable woman bring such a charge against three men jointly if it did not happen? She is a successful career woman and an authority on oceanography, enjoying sound financial circumstances. What motive would she have in bringing such an action if it did not occur? What purpose beyond retribution for an outrage against her person?

"Weigh up the probability and decide your verdict. Consider the individuals on trial.

"Hermann Schmidt. Lise identified him and Hilaire gave evidence of his involvement with the others at the brothel. Madame Sautet testified to his violation and rape of internees on a regular basis.

"Documentation of Nazi records recovered from the submarine confirms the Schmidt family business engagement in uniform manufacture for the German forces. That is fact. Also use of forced labour, confirmed by evidence led to this Court by Gerda Blom.

"What you must decide is, was Hermann in CHARGE and accountable after his father's death? You have heard testimony about stolen paintings and profit from theft. Some may even applaud stealing back from the Nazis what they had looted! Avoid the emotion.

"You have also heard testimony in mitigation from Gerda Blom, Natashya, Sophie and Ingrid, that he was a good man basically and a victim of war circumstances which affected his behaviour. The point is, was he or was he not guilty of the crimes for which he has been put on trial?

"Henri Saint-Laurent. Again the rape evidence is repeated. Was he involved?

"The Court has been given proof through records from the submarine that La Verite champagne was supplied to the Germans during occupation and forced labour used on the estate.

"It is alleged Henri made love with a young internee. Do you find any evidence of mistreatment or violation by HIM of prisoners on the farm?

"He is charged with conspiracy in the hiding of stolen Nazi booty and subsequent financial gain after the war. The question is, was Henri responsible or did his father, Arnaud, conclude the arrangements? Henri, granted, benefitted after his father's death, along with the rest of his inheritance, but did he decide at the TIME, or was it his father?

"The same issue is raised over the Gaston land deal. Was Gaston's deprivation done with the consent of Henri or was it his father's greed?

"The decision you must reach is this. WAS Henri responsible or was it his father? If Henri Saint-Laurent is NOT found responsible for the affairs at La Verite during the war, then you must find him Not Guilty of those charges.

"You will be required to make your recommendation regarding reinstatement of the Gaston estates to the heir." The judge's eye fleetingly caught Sophie's as his gaze swept the Court. Not a muscle moved in his face. Sophie pressed her lips together.

"Raoul Montpelier. In every group there is a leader. In this indictment of rape it would appear that Raoul Montpelier is the ringmaster." The smirk could scarcely be spotted on the Judge's face.

"Many threads of evidence lead to the door of Montpelier. Evidence has been led of involvement in the disappearance of Doctor Lavalle. It was even suggested that his death was caused by a mysterious substance, thought to be Zyklon B gas used to gas Jews in the concentration camps, with all the horrors that brings to mind. Possession of such vile poison must indeed be restricted to only a few people in the world. You may ask yourselves whether Raoul Montpelier is in a position to possess such lethal capability. He is not on trial for murder. No such charge has been entered. The issue you must decide upon, Members of the Jury, is whether or not Doctor Lavalle actually confronted Montpelier in his salon, based on evidence presented. If you are so satisfied he did, it would tend to confirm he had in fact followed the same thread," smiling at his own pun, "of the button and blazer trail, leading to Lise's rapist at an earlier stage than was first apparent. The demise of the good doctor certainly delayed exposure.

"Then Emilie Cohen described for us the lifestyle of Montpelier in his younger wartime days; a scenario of a man with base regard for women other than a source of carnal satisfaction. She speaks of his close association, collaboration and fraternisation with Nazi friends, with procurement of young girls to meet their lustful desires and wanton pleasures.

"The testimony of Rachael Goldberg reinforces the previous evidence, giving a horrendous account of his vicious, merciless mistreatment of her and constant violation of her person. He is clearly established in her testimony as a callous rapist.

"She goes on to allege that he was responsible for the deportation of her parents and later herself. The records of Drancy Prison prescribe her intended destiny as Dachau, which tells its own story. Showing us her tattooed number must dispel any doubts as to the authenticity of her version and whether or not it is more reasonable than any argument by Defence. Ask yourselves, could she be SO terrified of this man as to refrain from pressing legal rights to her father's former business and property because she was in mortal fear of her life? Is it possible? Your recommendations on the restitution of the former Goldberg property will be expected from you.

"Presentation of two paintings by the accused to brothel keeper Courtier, to secure for himself the carnal rights of 12-year-old Emilie Cohen, has exposed the gigantic fraud he perpetrated with objets d'art. Evidence has been led regarding numerous sales of those paintings chronicled as burned to ashes according to the Archives of Jewish Affairs in Berlin. Montpelier has admitted his incredible crime, which ironically saved many works of art of distinction from destruction. Proceeds from these paintings, hidden with the Saint-Laurent family, endowed them all with enormous wealth. Grand profit from theft.

"Members of the Jury, you will now deliberate on the evidence presented to you and this Court awaits your verdict."

Bang! went the gavel as a babble of conversation broke out.

"The Court will rise," sang the Bailiff as the Judge retired to his chambers.

Sophie smiled quietly to herself.

A subdued undercurrent of conversation evaporated when the court bailiff addressed the Judge.

"Your Honour. The jury has returned."

The stillness was broke again. "Silence in Court!"

Twelve pairs of shoes shuffled for an interminable period; bottoms settled.

"Foreman of the Jury; have you reached your verdict?"

"Yes, Your Honour," lips firm, voice steady, standing resolutely.

"How do you find the accused in the rape of Lise Delors; guilty or not guilty?"

"Guilty Your Honour!"

The court erupted. "SILENCE! SILENCE!"

"We place special blame on Raoul Montpelier as ringleader."

"Thank you Foreman. What is your verdict on the indictment of Hermann Schmidt as an active enemy of France?" looking up.

"Guilty, Your Honour. However we find mitigating circumstances as the accused was compelled by the Nazi powers to produce uniforms and he did not benefit personally."

"War crimes. Using French Nationals as slave labour – guilty or not guilty?"

"Guilty, Your Honour!"

At the rear of the court, Sophie bit her index finger knuckle. The Foreman continued, "However we see identical mitigating circumstances. The accused showed compassion by sheltering two Jewesses and for that personal risk we recommend that this be taken into account in his favour. We attribute the influence of Ingrid Penz for much of the unacceptable conduct."

The Judge nodded, writing.

"Henri Saint-Laurent. War crimes. How do you find the accused on the charges of collaborating with the enemy?"

"Not guilty, Your Honour."

"Forced labour?"

"Not guilty!"

Sophie collapsed with a sigh, breathless. She felt an instantaneous release of pent-up emotional excitement. 'Bless you Charles', she thought, 'Oh thank you Charles! You lovely Judge'. He had swung them. She had done it!

"In the illegal procurement of the Gaston estate, do you find the accused guilty or not guilty?"

"Not guilty, Your Honour. It was his father. We recommend retribution for the injustice by returning the land to the rightful heir. In addition we recommend financial compensation be paid."

Sophie tingled with excitement.

"Thank you Foreman. Accused Raoul Montpelier. War crimes. Collaboration with the enemy?"

"Guilty, Your Honour. Active participation. No extenuating circumstances."

"Theft of state property. Objets d'Art?"

"Guilty Your Honour. Active role. No extenuating circumstances."

"Theft of the Goldberg property?"

"Guilty Your Honour. We recommend restoration to the heir Rachael Goldberg, together with all stocks and penal compensation for her ill treatment and rape."

Nail-biting suspense in a silence of the dead fell on the court; minds speculating. 'What would the Judge's sentences be?' His pen scratched; notes shuffled. After an age he looked over his glasses, coughed. The silence was crystal; his gavel a gunshot.

"The accused will stand." The Judge's voice was grave.

"Hermann Schmidt. You have been found guilty of the gang rape of Lise Delors, now Lavalle. For the vicious, premeditated rape of an innocent young girl I sentence you to five years imprisonment. You are guilty of collaboration but with mitigating circumstances since you inherited the operation from your deceased father. You were not unduly enriched as the factory was bombed out. I sentence you to three years imprisonment. I take into account the Jury recommendation for showing compassion to the Jewesses by affording them sanctuary from the Nazis at some considerable personal risk. Two years suspended. You have been found guilty of the war crimes of using female Jewish forced labour. You committed heinous acts against them in the guise of discipline. However I take into consideration the Jury's comments and accept as valid the peculiar influence exerted on you by the elder Ingrid Penz on whom you placed much reliance and on whom you drew support in those early days. I sentence you to three years, two suspended. Sentences are to run consecutively. You will serve seven years in prison." He gavelled.

Hermann's knuckles were white as he gripped the rail to steady himself as the enormity of the stupidity of his complicity struck home. He had survived the war, yet brought his downfall on himself. He was shaken to the core.

"Henri Saint-Laurent. You are guilty of the gang rape of Lise Delors. Sentenced to five years. You are acquitted of the war crime charges brought against you and for illegal procurement of the Gaston estates. Nevertheless those lands do not belong to you and will be restored to the true heir, Sophie Gaston. You are ordered to compensate her with 50 million francs." The gavel fell on its wooden block. A whistle echoed through the courtroom.

Henri's right hand flew to his heart, which he thought had stopped! His knees buckled, causing him to sink to the bench. His warder gave him water, then lifted him upright. His mind raced. Loss of revenue from the Gaston estate, then compensation of 50 million francs on top of his wife's extortionate divorce demands, coupled to his incarceration for five years spelled ruin for his business empire. Reeling in shock he presented a pitiful figure, trembling in the dock; the once proud, handsome man was broken.

"Raoul Montpelier. You have been found guilty of the evil propagation of the gang rape of Lise Delors. I sentence you to seven years imprisonment. You have been found guilty of collaboration with the enemies of France. I sentence you to prison for five years. Guilty of theft of property. Three years. Guilty of the theft of the Goldberg property in conspiracy with the Nazi powers. You have been found guilty of the vile mistreatment of the heir, Rachael Goldberg and of conspiracy with the Nazis to exterminate her parents and herself. Five years imprisonment. Your sentences will run consecutively for 20 years in prison. The former Goldberg business will be restored to the rightful heir, Rachael Goldberg, including all stocks. You will pay compensation of 200 million francs to her.

"Your heirs will not benefit from your monstrous war crimes against humanity and the State. And you Sir, will spend many days contemplating the evil acts which have put you in that awful prison cell!" The gavel slammed down on the block.

Reaction was a whirlwind of hot air. A volcanic eruption in court. "SILENCE!" Bang! bang! went the gavel.

Raoul clutched at his throat, the stricture turning his face grey. He slumped to the bench on crumpling knees. Eyes focused on this evil species of the human race. A peculiar glee swept across many faces as they witnessed the tables turned on this despicable cretin. Justice had been done.

Lise Lavalle felt strange; she had expected a joyous elation, but it was not there. She felt avenged and for Pierre too. What she had set out to do, she had done. No heroics, simple retribution. Lise looked at Rex with a relaxed expression on her face.

He half smiled, holding her hand.

Three broken men were led below to the cells.

Sophie continued to sit for a few moments to reflect on the outcome. It had been fair. Scores had been settled; retribution made. She smiled wanly; one always had to honour one's debts. It was time to show her gratitude to a certain gentleman judge; the least she could do for 50 million francs.

The amount could buy an awful lot of gratitude, she mused with a smile 'Well done,' she said to herself quietly. 'It's over now.'

Chapter 54

PARIS

The memory of that last day in Court would always stay in Sophie's memory. The look Gerda flashed her was enough to kill: she would never forgive her. No word had passed. Ingrid, jealous of Sophie, ignored her as at Berghof. Sophie wondered if Ingrid's intuition had picked up vibes between Hermann and her.

Hermann, pleased to see Sophie, had kept his secret: Sophie knew his signals.

Raoul, thank God, she had never known.

Henri had been stunned when he had seen her – she knew by his twitches. She thought back to the time when Henri had been in trouble with his impossible father. 'Thank God I had the bastard killed', she thought. Henri had lived in dread of his father's bad temper and lacked the stomach to stand his ground even when unjustly scolded. On those hangdog days, Sophie restored Henri's broken pride, kissing his forehead, and comforting him with gentle caresses. 'Oh Henri, Henri', she recalled with compassion.

Charles Poirot had been marvellous. He had arranged a flat in his name whilst Sophie sorted out the legal affairs in Paris, enabling her to remain in seclusion from Andre.

Charles' influence secured an interview for her with Henri in prison. Even though he was seated at a bare table, with a single ceiling bulb etching his gypsy features and prominent eyebrows, the expression in his eyes told her that he was still moved by her beauty. Hazel eyes responded to his adoration as her hand groped to close on his. His reaction was unexpected.

"Come to view the vanquished have you? I'm nearly finished Sophie. You've got your revenge on our family. What more do you want?" he asked sarcastically.

"Henri, you've been an idiot to get yourself into this rape mess, but it's not all over for you. It doesn't need to be. I'll make a deal with you." He saw she was sincere.

His eyes narrowed. "A deal. What deal?"

"Well, I've got our family farm back and 50 million as well. La Verite shares have plummeted, which means that you may have to sell parts of the estate to realise enough to meet your divorce settlement and pay me out too. Right?"

"Looks like it." He gave a Gallic shrug. "And so?"

"Accept these conditions and I'll help you," replied Sophie.

"One. Divorce that bitch! No resistance. Pay her out on the devalued estate. Sell your yacht. Get clear of her completely. Completely! Do you hear me? The value has dropped and may go down further. Get clear of her.

"Two. Give me total authority over your estate affairs. Elect me manager of the estate. Managing director if you can.

"Three. Give me power of attorney over your personal affairs whilst you are in prison. I want to deal in your shares. I'll run La Verite efficiently and buy sections of the estate that have been sold to meet your commitments." Sophie paused as Henri chipped in.

"That way you could own the entire estate. I suppose you'll be happy then! Anything else?" he asked sarcastically with a hint of a smile.

"Yes. When you get out you stay with me. Then in time, if you are a good boy, maybe I'll marry you."

It was like a bombshell exploding.

"WHAT? I thought you were happy seeing me ruined!" he gasped, mouth open.

Sophie smiled weakly, but resolutely. "I've seen many men in my life, but there was only one Henri. It is time I settled down. I'm fond of you, my first love. Henri, you'll lose far less with me looking after your affairs.' Sophie didn't mention her intention to draw up an ante-nuptial contract: she had no intention of losing her family inheritance for a second time.

"Well! What do you say? Is it a deal?"

"Is it a deal? Sophie, I don't know what to say… yes, oh yes. Sophie, I missed you terribly when you left. I knew then there could never be another Sophie. She was gone from my life. And now you want me. I can't believe it!" His voice rose in excitement and he clamped his hand over his mouth in gleeful conspiracy in case the guard burst in. Henri was beaming.

"It's alright darling, the guard won't interfere – I gave him 100 francs to leave us for an hour. So my gallant knight," laughing at him, "I'm glad you accept."

*****

Ingrid had been badly shaken by the trial.

In the aftermath she sat in her hotel lounge bar when a large man greeted her.

"Guten abend. We both seem to have lost the same man!"

"Why? Who are you?" she responded nervously, startled by his presence.

"I refer to your husband. I had intended extorting a lot of money from the fellow by exposing his Nazi past, but the Court has beaten me to it! Blown my system you might say. As for the second question, I'm Erwin Ehrhardt, from the winelands of the Rhine, like Ribbentrop!"

"So am I! My father had a delicatessen in Bacharach. Hermann's father and mine were both early Nazi Party members. I grew up with the Hitler Youth and so on. But why do you chase old Nazis – have you gone Zionist or something?"

He scoffed. "No. I too was in Hitler Youth, then the army. I did their dirty work and they got the profits! I decided I wanted my share… that's all there is to it really. I am still a Nazi at heart. I also lost out on the trial. For 25 years I lived with Adele Mathieu; I believed she was French. Then I found out she was a Jewish bitch – Sophie! She deceived me for all those years; I'll bloody kill her. I used her for all those years to trap Nazi members. I called myself Andre Cartier."

"Hermann used me too! I built up the Vogel Fashions business from scratch. But we've grown apart," she laughed. "I got bored. I had a brief romance with Henri once. You probably heard testimony from that Ukrainian, Natashya!"

"Well we old Nazis should stick together!" Erwin smirked.

"Jesus, this rape business came as a hell of a shock. Common denominator the Judge called it. The entire past of those guys were exposed; two were special to me at one time or another. Crazy bastards. They screwed up their lives for a jump, and it was not even necessary. I used to fix up Hermann with broads. He had no need to rape that kid."

Ingrid noticed that as she talked, Erwin had been doodling with a pen, making a square, circle and swastika.

"Here's my business card. Look me up sometime," she said, passing it to Erwin.

"Thanks," he smiled. "I might do that."

*****

Sophie found Rex Trent and Lise very approachable. She told them of her appeal to Judge Poirot. After years spent with Andre she had left him and was scared for her life.

"If Karl Fleischer will testify against Andre being a Nazi, we can negotiate a safe passage for little old me. Andre has made money; plenty of it. He won't want to languish in jail at his age, he likes women too much. It is worth a try."

Rex arrived at the stupendous FRICK car showrooms in Munich. He was impressed by the swish office suite and success of Karl Fleischer. However Karl was devoid of arrogance when Rex spelt out his options.

"I've come to you through Andre Cartier's mistress. She has been living with him since the war. She told me Andre had been blackmailing you as a war criminal; you shot some guys in Italy – the whole story. She's left him and fears for her life. I want your testimony to his background, then I'll get him off your back for ever. I want to put pressure on him to save her. He's made a fortune, so rest assured he won't want to end up in jail. Give me a written testimony and we'll look after you if you are ever brought to trial. Is it a deal or do I have to blow you away anyway? Well? Was he a Nazi? His real name?"

Fleischer was ash pale. "Ja, I vill help you. Call his bluff. So my chanz of beink left alone depenz on it vurking too, Ja?"

"Correct. Put it on paper Karl."

"He vas a Nazi, Ja. I vud gif anyzink to see zat schwine ded," he spat out, starting to scribble. "Hiss name iss Erwin Ehrhardt – Untersturmfuhrer S.S. Death Head Unit. Ze trained killer! Lifs in Heidelberg."

To Rex, Erwin Ehrhardt was the epitome of Hitler's Aryan Race. Cropped blonde hair, square-jawed face, a big head on a bull neck, a broad frame dominated by massive shoulders and powerful arms. A lion of a man, even at his advanced age. He looked typically German, and Rex wondered how on earth Sophie had thought Andre a Frenchman. But he at least had the benefit of hindsight.

The two powerful men met on the highest platform of the Eiffel Tower, sizing each other up like two bulls about to do battle. Mouth clamped tight, Erwin listened to Rex stipulate the stand-off deal.

"You leave Sophie and Karl Fleischer alone. We have his testimony to your Nazi past relating to war crimes in Dachau where you practised killing inmates without any compunction or remorse. Also at Flossenberg camp. Fleischer knows he could go down with you if necessary. One down, all down. Sophie knows she'd be safer in jail. If you kill them, I'll hang you on that testimony. You'll go down for sure. I'll see to that. Alternatively, despicable swine that you are, you can get away with it all. You can retire with your stinking wealth; Uruguay perhaps? But no more blackmail, if you accept my stand-off terms. Well, what's it to be?" Rex stared into his steel-blue eyes.

Erwin had been sorely provoked and had stepped forward sharply, then checked himself; fists clenched. He sneered. "Brave bastard I must say. At one time you would have been dead by now, but I've matured." Erwin cupped his chin in his palm and stared at Rex with burning hostility. "Agreed! Now go, Brit Bastard."

Rex smiled. He'd enjoyed that. Got the guy rattled. He had an overwhelming desire to thump this ugly ex-Nazi thug, but he would have to strike first, fast and hard if he were to survive. Turning as if to go, Rex suddenly pivoted on his toes like a shot putter and with lightning speed smashed his elbow into the pit of Ehrhardt's stomach. It had the desired effect. His head shot forward and down. Rex whirled round and brought his knee up with a sickening crack under the protruding chin. In a split second his two clenched and balled fists came down with all his might to club the back of the bull neck. Moving away, the body crashed to the floor.

"Take that, Kraut shit," Rex shouted as he saw the body roll to the edge.

Years on the racing circuits had instilled a lightning sense of anticipation in Rex, who anticipated that one more roll and Ehrhardt would be over the edge. Blindly Rex grabbed and clutched a stout leg of the torso that was hanging through the lower rails. Without a second thought he hauled the big German back to safety.

"You're still a big shit," he remarked, dropping the leg and turning to get into the lift, leaving the blonde German bruised and bewildered on the 365 metre high steel structure.

Chapter 55

POST TRIAL:

NEUSTADT

Erwin thought it ironic that the submarine discovery, which should have been a source of such wealth, became the cause of his lucrative business collapsing. Blackmailing Schmidt and his Kordel/Vogel empire was new unattainable. Hermann was in jail, and Ingrid held absolute power over the group of companies. Court testimony had unequivocally shown that she had been a confirmed Nazi. Was she still? The idea came to him; if you can't beat them, join them. He would find Ingrid in Neustadt. He pulled out her business card.

Seated on a dark grey leather chair he took in the tasteful decor of pale wallpaper, watercolour paintings, soft grey carpeting and subtle lighting. Off centre, an outrageously huge pink pottery lamp demanded attention. It depicted a graceful female form bending backwards, slender arms reaching forwards to grasp a smooth sculptured cylindrical column, culminating in a larger rounded, somewhat triangular shape, on which rested the lamp. A second glance and he realised the significance of the shapes. She noticed his smile.

A low white bookcase was arranged along one wall, opposite a white leather couch. Nothing however in the luxurious office struck his attention more forcibly than the executive desk in black smoky glass, inlaid with maroon leather, on which stood a pen stand, cigarette box and lighter in pure gold. Ensconced in a high-backed chair of matching leather reposed the corporate head of Vogel. Everything epitomised taste, success and wealth. Close to, Erwin thought how beautiful Ingrid was; how strikingly attractive for her age. Her blue eyes, lovely face and full bosom gripped him.

"Kindred spirits, you and I; both reared as Nazis, both convinced. How do you feel now?" Erwin probed.

"Like you I glorified in the Third Reich. My dislike for Jews never left me. I've used them to advantage though. Hermann was not so adamant."

"With Adele gone and the Court exposure my operation is blown. I feel bitter... she cheated me."

"Did she know you were a Nazi?"

"No. But that was different!"

They looked at each other and burst out laughing. "Depends whose side you are on, hmm?" quipped Ingrid.

"To me they'll always be just Jews."

"So we are alike. I thought so. Well I'm unemployed at the moment," raising a smile. "What are the chances of my joining you to help run the businesses?"

"I have a management team structure, but you could help me on the market research side." Erwin nodded agreement, unsure what it entailed.

Ingrid gave him a history of their struggle to get established post war and their eventual success story. Erwin was impressed.

"And you? Tell me something about your side."

Erwin outlined how he had made his fortune with Adele's assistance. He described their twilight world of intrigue and deception, keeping one step in front and the excitement of the chase. From his tone it was obvious to Ingrid that he burned with anger over Sophie's betrayal, although she agreed with his decision on a truce as the most intelligent course to take. He didn't tell her that he had conveniently murdered Henri's father Arnaud Saint-Laurent, which had played very favourably into Sophie's hands. The thought stung him deeply. He couldn't undo it and disclosure would be lunatic. Sophie had one over him. She was the witness. It was a stand-off.

Ingrid cut into his thoughts. "Where do you live?"

"I have a house in Heidelberg."

"I love Heidelberg."

"I have quite a collection of memorabilia of the old days there, like flags, standards, badges, guns and so on. I'd like to show you. Would you come?"

"Yes. Why not," she smiled. "I've got a collection too; uniforms, hats, helmets, belts, holsters, boots; all sorts of things I can show you, but they're hidden in the castle at Berghof. We'll go up one weekend."

A week later Erwin drove Ingrid to Heidelberg and took her to the theatre, dinner and to his house. They found themselves compatible companions. Gravitation to the bedroom seemed a natural progression. Ingrid enjoyed a tingling excitement as she speculated on him as her lover.

She accepted his implied invitation as a matter of course. Handsome bastard she thought.

Ingrid climbed into his silk sheeted bed, waiting for him like a newly wed. He slid between the sheets and they began an exploratory touching, kissing and gentle petting, interspersed with sips of champagne. Relaxing and companionable.

He made love to her for the first time. Ingrid was all smiles. Erwin would fill in nicely. He was a better companion than toy boys, and more agreeable too.

He was wunderbar!

Erwin had landed on his feet. Ingrid liked him, and also needed to discuss business developments with him. When a business was still small, a wrong decision would not do much harm, but a major corporation would find it extremely costly. He was highly intelligent, she decided, and never underestimated his instincts. A man who had lived on his wits as he had done, possessed commonsense. That's really what life and success was all about.

"Darling, pour me a drink. I want to tell you something about the lingerie business background. Take the brassiere. It was invented in June 1889 by a Parisian corset maker, Herminie Cadolle. Her original aim was to save women of the privileged classes from being laced into canvas casings stiffened with stays of steel or whalebone. These corsets made it difficult for women to breathe, and even deformed their rib bones. Herminie was tired of seeing women tortured. She wanted to create an undergarment to support the bosom without constricting the diaphragm, so that they could actually breathe. She called it the 'Well-Being'. Then in 1913 in New York, a socialite by the name of Caresse Crosby was unhappy with the corset line under her evening gown and had her maid sew two handkerchiefs together with ribbons. A corset maker in Connecticut by the name of Warner paid Crosby about a thousand US dollars for a patent. It must be worth 10 million dollars today."

She went on to describe the background to her business.

"We have the benefit of nylon and manmade fibres. The object today is to produce a sexy, yet functionally light-as-a-feather bra; at its best when at its least. They are becoming increasingly expensive and more daring in the development of the 'no bra' bra. We produce lacy creations and dazzling see-through body stockings to tease the men, and have a large range of slips, briefs and cami knickers. We need your opinion on what, as a horny man, turns you on! We are also into swimwear and produce six styles in 100 different fabrics. I need you to give your candid opinion on appeal. Although we sell directly to women, the men are the ones to ultimately satisfy.

"Any questions?"

"How soon can I start?" he laughed.

"By the way, I've got a chain of sex shops which may interest you," she whispered.

Erwin was sent to Milan to negotiate in Italian and proved a great help in the business.

They got on extremely well in both business and play.

"It's time we had a short holiday," Ingrid announced one day. "Let's go to Berghof. Spend a few days there."

Once at the castle, Ingrid brought out her memorabilia. Erwin became quite excited and when the Wagnerian heavy music started, his mood changed. Ingrid got swept along in the mood of ethereal fantasy. She started snapping at Natashya when she gave instructions.

"Why do you put up with that bitch after her testimony against you? You must be mad!" Erwin scoffed.

"It is not that simple. This place is Hermann's, not mine, and he insists that she stays. She's been here nearly a lifetime and he trusts her to run the castle. So I put up with her shit. We try to avoid each other. Let's change the subject. We've got some pictures stored here. I think we should sell a few off. They must be worth a fortune by now." Ingrid showed him two which had been taken from the original consignment.

"We have a vault here with a lot inside. If we could get an indication of today's values we could consider what to sell. Paris seems the best place. What do you think?"

"Agreed. If you let me take some to Paris and see what they're worth, you can decide. Is that OK with you?"

"Yes darling, splendid! But right now let's fetch wine from the cellar and get quietly stoned. In between you can make love to me. Come here, her big boy," she purred, leading him, laughing, down the cellar steps.

Natashya watched their every move.

Ingrid had enjoyed Natashya's humiliation as Erwin shouted, "Bring food!" treating her like dirt, ordering her around in his drunken stupor. Nazi arrogance had been rekindled as they paraded about half dressed in the old uniforms.

Sickened by their antics, the thought that Ingrid may never be punished for her despicable conduct and crimes made Natashya boil with rage. What fuelled her anger even more was the conviction that they had been guilty of the murder of her wartime Slavonic compatriots. Disgusted, she went up to bed, leaving the drunken exhibitionists passed out on a chaise longue. Ingrid, half naked, and still balancing a peaked cap on her head, sprawled on top of Erwin and he lay with head thrown back, snoring like a foghorn.

The following morning Erwin stepped into the cellars after Ingrid. She pointed to an area and stood back as Erwin swung mighty blows with a sledge hammer at the plastered brickwork. Once loosened, he prised bricks free with a crowbar, exposing a vault door.

"Well there it is! Try the key," he instructed, brushing away rubble and dust with his shoe.

"I hope it still turns," said Ingrid tensely as she tried it. The key turned, and she quickly clunked the lever to open position.

"Let me do that," he instructed, grabbing the door handle and heaving the heavy door open.

"Here we go!" whispered Ingrid as she stepped inside, holding her kerosene lamp high so that they could see what they were doing.

"They are still here. Look!" She pointed to the neatly stacked wooden cases standing upended on battens.

"Open one. Let's see how the canvases are after all this time."

Erwin started prising open the first crate with the crowbar. Wood cracked and pulled nails screeched in the enclosed space.

Bitter, Natashya had stealthily followed them downstairs, watching from a dark passage corner. The noise was a perfect cover. Natashya saw her chance. Without waiting to think, quick as a flash, she swung the vault door closed with a bang and slammed the locking lever closed, turning the key.

"Open the door you bitch!" screamed Erwin, banging on the door with his crowbar.

"Fuck off SIR!" Natashya mocked, hurrying upstairs.

She realised that he would try to prise the back panel off the door to get at the mechanism, so she quickly returned and started working on the door. She visualised the big German struggling to get a purchase with his blunt crowbar on the flush-fitting panel. It was not giving in to his efforts.

In tears Ingrid begged, "Natashya, I'm sorry, let us out and I'll give you a million marks!"

"You fuck off," was the reply.

Natashya hurriedly stuck masking tape around the door, sealing off any cracks along the frame. Nearing completion, she lit an oily rag in the bee snuffer, which resembled a watering can and was used to smoke bees out from under the eaves. She pumped smoke through the nozzle under the door.

"Hey you stinking Krauts! How would you like to get gassed like you did to all those Jews! Go to hell, both you, and Madame," she mocked, "and take longer to die than my sisters you murdered. Go to hell, bitch! DIE!" she screamed through the steel protective shield. Sweat ran down from her armpits as she realised what would happen to her if that caged animal got loose. The smoke should slow him down anyhow.

She carefully sealed the bottom gap, depriving the vault of air, which would cause them to suffocate. A decision about the kerosene lamp would have to be made. Burning it would eat up even more oxygen in their prison. Turning it out meant total darkness. Did they have a match to relight the lamp? A slow death was a fitting punishment for those swine. Judging by the noise, the German required the light as he hammered at the inner door.

Natashya waited for two days before returning. Her fingers trembled as she got ready to pull the tape away. What if he was still alive? Fear made her wait another day.

She had been conditioned to solitude and talked to herself constantly. She had done so for years. 'There's no rush. Wait one more day. Make sure the bastard's completely dead!'

On the first day of their incarceration Natashya scrubbed the kitchen table spotlessly clean until its white wood gleamed. Her finger was bleeding from a cut she had made on her finger, but she continued to scrub the table every day until the once white table was smeared with her blood. A kitchen knife with her blood on it lay on the table. She bound up her wound and descended into the cellar.

'This is it, girl. Open it up,' she told herself. She boldly ripped the tape away, inserted the key, turned it and swung the lever, pulling the door open. They were stone dead. Bruises on Ingrid's neck showed that he had strangled her to put her out of her misery. A big lump on his head had probably been caused by knocking himself unconscious with the crowbar rather than experiencing a lingering death deprived of oxygen. They looked grotesque. It was the end of a Nazi era.

Natashya took the first crate and removed the canvases, carrying them upstairs. She decided to drag only the smaller crates upstairs. She would have to smash the big ones open and carry the contents upstairs. Eventually everything was in the kitchen and ready to load.

On the second and third days her familiar Citroen delivery van was seen around, going back and forth. She brought in sand and cement with some bricks from Windesheim where she thought no one knew her, and carried everything into the cellar in preparation. Once the canvases were removed, Natashya bricked up the door again and plastered over it.

Carefully she loaded the precious cargo in the Citroen and set off for Stromberg where she had arranged rental of a garage for six months. The paintings she stored there, under double locks to protect her millions of marks worth of art treasures. Once back at the schloss, she cleaned the van, then drove it into the castle garage. Opening the van's back doors, she cut her finger again and squeezed drops of blood onto the rear floor, then locked the garage.

Her wound dressed, she painted the newly plastered wall and threw sand on it to age it, and cleaned up every vestige of rubble and dust.

In the kitchen she took off her shoes and dragged their heels forcefully along the floor to the door before replacing them on her feet.

Thinking carefully, Natashya set the table for her evening meal, leaving a slice of bread with a chunk bitten out with her teeth-marks in it, and her knife and fork lying next to a half eaten meal on her plate. The coffee cup she knocked over, spilling half the contents and then overturned the chair. Perfect.

She dressed in an expensive stylish suit she had bought in St. Goar with money stolen from Ingrid's purse, and put her old scuffed shoes in a used plastic bag. Climbing into Ingrid's smoke-blue Mercedes Benz 380 SE she drove to Frankfurt airport, dropping her old shoes in a roadside rubbish bin along the way.

After garaging the Mercedes Natashya settled comfortably onto her Paris flight. Once in Paris she soon located Rachael Goldberg and Emilie Cohen.

"Let me take you to dinner and tell you my story," she offered.

"Nonsense! We'll have dinner with you, but WE are paying! You, dear Natashya, are OUR guest."

During dinner Natashya told them what she had done.

"I took the situation into my hands and there you are. So will you buy my pictures?"

"Of course we will. What a pleasure! You struck a blow for all of us!" they grinned conspiratorially. "We normally don't touch hot stuff, but this case is VERY different. Don't worry, we'll get you a fortune, bit by bit. Our money has bought us powerful contacts. We'll change your name Natashya, fix you up with a complete new identity, papers and passport. Where do you want to live?"

"Switzerland."

"Done… " said Rachael.

Natashya had had a series of relationships over the years. She enjoyed her independence and had no intention of becoming a slave to any man, which is how she viewed marriage. But she enjoyed sex, as long as it was on her terms. Her situation was indeed unique as caretaker at Berghof Castle, ensuring a freedom denied to most people. In consequence certain tradesmen calling at the castle whom she found attractive were invited inside for more than a pastry and a steaming hot cup of coffee.

Her postman friend was a fairly regular caller. Although mail deliveries at the castle were sparse, he would hurry along his route to find time to spend with his obliging mistress. She made his day, for sure.

Hot in anticipation, he rang the tradesmen's bell, rocking from foot to foot.

'Damn! Don't say she's out.' He knocked hard on the door, anxious now. Disappointment gripped him, when suddenly his eye caught sight of two blood spots on the pristine scrubbed kitchen step. He peered closer. Blood, definitely. He went cold, his original intentions abandoned.

Testing the door handle, he found it locked. Putting down his satchel, he skirted round to the kitchen window, peered inside and spotted the overturned cup and chair. Knowing Natashya's meticulous house-proud nature, which was fastidious to the point of irritation, he sensed trouble. What kind, he didn't know. He tried the locked front entrance, but there was no reply. No entry.

On his way through the village he reported at the Police Station. Telephone calls to Berghof were unanswered. Management at Neustadt couldn't understand it. Otto Kranz, financial director, drove up to see Ingrid. When he arrived the Police were investigating.

"Did you know her plans? Her whereabouts?" asked the Inspector. "There's blood on the kitchen table and doorstep, and there are heel marks and blood in the van out in the garage." The evidence heightened the Inspector's suspicions, and he rolled his cigar thoughtfully across his mouth. "I reckon they have murdered the housekeeper. It's her blood group. Motive? Killed for giving evidence in court? Would a person of Ingrid's position and wealth kill to avenge outrage at the woman's testimony? It wouldn't be the first time!"

Ingrid's Mercedes was missing, and her mysterious disappearance hit the headlines. Pictures of her and her new business companion, linked with romantic connotations, appeared in the press. Speculation was rife.

Erika, once a model with Ingrid for Vogel Fashions and since retired, saw Ingrid's face in the newspapers. In the next frame she recognised the man.

"That's him!" she shouted out loud. "He took out Grete that day she was murdered!" Erika bubbled excitedly to the Police Inspector. "In 1961. Remember?"

"Are you sure?" came the stern response. The cigar rolled across. "Positive! No doubt! Older perhaps, but that's him."

"He may have murdered them both," surmised the Inspector as he spat out the stub of his wet cigar.

Natashya wasted no time. She flew to Frankfurt, drove the Mercedes to Frick's in Munich where it was sprayed black, and the numbers ground off and stamped. She took delivery of a smaller Mercedes then drove over the Swiss border to Lucerne as Frau Putter. There she settled with her millions to this day.

Chapter 56

RETRIBUTION

Erwin, Ingrid and Natashya had disappeared. Only Rachael and Emilie Cohen knew Natashya's secret. They didn't know Sophie.

"She's been with that Erwin guy some 25 years! Okay she's Jewish, but we can't trust her with that secret."

"I agree… let sleeping dogs lie!" Emilie nodded.

But not Raoul Montpelier.

Rachael's eyes were cold and calculating. "Prison is too good for the swine! I'm going to give the bastard the same mental torture he gave me! He'll pay dearly for my parents' deportation. Do you want to help me?" she asked Emilie.

"Sure! It won't be easy – him in prison I mean. What's your plan?"

"You'll see. First I've got to get permission to visit him in a private room situation."

Rachael achieved it.

She was conducted with Emilie into an interrogation room. The door reopened and Raoul was led in. "Handcuff him to that chair with his hands behind his back please," she asked, smiling at the prison guard. "I don't trust this pig!"

The guard laughed, shoving the grey-faced prisoner into the high-backed wooden chair and securing his hands, then left them alone.

"Pig! We've come to show you the books! See how much money we're making. Here's last month." pushing the Sales Ledger under his nose. He squinted and grunted.

"Oh yes, we're becoming very wealthy with your old business, pig. Just think – you'll never be able to live like you did before – locked away in this nasty prison with no women to violate! Remember how you used to rape me? And how you took advantage of Emilie here, raping her when she was only 12? You are an animal. A filthy cochon!

"Emilie! Perhaps we should remind him of what it looks like."

All carefully rehearsed, they lifted their dresses, sans knickers and stood close before Raoul. His mouth dropped.

"You'll never savour this special magical delight for a lifetime, so we decided we'd remind you of what you're missing!"

Emilie had begun to fondle herself, making erotic noises to simulate rising ecstasy. Raoul's eyes were popping.

"Just THINK about it tonight lover boy! Come Emilie, let's leave this smell and go home. Oh, we'll be back next week. See you then. GUARD!"

The guard was in hysterics when he returned. .

Rachael slipped him a banknote that assured their welcome on future excursions.

Raoul Montpelier was committed for psychiatric observation. He was mentally ruined, a wreck.

Rachael, of all people, knew his Achilles heel.

He eventually went insane.

Chapter 57

PARIS / NEUSTADT:

DORMS

Rex and Lise were alerted to Ingrid's disappearance by Sophie. They nervously looked at the German newspaper article. The press luridly speculated how Ingrid and the housekeeper had been murdered and their bodies dragged away from the scene.

"I'm sure it was Erwin! I'll be next on his hit list! Revenge. I bet he's crazy with hatred." Sophie was clearly upset. "I've had this sent to me in the post," she said, handing an unopened envelope to Rex. It was postmarked Central Paris. Rex opened it and withdrew a paper with words and letters pasted on it. He read, "Don't worry. Erwin is dead." There were no names; no clues.

"I wonder! What do you make of it Rex?" looking at him for guidance, protection; anything.

"Well, not much. But if you'll come with Lise and me to Schmidt's factory in Neustadt, it could be as good a place to start as anywhere."

Like his father before him, Franz Schmidt inherited the business responsibilities sooner than he had anticipated. He had been rapidly appointed Managing Director of Kordel/Vogel Group whilst his father served his prison sentence. At 31, Franz had been partially groomed for his eventual role in the dynasty, with a good management team to support him. Gerda Blom, an old woman now, had kept a grip on the Vogel Fashions side.

"I wish you luck," Rex quipped. "What your father did, you shouldn't be punished for. In my opinion, your mother bears equal responsibility for his downfall. My father did business with your father remember. We knew him well. Perhaps I can help you on the nylon side. I also know a thing or two," he informed Franz, smiling. "Nevertheless your mother is missing and we are concerned about this lady's safety," turning to indicate Sophie. "Concerned that she may be murdered, which is what the press speculate happened to your mother. We want to get to the bottom of it and I'm sure you would be relieved to find out what actually transpired."

"Indeed," replied Franz, nodding. "I'll cooperate in whatever way I can."

"We want to see Berghof!"

"I'll arrange it," Franz volunteered.

Rex interviewed the Financial Director of Kordel Group, Otto Kranz, who had first visited Berghof. The Police had no evidence beyond the positive blood group identification of Natashya. The Inspector commented on how well Natashya had maintained the castle, and how clean it was.

It would be five years later, after Hermann was released on good behaviour and decided to sell some of the stolen paintings, that the grisly truth was discovered. It was a secret he had to keep!

After persuasion, Sophie agreed to take Rex to Erwin's house in Heidelberg. There was no sign of recent occupation, and no one in the vicinity had seen Herr Beckenbauer around for a while. Sophie was still apprehensive in case Erwin found her.

"He had a wall safe behind this picture which swung away from the wall, but I don't know the combination," said Sophie.

"People often use birthdays to remember combinations," ventured Rex. "What was his?"

"The day after the summer solstice, June 22."

"Year?"

"Let me think. He was 60, er... 1921."

"Let's try that: 22, 6, 21." He spun the dial.

"No luck," he said. "Let me reverse the numbers." His fingers spun the dial: 21, 6, 22. There was a click. "Bingo!" he cried, opening the door. Carefully Rex lifted out the contents which he spread on a table. His fingers rummaged through small ledgers, diaries, cash in various currencies, jewellery, false passports in different disguises. Then he came across an old photograph of a once fair woman. The photo was brown with age. On the reverse he read 'Worms 1924'. 'She must have been around her mid-twenties,' he thought.

"That nose! It must be his mother! I'm sure. It is just like him," exclaimed Sophie.

They rummaged further and found bank statements in the name of Ursula Ehrhart, even dated deposits had been made into the account, which also showed sundry withdrawals. Herr Beckenbauer's personal bank account statement reflected similar amounts made monthly by banker's order payments.

"Come. We'll visit Ursula's bankers."

The stiff German banker was reluctant to disclose any confidential information to strangers.

"But we have reason to believe that Herr Beckenbauer is dead." they protested. "The old lady is reliant on him for her income and may soon have nothing to live on. We need to find her to help her. The income will stop if he is dead!"

"It has already ceased," the banker admitted, scanning his client's printout. "She lives here," he informed them, writing her address on his business card.

"Thank you. You have been most helpful."

They found the 84-year-old woman still had a sparkle in her eyes. She lay back in a deep armchair, protected against the chill by a shawl. They saw that she wore mittens, probably in an attempt to ease the arthritic pains in her hands. Rex thought that she must have been a big woman in her prime.

"Erwin always provided for me. He has been a good boy to me," she mumbled through missing teeth in the lower jaw. Sophie interpreted for Rex as she explained.

"I lived with your son for 25 years. We have some sad news. We have reason to believe Erwin is dead. Has he contacted you recently?"

"No. No he hasn't," the slack flesh on her jaws trembled as she spoke. "Well I'm dying too, anyway. I don't have long to go. It's angina. Another heart attack and the doctor said that it will be my last. No excitement he said. I'm ready to go." She still managed to smile. "I've had a good life, but I'm tired now… very tired. I've kept his secret all these years. I could never tell him! I knew that he and I would both have been murdered if anyone found out." The old lady stopped as if to collect her thoughts.

"Found out what?" Sophie quietly prompted the old lady; having swiftly interpreted for Rex.

Her mouth silently opened and closed a few times before she looked at them.

"I'll tell you if you promise me you will not make mischief with it!" She screwed up her eyes, waiting for their commitment.

"I promise." Sophie was sincere.

With slow deliberation and some pain, the old woman reached for a drawer at her side, opened it and pulled out an ancient photograph.

They could see only the reverse in the mittened hand.

"I could never tell Erwin that the man I married wasn't his real father. This man was." She turned the photograph over.

They all gasped in shock at the infamous features, the toothbrush moustache and quiff of the former Austrian. Sophie clutched at her mouth; shaking. "Imagine if Erwin had known," she stammered.

"The Gestapo would have killed him!" Ursula Ehrhardt was emphatic. Her eyes then suddenly opened wide: she clutched her chest and her mouth dropped open. Her body jerked and she straightened up sharply. A sigh came from her throat then she slumped forward, chin on chest.

She was gone.

"Can you just think how history might have been influenced if he had known his real identity!" murmured Rex breathlessly, shaking his head.

"It doesn't bear thinking about," whispered Sophie, as she gently prised the gnarled and crippled fingers open to retrieve the Führer's photograph.

"I'll keep my promise," she said, looking at Rex and Lise. Her companions nodded in unanimous agreement. They would not divulge the long-guarded secret.

After an uncomfortable interval, Rex turned to Lise.

"Judge Poirot was right, you know. If it had not been for your miserable misfortune in the hands of those three once very rich men, whose lives have since been ruined, we would never have found out Erwin was Hitler's son. You were the common denominator."

www.ingramcontent.com/pod-product-compliance
Lightning Source LLC
Chambersburg PA
CBHW051638050726
47502CB00011B/1088